STRANGER IN *MY* LAKE

Robert Karp

Disclaimer

All characters appearing in this work are fictitious. Any resemblance to real persons, living or dead, is purely coincidental. Many of the places and institutions named in this book do exist. However, there has been no attempt to accurately portray, describe, or define how they work, how they function, or their mission. This book is fiction.

PROLOGUE
SUNDAY, JULY 4, 1976

The morning of the Bicentennial celebration day in New York City dawned bright and beautiful. Skies remained cloudless and deep blue throughout the day. New York Harbor and the Hudson River were dotted with dozens of impressive tall ships from around the world. Incredible U.S. naval military might was on display.

New York City was a perfect image of what the United States of America had become in two-hundred years. Its population, despite its geographically small size, was many times larger than the America of 1776. New York City was a mercantile power unrivaled in modern history. This city was emblematic of the dominance of America in the world.

In the thirty years since World War II there was a trajectory of growth in technology only dreamed of before by a very few. But dreams were part of what this nation was all about. The future now was of exaggerated importance to so many.

Visiting the World's Fair in New York in 1964 offered an exciting glimpse of a vision you could sense of the flood of great things to come from technology. And so you could walk up to what looked like a television screen with a typewriter like keyboard attached to its base and see the letters you typed show up on the screen. Then pressing a button a reedy monotone voice actually spoke those words: "Hel-up, I am trap-ped in a com-pu-ter."

An enduring image from July 4th, 1976 in New York City was of a group of four British Harrier Jump jets swooping down low over the Hudson River and then, just feet from the Statue of Liberty, suddenly stopping as one in mid air. Jet airplanes frozen in the sky. They stood in silent salute for moments that seemed an eternity for what that maneuver implied about signs of the future in our presence.

The information explosion from computerization and the revolution in personal communications would come faster than even the dreamers imagined. But not yet in 1976.

*   *   *

All of us have secrets.
Secrets accumulate over a lifetime.
Some secrets go to our graves with us.
Maybe that's good.

DAY 1 TUESDAY, OCTOBER 12, 1976

A lake? A pond? About a hundred acres. Crystal clear; spring fed. Fall in Vermont and quite a sight. Starkly impressive early this morning. Many of the trees with their varied colored leaves perched right up against the shore; water at the shoreline blanketed by the dropping leaves.

Scattered patches of mist covering parts of the lake. Other layers hovering at heights on the surrounding hills and mountain making the lake appear to be in a valley. Absolutely, incredibly still. Through the mist the water looked like glass. Fewer birds at this time of year but there were some singing from time to time. The only audible sounds.

When he pushed his row-boat into the water the repetitive sound of the oars cutting into the water and the water parted by the forward lurching bow became the only other real sounds on the entire lake. He hoped to get to his favorite spot at the mouth of the lake and fish for about an hour before he had to go back to go to school. It was very early but there was plenty of light for his trip. He glided past houses tucked into the forest on the shore. It didn't seem like anyone else was awake. No dogs were even barking.

He rowed near the outlet where the lake became a stream with a notable drop in height and could hear softly rushing water.

He directed the boat to a nearby small cove where the water was pooled and still quiet. As he drew closer he saw something through the mist in the middle of the pool. It looked like a big royal blue bubble, maybe two feet by two feet. A bright blue tarpaulin? He stopped his boat about twenty feet away and sat and stared at the blue bubble for a while. Nothing moved. The mist was thinning. He decided to row over to get a better view of this object in the lake. By ten feet away he could easily see the bubble was supporting two extended arms and two extended legs about a foot below the clear surface.

For a moment he thought about using his fishing gear to pull the body to the boat and row it to shore. Who could it be? He sat for a few minutes thinking about what was floating in front of him. Then he looked around and the quiet began to un-nerve rather than relax him. He saw nothing else in the water and along the shore it was still and peaceful. He heard nothing; no cars or activity on the roads that ringed most of the lake. He rowed rapidly to the close north shore and knocked on doors until he found someone to call the police.

* * *

The room was still dark. He lay, awake, for a short time. He felt her next to him. Her quiet, rhythmic breathing. She was asleep. He barely jostled her by moving and her sleep gradually lightened so he was able to speak softly to her to wake her further. He told her he had a few hours before his shift and pulled her closer to him and cradled one of her breasts. She continued to wake up, finally opening her eyes. The circumstances became clearer and she glanced at the glowing clock beside the bed.

She wasn't thinking about the timing of her cycle or birth control. She was calculating the time and the baby's likelihood of staying asleep, Kathy's sleep patterns, and when the dog might wake with any commotion and insist on going out. She got out of bed quietly and did the things she liked to do before sex. Shortly she was back in bed. They put their arms around each other and smiled and kissed. Quietly they made love. The bed covers stayed on. It was warm and comfortable. They were at ease with each other and their love-making was pleasant and relaxed, if not alive with passion. No one woke up who wasn't supposed to be up. Then their bodies drifted apart and they lay side by side, the first rays of daylight penetrating the bedroom.

As they lay there, pleased with the way their day was beginning, one and, just a few seconds after, another beeper went off. The beepers were on vibrate in their cradles above them on the headboard so the sounds generated were loud enough to wake them.

* * *

This was not going to be good. He used the phone first and called the State Police dispatcher. His call was brief. Then she called the hospital. Mrs. Arkady, their Russian émigré nanny, was away this month since Liza was on an elective rotation and had no overnight responsibilities. Without her, on a good morning, getting the household up and everyone off to the day's activities was like a huge ocean liner being turned in its birth. Now there was additional tension generated by the two early morning messages. Liza was no longer working regular hours in a less pressured setting in administration at the University of Vermont anymore. Now she was trying to *do it all*, raising a young family and do medical training.

Liza was out of bed quickly and put on her robe. Clearly the fun was over. Her face was all business now. She rummaged around the room picking things up and getting some clothes for the day.

"This means your mother is going to have to come and that's not great."

Ted was distracted, sitting up in bed, reflecting on the call he just received.

"Why do you say that?"

"Because she raises kids to be State Policemen. That's why. I'm surprised she doesn't have a bugle to play reveille every morning."

"I think we should be damn glad she's nearby and willing to come right over in situations like this. If you don't want me to call her then just tell me how you'd like to handle this? I've got to be out of here in about a half hour. The Mobile Crime Investigation Lab is on the way to Hubbardton where some kid found a body in a lake."

"Well this elective is turning out to be more work than I thought it would be. There's an urgent consult and if I say I can't do it they're going to think I'm not interested and not really a part of the team. I won't let that happen. I'll have to present to an attending by nine-thirty, at the latest. So I guess you better call *the barracks* and ask Major Mom to please come over ASAP."

Dressing themselves, getting two kids up, fed, dressed, and lunches made naturally took time. The arrival of Ted's mother and negotiating with her how she would complete the morning's responsibilities (always some variation in views) took longer than either wanted but it all did get done much sooner than usual. Liza had a thought maybe the kids were getting used to the demands of this life on all of them. Then she wondered, if that was the case, was that so good?

The dog was let back in just as the two of them headed out, still not as early as than they had hoped. Sheila Vallan, Ted's mother, actually relaxed Liza a bit as her mother-in-law's no nonsense, quick assessment of what needed to be done and somewhat surprising absence of any truly critical words about the situation was a relief. Maybe, after all these last few tough years, having a doctor daughter-in-law was beginning to sink in as a good thing.

Later that day Liza and Ted, probably at about the same moment, each had just a quick thought about the few minutes in bed making love. Not whether it was good or bad but that it was kind of a crazy prelude to another challenging day in the challenging world they were living in and trying to raise a family.

* * *

Little chatter on the cruiser radio as he got close to the turn-off for the lake. Nothing about the body he was on his way to see. Ted was anxious and still upset to be arriving later than he thought he should. He knew cases like this were an opportunity for him to demonstrate his interest and ability; to continue his rapid rise as an investigative trooper. As a deputy investigator Ted had achieved a great deal in a short time. His goal was to be one of the few chief investigating detectives for major crimes in Vermont. But he realized there was no easy solution for pursuing his career while also managing the requirements and sharing of responsibilities for his family life.

Turning off the paved road onto a one lane dirt road through woods leading to the lake he was surprised by what he saw twenty yards ahead and had to brake hard to stop his cruiser from hitting a cruiser in front of him. There were four vehicles ahead of his. In front of the lead car the dirt road elevated in a short 'S' curve configuration and the large Mobile Major Crime Unit van, more like an RV, was stuck on one of the curves and likely also on a branch at its roof. A crowd of troopers and staff were milling around surveying the situation. Clearly no one was happy and the time of Ted's arrival would not be anyone's topic of discussion today.

He backed up his cruiser, turned, and parked it out of the way, off the road. He took some gear and started off, walking around the van, heading down the lake road on foot. The mouth of the lake, where the body was, was less than a mile down the road. It wasn't much of a walk but all the equipment needed to ensure a complete and professional crime scene assessment was in the van. Ted figured he'd let the more senior troopers figure the van out.

Ultimately a homeowner brought a pick-up down the road from ahead of the van and some equipment was transferred to the scene. About an hour later, after chain saws and a few shovels were requisitioned from locals, the big van was freed and managed its way down the road, parking close to where the body had floated, about thirty yards from the shore.

Ted figured it would be best, after all this time, to document the scene and get the body out. After that the boy and those around could be interviewed. Until the body could be seen, face up, with the police tarp spread out, no one was likely going to be able to ID it.

So Ted went out in a private rowboat with a camera and a second boat had some poles and a very large net. The peacefulness of the lake in the morning and the nature of the undertaking helped to maintain the quiet. Inhabitants of the few homes that were still occupied in this second home community were standing at water's edge watching the police scene unfold. As Ted used his camera he made a note of which homes seemed to be occupied or, at least, which ones had people outside looking on. There was no way to know yet if people might be in any of the other camps also.

The homes around the pond varied from some smaller, clearly older cabins, to a few impressive appearing more modern lake homes. No telling how many homes were a bit back from the shore but Ted guessed at least twenty-five to thirty houses ringed the lake and dirt roads around the it.

After taking lots of photos, those on the boats had a long discussion about the best way to extricate the body. They decided to float it to shore. The mobile crime van arrived as they did with the body. Behind the van some cruisers fanned out to park. Then both an ambulance and a hearse appeared. Ted stood up in his boat watching them arrive together and he got a little upset with himself because he really wasn't sure which of them was supposed to take a body to the State Medical Examiner's office in Burlington. It was

Ted's nature he thought a chief investigating detective should know what the protocol was for this.

He only thought about it for a minute then decided the hearse, with an officer in the passenger seat to protect the integrity of the body, was probably the right way to transport it. He shot a glance at Detective Lieutenant Rondell and reminded himself to keep an eye out to see how the Lieutenant reacted to the transportation options for the body. However the body got to Burlington Ted knew he'd be involved with the autopsy, which meant he might get to see Liza from time to time during the days to come since the M.E.'s office was in the basement of the hospital.

The body was carefully hoisted from the water with four troopers assisting. They placed the it face down on the big tarp a few feet from the shoreline. He was an obese male wearing a royal blue dress shirt and dark blue khakis. The back of his head was covered with congealed blood matted to his dark black hair. The collar and some of the upper part of his shirt were bloodstained despite having been soaking in the water. He was missing one shoe but a sock was still on that foot.

Ted took more pictures. Then a trooper added another pair of gloves over the ones he was already wearing and began to check the back pockets of the man's pants. He didn't find anything. They turned him over. His face and hands were mottled. He appeared to be a middle-aged, Caucasian male, probably in his fifties. There were streaks of debris over the left side of his mouth and jaw and the upper left of his shirt suggesting he had vomited at some point. They repeated the process of photos and then checking shirt and pants pockets. Nothing was found in his shirt pocket. A key ring with two keys and a small multi-tool pen knife were in one pocket and a money clip with folded bills and a black vinyl case with some cards were in the other.

Ted brought the money clip and case up near the van and carefully removed the bills from the clip, emptied the cards from the case, and placed them on the hood of one of the cruisers for photos and examination. He was hoping to find a driver's license or other form of ID. When he opened the small case there were only four cards; no driver's license. One of the pieces was actually just some paper. It was smudged from being wet but still legible. One side had what appeared to be a phone number but no area code. The other side just had 'BINGO!' handwritten across it. The last cards sort of solved the apparent absence of a driver's license. The second and third cards looked like business cards, with 'OBJECTS D'ART' and an address on Sixteenth Street in New York City printed but no phone number. And the final card was a New York City Metro Card for public transportation. No name of anyone.

Nine bills were folded together in the money clip and their arrangement struck Ted. From outside to inside there were three one-dollar bills, then a five-dollar bill. Next two '$1000' bills and then one ten and a twenty. He had never seen a thousand-dollar bill before and wasn't certain they really existed. There was quite a stir around the cruiser as everyone came over to look at this find. They all chatted a little about the money and then Ted sealed everything up in clear plastic bags and inventoried it, knowing he was now responsible for everything he found.

No one in the small crowd of onlookers came forward to indicate any knowledge of who this man was. Lieutenant Rondell signaled some troopers to pick the body up and place it in the hearse. Then he told a trooper to ride with it to Burlington. Ted took notice.

*   *   *

Seventy-nine year old Doris Albertsen arrived in the Emergency Department (ED) via ambulance about five-thirty a.m. with a temperature of 39.4° Celsius (103° F). It isn't easy to get to 103° when you're seventy-nine. She was off the wall confused, very weak, and it looked like she had vomited recently. Her left lower calf was swollen and red with an unusual thickened and irritated region in the middle of the inflamed area. Mrs. Albertsen was delirious and appeared to be an infectious disease nightmare. Among other measures, after collecting some basic data, the ED staff put in a call for an urgent Infectious Disease service consult. That's when Liza was paged.

Liza arrived while Mrs. Albertsen was still on a gurney in the ED, albeit quite 'wired', with oxygen tubing and IV's, and monitoring equipment placed on fingers, arms, and her chest. Several were beeping a little too loudly to be easily ignored so early in the morning. A discussion was taking place about her clinical status and where Mrs. Albertsen should be placed; on the ward floors in a regular unit or in the medical Intensive care unit. Where she would go was not a call Liza would be asked to make but it didn't look to be a tough decision to her. She couldn't imagine managing all the lines and care this woman would require in a floor ward room. And her probable infectious illness appeared to mandate at least placement in an isolation setting.

Her *man friend* was in the ED but offered little information about the patient or her medical history. He certainly did not have any legal right to make health decisions for her. He knew there was some family in Florida but did not know who they were or what the relationships were. There was nothing available to the doctors to indicate whether Mrs. Albertsen had ever completed any documents detailing a desire for any limitations of treatment in just such a desperate situation as this.

Liza, and everyone who was talking in that group, had been through that discussion many, many times and the answer, invariably, in the absence of instructions from a Power of Attorney or a written document in their hands, was to do everything possible to treat all of Mrs. Albertsen's problems as aggressively and completely as possible. She was to be transferred to an isolation room in the ICU imminently.

* * *

So State Trooper Ted Vallan and Dr. Liza Vallan each began their day as part of teams trying to figure out, really, who their persons of interest were and what happened to them. Liza's team hoped to bring a patient back to health. Ted's team hoped to find out why someone had died…or, more likely, who had killed someone.

*   *   *

Ted Vallan was a seasoned six-year trooper but had been doing special investigations for only just over a year. He was about six feet and he, and for that matter Liza also, tended thin and wiry in appearance, reflecting years of running and activity. Ted thought he looked young for his position, even though he was about to turn thirty. He had perfected that policeman's flat, neutral facial demeanor but his youthful appearance rarely struck fear into others. Except kids.

As he set out to learn about the people and the lake community he was tasked with checking out he still looked a little green, probably because he was. He had little world experience having lived in Vermont his whole life, except for two years in the army. So he often still approached professional situations with some insecurity partly because he knew, uniformly to others, he looked young for what he was doing, and was also early in his career as an investigator. A whiff of a tendency to stammer when first engaging others when he was younger was gone but left him with a lingering, frustrating worry when initiating intense interactions, aggravating his unease.

It didn't seem to inhibit his progress on the force. He was advancing ahead of his peers and was working the path he desired: investigative police work. He worried Rondell and others thought he was most successful working on white-collar crime and he tried to make it clear to his superiors major violent crime was his greater interest. Solving the death of today's dead man was exactly what he wanted to be doing.

Bee pond was in west central Vermont in a forested region that wasn't really near anything. There are no big cities in Vermont and the area around the pond was especially sparsely populated. About twenty minutes, Ted figured, just to get to a 'mom and pop' store.

The region is dotted with small lakes and ponds inhabited more by second home resident's properties than true locals. A large majority of the mostly seasonal folks were from New York, New Jersey, or Connecticut, usually about a four or five hour ride away. Gradually a small but growing number of those folks were retiring to year round, or almost year round occupancy, so the *camps* were getting bigger and more established.

It was a cool, crisp fall morning, the sun now above the peak of the modest mountain making up the east border of the pond. A great day to be breathing the clear, fresh air and anticipating outdoor activities while the sun was out. Ted expected a number of residences were still occupied this time of year.

Early on he asked a local about the road they had all taken to get to the body. As he expected he was told it ended just twenty to thirty yards further west at the mouth of the pond. Another road on the south side of the lake did approximately the same thing. Both dirt roads came in from the east off the county road that ran along the shoreline and the base of the mountain and they ended at the west lake mouth. From there it was less than thirty yards from one road to the other across the stream and dense forest.

Ted was told getting across to the road on the other side of the lake required using an untrustworthy wide plank foot bridge over a shallow ravine. So anyone who drove in one side of the lake had to drive out the same way they came. Of course, since the body was found in a pool near the mouth of the pond it was even possible the body could have drifted there over night after being rolled or put into the pond from the paved county road that ran almost the entire east shoreline. There was often only a small, steep incline ten or so feet from the road down to the water.

*   *   *

"This is bullshit! Total bullshit."

Before he left for headquarters in Montpelier Lieutenant Rondell called Ted and Trooper Jeb Smith, from the local Castleton Station, into the van to talk about the investigation. Trooper Smith was a large man, at least ten years older than Ted, possibly older than Rondell, and he was obviously unhappy. Rondell and Ted sat, facing each other, around the small fixed table and facing benches located right behind the driver's seat, basically like a typical kitchen table set-up in an RV. Trooper Smith was not interested in sitting. He was too tall to stand up fully extended in the van so he hunched over slightly as he paced back and forth in the confined space. He had a two-day growth on his face, which was in fashion but not okay for a state trooper.

Smith continued in a raised voice: "There are at least thirty camps around this lake." He raised his large hand perpendicular to his head. "I am up to my neck in crap. I do not have time to figure out all these people. Look, it's the day after Columbus Day weekend, when we get a ton of these camp owners up from out of town. I can't spend my day going from camp to camp asking questions and filling out your interview forms."

Smith was reacting to the discussion Rondell and Ted were having about how to proceed with the investigation locally. They considered the body could have been dumped from the east road but they both thought it most likely, whatever happened, someone from one of the lake residences or someone in one was involved in this apparent murder. So far there was no easy way to eliminate any of the homes.

Rondell knew much of what Smith said about his responsibilities was probably correct but the trooper's attitude and manner did not sit well with his superior. He eyed him from his bench seat and moved his right leg from the way he had extended it along the top of the bench and began to sit up straight. But Smith was not done yet. "I asked Constable Shire to go to the town office to get copies of the grand lists for this area. And I think I know one of the officers of the lake association here and I'll try to find him to get their lists." He strode back and forth while he talked, then he huffed up a bit and dropped his bomb without even looking at Ted. "I'll do what I can but I have a ton of stuff to do. Junior here, from the city, will have to do his own legwork for this."

Ted didn't move but he felt his face flushing and his body tensed. "Fuck you, Smith." He was about to verbally start after Smith and trash talk about Smith's glorious job of intervening in domestic disputes in trailers but Rondell calmly took over the floor.

"Smith, I'm sittin' here lookin' at you and listenin' to you and I'm tryin' to decide if you might be intoxicated or if you are just one nasty bastard. If you think we're not going to do a job when someone dies…probably killed, then you are full of shit. So why don't you move on and do what you said you can do, now. And I'm tellin' Ted, right in front of both of you, to get in touch with you whenever he thinks he needs to or thinks you can help this investigation. I expect you to cooperate. Fuck the junior thing Smith; my eyes are now on you for a while…and lose that stubble on your face by tomorrow."

Smith was not noticeably affected by Rondell's words. He turned and bent down to get out the van door. In a sarcastic, but soft, tone Smith responded: "Okay Lieutenant, whatever you say." And he went out the door.

Ted and Rondell stayed sitting without either speaking for a minute. Ted was no longer red but he was still furious. Rondell intentionally relaxed his tone. "Ted, you know troopers like Smith live their lives and careers out here closer to the way the marshals in the old west did than doin' the kind of police work we do. They're practically always on call and have to cover large territories. Smith has been at his location, mostly on his own, for years and I'm sure what he has to handle can wear a guy down. You're probably doin' what he used to want to get into years ago, but he never got there. You know the force always has vacancies. For this pay and amount of work we try to keep what we have."

Rondell continued in his straightforward, explanatory tone. He began to slide over the bench to get up. His action indicated he didn't want to hear anything from Ted. As he got up and started to leave the van he turned to Ted. "So try to figure out a way to check out this neighborhood before Christmas, will you…junior and I'll speak with you after we get some autopsy findings in a day or so." The Lieutenant's voice and affect were so un-naturally humanized for him Ted understood his words as an indication of his confidence in Ted. It went a long way towards diffusing his anger.

The only thing the Lieutenant didn't do was give Ted a wink, but that was okay. Ted was on a track Jeb Smith would never be on…if he didn't fuck up.

Ted followed the Lieutenant out of the van and it quickly became all too clear he was now on his own. When Rondell drove away in his cruiser only Ted's and the major crime van were left. It was all quiet again now. Shortly, the van, with the photos, some gear and samples of this and that, and the $1000 bills and cards were packed up and it was off, albeit slowly and carefully on the small road, back to Montpelier.

It was still before noon on a beautiful and now almost warm day. Ted began to consider the obvious challenge, all the more thrown at him by trooper Smith, of how he would find out if the dead man and the circumstances of his death were related to this small lake community. Whatever the total number of camps there were a lot. He tried to think of options that would help him accomplish something in a reasonable time but the task was going to be daunting. First, even though others had spoken with the boy who found the body, he wanted to ask the boy some questions. Police had asked his family to keep him from school to be around for questioning.

The boy, Joe Angle, sat on some large rocks by the lake watching the police activity quite contentedly. A woman was with him who Ted assumed was his mother. Ted walked over but was intercepted after only about ten steps by an older woman who had been milling in a group of presumed lake locals also watching the police activity. In a firm take charge tone she spoke right up:

"Hi Trooper. I'm Edith Jones. I've lived on the lake forever. The fellow in the cruiser that just left said I should talk to you about what I know about our community. I can tell you I don't know who that man in the water was but I know which people who live here were around and who wasn't here over the holiday weekend." She reached into her pocket and unfolded a few pieces of paper. "Look here, I've jotted down the names and number of the camps, on both sides of the lake, and marked who's been around."

"Well, Mrs. Jones, that is helpful of you. Please hold onto those papers. Let me speak with the young man here so he can get on his way and then I definitely would like to talk about all this with you." As he finished he looked around and thought he should make a few remarks to the other five or six people still standing around. He already had several photos of all the bystanders.

"Hello folks, I'm Deputy Major Crime Investigative Trooper Ted Vallan from the Montpelier Barracks and I am part of the investigation of what was found here this morning. At this time we don't know who the man is who was found this morning or if anyone from around here is missing. The State Police are interested in hearing from any of you who think you might have some information about this man or the circumstances of him being here in the pond. I'll leave some of my cards on this stump here for you folks or for you to give to anyone else who might wish to contact us. Also I and probably some other troopers are going to try to speak individually with as many of you as possible about this situation."

[*Shout from the crowd*] "Was it murder trooper?"

"At this point we are not sure."

Ted then turned to Mrs. Jones and said he'd talk to her shortly. "Well Trooper, I'm just eight houses up this road on the lake side.

Please come up when you're done. Let me give you some lunch while we chat."

"Well thank you Mrs. Jones." And he tipped his hat.

Ted then continued on over to the lake's edge where Joe Angle was sitting with his mother. Joe was, rather amusingly, entertaining himself and his mother by cleverly twirling a small flat rock through his fingers then balancing it on the back of his hand and then quickly turning his hand over and catching it in his palm. About an hour before his activities caused a brief ruckus in the area. Joe was probably getting bored and started to skip some stones out on to the lake. At first some of the staff thought something might be going on in the lake. Then there was, briefly, some concern about him possibly disturbing the crime scene. But, actually, other than the lake itself no one was really sure where any associated crime scene might be.

Troopers and crime lab staff had walked the area near the mouth of the lake, including the shoreline right around there on both the north and south sides of the lake and a bit downstream into the woods. They found nothing. There had been a short discussion about bringing in divers but since they really weren't sure what they would be looking for, or where, no plans were made for now. Ted didn't even have the area fenced off with crime tape, again since it wasn't clear the area they were working from even had anything to do with what had been found.

Joe and his mother lived on the south side of the lake in a lakefront camp converted to year round use. Mrs. Angle said there were only three homes on the lake that were used year round that had kids in school and they all were off the south road. Each day school buses picked the kids up and dropped them off in a small turnaround at the county road. Mrs. Angle and Joe agreed there were four other south side homes occupied by year-rounders. The total number of camps on their side was only twelve. Mrs. Angle, in a somewhat annoyed tone, indicated to Ted that their side of the lake was pretty quiet and the north side was much bigger, busier, and crowded; filled with out of towners.

Mrs. Angle worked at the Rutland Regional High School lunchroom and her husband, Stan, home sleeping, worked nights in maintenance at the school. Joe's twelve-year-old sister was in school now. Mrs. Angle had nothing to say that might suggest any recent suspicious activity she had noticed last night or the last few days. She was unaware of any strangers staying in her neighborhood.

Joe seemed to be trying hard again when asked, probably for the third or fourth time, if there was anything else he might have seen or heard from the time he set out in his boat until he came to shore to run to report his finding. There was nothing unusual he could think of but he, once again, told of getting a creepy feeling that maybe he was being watched as he rowed to shore after seeing the body. But no, he never actually saw or heard anything.

Ted asked why he put his boat in on the north shore. Ted had a sense maybe folks on the north and south shores didn't socialize too much; split by more than just the short distance from each other. Joe said the north shore was closer, with camps close by. He would have had to row at least a half-mile to get back to his dock. Once he was on the shore he ran to the closest house and knocked on the front door. He had to go to the fourth house up the road before a light went on and someone opened a door. They called the police.

Ted gave each of them his card and thanked them for their patience, doubting there would ever be much more to learn from Joe. For the first time that day, though, Ted sensed a glimmer of a beginning of getting his arms around the challenge of managing the piece of the investigation that related to all the homes and people of this community.

Ted looked at his watch. It was a few minutes after noon. He was ready to walk up the road to meet with Edith Jones but decided he should first try to call his mother to find out if everything was okay after the quick exits he and Liza made early in the morning. He found out from the Angles all the camps on the lake were still on party lines so he didn't want to use a homeowner's phone. He took a chance and drove down the county road to a small grocery and gas station that only took about ten minutes, thankfully, not the twenty he expected it would. On his way down he asked a dispatcher to alert the Medical Examiner's office he would call the ME at about four-thirty. He knew this meant another pay phone. All the troopers knew their phone codes by heart but finding and using pay phones was usually inconvenient and often a downright mess in weather.

His mother told him all went well and everything was good. He decided he wouldn't tell Liza his mom actually said everything was 'A-OK, honey'. He told his mom he'd try to reach Liza, but if he didn't would she please let her know he probably wouldn't be home until seven or eight so no dinner (and also, he thought but did not say, no family bedtime chores). He was getting ready to say good-bye when a question came into his head.

"Say mom, way back, when you were a bank teller for a few years, did you ever see or hear anything about actual bills as large as $1000?"

"No, I don't think I ever saw anything bigger than a one-hundred. We were always told to have one-hundreds checked by a manager and that if anything larger was passed over to definitely not cash it. So I guess maybe they do exist but that's all I know about it."

"Thanks, Mom."

"But Ted, I'll ask dad if he ever heard about bills like that. Maybe he can get some information for you."

Ted responded instantly; forcefully, "Oh no, mom. Please no. This is police business. Don't ask dad." With some urgency he continued, "Doesn't matter if there really are or if any $1000 bill is fake. I will have to check with a treasury agent anyway."

They hung up but Ted was unhappy he had even mentioned the big bills.

Before he went to Edith Jones' he drove to the end of the north road and parked. Then he walked east up the road. Everyone was gone now. It was a strikingly beautiful day. Looking for any signs of recent activity he glanced over to the driveways of the first four homes, which all were lakeside. None had a vehicle in the driveway, even the home where Joe was able to ask the occupant to call the police. He was tempted to knock on doors and look around a little but felt he ought to get to Mrs. Jones' house since he had accepted her lunch invitation. So he turned around. He locked his cruiser and walked back up the road. He looked around the sunlit road. He saw a spur road going up a hill to the north, with two homes visible on a ledge.

Ted had a feeling one of the homes on this lake held some secrets relating to his dead man. It was difficult to accept a body could wind up here without some local help.

* * *

The Jones camp was much more house than anything like a cabin. It was two stories and had a garage actually attached to the house. Most striking was its location. It was placed, at water's edge, on a small peninsula which jutted about thirty or forty feet into the lake, assuring water views from three sides of the structure. Most of the shore there was a sheet of flat rock. There was no dock but a canoe was pulled up on the rock. A nice sized landscaped area with a permanent bench was placed to enjoy southwest exposure.

Edith Jones was a retired school administrator from Connecticut who Ted figured was probably going to fall into a category he seemed to know well: a no-nonsense lady. Her husband was a retired executive who was away for a few days at a senior tennis tournament. Their three grown children were scattered around the northeast. She was ready for Ted and they sat down to a simple lunch. He enjoyed and appreciated the size of the good chicken salad sandwich and the ice tea she offered. He hadn't eaten anything more than the apple he grabbed as he ran out of the house early in the morning.

"You know Trooper Vallan my husband and I have been at this lake almost from the time it was converted from a girl's summer camp in the early sixties. Some homes have burned down and there have been sudden heart attacks and other health emergencies but there's never been a stranger dead in *my* lake before."

Those words begged the question of whether there had ever been anyone Edith Jones *did* know who was found dead in the lake. But Ted had no reason to go there, at least not at this time. He also picked up on how possessive Edith Jones was about what she, several times, called '*my lake*'. And was it a lake or a pond? He thought it seemed to depend on who was talking. He'd have to check a map.

"It was busy up here this week, with the holiday. It's the last chance for a lot of the folks to close their places up for the winter. As I told you out on the road, I have some papers with a mimeographed list of the camps and owner information on the lake. On a copy of that list I made I checked off who, at least on the north road, was here at some time during the week. I put some question marks next to owners on the south road who I'm not sure if they were around or not.

"Ted? Is it okay for me to call you Ted?" Ted tipped his head indicating his agreement.

"You see, Frank, my husband, is president of the association so we have lists of everyone on the lake. Pretty up-to-date."

Ted put the two lists on the table next to each other. "That's very nice Mrs. Jones. I wonder if you might have another color pen or pencil handy so you and I can go through the list and check off camps you think are occupied today or maybe at least most of yesterday?"

"Sure, I can do my best. But, you know, two or maybe three of the camps on the north road had renters staying and, honestly, I'm not sure about all the camps on the south road."

As he had started to plan in his mind how he was going to approach getting educated about the folks who lived on the lake he had not considered vacationing renters. Virtually all of those folks would be considered strangers. While Edith scavenged for something green to write with Ted thought about what he was learning. He suspected, especially during this busy week, the dead body was probably not in the water more than last night. So finding out about the folks who were here, at least to late yesterday, seemed a reasonable way to initially start to weed through the large number of people and places to check out. He would also have to find out which camps had renters and then track them through those camp's owners.

When they began to talk about the lists of homeowners and properties Edith Jones volunteered another piece of valuable information.

"You need to get in touch with Scotty. Scott Golde that is. He's the caretaker for almost all the camps on the lake. He lives about five miles away and is always around, opening and closing camps, doing all kinds of repairs, and he does the plowing during the winter. Scotty probably has keys to every house on the lake." He wrote down Scott Golde's number.

Ted had some misgivings about what he might be getting himself into but he sat back in his chair and asked Edith Jones if she would go down the lists with him, one by one, and answer his questions about who owned camps around this lake. Her response expressed her reaction to what was going on.

"Trooper Vallan, this place is more than a bit of heaven to most of us here. We like our comforts but the more rural it stays the better for us. It seems like this has been our place of peace and refuge forever. Goodness sakes, we raised our kids here. A stranger, dead in my lake, just doesn't make any sense."

Ted was thinking about a number of things he wanted to do. Working on this list with potential persons of interest right away was important. He knew having his cruiser parked at the lake and for him to be seen walking around was important too. It would re-assure the locals and Ted was well aware crime scenes don't stay fresh very long. He took a few minutes and walked back down the road to retrieve his cruiser and move it to Edith's home. Also important, for later, would be to speak with the M.E. He knew he'd have to remember to call before four-thirty to be sure Doc Roller was still there.

Just before Edith Jones was finally able to launch into her take on the neighbors Ted voiced some consternation about where this Constable Shire was. Edith suggested the Constable wasn't really much of a presence around the lake and she suspected he didn't really ever get involved in actual police work. She described his bright red pick-up to Ted and told him she doubted he had driven by. Edith apparently kept an eye out for everything that was happening around this lake.

Since Edith seemed to have all the information the Constable was sent to get, what Ted wanted him for now was to report any findings from his walk of as much of the remaining south shoreline as possible looking for anything of potential significance farther from where the crime scene investigation team had been. After hearing Edith's quick assessment, Ted's hopes of assistance from the constable dimmed.

"Last night I was alone, because Frank is down in Providence. Did I tell you, at a tournament?" Ted nodded yes. If Edith was going to be a rambler the plan to spend this time with her might not work out and time was critical. He felt a slight sinking feeling as she continued on. "I guess I don't sleep as soundly when Frank is away. Except on summer nights the lake is very quiet at night. I probably read and turned off the light between ten and eleven. Sometime around then I think I was awakened from sleep…But maybe I wasn't exactly asleep yet." She seemed momentarily distracted by her memory. "Anyway, I heard dogs barking. Ted, do you know

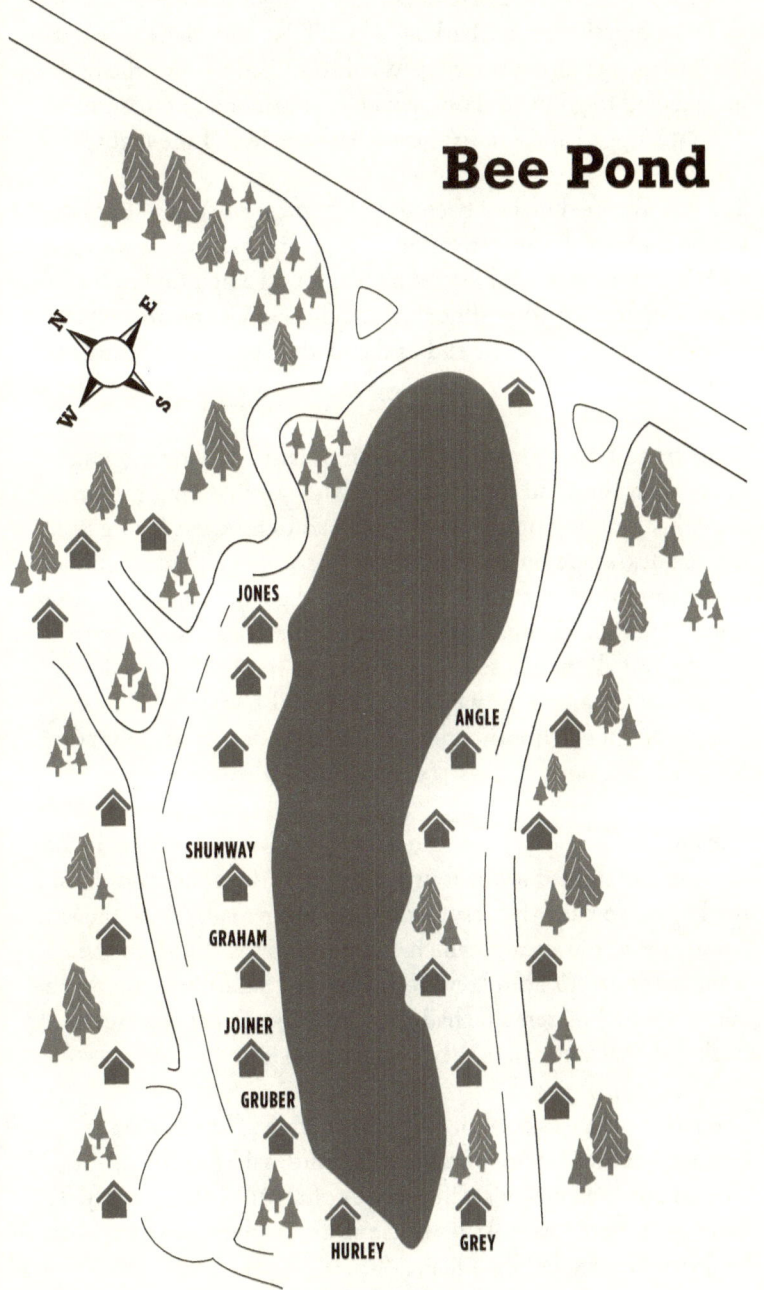

Bee Pond

JONES

ANGLE

SHUMWAY

GRAHAM

JOINER

GRUBER

HURLEY   GREY

how sounds travel on a lake, especially at night when everything else is so quiet? We have barking dogs all day and night here but not so much after the summer. What disturbed me was the barking just seemed to go on and on, maybe for most of an hour straight. Then it stopped and I didn't hear a bark the rest of the night."

Ted was ashamed he had been so quick to consider Ms. Jones might not be useful to his investigation. His spirits rose and he wondered, with her comments and lists, if he had found a helpful key for unlocking some of this difficult situation. He also realized all the times he was down at the end of the road he had never heard any barking.

"One thing I can tell you Ted", an air of familiarity developing in both her tone and usage, "anyone who was planning to leave early this morning on the north road had to have left before at least eight o'clock since the road was closed down then when your investigation van got stuck. No one could get out until after about nine. I mention that because I watched some cars leave as soon as the van and all the cruisers went down the road. As we go down the list I'll let you know whose cars I think I saw then." Was she a one-woman neighborhood watch? Was she too good to be true? Reliable?

The boy, Joe Angle, said he knocked at the first four houses before someone responded at the fourth and called the police. Edith said the Hurleys owned the very last house on the road, where the lake emptied into the stream, which Ted noticed was almost in the woods. They were from New York City and hadn't been up this fall and never had renters. Joe had put his rowboat in at the Hurley dock and that was where they floated the body.

The next house was occupied by year rounders, Ida and Franz Gruber, a retired doctor and his wife. Edith said the doctor was around but she knew his wife was out of town, visiting family. Ted had noted there was still no vehicle at the Gruber residence when he drove the area before lunch.

The third house was owned by the Joiners, also from New York City. Edith said she didn't think the Joiners had been up in weeks, but sometimes their children came, often only for the day, since two of them lived in the state now.

The fourth house was owned by the Grahams, from Long Island, New York. Ted knew it was someone at the Grahams who had opened their door for Joe Angle. 'Fred and Jane', according to Edith, had been up for at least a week. It concerned Ted that while the crime scene was very busy with police and people standing around there had been no car at the Grahams. And there still wasn't one there when he left his cruiser down the road around noon.

Ted started to feel almost dizzy as he contemplated all the questions he needed answered even just hearing about a few of the camps so far.

The fifth camp along the lakeshore was owned by Edna and Sam Shumway, from New Jersey, and they had not been up in a few weeks. They rented a lot and had renters for at least the long weekend, and maybe a little longer. Edith believed the couple was from New York City, but she wasn't sure. Edith said the renter's was one of the cars she saw drive away as soon as the mobile crime lab was able to be driven to the end of the lake.

Ted needed a break from going over the list. How was he going to keep track of who was who and sort out potential involvement? He changed the subject a little to have some time to let what he just learned sink in. "Edith, besides the doctor and you, are there any others who live here year round? Any local folks who still work and live here year round?"

"There aren't very many true locals on the lake, and they don't socialize much with the rest of us or even come to most association meetings. But they do pay their dues so they can get their roads plowed. A while ago some idiot went around the lake putting up posters hoping to recruit folks to sign up for a friendly softball game between the 'woodchucks and the flatlanders' which created a lot of bad will. It was only slightly better when the jerk then tried to switch it to the north road playing the south road. Since all the locals live on the south road that didn't really make a difference and there never was a game."

As she was finishing Edith pointed to a car going west, passing her house. "That's Fred and Jane driving in", she said. Thirty seconds after the Grahams passed a bright red pick-up also drove down the road. It stopped in front of Edith's and Constable Shire got out and started to the house. Ted excused himself and went out to speak with him.

The Constable was a large, friendly man, with a full head of gray hair. Like many locals in rural regions he was trying to manage several part-time jobs to maintain an income. As he shook Ted's hand he also proffered a sheaf of papers which were copies of the town tax records for the camps around the lake. Unfortunately, the way the Constable described his search of the south road, Ted was not very assured his skills were up to the task for a reliable police examination of the area, especially farther east of the mouth of the lake across from where the body was found.

Ted enlisted both Edith and Constable Shire to help him make a list of owner lake locations along the north and south lake roads and which camps had likely been empty or occupied by the owner or a renter the last few days. He asked Constable Shire to drive the south road with him so Ted could get a quick look at that neighborhood. From the cruiser he didn't see anything that struck him. Constable Shire seemed to know very little about the lake community.

When they drove back to Edith's Ted stayed in his cruiser and went through the laborious process, on his radio, of listing owners and phone numbers of the camps he wanted to have contacted by Montpelier staff. The afternoon was passing. Ted figured he still had time to speak with the Grahams right now. Then by four-fifteen he'd have to drive back to the payphone, ten minutes away, to call the M.E. After that he would come back and, hopefully, speak with Dr. Gruber if he was around.

When he finally was able to extricate himself from the clutches of Mrs. Jones' lengthy class on the history and inhabitants of Bee Pond he drove his cruiser down the lake road to the Graham's home. He parked just into the road end of their driveway and left his cruiser there, effectively making it difficult for a car to get out. It was immediately obvious to Ted someone was packing up the huge boat-like station wagon in the middle of the driveway and he felt he needed to make it clear, from the start, by where he left his cruiser, whoever was leaving was going to have to give him some time to get the information he wanted. All four doors and the back hatch of the wagon were open. The day was still warm and it was a nice fall afternoon.

A large, short-haired, tan dog greeted Ted with appropriate barking and tail wagging as he walked up the driveway. Fred Graham bounded from the house down the long diagonal steps from the front door to the driveway and came right at Ted with his hand extended and a big smile on his face. As he and Ted were shaking hands a stylish, blond haired woman carrying two brown bags in her arms and moving much more slowly walked down the steps and went to put the bags in the car. Then she also walked over to Ted and extended her hand.

The Grahams were from Roslyn, Long Island in New York. Fred was a mostly retired lawyer and Mrs. Graham, Jane, was still doing some interior decorating. The Grahams looked like they had jumped off the pages of the latest LL Bean fall catalog. There must be one for seniors, he thought. They looked fit. Ted supposed they were bright and sharp people. The continued smiles bothered Ted a little. They reminded him of the phrase *glad handing* and they seemed superficial in their manner. They were almost too pleasant. Notably, after the introductions, Jane Graham walked away and appeared to continue the process of loading up the car.

"Leaving for home?"

"Well yes Officer." Fred replied. "Our trip home is very long, so this time of year we plan to leave late so we hit the New York metropolitan area after the bulk of rush hour is over. We get home late but we usually don't have to sit in much traffic. I get to spend much of the day in my workshop here and, of course, we usually don't have to get up early the next day after the trip since we're no longer on regular work schedules. You're a long way from that type of schedule. Eh, Officer?" Fred laughed and made a motion as if to push a finger into Ted's side. But he didn't.

"Right. Mr. Graham, I understand the young boy, Joe Angle, came to your door this morning to ask you to call the police?"

"Yessir. He certainly woke us up, pounding on the door. You generally don't worry about your neighbors or seeing strangers up here so it didn't startle us too much. You know, I bet more than half the camps up here don't have their doors locked at night. Of course, we do because Jane is more relaxed with the doors locked, generally all the time.

"Anyway, it was pretty light when he knocked and I opened the door but I didn't recognize the boy and only later I recalled I had seen him before, from time to time, fishing in his rowboat. I'm a lawyer, you know Officer, so I took his concerns seriously. I tried to call the Castleton police and their calls were still being taken by the State Police at that hour."

"Mr. Graham, what made you decide to go right ahead and call the police just based on what a boy, who you said you didn't recognize, told you about seeing a body in the lake?"

For the first time Fred Graham seemed a little defensive in his answer. "At first I did think I should have the boy take me to the lake to show me what he had seen. Then, quite frankly, Officer, it was still very early and no one was out and, not knowing who the boy was, I decided I didn't want to leave the house. So I took his word for it and called the police. I actually even felt reluctant to let the boy into our house so I left the door open, with the screen door locked, so he'd hear me call the police. Then I told him the police would come shortly and closed the door." Ted made a mental note to check out the tape of the emergency call later.

"When the police arrived did you go down to the lake then?"

"Well, no, because we had left with Sporty, our dog, for a very early appointment for a grooming. You see, Officer, grooming in Vermont is quite a bit less expensive than at home in New York." Jane Graham continued to go back and forth loading the car, as though Fred was having a discussion with someone that didn't involve her.

Fred Graham didn't volunteer or seem to have anything to say about what had happened with a body found in the, or *his* (like Edith's), lake. Occasionally, he glanced at his watch.

Ted did not react to that. "Mr. Graham, what about yesterday and last night? Were you and your wife home? Did you or your wife notice anything unusual around the lake the last few days and, especially, last night? Hear any yelling or anything?"

Fred seemed to resign himself to the pace of the trooper's questions and shifted his stance and then walked a few steps so he could lean against the front of his car. He scratched his head. "Well it did seem like it was a bigger night for dogs barking than usual. Jane and I each remarked on that."

"Was there a time you noticed it the most?"

"I think it was the worst some time after ten. First old Gruber's dogs get going, then Sporty starts, and whoever else get going so it can be quite disturbing for a while. But, no, we didn't hear or see anything else that I recall. The lake was busy over the weekend, but I can't think of anything unusual going on or happening. Our direct neighbors, the Joiners, weren't here. The renters next door were a quiet couple who I saw each day going west into the woods for some hiking, I assume. We just waved hello a couple of times. Didn't even speak with them."

A Dodge Caravan slowly drove by and went into the driveway of Dr. Gruber's home. Fred waved as the doctor and his dogs got out and waved back. All the dogs barked. The doctor pulled some bags from his van and walked to his house with no obvious reaction to the police activity.

At this point Ted saw Mrs. Graham make a bit of a show of closing two of the car doors rather loudly. She was obviously hoping to get going. Ted, politely, asked her to come over.

"Mrs. Graham, I wonder if you noticed anything unusual the last few days or last night?"

At first Mrs. Graham paused and looked over at Ted with an expression that suggested 'why is he doing this to me?' Then she turned from her plan to go back up the steps and walked over to Ted and Fred. "No, Officer I really don't recall anything special from last night. The lake was beautiful. But…but you know, Fred, remember I had told you about that light over at the Joiner's?"

Ted looked at Fred. For a moment Fred had a questioning look on his face, then he reacted as though he knew what she was talking about and he continued her story. "Oh, yes Officer, Jane mentioned to me as she was going to bed she thought she had seen a light on in the Joiner's basement, just before. I was doing a few things. About ten minutes later I went over to the west window in our great room and looked over but I didn't see any lights on anywhere." Fred and Jane exchanged glances and Jane looked quietly furious with Fred as he then kind of shrugged his shoulders to Ted. It seemed obvious he was indicating to Ted he was pretty sure there had never been any lights on next door. Or, at least that was the way Ted took it.

"Are you sure you didn't see any other activity at that camp the last day or so?"

The Grahams were becoming unwilling folks to interview. Were they just in a hurry to get on the road or could there be other reasons? Fred answered for them.

"No Officer. Sorry, nothing else comes to mind."

Ted wondered why Fred felt the need to say 'sorry'? He decided to take a chance and see if the Grahams might not follow their usual better judgment in their desire to get on the road or to just end this meeting.

"Do the Joiners come up often? Do they rent their camp at all?"

"The Joiners are up a lot in the summer, less so the rest of the year, and I don't recall them having renters in a very long time." As he finished his answer he turned a little towards his wife and she nodded in agreement. "The Joiners have a bunch of kids and I think the two older boys are in school or working in Vermont; one in Middlebury and one in Burlington. We've seen cars with Vermont plates outside from time to time. We've just guessed or assumed they come down with a girl. Even when they are around we never hear anything from them. You know what I mean? But I haven't seen them this trip."

Ted patiently continued on, probably making it seem to the Grahams like there was no end in sight. "I see. Do the Joiners leave a key with you or anyone else for emergencies? I think it's important that I check their camp, after what has happened and what Mrs. Graham said she saw."

Fred shuffled his feet a little, trying to decide how he was going to answer. When he did the tone of his voice indicated he would respond like a lawyer, no matter how much he wanted to be done with Ted. Of course, there could have been other reasons also.

"Yes Officer, many people give a key to their neighbors in case of an emergency or a problem, and we do have a key to their house. And of course the boys each seem to have a key. But Trooper Vallan," and here he got more formal, "I can't give you our key from the Joiners without getting their permission. I'm sure Scotty Golde, the caretaker for most of the camps, has one also. If the State Police contact the Joiners I'm sure you can get Scotty to open up for you. Officer, we really have to get going. We are as innocent as bystanders could be in relation to what has gone on today and I can't open my neighbor's house for you and wait around until you have satisfied yourself there is or isn't anything in that house that could relate to what you are investigating today."

Fred Graham seemed to have got himself on a roll. His wife looked down at her shoes and slowly pushed some dirt around, appearing now more like she wanted Fred to handle this problem rather than evoking any sign of her previous impatience.

"Well Mr. Graham, after what Mrs. Graham said she saw I will have to get into that house very soon even if I have to disrupt the lock to get in. Just as you have to leave, I have to speak with the Medical Examiner shortly. If the body found in your lake today turns out, as we suspect, to be a homicide then what Mrs. Graham believes she saw will have to be checked out. Mr. and Mrs. Graham please write on this paper all the addresses and phone numbers we can use to contact you as this case is further developed. There is a good likelihood many of the camps on the lake, including yours, will need to be investigated shortly."

Fred and Jane Graham's reactions to this were difficult for Ted to assess. Ted hoped this opening would be accepted by Fred, who might hope by giving Ted his key to the Joiners Ted would not push to search his house. Sort of a compromise. But, clearly, Fred Graham had no intention of giving Ted a key. The question was why? Except for his increasing signs of discomfort and stubbornness in his interaction with him there didn't seem to be anything, so far, to connect this couple with the body in the lake. It was at least interesting that both the Grahams and Dr. Gruber apparently left the lake very early in the morning, after the body was found, but before the police arrived.

Ted had to leave, and he wasn't going to get a key to the Joiner's from Fred Graham. The discussion was getting confrontational and that served no purpose for Ted at this time. The nagging thought the Grahams, Fred, in particular, were fucking with him left a bad feeling though. Ted was tired, and now he knew he would have to check out the Joiner camp before he went home that night. Maybe, he thought, he was the one becoming confrontational.

He apologized to the Grahams that he had to step away for a minute and went to his cruiser to get patched through to Montpelier. He asked them to try to quickly call the Joiners and have them call the Grahams to ask them to give Ted their key. He also called the Constable and asked him to come over to Ted's location to watch the Joiner's house while Ted had to drive to a payphone to speak with the M.E.

Fred Graham's face was red when Ted came back. Now it appeared there was a power struggle going on; at least for Fred.

"Trooper Vallan, we have been very patient with you, but I can't think of any reason why this is still going on. We want to be on our way. We have nothing to do with what happened."

"Yes, Mr. Graham, I know you are anxious to drive home. But we haven't been talking very long and, in fact, as a lawyer I'm sure you understand, you and Mrs. Graham were here when what appears to be a capital crime may have been committed, steps from your home. You called the police to report the finding of the body and your wife reports some possible suspicious activity last night.

"I assure you I will be done for today in no more than five minutes. Please tell me if you think Dr. Gruber might have a key to the Joiners?"

Fred Graham paused for a moment. He had been in the process of getting huffed up about what he probably regarded as poor treatment at the hands of the police. But now he immediately seemed to sense a quick way out of this seemingly directionless conversation.

"Why yes…of course, I'm sure he has a key. His wife is away and that odd, old coot doesn't leave his place very often. Since his kids married off about a year ago we never see him out on the lake anymore. His wife is away so I'm sure he's home." Then he abruptly said, "I'm sure you'll have better luck with Gruber. He actually knows the Joiners much better than we do."

Not surprisingly, Fred Graham appeared happy to encourage Ted to move on to Dr. Gruber. Fred Graham seemed annoyed, naturally difficult, and was obviously insensitive to the day's events. Continued talking hadn't raised any new concerns since the report of the basement light came out.

Ted heard the beep from his cruiser radio and walked over to it. He closed the door so he wouldn't be overheard. Montpelier told him the Joiners said they kept a key under an ornamental pot at the edge of their deck and he had permission to use it to check the camp. Ted was immediately angry. He thought it was a good bet the Grahams knew about that key.

Intentionally, he walked back casually to the Grahams, who made it very plain to Ted they were packed, dog in the car, and ready to leave. That was fine with Ted, who now wanted them to leave before he did.

"Okay, Mr. and Mrs. Graham, it's okay for you to leave now."

Fred and Jane visibly relaxed. Fred had been preparing to continue to challenge whatever Ted said.

"You know, we've talked with the Joiners and they've given the State Police permission to go into their house. They told us where there's a key on their deck."

Fred had no visible reaction. Jane briefly contorted her face, looking confused, then almost shouted out, "Oh that's right. I forgot. There is a key under the big stone bench on their deck."

'Shit!' Ted thought. He had all but excluded them from serious consideration and now he would have to re-think the whole interview and keep the Grahams on his list.

* * *

Mrs. Albertsen was a small woman. Actually, looking through the glass partition of her room, tucked into an ICU bed with oxygen, bladder catheter, many IV lines and bottles, with monitoring equipment flanking her and surrounded by several nurses and techs, she appeared a tiny image, almost lost in all the surrounding people and paraphernalia. Mrs. Albertsen definitely was receiving intensive care.

Liza Vallan was a serious doctor. A no nonsense person (a little like her mother-in-law, actually) but well known to be warm, empathetic, and compassionate as a friend and as a medical resident. In short, she was on her way to becoming the primary care doctor everyone would want as their own. In appearance most would describe her as plain. Slim, neat, and well-groomed. Make-up wasn't on her list of daily chores. She had large and expressive eyes which were perhaps her most notable physical feature beyond her tendency to occasionally, fleetingly, glance away into the air during interactions, indicating thoughts and reflection being processed in her brain. She was always thinking. Some might have taken that mannerism as distraction but it really was, paradoxically, a sign of her alertness and intensity.

Lingering thoughts of being a doctor ever since childhood stayed with her as she took a different path and studied English Lit in college, wound up working at her alma mater, the University of Vermont, and met and married Ted. They agreed Liza would follow her dream and she enrolled in medical school, where she promptly became pregnant (and again in her first year of residency). Yes, there were huge challenges but here she was, in her last year of medicine residency, talking about a fellowship year. As she walked to a corner of a charting room with the Infectious Disease Attending and team so she could present the case of Mrs. Albertsen she knew, through it all just like Ted, this was exactly what she wanted to be doing in her life.

In the ED Mrs. Albertsen's temp remained up and blood pressure, pulse, respirations, and oxygen levels were not consistently stable. Before consults were obtained and the inpatient medicine team took over her care, rightly or wrongly, Mrs. Albertsen was started on a potent broad spectrum antibiotic for presumed sepsis. The origin of this infection now probably in her bloodstream could be from any number of places; possibly her lungs (pneumonia or aspiration; likely on x-ray and exam), urine (pus cells and bacteria in her urinalysis), skin (ill-defined inflammatory or infectious process on her leg), or other locations; even from a combination of locations. So when the Infectious Disease (ID) consult was completed Mrs. Albertsen actually wound up on three different antibiotics and a recommendation for Rheumatology and Dermatology consults to assess her skin findings and certain unusual lab results.

Ultimately Rheumatology placed her on corticosteroids and she promptly developed elevated blood sugars requiring insulin injections for presumed (cortico)steroid induced diabetes. In addition, she was placed on medications for deep vein thrombosis prophylaxis among a host of other standard treatments for this type of ICU case. Her wildness and delirium inhibited her from cooperating in any way and no useful recent or past medical history could be obtained. She repeatedly pulled at her lines which meant at least one staff member had to be with her at all times. Verbally her words made no sense; over and over asking to 'get out of this bathroom'. An initial hope that hydration and improved oxygenation might lead to less agitation was not happening and there was more discussion of possible treatment options.

The ICU medicine team took full control of Mrs. Albertsen's care in the unit before noon. As usual, a third year medical student was given the task of working with Mrs. Albertsen's companion to seek out other neighbors or, especially, relatives; anyone who might know more about her. Her friend went to her home and went through her wallet and a small pad with phone numbers which included a Florida number listed with the words 'my baby' next to it. This was relayed to the student. Since this probably was the important relative they hoped to find the team's senior resident made the call to who turned out to be Mrs. Albertsen's only child, a daughter.

After filling the daughter in on her condition the resident had three immediate goals: First to obtain as much medical history as possible; second, to try to get a sense of whether or not the daughter or anyone else was legally empowered to assist in making health care decisions for her. Finally, he hoped to find out if Mrs. Albertsen ever expressed any wishes about the extent of her care if she ever wound up in a situation like this.

It turned out the daughter spoke on the phone with her mother every few months, usually on holidays, and had not seen her for about three years. She did not seem to know much about her medical history but when queried about a large midline lower abdominal scar she first said, "that was me, a C-section", then she said she now remembered her mother had 'womb' cancer shortly after that and all her female organs were removed and that's why she never had any more babies.

It was after three and Mrs. Albertsen's condition had not improved in any material way. The senior resident repeated some of what was previously said about her mother's probable poor prognosis. Her daughter shouted into the phone "You must get my mommy better! You have to do everything. I don't want her to die. She has two grand babies you know." The daughter said she knew of no legal documents giving her any control over decision-making but said she was sure her mother would want everything done to get her well again. The daughter said she was going to make plans to come to Burlington as soon as she could, but was not sure when that would be.

* * *

It was about twenty to five when Ted connected with Dr. Roller. He had his flashlight and a pad out, standing at the pay phone at the edge of the store's parking area, almost in the woods. It was getting dark and he didn't know how long the call would take. Fortunately, it was not cold or nasty. The M.E., Dr. Roller, was clearly waiting for Ted's call. He spoke like he was in a bit of a hurry. Either he was ready to leave for the day or, less likely, he was in the middle of some other work.

"Yes, Trooper Vallan, I believe this man's death was intentional and, therefore, a homicide. The victim is a middle-aged Caucasian male, probably in his early fifties; obese and not in good health. The cause of death probably was drowning. But he did have a fresh heart attack. I'm sure it all started with blunt force trauma to the back of his head. Some kind of a board, at least three inches wide."

He continued on and Ted took notes as fast as he could. "Lots of water in stomach and lungs, and he had vomited so some of the stomach contents were aspirated into his lungs."

Ted interrupted, "You mean he swallowed his own vomit into his lungs?"

"Basically, that's correct. Not too much and not the reason he drowned or died. He also had food and alcohol plus some small stones and grass in his stomach."

"He was stuffed with stones so he would sink?"

"No, no. Just five stones, bigger than large pebbles but not by much."

"Can I see them?"

The M.E. paused for some seconds and spoke haltingly when he started again. "Sure…. Give us some time to get everything organized and cleaned up and I should have much more information about his heart, brain, and even some of the tox stuff."

Ted always stayed reasonably formal with the doctors he interacted with because, in small Vermont, he could never be sure who knew

Liza. He didn't want to ever make her career in Vermont any harder than it already was. "So, Dr. Roller, do you estimate a time of death?"

"With drowning after trauma and a heart attack he might have stayed alive a short time thrashing about or floating in the water. And the cold water impacts on skin changes. I don't think he had his last food much before he died and my guess is he was dead by midnight last night."

Ted thanked the M.E. and told him fingerprints and the usual things police do with a John Doe would be handled through the Montpelier Barracks. He asked that a copy of the preliminary findings of the post be sent to him over the new FACSIMILE machine at Montpelier as soon as possible. He called home, got a candy bar from the store, and headed back to the lake hoping Dr. Gruber didn't have early suppers.

Lights were on in only a few of the houses as Ted drove back down the north road all the way to its end. He parked between the first house, which was dark, and the second one, the Gruber home, which was all lit up. It was a little after five-thirty. He guessed his visit to Dr. Gruber was not unexpected, which would not be unusual given the day's events near this location. As he walked up the driveway he noticed Dr. Gruber's vehicle had a vanity plate: *STAMPS*.

A pungent odor greeted him as the Doctor opened his door just as Ted knocked, his presence pre-announced by the barking dogs. It was warm inside. Whatever was cooking was generating heat in the smallish living and kitchen area. This was another house that had two floors, a little unusual on the lake; so bedrooms were upstairs. When he entered the camp Ted was immediately struck by the remarkable number of knick-knacks all over the walls and on tables. A long table on the east wall of the living room had volumes of large binders, most likely filled with stamps, Ted figured.

Ted was invited in and the doctor gestured to a chair in the kitchen and he sat down also as Ted sat. The dogs sat too, flanking the

Doctor at the head of the table. Doctor Gruber was a rotund, short man with a kind appearing face. He was mostly bald with graying black hair circling his ears and the back of his head. His thin moustache was completely white. He hadn't shaved in at least a day. With his plaid shirt and baggy corduroys he was more likely to be mistaken for someone like a barber than a doctor.

From the moment they reached the kitchen the Doctor was chatting away. The Doctor retained a modest European accent.

"You see, Trooper, people become collectors for many reasons. For some der is interest in say stamps from a particular location, like a country. Or ma'be from a certain time in history. Some work very, very hard ta obtain every piece ever produced of what dey want so dey can hav a complete set, or as complete as possible, of what dey are after." Actually Ted knew a bit about collectors and their psyche. His father was an avid collector of many things.

"For me, I like old. What excitement ta know you are looking at somethin' from long ago. Officer, imagine possessing somethin' dat was meaningful long ago." His voice rose and he became quite animated as he spoke. "Ta know you have tings, like many of my stamps, dat were used so very long ago by da people who lived den; to me dat is interestin' and satisfyin'. Of course, for me, like most other collectors, I try ta get as complete a set, as possible, of whatever I'm accumulating."

Ted knew, from his father's activities, collecting can also be a way to try to make some money. But that didn't seem to be Dr. Gruber's interest. Looking through the doorway to the living room at some of what was on the walls Ted guessed Mrs. Gruber did some of her own collecting. He wanted to move on to questions about the doctor's whereabouts and activities the past few days but Gruber seemed interested only in providing Ted with a long story about his life and interests.

"You see, Trooper, I worked very, very hard for many, many years. Dey say as a doctor you are also often married ta your profession and I guess dat was true for me. What a pleasure ta be able ta read an study an be learning thins' all your life. Almost every day somethin' new ta learn."

When he heard this Ted could barely restrain himself. He thought, perhaps as a sign of his own pride in Liza, he should tell the Doctor about his wife, a colleague by profession. But the Doctor wasn't about to let him break in, and then his tone turned darker and Ted held off.

"You see, Trooper Vallan, retirement is a tricky thin'. Da kids are gone away somewhere an da patients are all gone. Why read da journals if der is no way to apply da knowledge ta your work? I used ta collect a few thins' over the years, but not much. Den I found myself retired an, over time, I have found dat collecting can be very, very stimulatin' and similar ta studying for da pleasure of learning."

Ted decided the best approach, at this point, was to be direct with the Doctor and take the lead in directing of the conversation away from the Doctor. He had a sense he was being treated like a house guest and, if he didn't get going with his questions, he might wind up expected to stay for dinner.

"Doctor Gruber, I have to leave soon and I know it's close to dinner time for you so I need to ask you about the last twenty-four to forty-eight hours; what you may have seen or heard, and where you have been during this time. I assume you know about what we found in the lake this morning?"

"Ah yes, of course Trooper." He sat back in his chair and rubbed at his day or two old beard. "You see, my wife, Ida, is away in da Carolinas visiting our new grandchild, so I have had da luxury ta not hav ta shave much for a while. Sorry." Ted shuffled in his chair to try to urge the Doctor on. The Doctor remained tangential and in no hurry. Ted sensed his desire to talk and, at least right now, his loneliness.

"Doctor, were you home last night?"

"Of course, Trooper. I let da dogs out around nine, nine-thirty an went ta bed early because I had ta go inta Rutland for a dental appointment at nine dis morning. When I put da dogs out dis mornin' it was quite dark. Dey din even bark for anythin'. I actually left well befor' seven so I could get ta da feed store dere before da dentist. Dey get me special stuff for da dogs and dey open real early. I took da dogs with me. Day love being in da car.

"When I drive back Edith Jones was out up ta road. Oh my, what she told me. Den I saw a police car next ta da Joiner's, near da Graham's. I guess you were da one talkin' ta dem."

"About the Joiners, Doctor. Did you notice anything over at their camp anytime the last few days?"

"No…no, can't recall anythin' ova dere lately. We don' see der cabin too easy from our place"

"You know I have to check all the empty camps and I'm wondering if you have a key to the Joiner's?"

"Sure, Troupa' Vallan, most ever' one shares dere keys around here case of emergencies. Lotsa people know dat da Joiners leave a key under da big pot on dere deck."

While the Doctor was talking Ted was thinking about the time Gruber said he left the lake and Joe Angle's report of no sounds and no response when he knocked on the first three doors. Someone's times may have been off. But it was a jolt when the Doctor told Ted about the apparently well-known location of the key to the Joiner's and that diverted his thought. Ted couldn't help feeling his strange conversation with the Grahams was now of more importance than he had originally considered.

Gruber clearly was a character. Just like the Grahams he seemed surprisingly incurious about what had happened just steps from his home. He seemed happy to be having a conversation, even with a stranger who was a cop, and told some of his life story, unsolicited.

Ted was tired and it was getting late. He had to get into the Joiner's camp and didn't know how long he would spend there. He knew the Doctor was staying around so he told Dr. Gruber he would probably be back to talk with him some more, perhaps later in the week. They shook hands and Ted walked out to his cruiser to get his flashlight.

It was completely dark and getting cool. The jacket in his trunk was almost a winter parka so he decided to continue his work, a little chilled, just in shirtsleeves. Ted didn't know if the Joiner's camp had any power on. If Jane Graham had only imagined a light on there might be no lights when he got inside.

He left his cruiser near Gruber's driveway and walked towards the Joiner's, crossing properties without going out to the road and around to their driveway. Using his flashlight he saw a steel basement storm door as he approached from the west. The walkway to the entrance to the house was on the other, east, side of the house. Since he was mostly interested in the basement, at least initially, he decided to check to see how that door was secured.

Ted was surprised and a little disappointed to find there was no lock on that heavy door. That meant absolutely anyone, in theory, could go into the basement at any time, with or without knowledge of the location of a key to the actual house. He pulled the storm doors open, left and then right, and shined his light down the six or so steps that went into the basement. No noises, no odors. He wondered, and was a little worried, about what he might find. Ted took a deep breath and slowly walked down the steps and onto what felt like a concrete surface.

As he hit the basement surface a loud noise blasted the room. Ted recoiled back a step and reflexedly put his right hand to his holster. The sound lasted about fifteen seconds. At first he wondered if he had set off some kind of alarm, which wouldn't have seemed to make much sense from what he was learning about the area. Just before the sound stopped Ted figured out it was a sump pump, maybe a little louder than most, that happened to fire at the moment his foot touched the cellar surface. Now he knew the power was on.

Regardless of the innocent explanation for the noise, it startled Ted and made him more anxious than he hoped he would be as he wandered around in a strange house. He couldn't find any light switches so he surveyed the ceiling with his light. In the center of the room there was a bare hanging light bulb with a cord. He pulled the cord and the light went on. He was in a room set up mostly as a workshop, plus utilities for the home were in the northeast corner. There were no steps to get upstairs into the house from the basement. There was just one small window, which faced east, making the light from this room visible at the Graham's…if someone was looking.

The room was nicely arranged and notably neat and clean. Almost too clean. Lots of quality tools and everything placed or hanging in well-organized fashion. But who could know if any particular tool from the workbench was missing? There were no signs of any projects in progress or scraps or dust. He could not see any indication of anything being stored in the basement at all. If someone had been in there the prior night Ted couldn't get a sense anything had been disturbed. He stood in the center of the room, under the light. He slowly did a 360 degree turn, with his flashlight directed to corners and walls. A dog barked for a few seconds. Not especially loud. Presumably one of Dr. Gruber's.

As he stood there, looking around quietly, he tried to convince himself since there was no way to get upstairs from the basement perhaps he didn't really need to check out the actual house above him tonight. Nothing looked amiss. If nothing happened last night in the basement Ted didn't imagine there was a great likelihood he would find anything upstairs where no light had been reported. Many different threads of thought were wearing out his mind. And he knew he was wanted at home. But, tired as he was, he was there now at the only site so far that had been reported to have any possible suspicious activity the night of the murder.

He turned off the hanging bulb and climbed out of the basement. As he was closing the steel doors the sump pump, which he had seen in the southeast corner of the basement, made another brief rumble. Ted walked to the back of the house and around to the east gravel walk that led to the front of the house, which faced south; the lake. Several steps up was a deck that ran the width of the front of the house. There was an unmistakable large pot at the west border of the deck; the front entrance was at the east end of the deck. He put his flashlight on the deck pointed at the base of the pot and rolled and tilted the heavy pot off its base. There were a few inches of space inside the ring of the base and a small container was sitting there. A house key was in the small box.

Ted used the key to open the door. The only lights were lamps. Even with several turned on he still thought things were a little dark. Another pretty neat place. Some throw blankets on a chair and couch that were not perfectly folded but it certainly didn't look like anyone had recently spent much time there. He walked around the main room and the kitchen, which was really just an extension of the main room. He looked in the single bathroom. No sign of recent use of any of the faucets; both kitchen and bathroom sinks were dry.

He came out of the bathroom and looked straight across the house to the entrance. Not a terribly well-lit area. He saw some debris on the carpet, off to the west, in an area he thought sure he hadn't yet been. When he walked over it appeared to be a dirt stain from a shoe or a boot. No, there actually were two stains and he decided at least one of them probably was a boot print. The prints seemed directed to the west, where a bedroom was, in the southwest corner of the house.

He walked into that room, probably the master, and turned on the two lamps on night tables flanking the double bed. Nothing obvious. No wrinkles in the cover of the bed. There was one closet in the room and he noticed the door was slightly open. He opened it fully but could not find any light to illuminate it better than his flashlight. It was a large closet. Nothing unusual struck him. Even the whiff of mothballs, probably coming from the neatly placed plastic bags filled with clothes stacked on the shelves, was pretty typical in a seasonal camp. Lots of clothes hanging from the bar across the closet. Then he looked down and something hit him. He reacted immediately. On the floor there were many, at least six or more pairs of shoes; all jumbled up. This was the only mess in the entire house.

He returned to his cruiser for his camera, some evidence bags, and his favored blue latex gloves. He started back but then returned to the cruiser again to take out some yellow crime scene tape. Just in case. Carefully avoiding the dirt on the carpet near the front door he took photos of the probable prints. At the closet he took some shots, especially of the pile of mixed up shoes. He knelt down on one knee and, with his gloves on, carefully pulled out each shoe, making a line, matching each one with its mate. He thought of the back of the card they found in the pocket of the body: "BINGO!" he spoke out loud, to no one. There were seven pairs that had matches and one adult male's that had no mate. The odd shoe was most likely the shoe missing from the body.

Ted took appropriate photos and then carefully put the unmatched shoe in an evidence bag. For a while his energy returned and he recognized the rush of adrenalin he had from his discovery. He thought about trying to track the Lieutenant down to tell him this news. It was after seven, actually getting closer to eight. When he considered the call a little more he decided the only unanswered question this finding raised for the night was whether the crime lab folks should examine the house and area immediately. On reflection Ted decided that was not going to happen so anything to talk about with Rondell could wait till morning.

He turned off all the lights and locked the front door. He put the key in its small container and put it in his pocket. The yellow crime scene tape looked like a crisscrossed candy cane the way Ted fixed it to the front door. He did the same thing around the steel basement storm door. Even though he knew that door could be easily opened, placing the tape usually at least deterred nosey neighbors from going where they were not wanted. He put everything back in his cruiser and sat, for a few minutes, thinking, and taking one last look around.

Only Dr. Gruber's had lights on in the immediate area. But Ted knew more homes had been occupied and lit up last night. He wondered if Dr. Gruber or anyone else, for that matter, was watching his activities of the last thirty or forty minutes? The Doctor had said it was hard to see the Joiner's camp from his and Ted noted just one, small, high up window on his house's east side. It was so dark that someone only twenty yards away would be invisible so it was possible someone was watching him. Just as Ted also thought some of the people in this small lake community were surprisingly incurious about the events of the past twenty-four hours, it didn't really matter for the progress of his investigation if he was being watched or not. He knew it was time to go home.

Ted finally drove home in the dark, exhausted and hungry. His head was pounding. He couldn't help feel a bit overwhelmed about the task ahead of him. And yet, he also sensed some satisfaction he actually had learned something very important about the investigation on just this first day. Finding that shoe in the Joiner camp made it very likely his John Doe hadn't been dumped into the lake from the county road. His body had some connection with someone at this lake. For a minute his body relaxed and he savored the thought of how important his finding was. But that didn't last long. He still had to consider the complexity of even dealing only with that lake community.

Just the few interviews he had conducted that day suggested a degree of possible suspicion for at least two homeowners. If many of the other residents of this lake community also had stories with odd wrinkles in them he still might wind up with a long list of people to consider as suspects in what was now definitely confirmed as homicide. The logistics of getting to interview all other homeowners or even finding out who was and who wasn't around was going to be a challenge. Then how would he manage to follow-up with those who were there last night but by now might be dispersed all around the northeast? He had a sense even getting back in touch with the Grahams would probably not go easily. Getting a key and warrant to search the house of an absent lawyer was probably not easily done. Certainly not without a ton of probable cause.

He already had Montpelier staff contacting homeowners whose camps had been empty and presumed most would agree to let him take a look around if staff phrased it that he needed to check for things like a break-in. But just the time to go through all of them would be daunting. In the early morning he would have a dispatcher read him the list of homeowners staff had reached who had okayed his inspection with the keys Scott Golde had. Camp owners who couldn't be contacted or refused him permission to go into their camps might be considered with some greater suspicion, but who knew? Getting to those camps, he sighed to himself, might turn out to be his biggest problem.

A killer was out there but Ted felt he might be stuck for quite a while slowly working his way through a huge number of useless interviews and camp inspections, basically looking for another needle in a haystack like that shoe. The legal wrangling that might be needed to do a complete job would take time and probably frustrate and anger him, and some homeowners. Sure, he had spent time interviewing some characters today but Ted didn't get the feeling he was with the kind of people who would or actually had killed someone. At least so far.

Who was this tubby guy in the lake? He didn't look like a local or the folks he had met around the lake. Why was he here, and then found dead? From a city? Like New York? There was no apparent connection to the lake. Learning more about his John Doe and the few odd things that were found on him was essential. That parallel path seemed to offer the possibility of leading more rapidly to finding out why this man wound up in Lake Bee (Pond?).

* * *

It was after eight-thirty when he prepared to enter what was usually a maelstrom he called home. As he suspected, more likely as he had hoped, the bulk of the routine daily excitement and activity generated by an almost five-year-old and an almost two-year-old were, thankfully, ended for the day. The kids were asleep and Liza was stretched out on the couch under the light from a standing lamp, reading from a journal. In front of her on the floor George, their chocolate Lab, only lifted his head when Ted walked in, barely acknowledging Ted's entrance. Liza did little more herself. She had a remarkable ability to focus on what she was doing. She was able to snatch small amounts of time and make them productive, especially for her medical education. She looked like she was trying to finish a page and then she closed the journal and exhaled an 'I'm tired' sigh and sat up.

Ted secured his weapon in a small safe then walked over to the couch and also gave a similar soft sigh as he dropped down, demonstrating his exhaustion.

They were each interested in what the other one was doing but their fatigue and the merry-go-round nature of raising little kids sapped some of their ability to get beyond a degree of even superficial verbal intercourse; light years from the way they had begun their day. Ted did indicate to Liza he was now involved in a big case he thought was really important to the force and, maybe, for his career. Liza seemed to understand the implication of what this would mean for his time and schedule for the foreseeable future. They each quietly sighed again and gently rubbed each other on the shoulder. Then Ted got up and went into the kitchen where he ate a small amount of leftovers and washed his and the few other dishes in the sink.

He asked how the kids had managed the day and how the case she had rushed in for early in the morning had come out. They talked a few minutes. Liza went upstairs and Ted let the dog out. A few minutes later he also went upstairs, looked in and kissed each of his sleeping kids, and went into his bedroom. He brought with him the lists he had accumulated from Edith Jones and Constable Shire.

In a few minutes Liza and Ted were in bed, each reading their own material. Beepers were arranged on the headboard as always. Thirty minutes later they turned off their reading lights, leaned into each other and performed a perfunctory good night kiss. Within minutes they both were as sound asleep as their babies.

*   *   *

DAY 2 WEDNESDAY, OCTOBER 13

A little before six Liza brushed aside the curtains in the baby's room and saw one of Ted's parent's cars in the driveway. Not just Sheila, but Thom also was there, ready to pitch in to help get everyone ready and off to their appointed activities. A warm feeling and genuine affection came over Liza for some folks who hadn't always been the easiest people for her to care about. The day was on.

Near seven-thirty Ted met Scott Golde at the east entrance to the south road to drive it and talk about the dwellings on that side of the lake. Constable Shire had reported finding nothing amiss on that road, but Ted's quick trip with the Constable was useless.

Scott Golde was parked just off the road when Ted arrived. His truck's driver's front door was open and he was sitting sideways, with his feet on the running board, drinking coffee from a thermos. Golde was a large, beefy fellow with a ruddy complexion, still tan from working outdoors all summer. The hand he extended to Ted was so thickly calloused it looked swollen. He appeared to be a pleasant and bright guy. Ted encouraged him to ride with him in his cruiser since he wanted time to pepper Scott with many questions about the lake community.

Before Ted could ask his questions Golde started talking. "Trooper Vallan, last year I met a fellow at the state Democratic Party meeting in Burlington. I think he said his name was Tom Vallan. Smart guy. You any relation?"

"Yes. Yes, that's my dad, Thom. He's a clever guy; got his fingers in lots of pots I guess you could say. He has a tough time sitting still."

"Well, you know Trooper, I don't think it will be too many more years and we will start to see Democrats begin to get elected in Vermont. All these young kids been coming here last ten years or so. State is definitely changing."

Very suitably for his job, Ted was apolitical. But not Liza. One of the things Ted occasionally worried about was whether his father's and wife's activity in politics could become a problem for his career in completely Republican Vermont. Ted responded with a neutral, "Well, we'll see."

Driving slowly down the road they saw Joe Angle and a man sitting at lake's edge in two aluminum folding chairs with faded vinyl webbing that was shredded in many spots. They were fishing. Scott confirmed the man with Joe was Joe's father, Stan Angle. Stan Angle looked a bit old to be Joe's father. Joe and Stan turned their heads to watch the cruiser pass. Their expressions were impassive. Scott responded to the obvious question of what he knew about Stan Angle. "I don't see Stan too much. They say he's working nights now, but I know he was living out of town for at least a couple of months until just very recently. Always a quiet guy. Never had any real conversations with him. Guess he's unfriendly or shy."

"Anyone ever mention where he was those last few months?"

"I heard someone say Stan was doing some kind of work near the New York City area, but, for all I really know, he could have been in jail or anywhere." Scott smiled and laughed.

Ted was disappointed when Scott Golde told him the last house at the west end of the south road, the Grey's, was not checked off on the list Ted showed him. That meant the Greys either hadn't been contacted or didn't agree to have the State Police check their home. Edith Jones had known very little about the Greys or their house. Their camp was located at water's edge, no more than thirty or forty yards from the other side of the lake where the body was found. It was the only house on the south road set off from the others and seemed more in the woods and a little hidden.

Since they were there Ted wanted to at least walk around it and more closely consider its proximity to the area where the floating body was found. The very end of the road made a slight hook to the right and ended at the driveway to the Grey house. The house beyond was built no more than ten feet from the shore. It was not easily seen from the road until you practically came right up on it.

As they stopped at the driveway Scott Golde told Ted the owners lived in New Jersey. Scott had a key with him. He indicated, without any particular hint of rancor, he hadn't done anything in the Grey camp for over a year since the Greys no longer seemed to request his services. He was aware the owners made a fuss with the association last winter, refusing to pay for the snowplowing he is contracted to do for the association roads since they said they weren't going to be up all winter. Everyone else always paid even if they weren't going to be up because the roads had to be clear for any emergency vehicles for a fire or whatever emergency. It struck Ted any structure that burned up here in most any season would be just a foundation by the time any fire truck could get to this remote spot.

As they each got out of the cruiser Scott told Ted he thought he might have seen a car in the driveway Saturday or, possibly, Sunday morning. He couldn't recall more than that. Since he said he didn't notice whether the vehicle had in or out of state plates Ted thought it more likely the plates were in-state.

The house was not in good repair. Scott directed Ted to a path that went south, around the back of the house. Scott said there were doors on three sides and a storm basement door at the west foundation. They went up and then down a small rise and just at the end of the southern exposure of the house there was a door, facing only woods, and it was open about three inches.

Ted, and then Scott, stopped talking and Ted motioned to Scott to walk back to the road with him. At the cruiser he pulled out two of his prized blue latex gloves and a flashlight. He un-snapped his holster and asked Scott to stay at the cruiser and please try to be patient. He walked back to the open door. He put the flashlight on and, while staying outside, peered in. Then he knocked loudly on the door and announced who he was, starting and ending again, quite loudly, with "State Police". There was no audible response.

He stepped back and pushed the door completely open using the back of the hand with the flashlight while keeping his other hand on his holstered revolver. Nothing. This was one camp where the power was not on. It smelled musty and it was cool. He saw he was entering through the kitchen. He carefully pulled some curtains open and moved into the main living area where he did the same to get some light.

First he felt the mouse droppings under his boots, like coarse sand. Putting his light to the floor he thought he detected a possible path of droppings heading to a door on the northwest side of the house. He walked that way and cautiously opened the door. The room smelled like garbage, not overwhelming but unpleasant. There were windows at two exposures and he pulled all the shades up, which let a fair amount of light into the room.

This was probably the master bedroom. There were a bunch of rumpled blankets on the large bed. Ted carefully pulled them to the side to make sure nothing was underneath but there was something. There were no sheets. What he found were some streaks of dried blood on the mattress cover.

The mouse droppings were more directed to a corner next to a bathroom, where a wastebasket was tipped over. McDonald's wrappers and some pieces of buns were at the tip, along with Mountain Dew bottles and, as best he could see, two bloody tampons. The toilet in the bathroom had some waste in it. Always sure to get a reaction from Ted, or anyone, when considering what someone was thinking when using a toilet in a camp with no water or power on.

As he walked out he noted several candles had been used. Amazing they hadn't burned the place down. Walking out the kitchen door to the driveway he thought, 'so much for the investigative skills of Constable Shire'.

Ted told Scott Golde he would need some time to document what he had found. Scott said he would do some preliminary work for the winter removal of the dock and float at the next camp while Ted completed his investigation of his findings at the Grey's camp. Ted removed his camera, some plastic evidence bags, and crime scene tape from the cruiser.

Back inside the camp he took photos, inventoried what he saw, then folded the bloodstained mattress pad and placed it in one of the plastic bags. Finally, he carefully removed the tampons from the tipped wastebasket and secured them in bags also. His only real goal was to secure the things with blood so typing could be done to rule out any association of this break-in with the death of his John Doe. He was pretty sure they were unrelated.

Back outside Scott Golde came over as Ted was placing the evidence bags in the trunk of the cruiser. After that they went back to the camp with some wire Scott was able to find next door and made an effort to create a barrier by wrapping it around the broken door so any entrance through that door would be a defiant act of breaking in, again.

Back at his cruiser Ted used his radio to get patched to the Castleton Station. Not a great surprise that Trooper Jeb Smith responded to the call. There was no love lost between these men.

Ted knew Smith had no interest in speaking with him, and his gruff manner was transmitted through the radio. Ted was all business and told Smith he had just happened on a B&E at the lake he was working. Probably unrelated to his murder investigation. He kept on talking and told Smith he had documented the scene with photos and would be taking the only pertinent evidence for his investigation back to Montpelier. He assured Trooper Smith he would have the relevant results and copies of the photos sent to him in Castleton.

When he finished what he had to say to Smith Ted was not surprised at Smith's response.

"Vallan, since you found the crime and started on the investigation that means it's your responsibility to complete the investigation and report."

"Bullshit, Smith," He said with great emphasis. "Some Castleton College kids enjoying their Mickey D's after sex in someone else's house in the middle of nowhere; that's your job. See you around."

He clicked the radio off. He couldn't help showing a grin and feeling some satisfaction. Scott Golde was standing beside him during the conversation and chuckled quietly. As Ted turned and their eyes met it was clear Golde knew a little bit about Trooper Smith also.

*   *   *

Ted satisfied himself that evaluating the homes and homeowners on the south side of the lake was not going to be nearly as challenging or time-consuming as figuring out the folks on the north side. There weren't many camps on the south road and they were small and, except for the Grey's, the area wasn't very wooded. You could see several houses from any one house. Scott Golde was unaware, in particular, of any renters last week.

As they slowly worked their way back east towards the county road Ted slowed further and stopped when they were as close as the road went to Stan and Joe Angle, who were still fishing. Ted opened his door and got out and called over to them. "Fellas, I'm going to drop Scott Golde off at the county road then I'm gonna come back to talk to you for few minutes."

The fishermen looked at him but had no visible response to his words. They drove on and when Ted let Scott out at his truck they arranged to meet a couple more times over the next few days to do more thorough examinations of empty camps. Staff at the Montpelier Barracks were still contacting homeowners to get needed permissions for Ted to use Scott's keys to get into unoccupied camps.

* * *

He parked his cruiser in the dirt driveway. Most of the camps had driveways covered with gravel they would replenish periodically. The Angle house's driveway was dirt, pocked with depressions and some ruts. The home was a small cape, falling, as so many other Vermont homes, not so graciously into disrepair. It was another Vermont property with a perpetual 'For Sale' sign at the junction of the road and the driveway. A beat-up old Dodge Dart was parked just below the deteriorating wood front steps.

It was unusual for Ted to find local, year round, Vermonters living in a lake-front house. Lakefront anywhere in the state was valuable, meaning the cost of both the camp and its taxes were often prohibitive for most locals. Maybe they were long-term renters and so not considered the same as vacation renters. Ted walked to the west side of the house and started to the lake. Only the boy, Joe, was there now, the second chair still present but unoccupied and the second rod was gone. Joe had put his fishing gear down and was skipping rocks on the lake surface.

"Hi Joe. Looks like skipping rocks is something you do really well."

"Plenty of time around here to toss rocks. Say, my dad told me to tell you he had to get to bed so he's in the house. He works nights and had been fishing with me way too long. He's been up since late yesterday afternoon."

Ted tried to keep a neutral look on his face as he thought about possible reasons for Stan Angle's action. He knew he should make a quick decision. Ted would either accept what Stan just did and not question him today or he should go to the house and challenge Stan's action. He decided to keep talking with Joe for now while considering how to react.

"How come you're not in school Joe?" Just a friendly, informational tone. Ted wasn't interested in being anyone's truant officer.

"Oh, I have a half day today for teacher's conferences. I'll be leaving with my mom in about a half hour. She works at the school lunch room, you know." While they were talking Joe put his hand in his pocket and pulled out what looked to Ted like the very flat stone Joe was twirling from finger to finger when he first met Joe a day ago. Joe started rolling it from finger to finger just as he had done then.

"Joe I just want to tell you again, as I did yesterday, we don't really know what happened to that man you found or how he got there. It's very important for this investigation you keep all this, everything that you've seen and heard, to yourself for now. If you need me to explain to you why that is necessary, I will."

"No Officer, I think I understand why. And my dad pretty much said the same thing."

Ted and Joe were both transfixed with the neat way Joe fluidly twirled the stone in his hand from finger to finger.

"Say, you roll that stone really well. That your *lucky* stone?"

"Well …I, I guess maybe it is now. I just found it yesterday while my mom and me were sitting on that stump on the shore watching what was going on and waiting for you to talk to us. It's a little small to skip. And last night I saw it looks like it has some kind of marking on it."

"Really. Can I take a look at it Joe?" Not surprisingly Joe, an affable, relaxed appearing teenager flipped the stone, like a coin toss, to Ted. Indeed, the stone had a bunch of unusual features. Barely larger than a quarter and, uniformly, about an eighth of an inch thick, it was almost perfectly round, except for a small nipple like bulge. About a quarter of an inch from the tip of the nipple protrusion was a small hole in the stone. One side was blank but there definitely was some kind of marking on the other side. The marking was faded and meant nothing to Ted. But it was definitely a stone. Ted couldn't imagine it could be a coin or anything like that.

"Was it on the shore or in the water when you found it? Have you ever seen anything like this before?"

"No, no I've never seen anything like this before. It kind of stood out a little from the other rocks right on the shore. It was so smooth and round compared to the others."

Ted was impressed with this stone but had no idea if its presence at that location in the lake should mean anything to him. Of course he remembered his John Doe apparently had some stones in his gut on autopsy and he assumed that was maybe why he was more interested in this object than he would have been if Doc Roller hadn't mentioned them yesterday. Anyway, he decided he should hang onto this stone for a while. He didn't make a fuss about taking it from Joe and Joe didn't react like it was a problem or big deal to him. Ted liked Joe. He decided, for now, not to press Joe's father on why he walked away or where he had been the last few months.

*   *   *

Day 2 ICU Wednesday

Before formal rounds began the students, residents, and fellows on the ID (Infectious Disease) team each hurried to see the patients for whom they had completed the initial consult for the team. A small number of patients were actually on the ID service so their status would be updated by meeting with the appropriate medicine floor team. When both teams met on rounds that often meant almost ten people in white coats squeezing into a small, usually doubled bedded room.

Rounds with the ID attending would start at nine-thirty and most of the patients would be discussed. That meant Liza only needed to see three patients before rounds. But ID was a *cross the t's and dot the i's* service, very labor and time intensive, especially in tracking down all the cultures and other lab studies that would be pertinent. ID and Rheumatology consults were generally among the most comprehensive reports in Internal Medicine.

The ID team always began formal rounds with the attending physician on service for that month in the ICU. Presumably the sickest patients. Sometimes so much time was spent there with those incredibly ill and challenging patients the remainder of rounds became a rushed struggle to be done before about noon.

As soon as she arrived at the hospital Liza went to the microbiology lab to check on cultures and then to the ICU to see Mrs. Albertsen. Vital signs were significantly improved but that was about it. Urine output was poor. Mrs. Albertsen remained delirious. Very confused and still thrashing about in bed trying to pick at her peripheral lines. She looked exhausted and was still not taking anything by mouth. The unusual red splotches initially exclusively on one leg now appeared on three of her extremities. The lesions were thick and firm and obviously tender. She recoiled if one of those extremities was touched. Laboratory values from very early that morning showed further worsening of liver and kidney function. No meaningful microbiology data had developed to suggest any recommendations for changes from the consulting ID group.

In many ways the environment in the ICU seemed to contradict a basic tenet of healing. It wasn't really a place to rest. The unit was active 24/7. Lights were never more than barely dimmed. There was a tonic level of noise; sounds from equipment and machinery. That hum was frequently punctuated by louder sounds, especially the voices from staff and patients.

Mrs. Albertsen looked awful. Her clinical picture and likely prognosis were nothing Liza hadn't seen many times before for patients in this age group. Lying flat on her back, tethered to so many lines and tubes she was unable to control use of her extremities. Starting days before she came to the hospital she probably had no meaningful nourishment, which continued now. Thoroughly confused, obviously anxious, and agitated. She was profoundly weak.

Would it be possible for any elderly person to physically tolerate the insult of serious acute illness when virtually every part of her had been destabilized? The massive functional decline of Mrs. Albertsen foretold her end. Liza and most of the physicians attending her knew it. But only a few wondered, like Liza did to herself, whether it was cruel to Mrs. Albertsen to put her through treatment that was only going to worsen and prolong her great suffering when there was little doubt about her end, shortly.

Nothing like that was discussed and all the consult services and ICU team each concentrated on trying to determine why Mrs. Alberstsen was so ill and what disease treatment might make a difference for her. It fell, through the well-established pecking order of responsibility, to her assigned intern on the ICU team to call Mrs. Albertsen's daughter and fill her in on her clinical status and issues. The intern was advised to alert Mrs. Albertsen's daughter things were not going well and she remained very critically ill.

* * *

DAY 3 THURSDAY, OCTOBER 14

Ted drove to the Montpelier Barracks from home. He picked up the two $1000 bills to bring to bring to Burlington to show them to the U.S. Treasury Agent for the area. That office was in the Federal Building downtown, naturally, on Main Street. After he signed out the bills he headed west to the city. Then he made a silly mistake that would annoy him all day and generally left him cranky about events that day.

He hadn't called to speak with anyone about the bills before he brought them over. He just assumed the treasury agent would want to take custody of the bills so they could be evaluated, he guessed by somebody, for authenticity. He left an appropriately documented file, with photocopies, in Montpelier.

Ted parked and went into the main lobby and read the directory. He found the location and climbed the three flights, two steps at a time, his usual practice, and walked to the office and went in. The room and the reception desk were empty. Since the door was unlocked he assumed someone was around. He stood at the desk a few minutes, hoping someone would appear. Didn't happen.

The space was small. It looked like there were just two offices down a very short hall, and he could see what he assumed was a coffee room farther down at the end of the short corridor. Ted walked to the entrance of the hallway and asked:

"Hullo, is anyone around?" Pause. "Hello?"

He heard some stirring in one of the offices. A chair squeaking as it moved on the floor. A surprisingly long minute after that, just as Ted was preparing to knock on the door of that office, the door opened. A tall, chubby man with a tie, his shirtsleeves rolled up, and a none too pleasant expression on his face, a frown Ted thought, came out of the office. His clothes looked like they might have just dried after getting soaked in a rainstorm. Ted doubted it had rained yet.

"That son of a son of a. Not coming to work today is gonna screw my whole day. How will anything get done?" Ted retreated to the reception area and the agent, he presumed, would follow him there. All business: "Yes, what is it Trooper…er, Trooper Vallan", as he read the name tag? "This day is gonna be some day." No hand extended.

Ted extended his hand. "Yes, Ted Vallan. And you are Agent…?"

"Smith, Agent Charles Smith."

He let Ted take the lead. Ted explained the reason for his visit. Agent Smith evidenced very little interest in how the Vermont State Police came in possession of the two large bills. Agent Smith looked at him as Ted spoke and his expression seemed to be asking what Ted wanted him to do about the bills. So Ted told him.

"Well, I don't know anything about bills like these." He opened the folder under his arm and removed the plastic bag with the two bills and put them down on the receptionist's desk. Agent Smith made no effort to examine them.

"I don't know if these are real or if there ever were or still are bills that large. If real bills this large do exist then it's important to a case

I'm working to find out if these are real or counterfeit. If these are just joke money that might be significant since, to this point in the case, I've been assuming they might be real."

Agent Smith apparently had heard enough to satisfy himself what his role was so he didn't bother to inspect the bills or ask Ted anything more.

"Could be real. Some big bills still around. I don't know squat about that kind of stuff. You need to talk to Milt Frober. He's the agent in this district handles that stuff. He's out of Albany. I'll get you his number."

Ted was a little startled. "Don't you want to take these bills and send them to the agent in Albany? I've got copies and I've written down everything on them. I need to know if they're real."

Agent Smith was busy writing down the info with Agent Frober's name and number while Ted spoke and handed it to him as Ted finished. Ted felt dumbfounded.

"We can't help you here. Got no safe mechanism to transfer them to Albany. You guys may have to do it." The agent looked at him like Ted was taking up his time. Then he seemed to pause and think for a moment. He said he would copy both sides of each bill and send a FACSIMILE to Frober, in Albany, sometime today. Ted felt there wasn't much more for him to say so he nodded and watched, very carefully, as Agent Smith took the bills out of the plastic and copied both sides of each of them. Ted made certain both bills were back in the plastic bag the agent returned to him.

A phone rang in Agent Smith's office and he gave Ted a 'we're done' look and made a move towards his office. Ted nodded and turned and left. "Thanks for not much" he mouthed under his breath. On the stairs going back down he thought at least the Agent said such bills could be real. That was justification to pursue this with the agent in Albany.

Ted was annoyed. He expected to leave the actual bills. He was planning to go from Burlington down to Lake Bee. He didn't think it was a great idea to bring the bills with him to the investigation site. Shit. He could, and would, bring the bills to the Williston Barracks, about ten minutes away. There would be paperwork but he would be able to get them safely locked up there and get on his way south to the lake...or pond, whatever it is. He never looked it up yet.

Since the treasury office visit was quick he had some time he hadn't counted on. Before he drove to Williston, he decided to call the M.E. to see if he could drive over while he was in Burlington now and get the information the M.E. promised him, instead of on Friday. This time Ted definitely thought to call first. He drove to the Burlington Police Department where there always was a desk troopers were free to use.

After a quick *shoot the shit* with the duty sergeant he sat at a desk and called the M.E.'s office. The secretary who answered was non-committal about where the M.E. was. After hanging on for over a minute she came back on the line. Ted had the sense her tone probably echoed the way Dr. Roller had spoken to her. She told him, rather firmly, the Doctor had told him he wouldn't have more information for him until, at the earliest, on Friday. He got the 'don't keep calling' implication of her words. He was surprised, though, to hear what he was asking for might not be ready the next day; Friday. The M.E. report in his last capital case (Ted's first) had moved along very quickly. That was a domestic violence case. He wondered if any of this meant anything about this case.

So he set out for Lake Bee, first stopping in Williston to lock up the $1000 bills.

The weather had turned cold and damp. His plan for the day was to complete checks of the camps made accessible to him by owners near the west end of the north road. On Wednesday afternoon he was able to spend time at the Hurley camp, the last on the road. It was one of the larger houses. All power and water was off. He found nothing to register any concern although he noticed the mice were already moving in for the winter.

Today he hoped to check as many houses along that road as he could get to, working his way east. Nothing further was found at the Joiner's by a crime lab team so he skipped that camp. Ted was pleased the folks just east of the Graham's, who had the renters last weekend, were on his list from the dispatcher. A good look at that camp seemed important. But he saw no indications of concerning activity or that anything was obviously moved or otherwise disturbed around that camp or the almost eight or so other houses he was able to enter toward the west end of the road. And, maybe just as importantly, Edith Jones, his local eyes and ears, sought him out and reported nothing new that was notable.

Ted was extremely appreciative of the time Scott Golde was giving him and he wanted to make sure Scott was not put in an uncomfortable spot by allowing the police to inspect any camp without an okay from the owner. So he made sure to show Scott the list of names with those contacted who agreed to a search of their camps. Scott Golde then gave Ted the keys to those camps on the north road he hoped to evaluate that day.

As he moved from house to house his spirits sagged. He had been through a bunch of camps with, except for the Joiner's on Tuesday night, really nothing to show for it. Of course, he wasn't even really sure what he was looking for, beyond obvious signs of a disturbance. Maybe blood or maybe another body. Anything subtle had a good chance of being missed. Frustrated, some anger directed at the M.E. welled up in him. The slow flow of information from that office about his John Doe was stifling progress on that avenue of investigation.

He wanted to contact police in New York City but felt he still didn't have enough for them to pursue the case at their end. His own lab had told him that morning there was no match for the dead man's prints in the Vermont state database. There had been no missing person report anywhere close to his John Doe's description in Vermont.

All the time he was methodically looking through those camps he was feeling stymied because he couldn't search the two camps, the Graham's and Gruber's, he considered possibly more important than any others on the lake, so far. He knew he had no grounds for even considering search warrants for either of them. He also still wasn't sure what the deal was with Stan Angle, and interviewing him remained a priority. Unhappy as he was, thinking that checking all the unoccupied camps was going to be a waste, Ted felt he had no option. For the moment, he also appeared to have the time.

*   *   *

Day 3 ICU Thursday

When Liza entered the ICU early in the morning she was greeted by the intern. He wanted her to know Mrs. Albertsen had improved overnight. He was more than a little excited as he told her all vital signs remained good and the patient was having lucid periods. She actually took some broth by mouth just a half-hour before. Liza reviewed the chart, put on a gown, gloves and mask, then walked into the cubicle where Mrs. Albertsen was residing. Indeed, she was more alert, following Liza's movements around her bed, suggesting improved awareness and attention. Liza would not have faulted the patient for assuming she was one of the nurses since Liza was one of the very few female physicians patients would see in the hospital.

Liza was impressed. Mrs. Albertsen did seem less delirious. Other than that though she didn't find much, or really anything else, especially encouraging. The patient developed loose and oozing diarrhea in the middle of the night and a rectal tube had been added to her long list of tubes and wires. A nurse told Liza Mrs. Albertsen had 'sparse padding on her skinny bottom' and her skin was already breaking down, necessitating the rectal tube for skin protection (and also, Liza knew, to lessen the need for staff to constantly be changing soiled bed pads).

Close to nine the members of the ID team gradually assembled in the ICU to begin rounds for the day. Not surprisingly, several other consulting services were in the unit beginning their daily rounds starting with their sickest patients also. There was a brief kabuki like dance movement as several small groups, members of each group moving in unison like a school of fish, jockeyed to either be first with a patient or rush to another patient who wasn't being seen yet.

It happened both ID and Rheumatology began their group motions just as the ICU team arrived at Mrs. Albertsen's bed. So each team decided to listen to the intern's update on her. That necessitated having the discussion in a charting area just a few steps from the cubicles with the patient beds. At least fourteen or more physicians and a couple of nurses scattered about the small area for the discussion. This turned out to be very unfortunate for the young intern who had the responsibility to update everyone in that area about the patient's status.

This type of quick meeting was by no means unprecedented. The intern was actually kind of excited to be able to tell all these interested staff members Mrs. Albertsen might be getting better; beginning a long road back to health. He spoke as though he was convinced. He reported on the events of the prior twenty-four hours, her vital signs, which continued to be good, and her return to periods of lucidity and less agitation. He described the increase in the number of lesions on her extremities but said older ones now appeared to be fading a bit. And he mentioned the diarrhea. Finally in his review he updated the latest lab data. That's when he made his error.

Listing her latest blood chemistries he reported her kidney function blood results as distinctly improving. This raised a few eyebrows, as consideration for adding kidney dialysis was being anticipated since the day before she had nil urine output and her kidney chemistries were just short of disastrous. Although the kidney blood tests were slightly lower, the way these levels move clearly allowed for no such interpretation. The large group in the room knew the intern was interpreting these results as though kidney function measurement changed in a linear fashion. But, actually, it moves geometrically, which meant, at the very high levels being measured in Mrs. Albertsen's blood, only a much, much larger drop could justify his claim of improving kidneys.

His error led to some awkward moments before a senior resident on the ICU team clarified his comment. In the great scheme of things the mistake didn't make much difference and might not have seemed to many to be a big deal. But in the world of an academic training program it was very unfortunate. More than just perhaps marking this intern, indefinitely, for his apparent knowledge gap, it placed a psychological burden on the intern for having screwed up in front of many levels of peers and superiors. Internship was defined as demanding and intense. The intensity of this man's internship had just been ratcheted up by several orders of magnitude.

Ultimately, after discussion and input from all involved resources, there was sort of a consensus Mrs. Albertsen probably had an underlying, ill-defined, autoimmune disorder, greatly fueled by infection. The use of large amounts of corticosteroids appeared to be helping her, while at the same time steroids, being the ultimate double-edged sword, also were contributing to many of her problems. ID advised stopping one of her antibiotics hoping that might impact favorably on her diarrhea. The steroid dose needed to be continued. Dialysis was not to be started today, but remained likely soon.

After rounds the senior resident called the intern aside. He wanted to talk with him about the phone call he was about to make to Mrs. Albertsen's daughter, whom he had promised to update daily. The intern was advised to remain very conservative in his estimate of the patient's status and prognosis. The senior resident was clear to the intern her survival remained greatly in doubt and everyone involved in this case was extremely interested and hopeful permission for a post-mortem (autopsy) exam be obtained if and when she died.

When he called Mrs. Albertsen's daughter he truly intended to follow through as instructed. But in this, their second conversation, the two seemed to bond a bit and Mrs. Albertsen's daughter was so distraught and also seemed so dependent on the intern he found he felt he had to be somewhat encouraging. So he mostly spoke to her about her mother's improved alertness and ability to take sips of liquid by mouth.

* * *

At the end of the day Ted called the state crime lab. There wasn't much new about the body. Ted said he was anxious to contact the New York City police but didn't have much for them to go on. A tech told him he had read there was some success around the country getting identifications sending enlarged fingerprint copies to other jurisdictions over the new FACSIMILE machines.

He called Lieutenant Rondell and they reviewed the parallel tracks Ted was pursuing. Rondell made it clear, despite the likely low yield, he agreed the camps and people around the lake needed to be evaluated and checked as completely as possible; sooner than later. He told Ted he was not anxious to have someone find a body or obvious indication of involvement weeks from now. Ted got it.

As far as better identifying the body and its apparent connection to New York City he advised getting started with the NYPD on Friday. Something might be out there already they might be able to connect to their John Doe. Who knows? Ted didn't voice his growing frustration with the M.E.'s office. The Lieutenant didn't comment that he thought the report was slow in coming so Ted said nothing.

Finally, sitting in his driveway, before he got out and went inside his home for the night, he checked with dispatch for messages. There was a note from Treasury Agent Milton Frober with a phone number from his Albany, NY office.

* * *

DAY 4 FRIDAY, OCTOBER 15

When the household began to stir early Friday morning it was noticeably dark. Sounds of the morning birds were gone. It had actually been a late fall but the leaves were falling regularly now and, at least in northern Vermont, the shine was off most of them. Rain and wind during the night helped the leaves along on their journey to the ground. Finding time to do some leaf raking would be necessary on a regular basis for the next few weeks.

A trip to Lake Bee was still on Ted's list but first he planned to go to the Montpelier Barracks to try to contact the Treasury agent in Albany. In his mind he argued with himself about what time he could call the M.E. again to find out if there was additional information he would want to use when talking to the NYPD. He was determined to definitely contact the New York police today, since it was Friday. Not too late in the day was probably a good idea on a Friday.

Family affairs were settled. Liza was up extra early because she needed to be at the hospital exactly on time. They talked about a barbeque planned at his sister's house on Saturday afternoon. Everything had a little more routine feel again, at the end of a stressful week. Liza didn't say anything to Ted and he didn't say anything to her but that morning they each had a thought about Mrs. Arkady who wouldn't be back for another two weeks. It was still a long time before life would get easier for them. Neither wanted to admit that to the other.

"Man, it's cold this morning!" Ted was the first to leave but quickly turned around and went back inside to get his regulation vest and alert Liza to the needs raised by the drop in temperature. Liza was already planning accordingly for the kids since she had been the to one to let George out as soon as they woke up.

At the Barracks there was nothing from the M.E., which really didn't surprise him. He wanted to get going so he called the number he had for Agent Milton Frober. Ted was pleased he answered himself.

"Trooper Vallan, good to speak with you. Agent Smith wrote a few words on the photocopies he sent me through the FACSIMILE machine. I gather you have some questions about 'high denomination' currency?"

Ted immediately wrote down and underlined 'high denomination'. If that was what this stuff was called he better incorporate that into his reports. Besides, he liked the term; it surely fit. Agent Frober listened, patiently, while Ted reviewed the story of his John Doe and the specifics of finding the two $1000 bills.

"So, Agent Frober, I have no idea if these bills are real. And, of course, I have no idea if they have anything to do with my dead man's death."

"Well, Trooper Vallan, there's no reason they can't be real, and the fact your body was carrying two of them actually makes it more likely they are real. If someone was in the habit of carrying around a souvenir or *lucky* fake big bill they usually would only have one. What would be the point of having two?

"On the other hand, why would anyone carry real $1000 bills around, especially in the Vermont woods? As you can imagine, you can't walk into a store, or even a bank, and just have it cashed.

Maybe in a very large city, but even there, I'm not sure any more. So bills like these show up in less straightforward transactions."

Ted still wasn't at all clear where bills like this originated from and why they were news to him. So he asked the Agent to explain this to him.

"I'm sorry, Ted, I should give you some background. You know, dealing with all kinds of monetary and currency issues is what I do and sometimes I forget things like 'high denomination' currency is very rare for most people, including law officers.

"I guess you'd be surprised to know that dating as far back as the late 1700's various colonies and then states printed $500, $1000, and even $5000 and $10,000 bills, or certificates. Since the early 1860's federal banknotes with those denominations were printed. If you think about it you can easily understand large denominations were probably pretty common and useful in places like banks and brokerages and other places where large amounts of money were moved from place to place before there was any way to move money electronically. No $5000 or $10,000 bills this century.

"In 1928 paper currency was changed to its current size. And, while nothing larger than one-hundred dollar bills are printed now, back then millions of $500 and $1000 bills were printed. In fact, Ted, the last $1000 bills were printed in 1945…or was that 1947?" Agent Frober's tone changed and he was clearly upset he wasn't absolutely positive which year was correct. He seemed so shaken Ted worried he might not be able to complete the loop on this story.

He recovered. "Anyway, you could still order $500's and $1000's from banks in the early sixties. But the treasury officially discontinued them in 1969 and since then the Federal Reserve has tried to get them out of circulation."

Both Ted and Agent Frober knew why 'high denomination' currency was not only no longer needed but had a distinct downside now. The agent spoke about that anyway.

"Large scale financial transactions are now electronic so bills like that are no longer of any commercial use. What has happened with bills that large is a notable frequency of counterfeiting, but, more importantly, they become useful in a variety of unlawful activities, such as money laundering and, more recently, in the drug trade. So we're trying to get rid of them.

"But you can imagine what happens when you try to take something like currency away from general availability and use. Sure, it becomes a collector's item. In the 1950's U.S. paper currency started to become collectable and that continues. Maybe somewhere around two-hundred thousand $1000 bills are still out there. That's considered pretty rare."

"How do you know what these bills are worth today?"

"Trooper, I'm not aware of all the specifics that make one $1000 bill worth more than another, but, beyond condition and things like that, I know dates of printing series, low serial numbers, and things like that can make a difference to collectors. I think there were only three printing series, 1928, 1934, and 1934A, by far the most common.

"If you look at the bills you have you see they are from the 1934A, the most common series. But their serial numbers are low and they are sequential. Whether that was a random occurrence, who knows, but a series of bills with low sequential serial numbers usually are worth a bit more."

Ted asked again. "So what do you think these bills might be worth today?"

"Sorry. To the bank they're worth $1000; face value. To a collector I have no idea. Maybe unless special at least about $1500?"

Ted wanted to bring the discussion back to his case. "Milton, do you have any thoughts about why my John Doe had these large denomination bills folded in his money clip when we found him? Any experiences with this?"

"Just like now, we get these bills from time to time. Unless a citizen or, more likely, a law enforcement agency involves us because of a crime or maybe a need to establish authenticity, we don't seek them out. Your bills, given the circumstances you've told me, would seem to have every indication of being associated in some way with some form of criminal activity. If you're asking about challenges moving bills like these the answer is they're very easy to move. The only concern is always if they are real currency."

That was what started Ted's adventure with those bills. So Ted said, "Wouldn't it be worthwhile to find out if these bills are real or counterfeit? That might make a big difference as this case unfolds, don't you think?"

There was a pause and Treasury Agent Milton Frober answered: "Frankly Ted, that's why I'm kind of surprised you've only sent photocopies to me. I don't know why you and Agent Smith didn't arrange to get the actual bills here to me in Albany?"

* * *

Day 4 ICU Friday

Liza arrived at the hospital just after eight and went directly to the ICU with her coat and book bag. She wanted to begin to prepare for rounds and also make sure she had all the chart information she would need to give a brief presentation of the ID components of this case at the one o'clock Rheumatology conference. After seeing Mrs. Albertsen and looking at her chart she would quickly run to the lab and update whatever might still be growing in the microbiology lab.

She put her things down in the charting area and glanced over at Mrs. Albertsen's cubicle. Uh oh. It was dark. She walked over and the bed was empty, with clean sheets, and all the monitoring apparatus turned off; quiet, near the bedside. She quickly surmised Mrs. Albertsen had died. A nurse confirmed she died just a few hours before, after an awful night. Liza didn't ask. She had lived through many of those awful nights finally terminating in a patient's death. She hoped they had not worked on her too long to try to keep the poor lady alive.

Liza and others were pleased to find the intern who was in contact with the family was on-call last night and kept the daughter aware of what was happening. At Mrs. Albertsen's death he informed her daughter and successfully obtained the autopsy permission everyone felt was so vital for this perplexing case. Liza was pleased they would probably be able, eventually, to better understand what happened to Mrs. Albertsen. She also wondered if the outcome might not have been so foretold if management offered to this elderly patient had, right from the start, included a stronger effort at promoting aggressive support for all her faltering body issues caused by her age and illness.

In any event, she also had a compassionate thought about the intern who embarrassed himself so publicly, hoping he might garner improved feelings of self-respect from accomplishing the, often not so easy to get, autopsy permission. In a teaching hospital post-mortem examinations were highly valued and the intern would be praised. With an autopsy pending it was decided not to discuss Mrs. Albertsen's case that day, but wait another two weeks for the next biweekly rheumatology clinical conference. Another case, not involving Liza, was to be discussed at the session for today.

* * *

Ted had no answer he thought worth expressing for the final comment from the treasury agent in Albany. He was pleased the Lieutenant agreed to have a courier bring the real bills to Milton Frober at the Albany US Treasury office right away. That was a brief saga he didn't want to stew about any longer. That agent Smith was a jerk. He took a breath and called the M.E.'s office.

The post-mortem was done on Tuesday and Ted still didn't even have a copy of the preliminary, much less complete, findings. It was approaching mid-morning and he wanted to either get to the lake or call the NYPD, depending on what he could get from the M.E.

The woman he spoke with in the M.E.'s office seemed to be ready for his call. She was pleasant but, again, firm in her words. The M.E. would be able to get him the report but not until later in the afternoon. She explained he was in court and had an autopsy to do as soon as he returned. After that he would be able to get to his paperwork. Ted knew the M.E. in Vermont also completed post-mortem examinations for the hospital, in rotation with the other pathologist. He didn't know, at the time, the post waiting for Dr. Roller was Mrs. Albertsen.

The M.E.'s secretary told Ted she already had the FACSIMILE number for the brand new machine at the Montpelier Barracks. She would send out the report as soon as it was ready. Ted wondered if the M.E. had consciously decided he'd rather work with him in print, via machine, instead of over the phone. He couldn't help wonder about the limited support he was getting from the M.E. office. In any event he decided he might as well try to begin to work with the NYC Police Department and use the limited information he had in hand now.

Since Wednesday he actually had been carrying around a number to call for the New York City Police Department that someone in 'Administrative Relations', whatever that was, had secured for him after he reported his interest in the address on the card in his John Doe's pocket.

* * *

"Hi troooUper Vallan. I'm Janice Delario, adminis'tative assistant to Cap'n Taylor, Man'hattn' Sout', 10th precinct. Gloria Jefferson from central he'quarters told me youse be callin'. Tell me something bout what youse got so I can figure what we need to do to help youse."

"Thanks, Miss Delario. I……"

"Janice, hon, call me Janice."

"Oh. Oh okay, Janice. I'm Ted. We found a body in a lake four days ago and we are unable to ID the man. It's a homicide. On him we found a business card listing a New York City address on Sixteenth Street. We also found a piece of paper with a phone number but no area code and all we know about that is it isn't from the 802 area code in Vermont."

Janice interjected: "What 'bout some youse otha' area codes?"

"Ma'am, there only is one area code for Vermont." He heard a soft sigh like sound in response. All the time they spoke he also had the sense she was chewing gum.

"I guess tings are a little busier down here. So, trooo…Ted, I'm listening to ya' problem and tryin' to decide if sending a black and white to check out dat address is good enough, but I'm tinkin' you may need more den dat so we gonna need to get you hooked up with a datective. Okay?"

"Sure…."

"Look, you got copy machines up der youse can send stuff, don't youse?"

"Oh, of course." He replied with a conviction that belied his only recent experience with what he regarded as a very new, complex machine and concept. Did she mean FACSIMILE?

"Well here's our number, 212-555-0102. Got that? Now send me what youse got. Descript of your John Doe, dat address, and dat phone numba' and anythin' else youse think we should know. I'll get a team to follow up and let youse know."

"That's great Janice. I'll send it to you right now. Do you have any idea when I might expect to hear something back?"

"Tough question, Ted. We got plenty John Doe DOA's 'round here. Checkin' them out is usually a pain in the ass. Not always a prior'ty, if youse know what I mean. Are you shore he was killed? Dat should move your boy up the list. Wit weekend comin' maybe take two, tree days."

His frustration welled up in him. He should have started to work with the New York City Police days ago instead of trying to wait for the M.E.'s report. Ted didn't want to hang up until he had thought of everything he could do to light some kind of a fire at the NYPD. He wanted to create some urgency to ensure speeding up the apparent big city bureaucracy he was already sensing, to get the information he wanted.

"Say, Janice, If I drive down tonight to help out do you think you can find me a detective to work on this with me tomorrow?"

"Troouper." now more formal, "We can only do what we can do here. I'll let the Cap'n know youse say youse got a murder so youse in a rush. He'll make an assignment. Pleez send dat stuff and we'll see what we can do here. No use youse coming down just yet." Then she relaxed. "If youse do ever come down here to da city Ted, bring me some of dat Vermont maple syrup, will ya Ted?"

After hanging up he sat there, swiveled his chair around, and looked down the corridor behind him that ended at a large window framing some trees and natural light, registering a rural scene in his mind. He tried to imagine police life in a huge city like New York. With thousands of cops who could keep track of who? Getting anything done might be so much more complicated. He wondered what his life would be like in that setting. He had difficulty even projecting an image of himself into what he assumed in city precinct stations were huge open areas, like in an armory, with probably hundreds of people sitting in small cubicles.

When Ted thought of big cities he always imagined everything and everyone moving fast. His work in Vermont was moving slowly. What if it was worse in a big city? Now he was beginning to think everything in cities might just crawl. He imagined people and tasks actually physically wrapped up in some generic red tape. So diverted trying to get unraveled that things Ted might call making progress wasn't anybody's real concern.

Janice wanted him to think she's in charge of a lot. He wondered if that was true. He wasn't sure if she was even a cop. Probably not. A secretary? But he guessed she had some power and was a person to try to have on your side to get things done. He wrote in the left margin on the yellow pad he was writing his notes on: 'Bring syrup to Janice. NYC, 10th precinct.' and put an asterisk next to it and then underlined it.

He didn't leave his desk until he had typed up the FACSIMILE to send to Janice. He wanted it to be as complete as possible, but after that phone conversation with Janice, he thought he actually had to try to be precise about what he had and what he was hoping to find out. From the call he had a feeling whoever was going to wind up with these papers might be a bit touchy about getting too little or too much information and requests. Just like Goldilocks, he guessed the cop he was reaching out to would want it all to be just right. He also remembered he wanted to include the photocopy of the prints he had in the transmission.

Despite thoughts, right now, reflecting his tendency to assume New York a monster sized place filled with police with crazy personalities, Ted recognized he was excited when he considered there was a good chance he might have to go there at some point for this case. Unless there turned out to be no New York City connection there were things he'd have to do and see for himself in that place. For about twenty minutes he tweaked the things he put in the transmission then sent it off to Janice.

* * *

Arriving at the lake around noon he noticed cars in the driveways of two houses which were unoccupied all week. One was the Shumway camp, just east of the Graham's, where the renters from New York City had been over the Columbus Day weekend. The Shumways were from New Jersey. They came up for this weekend expressly because of what they had been told by staff from Montpelier about the incident. They were just arriving as Ted drove down the road. He diverted into their driveway and spoke with them. It turned out they were pleased at the coincidence and preferred to enter their home with Ted alongside them even though he had been in the camp earlier in the week to look it over.

All agreed nothing was amiss. They knew very little about the recent renters. In fact, they commented they had never been really clear about how the renters found out the Shumways rented their camp from time to time. Mrs. Shumway recalled the female renter explained she had been given their number by Janet Grey, whom Mrs. Shumway said she barely knew. Ted took note also, having had the impression from Edith Jones and Scott Golde the Grey's had never been considered regulars in the community social group.

But both of the Shumways were pleased how neat and clean their place looked. Ted knew he wasn't going to get anything more from the Shumways and politely thanked them and made his exit. If he had previously wavered about ever needing to speak, in person, with the renters, he now leaned toward believing he should. Another reason to consider going to New York City.

A few houses further east up the road where the other new car was he drove into the driveway to speak with those folks. Before he left his cruiser to go to their house he checked his lists. This was one of the two camps Montpelier had been unable to make contact with the listed owners. The owner's address was Connecticut but the car in the driveway had Massachusetts's plates. Probably renters Ted assumed. He still went to the door, hoping he might be invited in and get a chance to look around, at least a very cursory check to rule out any major findings.

Vern and Mary Schmidt were in the house and were the owners. They were very pleasant and respectful to Ted and immediately invited him in. They hadn't been up to the lake since before labor day because they moved to Massachusetts the last week in August. Their new personal information had not been updated yet on any of the lists Ted had. Why their phone number in Connecticut had continued to ring was a puzzle to them.

The Schmidts were there to close their place up for the winter. They had no idea what had happened earlier in the week and their visible reaction to that news confirmed their words. So Ted received an escorted tour of their place. Once again, all agreed everything appeared to be in place with no signs of the kind of disturbance Ted was looking for. The Schmidt's shock and questions kept him there longer than he wanted. He declined a drink of juice or water and politely moved to the door, tipped his hat, and left.

He still had a few sets of keys from Scott Golde for places near the county road he hadn't checked. A few homes on short spur roads up the hills north from the north road also remained on the list. He had been in or had spoken, personally, with the owners of most of the homes in the community. The total was thirty-one. There were nine to go.

It was approaching one-thirty. Ted wanted to be back in Montpelier in time to meet with the Lieutenant and digest the report coming from the M.E. He wondered how it would look to the NYPD if he had to send them information from the autopsy that radically altered what he had sent in the morning. By now there wasn't much time left for him to do anything more at the lake. Ted remembered one old cabin on the paved county road directly on the lake he had not looked at. He decided to check it out and then drive to the Barracks.

The structure was actually only the remnants of a tiny cottage that had been uninhabited for years and was, literally, falling into the lake. The space between the cottage and the road was all dirt and served as a parking area, probably mostly for fishermen, who then carefully navigated the short, but steep, incline down to lake's edge. No beachfront.

Of course people park at a place like that for many reasons. To think. To neck. And whatever else. Probably at all times of day or night, he assumed. The flotsam and jetsam of their presence was all over the dirt patch. The question was whether anyone ever occupied the cabin for short periods. The cabin leaned a good thirty degrees down the incline to the lake. Ted wasn't overjoyed to climb into it but decided he had no choice. Worry about skipping *the* camp with the important clues he was searching for probably reflected an obsessive personality trait more than the likelihood of finding anything useful in this shack.

He put his trooper's hat in the backseat and picked up a ball cap with 'State Police' emblazoned on it. He took his flashlight and checked that all the equipment attached to his body was secured. The window cutouts were boarded up but the entrance only offered a hint of having been covered with boards sometime in the past. What had been there at one time were now mostly broken off or cut, so the doorway was easily breeched. Inside was very dark and the scent of wet, rotted wood was strong. He moved his light from quadrant to quadrant and took only one short step inside. That was enough to disturb some birds, and maybe, he wondered, some bats.

Remnants of a few walls and some plumbing were still there. The floor in front of him looked intact. The cone of his light revealed some blankets in one corner and maybe a sleeping bag along the west wall; the lake side. He suspected there was a tiny porch on the other side of that wall which he had seen when he looked around the outside before entering. Any type of kitchen and then bathroom were along the south side of the cabin. There was no obvious indication of any significant recent activity or commotion. The place was very dusty and cobwebs seemed to rule the area, appearing as though they hadn't been disturbed in some time.

Ted wanted to back out and cross the place off his list. But his eyes kept being pulled back to that clump of material in the northwest corner of the main room. It looked like a sleeping bag, but it took up more space than he thought an empty bag should. What could be in there? He remembered his findings in the Grey camp. Sometimes an investigation leads to serendipitously stumbling onto other crimes. If he found something he could have the satisfaction of calling Trooper Smith again, which would be no small pleasure. But first it would be Ted's responsibility to find out if this really was anything of concern.

Moving a step more into the room impressed Ted with how steep the incline was. Instinctively he held on to the door frame as he shuffled further in. It was damp and everything looked rotted. Shortly he would have to let go and move to the far wall where the stuff he was looking at was. He held his breath, gently let go of the door frame, and walked and slid the four or five feet to the far wall. He put a hand on the wall and stood still. So far so good. The bag on the floor reeked of mold. Nothing was moving and now he didn't believe a full sized person could be inside. He pulled out two blue latex gloves and tucked his light under his left armpit.

He bent over and started to pull the material apart to unfold it. Something of some weight was inside some of it. The amount of dust that flew into his face when he disturbed the material suggested it had not been placed there very recently. Still hunched over he used both hands to lift it. Four or five empty liquor bottles tumbled out and he could tell there were still more in there. He figured someone probably slid the bag, filled with empty bottles, across the floor from the door.

Waste of time. He let the bag fall and stood up slowly and extended his back to stretch. His head hit a beam and he jumped a foot forward. Suddenly the floor started to give way and his left foot fell right through a rotted plank. 'Oh shit! This was not a good idea' he thought

His right leg and torso remained above the floor. It was a good bet absolutely no one had been dumb enough to enter this place in a very long time. Ted perched the flashlight at the junction of the floor and the west wall. Slowly he placed both hands firmly on the floor and tried to gradually hoist himself up from the hole.

Putting pressure on the floor seemed to cause the entire structure to begin to creak and actually increase its list. "Oh man!" He stopped and stayed still. Getting out of there was becoming a serious priority. It was daylight and there was no reason for anyone to stop where his cruiser was parked outside. He had no way to communicate with anyone. Ted accepted he was suddenly alone, in a very dangerous situation. Even at this worrisome moment it wasn't lost on him that part of the reason he probably had decided to go in was his hope of having another reason to piss off Trooper Smith. Now he was in trouble.

He tested again, putting some weight from his arms on the floor, and everything stayed quiet. Slowly, carefully, he began to hoist himself up once more. This time it went smoothly and he extricated himself from the hole. He wanted to get out of that shack immediately.

He decided to stay low and crawl to the doorway. Best to move slowly. Ted hoped the worst of the danger was over. He was sweating and had some cuts and scrapes. On his knees he positioned himself facing the doorway and felt no movement. Before he started to crawl out he leaned back to the wall for his flashlight.

With a loud crack the whole building started to slide.

"Shit!"

He jumped up to try to make a dash to the doorway. Below his feet another large area of floor boards gave way and, instantly, he was down another hole. As he dropped through the flashlight flew out of his hand.

For a few seconds everything was dark. He was conscious but a little woozy. His left shoulder and leg hurt. As his eyes began to accommodate to the low light he wasn't sure if he was inside or outside the fucking cottage. His feet and lower legs felt cold. Probably in water, he decided. Ted's body, proper, seemed to be wrapped and stuck in a cluster of beams. It was most likely he was under the cabin, tangled in the remnants of its supporting wood beams. The structure was sliding into the lake. The question was whether, at some point, the cabin would collapse on the beams he was stuck in and crush him or drown him. Even if it didn't collapse much more he doubted there was room to extricate himself by trying to swim under and out from it.

Ted was anxious and worried but felt no sense of panic and that helped reassure him. Rather he was focused on determining how to get out. His situation required him to find a way to unwind himself from the beams all around him and crawl up and away from the building without provoking it to collapse or slide any farther. He knew that could happen at any moment regardless of whether he moved or not. Since he had no control over that he did not dwell on it. He chose to think of himself as a stick in a *pick up sticks* game where it was his turn to move out without disturbing all that was around him.

After all, his arms and legs still worked, even though they ached and beams limited mobility. He was breathing fine and his head, eyes, and ears worked. He told himself he felt too good, still too much in control, to see this as a prelude to the end of him. How to get out?

He decided he was standing on wood, presumably a beam. It felt like the water line was slowly progressing up his legs. Everything was sinking. The broken floor boards were about a foot above his head. Ted couldn't imagine a way out from below or on the sides. Since he had slipped down into this fix it seemed to him trying to slowly unwind his legs and pull himself up to the, albeit unreliable, floor was his best option out. Same way out as in.

If he was able to get to the point where he could pull himself up and out he had no idea if the weight on the boards from actually doing that would just set the building sliding more. The beam he was standing on might stay where it was but he doubted it. He guessed everything was going to descend further, including him. He was in a bad spot.

He couldn't see well though there was some light to his west. The day had clouded over and the days were already getting shorter. Who knew how long before he wouldn't see anything? Every now and then he could hear a car whiz by on the county road. The chances anyone would decide to stop where a State Trooper's cruiser was parked were nil. Maybe Scott Golde would but he was about it. If he couldn't get out when would someone find him?

There was no sense trying to pull himself up while his body was still twisted around several beams. He considered but tried not to think about the chances he would be able to pull himself out of the hole even if he could work his limbs free. Doing a pull-up with his wet boots and all the gear strapped to him was certainly something he hadn't done since basic training in the army many years ago. Maybe he never had done that.

Everything stayed quiet and he decided it was time to move. First he untwisted his arms, which turned out to be easier than he thought. He could tell his left sleeve was cut but he didn't sense the wetness of blood. He thought about trying to take his belt off but decided trying to do it might jar his surroundings. Very gently and slowly he moved his left foot around until he found he could bend his knee without restriction. He left the leg dangling and put more weight on his left arm, which rested hooked around a beam. He reached up and was able to secure a handhold with his right arm on a floor board at the edge of the hole. He tugged, just a little, and it seemed firm.

Then he slowly moved his right foot from the beam he had been perched on. He had to do quite a wide arc of motion, essentially extending it far out to the right and sliding it over a beam and then under another before he could bend it freely. With every motion there was soft creaking around him. The lake water might have been cold but Ted was drenched with sweat. Once his legs were hanging freely he knew he wouldn't be able to hold that position for long. Strength in his right arm would not continue indefinitely. So it was time to pull himself out of the god-forsaken hole and crawl out of that structure as quickly as he could. He tried not to consider what he should do if the building started to slide again.

His left arm was sore from the cut, but he had no difficulty extending it to the hole in the floor. It was his right arm which facilitated that action and it was right arm fatigue that worried him the most. Too much concentration on running and not enough strengthening exercises, he thought.

He bore down hard, flexed his legs so they were free of the water, and slowly hoisted himself up, red faced and grunting all the way. As soon as he could put his right elbow flat on the floor he paused to re-trench. Then he, again slowly, but persistently, pulled himself completely out of the damn hole. He was dripping with sweat and thoroughly exhausted.

For the first time during the entire miserable episode an image of Liza, and then his kids, flashed before him. He didn't know if that was a good or bad omen, but he thought he better keep moving. There was no time to think about any of that. He shimmied, on all fours, slowly towards the doorway. He heard cracking and felt movement in the floor he was moving across but kept on going.

The house was listing further but he continued sliding forward, on his belly, to keep his weight as evenly distributed as possible. At the door frame he grabbed for the wood and suffered a cascade of splinters in his hands through his gloves. Once again, because of the angle of incline of the cottage, he had to pull himself up, in pain, to reach the doorway. As he poured himself out, head first, it was no surprise to Ted when the miserable old shack took its ultimate dive into the lake, trying to pull him back down by his legs with it. He could hear whatever was under it breaking apart as the weight of the cabin crushed and compacted it.

Three quarters of his body was outside when the big crash happened behind him. As he was wiggling his way out completely he was struck by how bright it was again; still daytime. He looked up from the ground as two cars going north on the county road passed. He could only imagine how those people reacted to the sight of a Vermont State Trooper lying, filthy, on his belly, halfway out of an abandoned shack that had just fallen into the lake. Thank goodness they just kept driving.

He made it out. He was alive. Ted Vallan was almost overcome with emotion. Another cold sweat.

Every now and then in life there are moments when something very dramatic, even life affecting, happens only to you and has a profound, personal, emotional impact. For the rest of the world, unaffected by that event, life goes on as usual. It's a very strange feeling. The closest thing it reminded Ted of was when Kathy was born at five in the morning and several hours later he was at his desk doing routine work, appearing to others as though nothing much was different about that day. He was, of course, ecstatic and overjoyed. Yet, for the rest of the world nothing had changed.

Just like the days his babies were born, today he recognized something remarkable in his life just happened to him. He felt an exhilaration about his escape and being alive few others would understand, much less ever hear about. His arms and shoulders, especially his shoulders, were very sore. They would ache for days.

Only as he drove back to his Barracks did he begin to consider himself unlucky to have had such an experience. As usual for Ted Vallan he began to second guess the dangerous episode, especially how he let himself get into such a spot on his own. But just a little. He also decided he would let the Lieutenant decide if the police or highway department, or whoever, should be notified about a shack that fell into a lake.

His shirt was torn and his pants and shirt were filthy. It was close to three and even after all this he wanted to get to the Barracks to at least look at what the M.E. sent him. Going to his home first wasn't out of the way and Ted could quickly wash up there and change clothes. He was in a hurry. Here he was, in a place most of the rest of the world would call the middle of nowhere, and he was racing the clock. It wasn't regulation but he turned his light on. No siren, just the light to get him some right of way.

In his cruiser he called in and asked if a report from the M.E. had arrived and was angry when told there was nothing on the machine. This report was becoming a challenge. Didn't make any sense. All the more reason to get to Montpelier and call the M.E.

At home no one had returned yet. He took his belt with all his equipment off and noticed a few cuts in the black leather. Stripping off his shirt his right shoulder already felt stiff and sore. He washed his bloodied hands, face, and trunk and toweled off. He left his pants but put a clean shirt on and transferred his name tag and pins. As he dashed out of the house his mother drove into the driveway with his kids. Immediately she noticed the water lines on his still damp pants legs. A quick wave as he walked to his cruiser signaled her he had to go, urgently. He hoped switching on his flashing light would satisfy her.

It was just before four as he arrived at the Barracks. Speed helps.

On Ted's desk there was an eight-page report from the M.E. Prior to beginning to read it he looked at the very tiny print at the absolute bottom of the page that gave the transmission time as three twenty-nine. Well, at least it had arrived. He sat back and took a big breath. He was starving. He had nothing to eat since early in the morning. Before studying the report, he walked to the vending machines and got a candy bar. For the first time he could ever recall it occurred to him he should find healthier snacks than candy bars.

The autopsy report looked like it went forever. First, under *'Gross Appearance'*, there were detailed descriptions of the body's appearance, stripped of all clothes. He noted an asterisk that was explained on the next to last page. There, since this was an M.E. case and not a routine post, the clothes were cataloged and also described in some detail. Then, still under gross, the internal organs were listed and described; intact and cut apart. That took a few pages, and then the microscopic slides were listed, apparently confirming his heart attack and emphysema, and other things.

Finally, the last two pages pertained, exclusively, to the forensics. Essentially a summary, it detailed everything, like clothes, body condition, trauma, stomach contents (especially as reflecting time of last meal), pertinent organ damage, and blood alcohol level (John Doe was legally intoxicated at his time of death). Then there were determinations, with explanations, of time of death and causes of death. There was a sequence listed under cause of death starting with the head injury and the presumed consequences from that.

"What the fuck?" A few desks away, the solitary remaining trooper in the room glanced over after Ted's expletive.

Ted put in a call to Dr. Roller. He was exhausted, his shoulders burned, and his sore hands were throbbing. He doubted his ability to concentrate well. He read the report over two times, trying to read slowly the second time. He found only one surprise in the entire report. There didn't appear to be anything new or different that might help Ted very much. The surprise was that those goddamn stones weren't listed.

The way this day had gone Ted had slim expectation Dr. Roller would still be in. The secretary who answered was stiff and formal in her agreement to see if the Doctor was still in the office. Ted was very firm, telling her it was important he speak with the Doctor today. Ted wasn't sure he had a right to be but he was angry with Dr. Roller. His investigation was moving at a glacial pace and he couldn't even get a straight autopsy report.

When Dr. Roller came on the line they each were more formal than in the past. Ted tried hard to maintain a patient tone but his firmness in questioning the M.E. even surprised Ted.

"Dr. Roller, I finally," Ted regretted that immediately, "have your report in front of me. You know, I guess it's got as much as we're going to get from that man. But Doctor, do you remember when you gave me the preliminary report over the phone on Tuesday and you told me there were some small stones in his stomach?" He didn't wait for an answer. "Well I have the report in front of me and I see nothing about any stones. Does that make sense to you?"

"Trooper I have the report also. Let me take a quick look and see what's here. I do remember you asked me if those small stones helped make him drown."

Kind of a gratuitous comment since however those stones got there it wasn't Ted who fucked up on the report.

"No, you are correct Trooper Vallan. There must have been some oversight or small mix-up when diener Hardy put the final report together. You know it's generally just water, food, drugs, or alcohol we find so I guess he forgot. Weren't those just some pebbles? I'll speak with the dieners and have one of them check again and correct the report. Listen, I'm sorry about this. I'll make sure Jimmy gets this all straightened out right away. Jimmy is still here, I think. I'll talk to him. Oh, and how many stones did you say I mentioned when we first spoke?"

Ted wasn't really sure why he said it, but instead of the number five he recalled, he found himself saying "Six; six small stones, Doc." It was one of those moments when an impulsive action might help or confuse an investigation. But Ted didn't want this seemingly very minor issue to occupy his time unless it just wouldn't go away. "Dr. Roller, I will definitely stop by on Monday. I assume Mr. Hardy is an assistant, and I'd like to speak with him also."

The M.E.'s tone wasn't especially friendly or nasty but he got Ted's point that any fuck up in a big case was a concern to the police. As they were about to hang up and Ted was thanking him, Roller said: "By the way, this morning one of the secretaries in the department told me she had a phone call late yesterday from a woman asking if we knew anything about a white male in his early fifties. The lady said she called the hospital looking for him and they suggested she speak with our department. All she would say was he was an acquaintance who she knew was coming to Vermont for business. She should have heard from him by now so she was worried. Of course our office didn't tell her anything and suggested she call the police. At least I hope she didn't say anything about our John Doe."

Ted sighed audibly. "Thanks for telling me, Dr. Roller. Can you give me the secretary's name so I can speak with her also on Monday?" The call ended. Ted was worn out and losing some self-control. "What the fuck?" He said aloud again. 'Nice of that office to let me know; only a day late and as they close up for the weekend,' he thought. "Shit!"

* * *

It was dark when his cruiser pulled into the driveway; almost seven. Ted removed his boots as soon as he was inside then secured his weapon in the small safe he kept for just that purpose. Upstairs he quietly walked into the baby's room where Liza was rubbing his back in the crib. He appeared to be out. Kathy was sitting on the floor, quietly playing with her dolls. He kissed Liza and Kathy but was cautioned, by Liza raising her hand, not to go near the just asleep baby.

He went downstairs to put a plate together of the food left out for him. A while later Liza came downstairs and started to pull out a chair at the kitchen table.

"Lize, you look exhausted."

"Yeah, well you look beat to hell yourself."

"Babe, I've been thinking. I'm gonna rack up a ton of overtime with this case. Maybe we should call Mrs. Arkady and…."

"No, I don't think…" She already had some ideas about what they would do with that money "…Ted! Look at your hands!"

Ted, sheepishly, slowly put his knife and fork down and turned over his hands, palms up, to Liza. There were a bunch of splinters; some already had surrounding redness and some swelling. His hands were a mess.

"I don't know if I can take care of all of them."

Ted's face lightened. He had not a doubt she could do it. He was supremely confident she could do it. He thought she was the best doctor in the world. He once fantasized if they were on a hiking trip and his appendix burst, Liza could operate right there and he'd be fine.

"Of course you can. They don't feel that bad. Let me finish eating then you can operate."

Of course, Liza did, successfully, clean up his hands and, with sterile technique and equipment, remove about five, large, nasty splinters. When she was done his hands, wrapped up in bandages, were almost useless to him. They both knew he would take them all off for his shower in the morning. As he told her about his lake experience while she managed his splinters he agreed to let her help him wash his trunk and legs in the shower that night to get rid of the filth.

At first he teased her when she asked what happened. "Do you mean on my case, or do you mean to wind up with hands like this?"

Liza didn't think he was funny. "I mean your mother told me she saw you rushing from the house and your pants were all wet. Now your hands look like shit. Those are the things I'm asking about."

While they were tied up working on his hands Ted offered a long version of his afternoon in the crumbling shack. He left it to Liza to decide if he was scared or frightened for his life during any of it. If she was horrified, or even angry, she didn't let on and Ted was pleased. Next he took that shower with Liza's hands on assistance, which he really enjoyed. Out of the bathroom they sat on their bed and tried to decide if it was worth it to go downstairs. They settled on staying in their room, each assuming their usual spot on the bed, but remaining above the covers.

"How did your case presentation go today?" He was pleased he remembered to ask.

"It didn't" She responded. "I mean it was put off. The patient died early this morning and it will be best to wait for the results of her autopsy before discussing it."

Autopsy. The confusing and a little crazy autopsy of his John Doe came back in his mind.

"Man, the autopsy report I've been waiting for has become a real mess. I hope you get the information you need in a reasonable amount of time. You know, I've been waiting since Tuesday and I still don't think I have a complete report. I mean I have a cause of death and all, but, just today, I had to point out to Dr. Roller that the supposed final report he sent over late this afternoon is missing stuff. That's crazy"

"I did an elective in med school in pathology and I found Dr. Roller to be really organized and pretty sharp. What do you mean?"

"Well, I don't know. It's probably nothing. I talked to him on the phone, late Tuesday afternoon, right after he finished whatever it is they actually do to dead people." Ted was a little loose after all that had happened.

"He listed his findings for me. He said the guy died of drowning but had been creamed on the head and also had a heart attack. But, you know, I was startled when he said the guy had some shit in his stomach and I guess I surprised Roller by reacting to that. He told me how the guy died, and he mentioned there was food and alcohol but also some blades of grass and five stones in his stomach. I remember he said five stones in his stomach. So I guess, like an idiot, I asked if he thought the stones were used to weigh him down to help drown the guy. Doc Roller seemed to me to react like it was a dumb question and said of course not. He said they were just small stones."

Liza was getting weary of this lengthy story and looked like she was fading a bit on the bed. She was trying to stay awake and listen.

Ted was awake and re-living the whole thing in his mind, including his contact with the M.E. late in the day. He couldn't decide if any of this meant anything he should be concerned about. He couldn't help himself; he wouldn't let Liza drift off. He gently tapped her arm. She looked over at him and when he thought he had her attention he continued.

"Well it seems to me it took an awfully long time to get that final report today and I may have burned some bridges with that office the way I kind of pestered them for it all week. And then, after the M.E. and I had this really strained conversation about what I want to tell you about; as I'm just about to hang up, he tells me someone from out of state called his office a few days ago nosing around about my John Doe! Do you believe that? Never let me know until four thirty on Friday! Man…."

"What was it you wanted to tell me about the autopsy, babe?"

"Right. So when the official report was sent over by FACSIMILE and I read it, I knew I was tired from my crazy fall into the lake and it was hard to concentrate on all of it. But I did see the report didn't include much about what was in his stomach and didn't even list those damn stones he had made fun of me about. When I called him to ask about it that's when he got kind of stiff and acted like I was taking up his time for nothing.

"Of course, he did agree he remembered telling me about what he called 'some pebbles' and had to admit they were not in the report. Seemed like he was cussing out one of his workers. I thought I heard him mutter a name; Hardy, I think. Anyway, he promised me he would clear it all up by Monday. Monday! At least I didn't have to contact the New York police and contradict any of the info I already sent them about the dead guy.

"I don't know. Just seems to me all this should have gone more smoothly, you know? Stupid stones. Now everyone is mad at everyone."

Then Liza said something that ignited everything.

"Ted, if there were a few stones which really were only pebbles they could easily wind up in the stomach of someone who drowned. But it's not easy to swallow one or certainly more than one stone of any real size. The esophagus, the swallowing tube, expands a bit when something goes down it but there's not a lot of room. A stone that gets into the stomach might be too big to pass from there into the intestines or could get stuck in intestines. Or, a stone might just sit in the stomach a long time. That's unlikely but I guess that could happen. Anyway, a stone, or stones of any real size, certainly bigger than probably a quarter, would be unlikely to get swallowed with water in a drowning. That's what I think."

Ted wasn't sure he understood exactly all the things Liza was saying. But, for the first time, he had a thought that how those stones got in this guy's stomach wasn't clear. He lay there thinking about it while Liza dozed off. He nudged her hand and was about to tell her to go to bed when a thought came into his head.

He got up from the bed and walked to his dresser. With his bandaged hands he couldn't really pick anything up. He looked through the change he had in a pile there. Sifting through it he slid out the stone he had taken from Joe Angle the other day. Maybe just a spit bigger than a quarter, he figured. He worked the stone to the edge of the dresser and pushed it off into his other bandaged hand. He took it over to the bed and sat down next to his softly breathing, sleeping wife.

"Babe, I'm sorry to wake you, but I want you to look at this. And, if you're gonna go to sleep you need to get undressed. I'll let the dog out. I need you to look at this first, please."

Her eyes opened and she gave him a dreamy look but she was waking up. He put his fat clumsy hand in front of her and she picked the stone out of it. She moved it around in her hand, turned it over, and held it up, trying to see the faded image etched on it.

"What do you think of this?"

"You mean could it make it into someone's stomach? Well maybe. But if it ever got in it probably would never go through and make it to the rectum and come out on its own. Too big. And I think even if someone could swallow it, it's very doubtful it could ever be vomited back up. Too big.

"But you know, Ted, this isn't just a stone. Something's written on it, and the way it's shaped, with that hole in it, it's been worked on by somebody."

"Yeah, I know that. The kid who found the body found it at the lake's edge near where we pulled the body in. Any idea what the scratching on it could be?"

Liza was up and the stone interested her. She kept looking at it as she spoke. "I have no real idea. If I were to guess, I'd say it's a rune."

Ted was amazed. "You mean you know what it is? What's a *rune*?"

"I think the symbol that is etched on it reminds me of something

Old Norse, you know, like ancient Scandinavian and Germanic symbols from hundreds of years ago."

Well, he didn't know. She was the English major. Any education he was getting in the humanities was coming from her direction as she chose books for him to read and then they would discuss them. He loved it.

"So, if it's a thing you call a *rune*, does that mean it's something ancient?"

"Oh no. I'm sure you can buy all kinds of things with different rune images on them from a lot of places. I think I've seen them considered good luck pieces or symbols for many things. Who knows where it came from or what that symbol might mean? Runes were around for hundreds of years, in many variations, so there must be many different types of rune symbols. I don't know if there was a way to really do what we call writing with runes; but maybe."

Ted couldn't help himself. "If more stones like this were in that guy's stomach it might mean something. I don't know what, but it could mean something. And not showing up in the report; that just makes me wonder some more...."

"Liza, how do think I can find out some more about this stone?"

"First of all, you could try to track down old professor Symthe at UVM. He was there when I was there. His thing is ancient languages. He was real old when I was there but he might still be around. If not, there should be someone teaching what he did. I don't know how much more anyone else will be able to tell you about this stone.

"I would say, though, if you got a look at those stones from the guy's gut and they are similar, then you might be able to get some real information."

That simple comment served as prelude to the future permanent difference of opinion on how it came about that Liza Vallan went to the autopsy area the next morning. Over the decades their *he said, she said* views about that event were not untypical of remembrances of an important occurrence in many long lasting relationships. In this case, ownership for the decision was attached by each to the other. In any event, there must have eventually been agreement for Liza went to the morgue in the morning.

*   *   *

DAY 5 SATURDAY, OCTOBER 16

Liza wanted to get there early, but not so early she would arouse unusual suspicion if a staff member or security guard happened on her. About nine thirty on a Saturday morning seemed good. If there was a post-mortem exam going on then she'd have to forget about it and just turn around. It was more likely this part of pathology would be closed up for the weekend.

She walked down the stairs to the basement level. Morgues tended to gravitate to windowless basement regions for pretty obvious reasons. As she was ready to reach for the doorknob to the area she realized it would be locked today. Liza had no problem calling security to have someone come to let her in. A resident wanting to enter the suite would not be too unusual. She turned to go down the hall to a phone on the wall. As she did that it struck her it wasn't totally black behind the frosted glass which made up the top half of the door. Maybe one of the lights was left on inadvertently.

Five minutes later a security guard, who Liza happened to have a nodding acquaintance with from all her years in the hospital, arrived and they chatted as they went down the corridor back to the door. The guard took out a hundred keys on a huge ring. He turned the door handle as he inserted the proper key causing the door to slide open before he had inserted the key all the way.

"How about that" he said. "I'm gonna have to report that.

Somebody was sloppy. Hey, it's totally black in here. Let me find some lights for you, Doc."

"Oh no, but thanks. All I need are the lights over 'round the corner, off to the right, where the specimen cabinets are. I know the general area where the things I need will be."

She saw no reason to light the whole place up to further advertise her presence in the morgue. After he left Liza headed to the row of cabinets which took up an entire wall along the far end of the suite. The room's walls and partitions were set up so the door to enter was not visible from where Liza was. So far so good. She was pleased with her progress and relaxed a bit.

The problem was she wasn't entirely sure what she was looking for. She wasn't positive but thought one cabinet, in particular, was reserved for M.E. cases. And in that large cabinet she thought specimens were cataloged by date and initials, not name. The other cabinets were ordered by medical record number and initials. Ted sent her armed with all the information he could think of about his John Doe and she brought the pertinent information for Mrs. Albertsen if she had to explain her presence.

If interrupted she would plead ignorance of the filing and storage system. It was her only defense for looking in a forbidden location. That seemed a plausible excuse to her so she felt comfortable as she searched the area. Ted didn't want her to take anything. All he wanted her to do was try to actually find if there were some stones. Or, at least, a jar hopefully labeled 'stomach contents', although Liza told Ted it would say 'gastric contents' not stomach. Checking such a container by looking through it to see if there were any flat stones inside would have to be good enough. Ted was worried those stones were gone.

Liza had blocked out any fear that she was all alone in a poorly lit morgue. When she thought she found the correct cabinet she was excited. Parts of the cabinet were locked but there were a fair number of gross specimens on accessible shelves. As she looked at some specimens and labels it did register with her she was staring at body parts and she felt a slight chill and a renewed reaction to where she was.

Liza worked as methodically as she could, while trying to move along, checking specimen jars. Halfway through inspecting jars on the shelves the complete silence in the large area was broken. She thought she heard a sound like a shoe squeaking on the floor somewhere. Liza realized it wasn't going to take much to make her anxious and a little frightened. She stopped what she was doing and turned around and stared and listened. Nothing... But it was too late. Now the whole place and her appointed business began to terrify her.

Once that happened it became impossible to banish the thought there might be someone else in the suite besides her. No rhyme or reason for it other than that sound but Liza thought she was not alone. It changed everything. The adventure was over. Should she continue to try to find what she was after or leave?

Another sound. Perhaps a slight creak from an interior door somewhere. That was it. She'd had enough. It was time to go. She was terrified about how she would get out. For a second she thought about looking for a phone so she could call security. But what would she tell them? The whole idea was to call as little attention to herself as possible. Now remembering the light when she first looked through the frosted glass and the unlocked door all fell together increasing her fright. Her heart was racing.

To leave she would have to go almost in a 'U' path around a wall from where she was to the entrance corridor. If the lights went out as she moved there was nothing she would be able to do about it and she would be in total darkness. Both she and Ted had ruled out bringing a flashlight, given what that would indicate if she was interrupted. Before she left she turned back to the cabinets and quietly closed all the large doors.

She turned again to leave and tried to look straight at where she wanted to go, not letting her gaze be diverted by anything around the large room. Her body literally flinched as she heard a large door swing open and the entire room was suddenly filled with light as each bank of lights switched on successively.

"Hey! What's goin' on in here?" A loud male voice from the main entrance. Liza froze. She wasn't sure what she should do. A lady alone in the bowels of the hospital in a spot that usually wouldn't be open all weekend, so maybe not again until Monday morning, didn't put her in a great position. By now she was more worried about her physical safety than her excuse for being there. Should she try to hide and wait this person out? What if, as she suspected, there was already someone else in the suite? She willed herself to take some deep breathes and try to calm down.

Footsteps coming to the base of the 'U'.

Liza decided her best option was to first try to defend her presence with her hospital ID and the need to see Mrs. Albertsen's stuff, even if she'd never done anything like that before, nor heard of any resident or student doing it either.

Around the corner, in a huff, came James Hardy, one half of the two dieners, or pathology assistants, who help with the autopsies and maintain the morgue. Most all dieners, by the nature of their occupation, usually achieve some degree of negative notoriety in a hospital community. Warm personalities often were lacking and a surprising number of them fit their stereotype of being creepy and not too bright.

The Burlington hospital pair had their own history and legend, partially just because they had been around for so many years. Also, this one, James Hardy, was quite tall and thin and the other, Tim Jackert, was short and fat. Their appearance and one having the Hardy surname was enough to earn the tandem the well-established sobriquet of 'Laurel and Hardy'. Tim Jackert's last name helped get him another nickname used from time to time behind his back. Neither one of them liked 'Laurel and Hardy' and scorned its use if they ever overheard it. The morgue was their own little fiefdom. There they were in charge and let everyone except the pathologists know it.

James Hardy's loud, accusatory "Who are you!" turned into "What are *you* doing in here?" as he quickly had some recollection and recognition of Liza and who she was. Knowing she was hospital staff, and probably a resident, didn't seem to have the effect she hoped. He was fiery mad.

"You're not supposed to be in here now. What do you think you are trying to do standing there at the specimen cabinets? Huh?"

His tone and the way he came down the short hall at her increased her terror. She wondered why he was so angry at finding her there? She knew he was different, but was he crazy? She decided she had to try to stay as calm as possible and go with her bluff. She would watch him closely to see if he was going to settle down, at least a little.

"Mr. Hardy, I'm Liza Vallan, one of the internal medicine residents. I was taking care of this woman." she flashed the ID information for Mrs. Albertsen, but he barely gave a glance at it. He was still steamed. "She was posted yesterday and I have to give a talk about her on Monday so I needed to see if I could find some results from the post." She sure hoped he wouldn't be so concerned about her being there he'd check-up and find there wasn't a conference on Monday. "A security guard let me in." Liza was pretty satisfied with her performance but the diener's eyes were still glaring.

He continued to shout. "Then why are you standing in front of the M.E.'s cabinet? You should know the ones for the regular hospital start at the other end of the wall!"

"Well sorry, Mr. Hardy. If I ever did know that I guess I forgot. I just barely got here anyway, and I haven't really looked at anything. I don't suppose you'll help me try to find the specimens for Mrs. Albertsen?"

Hardy seemed to recall Mrs. Albertsen from the Friday post and that helped. He stopped huffing and let his clenched fists relax. An emphatic "NO!" Then, not screaming but very stiff and formal: "Listen Doc, you're not supposed to be in here so you got to leave right now. Understand?"

Liza thought she was playing it well. She figured she had talked herself into a way out and she wasn't going to mess that up. If there was a third person in the room that was going to be the diener's problem, not hers.

"Okay, Mr. Hardy, I'll have to wait till Monday then. Didn't mean to cause a fuss."

Anger and suspicion remained displayed on his face. She walked slowly around the 'U' and out to the main door, fearful Hardy hadn't bought everything she said. Arriving at the main door and finding it was locked from the inside stunned and further scared her. She wondered why he had done that as she unlatched it and darted out. Liza closed the door behind her and once down the hall and inside the stairwell raced up the stairs and out into the main lobby. She took a deep breath, slowed down, and walked directly to her car in the staff lot.

* * *

On her way back to Richmond Liza re-lived her experience in the morgue and with the diener. By then she was disappointed she was returning home without the information Ted wanted. She wasn't afraid any longer and that felt good. She couldn't decide if she had been more afraid of the unknown, feeling she wasn't alone while there, or the intense anger and threatening behavior of the diener. The diener scared her but the sounds really frightened her.

Five minutes later, on the road, Liza was more concerned with judging the temperature and what the weather would be that afternoon so she could decide how to dress the kids for the barbeque at her sister-in-law's. Pulling into the driveway the three of them were running around with the barking dog. The baby moved around as much as a twenty-two-month old could. Neither of the kids had enough clothes on for the chilly fall day. She, as well as anyone else, could see they were having a great time so she bit her lip and determined not to say anything about that to Ted.

Ted swooped both kids up and jogged over to her car. He was sore, but he still felt that high from surviving a near disaster and was energized. "So how'd it go? Success?" He looked hopeful.

"Well, if you measure success by the fact I'm back alive then it went great. Ted, I'm sorry, it wasn't what I thought it would be like. Sounds in the place creeped me out and Jim Hardy, one of the really creepy dieners, showed up and went crazy finding me there. Sorry, I was glad to get out of there. I was in the right area and, for a minute, I think I was getting close to finding some of your guy's stuff. But everything fell apart very quickly. That diener had fire in his eyes when he found me there and I bluffed my way out as fast as I could."

When the all too precocious Kathy, already practicing to be a clone of her mother at almost five, piped up: "What's a de-nay mommy?" Liza knew the discussion was over for a while. Ted wasn't entirely sure what *diener* meant and wouldn't have minded an explanation either. But he could wait until later. What he just heard made him feel terrible. He had let Liza do this. In a few hours, after the barbeque when the kids were asleep, the everlasting disagreement over who instigated that ill-fated adventure would begin, never to be resolved in their lifetimes.

The kids were over excited and being with cousins and grandparents would make for a miserable afternoon for everyone if they didn't get decent naps first. They had a light lunch and then the kids were put down. Ted had hoped he could find out more about the morning while the kids slept but Liza determined to stay in the room with the baby, ostensibly to ensure he would sleep. Whether she used that as a means to avoid talking with Ted was open to conjecture and personal perspective.

Ted spent the quiet hour or so while everyone slept thinking about his case. He was on his fifth day and he still didn't know who his murdered dead man was. Reams of notes were accumulating but the case appeared rudderless. Even the few pieces he did have weren't fitting together. The puzzle in the center of the table remained almost empty. Any new pieces he was getting were still sitting off to the sides.

It gave him a slight chill when he thought how little he had after all this time. He was working on this as hard as he could. He knew he would be judged by what he solved, not what he did or how busy he was. How could he have so little after five long days? Were his superiors hovering over him and getting impatient? Not yet, but that might come soon. With the craziness of the post he had to deal with late Friday he barely had a chance to speak with Rondell, who only managed to tell him he looked like shit and not much else. There would be more complete meetings coming. He knew it. Probably first thing on Monday.

Thank goodness for the weekend so his hands and aching shoulders could be rested and heal up. He was sore, but no lasting problems and his hands, he thought, looked great, just sore. Rondell made it clear to him he was welcome to work on the case 24/7 if things were moving along, but otherwise, if it was quiet, thinking and planning were fine for the next two days.

He determined to sit with some paper after the kids were asleep that night and write down what he had and try to place things into at least the two parallel paths he needed to pursue: The probability of someone at that lake being involved in the murder, and finding out who the hell his dead man was and what he was up to.

Knowing someone was looking for that guy could turn out to be a solid lead. There had to be others leads he should find. With aid from the New York City Police an uncertainty, Ted slowly sensed an increasing importance for going to New York City, if only to try to light a fire under the NYPD.

* * *

DAY 6 SUNDAY, OCTOBER 17

All he planned to do was take the baby for a ride during his nap after lunch since Henry always went out right away as soon as he was in a moving vehicle. Ted knew he was capable of sleeping two or more hours. He had been raising hell all morning and Liza thought he might be coming down with something or had over stuffed himself at the barbeque yesterday. In any event, as always, he was out by the time they reached the end of the short street they lived on. Both kids always looked like dolls when fast asleep in their car seats. Ted was happy to see Henry get some rest.

He didn't tell Liza but he knew he was going to head for Lake Bee. He brought a diaper and a snack and juice for when Henry woke up. He took their small sedan, not his cruiser. He figured he had almost entirely avoided putting his kids, especially Henry and his car seat, in a public vehicle, and this trip was no reason to do any differently. He was not in uniform and took no weapon. So off they went on a beautiful fall day. He thought when Henry woke up, if it was warm enough and they were still at the lake, he could let him throw some stones into the water from the public boat launch just off the county road.

Ted wanted to drive around the lake to see if there was any activity on a weekend afternoon even though the summer season was over. He also wanted to be sure to see how the water current was directed when any wind came up in mid-afternoon. If he had time he thought about driving as far as he could on the two or three small spur roads he hadn't fully investigated yet.

The lake community was quiet, and there was a moderately stiff wind blowing southeast to northwest, towards the stream at the mouth of the lake where the body was found. So this was the third time he had seen the small waves directed that way, suggesting any floating object would, eventually, have a good chance of winding up near the stream where his John Doe was found.

He decided to drive down the south road first just to look around. Slowly, maybe so slowly his driving might, unintentionally, cause some on the lake to notice him and assume he was an uninvited stranger, he navigated down the road. Around a bend he saw the elusive Stan Angle working on his beat up old Dodge Dart in his driveway.

What to do? This guy had shown signs of aggressively avoiding him at least once and that worried Ted. Here he had him in a setting where he couldn't walk away so easily. But Ted had Henry with him. He rationalized to himself Henry was still early in his nap and he had some time. He could pull into the driveway and crack some windows and he wouldn't be more than a few feet from his car while he spoke with Stan Angle. He never considered what he would do if this fellow's behavior became a problem while they talked and something dangerous might happen. Neither Liza or Lieutenant Rondell would be pleased about any of this…and his service weapon was at home.

He drove into the driveway. He could see Stan Angle's first impulse, on standing up from the engine area he was leaning over, was to walk to his house. He appeared to recognize Ted. But he stayed. He stood there, a scowl on his face, while Ted got out and quickly looked at the baby and the windows in his car. He would be no more than seven or eight feet away and was sure he would hear him if he stirred.

Stan was wearing in a sweatshirt with cut sleeves and black jeans speckled with old paint stains. He was medium height, stocky, and unshaven. Before Ted could introduce himself and, he presumed, shake hands, Stan Angle spoke, in a resigned but angry tone.

"What do you want from me?"

At least he didn't tell him to get off his property, Ted thought. And he did know who Ted was.

"Mr. Angle, you know I'm investigating a homicide. Your son found the body on Tuesday. I have to interview everyone who was around the lake last week. I've been looking for you and had difficulty getting to speak with you."

Before he could continue Stan interjected, "You ain't really interviewed Maggie, my wife, have you?"

Ted stopped. He didn't have a good answer to that. Because Stan was right. On the day the body was found Ted had not really asked Joe's mother anything much more than to find out what she did for work. Ted knew the implication of Stan's words: That Ted considered him under suspicion. Stan's suspicion about Ted probably was correct.

Stan continued on. He spoke in a slow, measured way, his anger barely contained beneath the surface. "You think I could have something to do with your body. You probably have checked me out and figure me as a good bet for any trouble around here. Well then you know I got a record. I done stuff I paid the time for. And I done stuff I ain't never been caught for too." He tone was a little too proud when apparently feeling the need to highlight he wasn't always caught. He made Ted a bit nervous.

Actually, Ted had not yet thought to consider if any of the people he was trying to speak with around the lake had any criminal histories. He silently agreed with Stan that if he did do some searching Stan looked like someone he'd expect to have been in trouble; have a record. Best to try to move along and ask the questions he wanted so he could assess for anything that might tie this man to the crime or, hopefully, make him less likely to have had any involvement.

"Listen, Stan, what I need to know is where you were last week when this all happened? And I need to know if you saw or heard anything unusual around then? I'm also asking folks about their connection to the lake, how long they've been here, and what they do." Which wasn't entirely true, but he sure wanted to get an answer to the question about where this man had been for the last few months since lake gossip was he hadn't been around. "I don't want to keep….uh oh."

He heard a cry from his car. He nodded to Stan and walked to the car. Henry was wiggling in his seat; clearly awake. He picked him up and held him to his chest so his head was on his shoulder and he became quiet again. He was sweaty, with that moist, vinegary baby smell. With his hand cradling his bottom Ted could tell he had peed in the diaper. He didn't smell any obvious poop, thank goodness.

He had come this far with a reluctant Stan Angle and was anxious not to break it off now. Henry resting on him, sleeping again, he walked back over to Stan and, rocking slightly back and forth, he tried to continue the interview.

Stan never said a word about the unusual situation but, maybe because of it, seemed to oblige the Trooper and, unprompted, spoke.

"My wife told you I was working that Monday night. I work nights as a custodian at Rutland Regional so had to leave here around nine to get the place set up for the morning. No Columbus Day holiday in that school system. I slept all that afternoon and I ain't seen nothing when I left. I seen your police vehicles across the lake when I come home in the morning, but that's it."

Henry shifted his head and Ted intensified his back and forth rocking. This was not the time to leave. Having Henry on his shoulder may have cut into some of Stan's anger.

"Everyone seems to want to know everyone else's business 'round here. I was away most of the summer and that set lots of folks to some nasty guessing. Well, screw them. I was back a few days now and then, just nobody saw me." He was pissed.

"Really. Think about it," he said. "Custodian can be a year round job, but I got to make as much as I can for me and my family. So I could get the summer off since they only need a light crew then anyway. I took a good job at a fancy resort near Lake George and, on weekends, I worked nights at a fancy dinner place, Scone Castle, in Whitehall in New York." Getting angry again, but more at his situation in the world. "You do what you fuckin' got to do."

Henry was definitely up now. Any effort by Ted to query Stan with any subtle or even trick questions would be lost in the midst of trying to get Henry to lay low any longer. Who knew what the whole story was with this guy? It would probably be a lot of work to check out all the jobs he mentioned but it might be necessary. He did make a mental note to look up Stan's record though.

Ted thanked Stan for his time and was careful to let him know he might be hearing from him again. He took Henry to the car and wanted to strap him back in the car seat, but he stiffened and hope of driving even a hundred yards and then changing him wasn't going to happen. So he gave a furtive glance to Stan, who was watching him, and proceeded to change Henry's diaper.

All dry, strapped in, juice in one hand and a cookie in the other, Henry and Trooper Ted Vallan backed out of the Angle driveway and headed home. He fervently hoped Henry would stay as mum about the afternoon's events as he planned to.

* * *

That evening, around seven, Ted got a call from a Montpelier dispatcher telling him a detective from the Burlington Police Department wanted to speak with him. Ted virtually repeated, out loud, what the dispatcher was telling him so Liza, sitting nearby, could get the gist of the call and let him know if she was willing to monitor the kids so he could take the Burlington PD call right away. Liza nodded her ascent. The dispatcher must have wondered, on her end, what kind of a weird guy Ted was, parroting her call back to her. She patched the call through.

"Trooper Vallan?"

"Yes."

"Hi. Corporal Hank Jackson, with the BPD. I got the duty today. I'm calling to ask about a possible missing person. Probably a little preliminary but I have some time and I thought I should make some inquiries.

"One James Hardy from Burlington, who works as a pathology assistant at the hospital, was reported missing by his family a few hours ago. Now he's only been gone today so he might have headed somewhere for the day and just isn't back yet. His family is worried and are telling me that's way out of character for him. They call him a home body who sits with his beer and watches the tube when he's not working. Especially football on Sundays. Anyway, the reason I'm calling you is the M.E., Dr. Roller...You know who he is, don't you?"

The corporal was hell bent on getting his story out. Ted already had made a connection he couldn't figure out. He knew from Liza that was the name of the pathology assistant who walked in on her yesterday. How his possible disappearance could have anything to do with Liza stumped him. Ted squeezed in the answer the Corporal was looking for.

"Yes."

The Corporal sped on. "Well I told the family I'd make a few preliminary inquiries today. So I contacted Doc Roller and he told me some things and then suggested I speak with you."

Ted was still looking for a connection. 'Those damn stones?' he wondered to himself.

"Doc told me that he was working on a case with you and this fellow James was also involved. Doc said something wasn't going too smoothly and he had yelled at James on Friday about it. Could be nothing. But Doc said you had brought up a question about maybe some sloppy work. If this James is really gone Doc wonders if that case could be related in some way.

"Course there are probably ten other things could be going on in this guy's life. Who knows?"

Ted offered the Corporal nothing more than confirmation of the M.E.'s comments. He asked the Corporal to alert the BPD to keep him informed of anything they developed on the man and they, cordially, hung up. 'Must be something about those stones', Ted mused. Dr. Roller couldn't seem to keep his report straight about them and that's why Liza ventured to the morgue yesterday. Ted was in a light mood. 'Be wary of stones in a dead man…or maybe, be wary of a dead man's stones', he thought to himself and smiled. 'A dead man and his stones don't talk. Wait till Liza hears about that diener.'

* * *

DAY 7 MONDAY OCTOBER 18

Ted glanced at his watch as he drove to the Montpelier Barracks. It bothered him he wouldn't be at his desk by eight but there was no time-clock to punch and there was never going to be any question about the hours he put in. He was feeling good, more relaxed than he could recall since that body showed up in Bee pond…lake or whatever it was. He still wasn't sure. He even heard one of the camp owners refer to it as 'lake Bee pond'!

How could he not feel good? He was still alive after a near death experience on Friday. Effects from the adrenalin high from having survived still affected him. Despite some residual soreness in his hands and shoulders he had nudged himself out of bed very early to run.

With the early hour he was able to take a quick four mile run before the kids were awake and the morning zoo began. Running by five-thirty now meant going out in the dark. He wore a large reflective vest and he had just started again using the neat headlight strapped around his hat that Liza got him last Christmas. It burned through batteries. Liza's real plan was for them to share it. It was a good idea for both of them. Too busy and childcare responsibilities meant rarely ever running together anymore.

Ted recognized some of his improved mood and feeling more relaxed this morning was from his run. He thought maybe in the future he could figure out a way to run during the day, like at around noon, at the Barracks. He knew there was a shower and assumed anyone could use it.

While mulling over ways to ensure more regular running as his job responsibilities got bigger he drove into the parking lot behind the Barracks. He got out, walked through the unlocked glass door, punched in his code at the inside metal door, and headed to his cubicle, one of about ten in the main duty room. His most immediate goal was to complete some case related paperwork needed for the bean counters to justify his work time.

His bigger goal required him to go to Burlington and meet, face to face, with Dr. Roller to resolve any confusion about the post and those fucking stones. He had his stone with him. While in Burlington at the M.E.'s he planned to check out the story about who had called looking for a missing fat man. He was already days behind on that one, courtesy the M.E.'s office. He wanted to find out more about the diener, James Hardy, and if he was still missing. If so, he'd then go to the Burlington PD and discuss the status of their investigation. Finally, before he left Burlington he hoped to stop by the Ancient Languages department at UVM and show someone the stone Liza called a rune. It would be great if his stone meant something to someone.

Having left so late on Friday he was surprised when he saw a yellow sticky already placed in the middle of his desk so early Monday morning. Some of his good feeling was chipped away a little when he saw the sticky was from Lieutenant Rondell, with the time listed as eight-fifteen, asking Ted to come to his office at eight-forty-five. It was eight-twenty. Out loud, to no one, he barely whispered "nuts!". No, he didn't have to be in by eight but he sure wished he had been at his desk when Rondell showed up. Rondell's office was down a corridor and there was no way he would know whether Ted was at his desk without walking over or calling.

Ted pulled some papers from a drawer, but he was distracted now. Forgetting the bean counters he had less inclination to even draw up the outline he also planned to put together this morning. He needed to sketch out what he wanted to get done over the next few days when he was back in the field. This afternoon, when back at Montpelier, he planned to start to track down the people he was going to have to get some assistance from at the NYPD… 'Oh man, New York City!'

Even contemplating going to New York City gave him a tug in his gut. What mixed feelings he got; part excitement; part true fear of the unknown. At this point he held out little hope the type of assistance he had received so far from the New York cops was going to be nearly enough to even get him a real name or the needed information that was still mostly a blank in this case. Maybe Rondell was thinking of sending someone else and that's what he wanted to talk with him about.

But it was Ted's case. Now, even after Liza's strange business in the pathology area and that odd diener's disappearance, he felt he should be the one to go and finally find out whose body this was all about. He knew Liza would not be happy with him going, open ended, for at least two or three days. Maybe his parents would stay with them.

Yes, that probably was what the Lieutenant wanted to speak about to him. As he sat at his desk, still feeling a little uncomfortable about not having been there when Rondell came by, he accepted he would be disappointed if he didn't get to go to New York; because it was his case but also, he admitted to himself, to miss a chance to check out life and people in a big city. It was time. It also was time to go to the Lieutenant's office.

Lieutenant Rondell, as usual, looked all business when Ted showed up at his open door and was told to come in and have a seat. The Lieutenant's office was one of the larger ones in the building. His desk wasn't any larger than those in the cubicles but he had a side table, a copier, and three chairs placed near the desk. There was no sign of a sophisticated investigative operation. Basically nothing in the building impressed of high tech for its time and that was the way it was for the Vermont State Police in 1976.

There were two plaques on the wall behind the Lieutenant, a cork bulletin board on his left wall, and a window looking out on woods to his right. The window faced north so there was never much direct light. The corkboard was almost filled up with papers tacked to it. Notably, everything was absolutely neat and in perfect rows. On his desk two small framed photographs faced him. Ted knew, from prior visits to this office, the photos were of his wife and girl and boy.

The Lieutenant's face appeared bland and unemotional which wasn't unusual. He motioned to Ted to sit in the farthest chair from the door, next to the window. After Ted was sitting Rondell said: "Ted, have you ever heard of "Applegate's Better Collectables Weekly"?"

"Well sure." He relaxed a little. "That's a really well known trader's magazine for people all over the country who are collectors of a million different things. It's called the "ABC" by the folks who use it."

"Really" Rondell said. "How is it you know this?"

"My father is a collector of old novelty 45 RPM records and has used the "ABC" to make trades and deals for years. I kind of grew up with it around the house."

"Novelty 45's? What does that mean?"

"Oh you do know about them. Remember from the fifties and sixties songs like "The Purple People Eater", "Itsy Bitsy Teeny Weeny Yellow Polka Dot Bikini", and lots of others? Sam the Sham and the Pharaohs' "Little red Riding Hood"?" Ted started to sing:

> *"Hey there Little Red Riding Hood*
> *You sure are looking good*

You're everything that a big bad wolf could want....
Listen to me!"

The Lieutenant's left eyebrow elevated, reflecting his surprise at Ted's sudden crooning.

"My father, Thom, is actually a pretty clever guy. He got interested in novelty songs, and there were a lot of them, way back. What he did when one came out he thought was in that category, he didn't just buy one, but he got five or ten copies. So, pretty quickly, he was able to get into the game, so to speak, and had the ability to make trades and, by now, make deals for some decent money."

"Really." Rondell's face was still slightly contorted in response to what Ted had just done. At that moment there was a buzz on the Lieutenant's phone. He answered and said, "Send them in."

As two men walked into the room Ted's eyes were still fixed on the Lieutenant and he watched as Rondell's visage turned to stone. The Lieutenant didn't get up but Ted quickly figured he better, so he stood to shake hands. First, with the one in uniform, Detective Sergeant Steve Dixon, who Ted was well aware, was in charge of Internal Affairs. Now *Ted's* eyebrow went up. He also knew the other man, who was dressed in a suit. He would not quickly forget their recent interaction at the Federal Building in Burlington.

The man introduced himself to Rondell and then, stiffly, to Ted, who clearly remembered him as Charles Smith, the asshole treasury agent who had spoken with Ted about the $1000 bills he found. (The agent had used the word 'recovered'.) This morning Agent Smith looked older, with small jowls on his cheeks and the beginnings of a paunch. His suit wasn't pressed and Ted guessed he wore it daily as his regular work clothes. The contrast between the three men in uniform, who all looked and carried themselves with an almost military bearing, and the treasury agent's trending to sloppiness was obvious.

Everyone sat and Ted told Agent Smith that Milton Frober, the agent Smith had directed him to out of Albany, had been very helpful and had given him some good information. Smith seemed disinterested in hearing anything from Ted. His face still wore a frown.

Smith sat for a moment and then spoke directly to Ted. "Trooper Vallan are you familiar with a weekly paper called "Applegate's Better Collectables"?" Ted immediately stiffened in his chair and shot a glance at Rondell. This time he told these men most of the same story he had just told Rondell, but his demeanor was completely different; subdued and direct. He had no intention of singing to them. Ted motioned to Agent Smith's suit side pocket and said he could see the agent had a copy of an "ABC" with him. Smith moved around in his chair indicating he wasn't too interested in listening to Ted and wanted to move on. The other two men just sat, listening.

Smith cleared his throat and spoke a bit officiously and pompously. "Trooper Vallan, we have people who have contacts with us who monitor magazines like these looking for any indications of possible financial improprieties. Yesterday it was brought to our attention there may be something going on related to someone trying to unload some $1000 bills."

If he hadn't been sitting in this small room with these three stone faced men Ted might have tried to convince himself this was good news and possibly a piece of the puzzle he was working on was coming into place. But that idea didn't fit this setting. His brain was rushing and he didn't like the most obvious thoughts coming to him. Among them were some vague ideas about his father, who he identified with the "ABC". But he quickly came to the logical conclusion whatever was about to come out was about himself.

"Trooper Vallan this week there is a listing placed in the 'Bill Collectors' sub-section of the 'CASH – Coins, Bills, and Notes' section we believe comes from Vermont. It looks like it may contain a code of some sort but it clearly states an interest in moving some $1000 bills. Maybe you'd like to take a look at it." Agent Smith pulled out his copy of the "ABC" and, with a needlessly dramatic motion, opened it to a page he had dog-eared. "I'll read it before I hand it to you." Clears his throat. "Selling or Trading; information about circulated $1000 bills. Several genuine, circa 1926 available. Vonn Talley, Box VT."

Ted froze in his chair and felt a warm flush racing across his face. He wasn't angry about the way this jerk was coming at him. It was his recognition of what the ad meant and that he was quite sure what its genesis had been.

Agent Smith practically taunted Ted. "Does this ad mean anything to you, Trooper Vallan?" Ted wondered if all people named Smith were assholes or just the last two he had met. In fact, Ted was one of those people who came across as so genuine and honest even his enemies tended to warm to him. Not these Smiths.

"Yes, I think I know who placed that ad and I know why." The three other men in the room reacted as though they had just been slapped in the face. They all shifted in their chairs like they were leaning, ever so slightly, a little closer to Ted to hear his response.

"My father is almost sixty-two. He spent many years as a foreman in a small machine shop in Colchester. The owner abruptly closed it about eight months ago and there really hasn't been any meaningful work for my dad since then. We all have seen how having time on his hands has affected him." Agent Smith's scowl increased, if that was possible, and he opened his mouth as though he was getting ready to interrupt words he deemed were extraneous to the main issue.

Ted lifted his hand ever so slightly to warn him off. "'Vonn Talley' is the nickname my father has used for years in his dealings with his record hobby. He mostly reversed first letters of his name to come up with VT. So Thom Vallan became Vonn Talley." Ted shifted in his seat.

"It looks like I made a big mistake when I was asking my mother about big bills like these." Eyebrows raised again, this time around the room. "You see my mother had been a bank teller for some years way back. We had just found those bills at the crime scene and I was wondering if there ever were bills in such a denomination. I called my mother mid-day to check on my kids. As I was about to hang up I decided to ask her if she knew anything about $1000 bills. She had some anecdotes but basically didn't know if real ones existed or not. Then she told me she'd mention it to my father to see if he could help out. Immediately I realized my mistake and asked her to please not mention it to him or anybody. I guess she didn't listen to me. All the time she's trying to find things for him to be occupied with. I guess neither one of them understood the problems their involvement could stir up." Ted shifted again in his chair and mostly directed his next words to Detective Sergeant Dixon.

"I will go over there today and sit with both my parents and explain that my father is interfering with a criminal investigation and it must stop. I'll make sure if my father gets any responses to that ad I will show them to Lieutenant Rondell and forward copies to Agent Smith. I'll make sure the ad doesn't run again."

Everyone in the room was tense.

Agent Smith spoke up, almost as though Ted had never said anything. "Trooper Vallan, how do we know you had nothing to do with this ad?" Ted sensed he hadn't defused anything and, there was a good chance this thing was be about to get bigger. "Every part of this ad could have come from you. Our people think there is a code in there that indicates the person who put that ad in is fencing four $1000 bills with markings dating them to 1934. The two bills you turned in date to the 1934 series, you know."

Ted was desperate to understand what code he was talking about. But neither he nor the other troopers seemed ready to ask that question. What mattered right now was Agent Smith was trying to implicate Ted in the felony of stealing from a crime scene. From speaking with Milton Frober he remembered the bills he found were series 1934A, not 1934. Would it make any sense to correct this asshole?

Detective Sergeant Dixon leaned forward and spoke to both Ted and the Lieutenant. "Ted, this is all new information we just heard about late last evening. I'm not sure your explanation won't clear things up eventually…but for now you are going to have to be removed from this case while we investigate what's happened and all of Agent Smith's concerns."

Agent Smith didn't seem, again, to care much about what others were saying. "Actually, we want that box to stay open for now and, beginning today, we expect to be monitoring the call in mechanism for retrieving responses. But first, we don't want anyone speaking with anyone else about that ad and the box. Troopers, our people have answered that ad and we intend to follow-up with whoever is involved."

Ted felt almost helpless. He doubted there was much he could say that would make any difference with what his father was stumbling into or the case Ted was working on so intensely. He couldn't deny his fuck up, but he wasn't at all sure this jerk Smith was making much sense. He decided his best chance to keep his job and this investigation was to try to wait out Smith and then plead his case with Dixon and Rondell after Smith left. He could easily sense the other troopers were put off by Smith's bluster and *case solved* approach to this increasingly complicated situation.

He didn't want to see his father in trouble but he knew his father wasn't trying to move any bills, much less monster bills. However actively the feds worked on this little detail they would soon find out it was just a stupid mistake by an amateur. Any effort they made to lean on his dad would quickly fizzle into nothing. No one in that room, including Ted, knew his father already had the one hit he decided was worth pursuing and had erased that message from the box. Last evening, virtually minutes before the reply arrived from the feds, he cancelled the box.

Agent Smith stood and faced Sergeant Dixon and began speaking. "My office will keep you informed as events unfold." Clearly Agent Smith was anticipating a significant investigation. Then, as he turned to walk out of Rondell's office, he tipped his head and, out of character for his somber demeanor, said "Fellas."

Ted prepared to do whatever he could to defend his continuing involvement with his case. He knew he better wait to see what his superiors were going to say before he spoke up. Dixon and Rondell looked at each other and, after a pause, Rondell spoke.

"That Agent Smith comes across like a dick; a real asshole."

Ted was quietly elated. He thought the sergeant would probably try to get some direction from the Lieutenant. Rondell's words might be leaving some sort of an opening for Dixon to let Ted make his case for staying on the homicide case. Dixon put his hand on his chin. He said nothing but visibly turned in his chair and faced Ted. Ted felt he was being afforded an opportunity to speak. Ted figured he should speak to both men and not direct his words to Sergeant Dixon exclusively.

"A week ago a body was found in a lake, the victim of a homicide. There has not been a great deal of evidence found so far. An assistant in the M.E. office who assisted with the autopsy of the John Doe is now missing. What *I* have found" (he made the I forceful, to stress his control of the case, to this point) "is a stone with engraving on it that could be related to stones found in the dead man's stomach, and two $1000 bills. The bills are now at the U.S. Treasury district office in Albany where it will be determined if they are real or fakes. My guess is Albany thinks they are real and that's why Agent Smith contacted you. I am working" (a bit of a stretch he knew) "with the NYPD to ID and get information about the John Doe.

"There is no doubt the ad in the "ABC" is related to what was found on the body because the ad is obviously from my father. My fault. Sloppy and inappropriate on my part. But there is no reason his foolish idea of trying to help me by thinking he was going to learn more about that type of currency through an ad would have anything to do with this real case. Look, by doing ads in papers like that my dad has made friends and contacts, and those kind of people routinely pass along all kinds of information about things they mutually collect."

Then Ted's voice rose and his words were emphatic.

"I found and photographed all the bills found on the John Doe, and there were a bunch of people standing at the scene who watched me do it. Until we opened the clip with the money, on the hood of a cruiser, not I or any one of the people standing there had any idea of what was between the smaller bills surrounding the two large bills. A couple of hours after that I talked to my mother about a $1000 bill. And you know what happened from there. To get the ad in the "ABC" issue being talked about my father had to have put it in immediately or it would never have been printed in the issue Agent Smith brought. And there's no code in that ad that makes any sense to me.

"Since the body was found I've practically lived at that lake, interviewing and, yes, searching camps. Some camps were occupied, but most were empty. But even if I found a bunch of $1000 bills and, totally crazy and committing a felony, decided to try to sell them to a hobbyist or whoever (and I don't even know why that would be a good way to sell them) I couldn't have an ad in the current issue. Even if I was working with my idiot father it still wouldn't have been possible to place that ad after the first afternoon of the case.

"What my dad did is not a crime. Turns out $1000 bills do exist and can be bought and sold legally without any government control. The idea the feds think they are doing some kind of a sting is as crazy as what my father thought he was doing. With the feds shutting off the only simple way to settle this whole crazy business by not letting me bring my father here to tell you what he did, there's nothing else I can say to resolve your concerns. There's nothing here that makes any sense that should have the department worried about me being a criminal. If I'm taken off this case right now it will become a mess." To himself Ted thought that more accurately he probably should have said *more* of a mess. "How long are the feds going to play their game and waste their time tracking amateur collectors as they go back and forth about big bill collecting? It's a dead end for them and a needless delay with me off the case until the feds lose interest."

Ted surprised himself with the forceful way he responded but also the way he mapped out the situation for his superiors, offering them a clear path to keeping him on the case. Rondell and Dixon leaned back in their chairs and listened, thoughtfully, as Ted talked. Rondell looked at Dixon. After a minute of silence Dixon spoke.

"It's always challenging when another law enforcement agency comes to us with questions or information. The State Police never want to miss criminal activity within our own ranks. It does happen. The feds can't tell us what to do. They only tell us what they think or know about a situation. Suspicion of a criminal act is a justification for relieving a trooper from active duty. It's a big step to do that, and you can imagine what that can do to a trooper's career."

The Sergeant shifted his glance from Ted to Rondell. "It does seem unlikely there is much going on here with this $1000 bill business beyond some poor judgment on Trooper Vallan's part for sharing police business with his parents." Dixon's face seemed to express an inquiry looking for some sort of sign from the Lieutenant about Dixon's take on all this. Rondell's expression didn't seem to change appreciably to Ted.

After a short pause Dixon continued, probably deciding Rondell was leaving the decision up to Internal Affairs. "I think it's okay for Trooper Vallan to stay active and continue to work this case. Agent Smith needn't know what we're doing. But if there is any information we get which even slightly changes what we have been told the force will go ahead with a suspension and further internal investigation." Ted wasn't sure if he could relax yet. He looked from Dixon to Rondell.

"Sergeant Dixon, I'm glad you agree Trooper Vallan's response to our concerns is credible and reasonable. It is unfortunate the feds are insisting they have happened on criminal activity. But that's the way it is. Ted, you can't speak, at all, with your parents about any of this until we get an all clear from the feds. I hope Sergeant Dixon will have someone check with Agent Smith's office every few days to find out what does or doesn't develop from their work. And I agree with the Sergeant if anything strange or unusual comes up for a while, for anything related to you, you will, at the least, need to leave this case, and Internal Affairs will have to get involved again."

Ted stood up. He had dodged the bullet. He kept a serious expression, nodded to each of his superiors, and walked out, assuming Rondell and Dixon had more to say to each other.

Back at his desk, even before he looked at his messages, he re-lived the experience. Even if he despised the manner of the treasury agent he could understand how the ad might confuse the feds. But they should have been willing to consider Ted's explanation before launching any kind of investigation. That was sure going to be a waste of time.

He felt reassured about the force with the way Rondell and Dixon allowed him to explain what logically happened and also how critical he is to solving the case. Ted was sure his superiors believed him. He recognized the way he handled the thinly veiled charges made by Agent Smith signaled a more aggressive behavior than his usual demeanor. Maybe just a temporary, small blip from his usual more self-effacing manner but maybe not. Ted realized developments in this case were challenging his standard approaches and reactions, even about himself. What he still couldn't figure out, at all, was just what his father thought he was doing? What an idiot!

* * *

What was the point of trying to plan each day when something almost routinely turned up to thwart it? This was certainly not starting out anything like the day he had in mind. He had to get moving and find a way to shake off his amazement and anger over what he just went through. Calling the BPD from his cruiser helped. The police told him the diener, James Hardy, was still missing. He did not show up at the pathology office today.

With that news he decided to go to the M.E.'s office at the hospital first. When he walked in he could sense the tension of the staff. The place was abuzz about James Hardy's disappearance. Staff stared at Ted as though he was an inquisitor coming after them. Of course he had never assumed any of them were curt to him last week because there was anything sinister going on in that office. Now anything seemed possible, although unlikely. Instead of quizzing the secretaries about Hardy, which was for the BPD as far as he knew, he wanted information about the woman who called on Thursday.

The secretary who took the call was defensive from the start. No one in that comfortable office felt comfortable just then. She repeated the details of her interaction and there was very little beyond what Ted already heard from the M.E. on Friday. The caller was a woman who, initially, seemed concerned but relaxed on the phone. Hospital information had transferred her call. It wasn't clear if the hospital or the woman suggested trying the morgue. The woman did say she was calling from New York City. She never formally identified herself or left a phone number or any other way to contact her if the fellow she was inquiring about did turn up there. At the end she did say the man she was looking for didn't know his way around Vermont at all.

What the secretary didn't say, and what Ted was more interested in now, was whether there was any reason to think this caller received enough information to assume the man she was worried about was now in the morgue. The secretary's face flushed and her eyes became watery. She knew the rules. The secretary recounted how the caller started to cry and say she just knew it was him and insisted on describing 'that fat old lug, but I loved him' and the secretary thought she, maybe, had indicated they had a John Doe with a good likelihood of being that man. Whoever the caller was she got what she wanted.

Ted asked to see the M.E. now. There was a look of great concern on Dr. Roller's face as he got up when Ted came in. James Hardy was foremost on his mind.

"Trooper Vallan, the Burlington Police were here earlier for an hour. This is terrible. You probably spoke with them yesterday. I told them I had yelled at Jimmy on Friday after the mix-up with those stones we talked about. I don't usually yell at anyone. But he didn't seem terribly upset. He said it was his responsibility and he would take care of it. To just disappear like this. That's not Jimmy. And he didn't seem that upset."

Ted had so much to do. He was happy to let the BPD take charge of this and would go over it with them, hopefully, shortly. He did get the M.E.'s point something unusual had happened. He wasn't about to say anything to Roller, one way or another, about Roller's apparent feelings of guilt for yelling at his subordinate when he had clearly fucked up.

"Dr. Roller, what about those crazy stones? I assume you do have them?" expressed in-artfully given the definite disappearance of diener Hardy.

Very flat. "Yes, we can go out on the floor to the specimen cabinets." Ted assumed the M.E. would have already checked and would have them on his desk. Maybe that wasn't a good spot for specimens. Ted noted, even all lit up, the whole large area was creepy. Liza was something else.

The other diener, Tim Jackert, came over and went right to the cabinets and retrieved a box containing several glass jars. There was a large table a few feet away and the diener placed the box there, fetched three pairs of latex gloves, and opened the glass jar of interest. A metal tray was on the table and the stones were slowly pulled out and placed on it. Ted counted, four, five, six; all small stones non-descript, each a different shape, none larger than a nickel.

The M.E. had no visible reaction. Ted was furious. He told the M.E. he thought they should take the tray to his office to talk about them. Doc Roller looked puzzled and muttered something about that being irregular but didn't argue. Once they were alone in Roller's office Ted removed the stone he had been carrying for several days from his pocket. He didn't say anything, he just held the stone up so the M.E. could easily see its size and structure. Roller's expression devolved into a sheepish look. Then he appeared visibly ill. He knew exactly what Ted was suggesting.

"Oh my goodness. I do remember now. Even covered with all the matter in his stomach the stones looked more like this one than these pebbles. I don't think the stones in this tray are the stones from that man's stomach. Oh, this is just terrible! Trooper Vallan, I don't know, I just don't know what to think. Why would Jimmy even conceive of doing anything like this? It just can't be."

Dr. Roller looked genuinely astonished and shocked. When Ted told him that on the phone Friday Ted added one more stone to the number Roller had listed for him right after the post, he was speechless. Ted talked with the M.E. about the other diener, Tim Jackert, but decided not to interview him until he learned more from the BPD. Finally, about to leave, Ted cautioned Dr. Roller not to say anything to anyone about his post or the stones. He requested whatever paperwork was necessary so he could take the stones on the tray with him as evidence.

At the Burlington Police Department Ted was stingy with the information he shared with the Detective on the missing persons case. The Detective thought something had happened to Hardy, but so far they had nothing. He and his car were missing. Ted made it very clear to the Detective he was very concerned the disappearance could have something to do with a capital case he was investigating. He told the Detective any information developed by the BPD had to go through him before release to other agencies or the media.

James Hardy, missing from his own community, was already a public concern. John Doe's appearance in Vermont had stirred almost no public awareness.

* * *

Any further information he could get about the stone he was carrying no longer seemed like only busy work. Ted had to believe that stone meant something. He also hoped it had never been in the dead man's gut. At UVM he took advantage of his cruiser and figured he probably parked in a protected spot for faculty. The campus was notorious for growing vehicle congestion and lack of parking.

Liza had sketched out where he was to go and Ted found the building without any difficulty. What he didn't find was anyone who he could speak with. The professor Liza told him about retired long ago. He was given two names, neither at the school that day. Tuesday both would be in all day.

He made some calls then walked across campus to the medical center and met Liza for a late lunch. After that he headed for Lake Bee. He was almost done with looking at some part of every structure around the lake. He thought it unlikely but hoped those stones would mean something. Going from camp to camp was what seemed more like the busy work now.

* * *

DAY 8 TUESDAY, OCTOBER 19

"Teddy, guess where we are?" His mother had an ironic life view. Both his parents reserved 'Teddy' for more direct family related situations since Ted became an adult. She had just paged him on his beeper.

"Mom, I have no idea. What's going on?"

"Well I'm in the waiting room at the hospital. I brought dad in because he isn't feeling well and they're taking him into the emergency room."

Her pauses in filling him in were annoying, but he was quite concerned. "What's wrong? What happened?"

"This morning he told me he didn't sleep well last night. All morning he hasn't looked good. He said he's weak and a little queasy. When he told me he felt funny in his chest I said we should call Liza or go to the hospital. He refused for a while but he's not better. He wouldn't let me call the rescue squad so we drove over just now. They're taking him into a room."

Ted looked at his watch. It was about noon. Just like his father to delay getting evaluated. And, he thought 'What the fuck has he been up to? This crap with him might be getting worse.' "Well mom, stay close to dad and ask the staff to page Liza. She could be out running but keep trying her until you get her. She will come down and talk with the doctors. Then she'll tell you what's going on and will call me. I'm in the middle of something right now and I really need Liza to tell me what I should do. I'll get there as soon as I can."

He thought for a minute. He decided he should wait for Liza to get back to him. He never doubted for a second she should be the decision-maker for these kinds of problems. His only worry was whether his mother would agree. Dad would do anything Liza said.

So he returned to the side deck of the Gruber home where he had started to interview the Doctor's wife, Ida Gruber. Ted then planned to meet with Scotty Golde to look at the absolute last few unoccupied homes yet to be checked. They were all up in the woods, away from the shore, and even less likely involved in the case. He realized he might have to delay inspecting them if he had to go to the hospital.

Ida Gruber returned to Vermont from South Carolina a day or so ago. He doubted she would have much to add to his investigation but the location of the Gruber house and the other few homes on this part of the lake meant those camps, next to the Joiner's, were places Ted needed to know as much as he could about all their owners. She was sitting in a chair with their two dogs playing at her feet. The dogs were medium size, pretty identical looking, mostly black, mixed breeds. They barked playfully. Ms. Gruber tried to shush them as Ted walked back.

Before his mother paged him Ms. Gruber had told him she was a retired nurse so he had told her about Liza to try to make the interview seem as sociable as possible. She was very pleasant but seemed superficial, making light of his questions. She was overweight and easily fit anyone's definition of dowdy, with too much make-up. She also appeared to be probably at least ten years younger than the doctor, who he assumed was around seventy.

The dogs barked a little louder so Ted decided to comment on it, asking if they were big barkers.

"Oh no, they can get riled up, from time to time, like any dogs can. But no, they usually stay pretty much quiet. Don't you boys?" The last words in baby talk, barely a question.

Ted detected some defensiveness in her responses about the dogs. It put him a little on edge. He decided to probe one of the areas he had been considering ever since they found the big bills.

"Your husband told me he has many hobbies. He showed me his workshop and it's really something. He told me he's also a stamp collector."

Without any prompting she chimed right in: "Oh my yes, the Doctor never has any problem staying busy. He seems busier with all his interests now than when he was practicing. He still keeps up with his collections of stamps, coins, and pretty much anything that's old. Busy, indeed. He's not one for watching much TV."

Ted tried to keep his face impassive, but he was impressed the doctor had only mentioned stamp collecting to him. "'Anything that's old', Ms. Gruber? What do you mean?" he asked.

"Oh, well you'll have to ask him to really explain that to you. But, to me, it seems the older the better. The Doctor says really old things are magical to him."

*   *   *

On his way to Burlington Ted got the word his father was believed to have had a heart attack. As soon as he arrived at the hospital he went directly to the Coronary Care Unit. His mother told him Liza had just left to get the kids since Sheila would not be able to pick them up that day. She wouldn't be back and he would see her when he went home. His mom said his father seemed fine, joking away with the nurses, making light of the whole business. She said they were looking for a bed for him in what they called a 'step down' unit since he was doing so well.

Sheila had a look of uncertainty on her face when she told him the doctors thought his attack was very mild. To her a heart attack was a heart attack and it couldn't be good. Ted recalled phrases he had heard from Liza, establishing a woman can't be 'just a little pregnant' or you can't have a 'touch' of TB. "You are or you aren't" she had said. Maybe his mom was reacting to the reality of both of them getting older and the inevitability that excellent health and freedom from illness rarely go along with a long life.

"Dad, what is going on with you?" He wanted to see how his father would respond to that open question given what he had learned about him yesterday.

"Ted, my only problem is what to do with myself to stay busy and figure out how to make a couple of bucks. I'm feeling fine. Not sure why I'm in this place."

"Way I heard it you been hanging out at home feeling like crap and it's good you're here now, don't you think?"

Thom Vallan shrugged his shoulders. He seemed like he didn't have a lot to say and that was unusual for him. "Oh I guess I'm okay now. Sure glad we been paying into that COBRA since my job went up in smoke. Should make a big difference in paying off all this. Big relief."

Ted wasn't sure what a COBRA was but figured it had something to do with insurance and it sounded like a good thing, especially for a guy sitting in a bed with tubes and wires everywhere. He made a note to himself to try to remember to ask Liza what a COBRA is.

"So you just got sick yesterday and it kept you up all night, huh?" No response. "You weren't jacking up your car or chopping trees yesterday, were you?" He had given his father an opening to spill whatever he was doing with his "ABC" scheme if he was going to. Nothing. Shook his head 'no'. Ted knew that was enough for now. Unless he thought his father was irretrievably dying he saw no importance in upsetting him now about his cockamamie $1000 bills post, whatever it was he was trying to do. Someday there would be a time for talking about that.

"Well I thought you looked fine at sis's barbeque. Maybe we all ate and drank too much." He knew he and his father were good for one beer and that was it, but it seemed like a way, if his father was suspicious of Ted's words, to let him know he wasn't going to probe anymore.

His mom walked in and had that take charge look about her. "So Liza and the Doctor told us dad's going to have to stay around the house for a few weeks. At some point he will have to take one of those treadmill stress tests. They also said there's something they do called 'heart catheterization' that means staying overnight in the hospital and getting special heart arteries tested. After that depends on what they find."

"Mom, I've been talking with Liza about seeing if we can get Mrs. Arkady to come back now instead of the beginning of November. There's too much going on, and now you and dad need to lay low for a while" He knew Liza wasn't in favor of this but the situation at home had changed quickly.

"Oh Teddy, don't be silly. You think dad and I are just gonna sit in chairs at home and stare at each other for weeks? Come on. Thom can sit in your living room as well as his own. And the same for being in a car. The kids rarely rile him."

Debatable, Ted thought.

"And that Mrs. Arkady. 'Quick to slow, quick to slow' and her million other, what Liza calls 'maxims', whatever they are. Your father says things like 'that's what makes horse races'. That I can understand. But half the time who knows what she's talking about. And with that too cute talk and accent."

Ted knew his mother wasn't a Mrs. Arkady booster. He guessed she was a little jealous. The kids loved Mrs. Arkady. She had a warmth and affection that swallowed them up. Amazing, he thought, considering what she had endured in life.

Sheila even sacrificed her daughter, his sister Ellen, who didn't have to work, to encourage him to hold off on Mrs. Arkady.

"When Ellen was here she said she will help out a little more now."

Ted left it up in the air. "We'll talk some more about it. I don't want dad to feel any pressure." Thom Vallan waved the idea off with a flick of his wrist. He really did look fine.

"I'm pretty sure I'm going to New York soon for the case I'm on. I was thinking of leaving sometime tomorrow but I think I'll try to plan for early Thursday morning instead. I want to hang around another day to make sure you're okay before I go."

He was kind of surprised neither parent quickly spoke up to tell him he shouldn't worry and go ahead and do what he had to do. No, they both reacted in agreement. Ted had plenty he could do until Thursday but wasn't happy. He got the message they needed his support. If his father continued to do well and was discharged on Wednesday he would take the time to bring him home and stick around to help out. His case was going nowhere fast anyway, he lamented to himself.

*   *   *

He had struck out finding anyone to help him at UVM yesterday but now he was just across the street and decided to go back and try again. At the Ancient Languages office he was directed to a young assistant professor who looked barely older than Ted. The man seemed anxious to help and looked at Ted's stone a long time, twisting and turning it over and over. The upshot from him was basically what he had been told by Liza: A *rune*, and all that implied historically and as souvenir talismans, sold for centuries since and even now. He said if he had to guess he thought the faded symbol on Ted's stone stood for *water* or a *lake*. Ted thought that was interesting.

As he twirled and twirled it around the young prof had a puzzled look. He told Ted there was something about this stone he couldn't place but somehow it reminded him of something; he just couldn't recall what. Of course that elevated its mystery to Ted.

Ted was excited when the prof told him the pre-eminent rune expert in the US was at the Scandinavia House in New York City. The prof had the man's information and Ted wrote down his name, location, and phone number.

Driving back to Montpelier he ruminated over how much time, a week now, had gone by since the case broke. He still didn't have a name for his John Doe, much less any strong leads about who killed him or why. He could work on some things until Thursday but New York City was the place he needed to get to next. Anyone at Lake Bee who could be involved was going to take a lot more work to filter out. He couldn't help hope he would find some key or better direction to put some pieces together in New York.

At the Barracks he checked his desk. A message from the BPD dated a half hour before he arrived said the missing diener's car had been found at the Rutland Bus Station lot, which is about sixty-five miles from Burlington. So far there was nothing more. Ted decided to call a Lieutenant he was friendly with in the Burlington PD. As he picked up his phone he was buzzed from dispatch.

"Ted, a Detective from the New York PD is on line two for you."

"Hi, this is Ted Vallan."

"Officer Vallan, I'm Jack Nichols, a detective in the 10th precinct, NYPD. Janice Delario asked me to check out some things about a John Doe you got; possibly a homicide." Ted was a bit startled by the lack of an accent after talking with Janice.

"Thanks for looking into this and calling, Detective Nichols. I appreciate hearing from you so quickly. Hope you have some information for me."

"Well, so far, I did two things. I got that phone number you sent over to the phone company and I drove over to the address you have on that business card. The phone guys plugged in that number with all the local area codes and came up blank. You sure you checked it out where you are?"

"Yeah, Detective Nichols, we only have one area code, 802, for all of Vermont, so it was easy to check out."

"Okay. So I drove over to the address on Sixteenth Street. I showed the Sooper your guy's picture and he recognized him but didn't really know anything about him." Ted wondered what a 'Sooper' was?

"Picture was helpful, even dead, cause after he saw it he was willing to let me inside the guy's place."

He paused and Ted thought he heard some papers being moved.

"So it's a tiny place in a beat up old walk-up loft building, kind of set up to like maybe be an office or showroom of some kind. Little fancier chairs, even wallpaper, then might have guessed from the building. No names on the door, just '3G'. I looked through a few drawers and things. Nothing really there. I found some of the business cards you described and that's about it.

"Funny thing is, before I went over there, when I was checking your phone number with the phone company, I asked if there was a phone listed for your guy's address on the card. They said yes and gave it to me. But when I was in there I didn't see any phone. Anyways, your guy paid for his monthlys, rent and phone at least, in person and in cash. He gave his name as Harry James, but who knows."

"Huh?" Ted said, confused about what all this meant. "Detective?"

"Jack" Nichols said.

"Sure. Please, Ted." he replied and continued, "Jack, when do you think you might get an ID from the prints I sent down by FACSIMILE? I get a feeling this fellow probably has a record."

"Yeah. Likely. I agree. Shouldn't be more than another day, if not today. We may need the originals though. That page came through real grainy. Good chance it can't be used."

"Okay. I hoped to be coming to New York tomorrow but some things have come up and I have to wait until Thursday. Can I go look at the place myself when I come down and maybe meet up with you before or after?"

"Sure. I marked off the place as a probable crime scene and that got me the sooper's key from him. Come down to Twenty-third Street and pick it up from Janice and if I'm here we'll chat. Otherwise later for sure when the prints and things are done. Oh, and say, Ted?"

"Yes, Jack?"

"I don't know what your resources are up there, but if that phone number didn't make a hit in your state you might want to get a check run for the states with codes that border Vermont. You know, north, south, east, and west."

Ted wondered if Detective Nichols knew there was no state north of Vermont. But they have phones in Canada also and his suggestion wasn't a bad one. "Thanks, Jack, I will have that checked out."

*   *   *

That evening, while they managed dinner and the kids, Ted asked Liza to review all she knew about his father's episode; what it meant for his future, and what, if anything, needed to be done now.

She explained it all to him in a way he could understand. One feature of her discussion they each took note of was what the doctors had hypothesized about the timing of his heart attack. They both knew Thom did not agree to go to the hospital until almost mid-day. The blood tests at the hospital reflecting heart muscle damage could be looked at two ways. Either Thom Vallan had just had the very mildest of heart attacks or, more likely, the blood tests were only catching the tail end of the acute heart muscle damage since he had been sick for a while and the enzyme levels had returned to very close to normal. The cardiologist Liza spoke with guessed the actual attack probably began later on Monday, maybe even as long ago as late that afternoon.

Ted didn't say a word about that to Liza. He was concerned and worried about his father but he also couldn't help wondering what he might have been doing that he fought for so long against going to the hospital despite feeling bad.

What he did do was bring up the subject of Mrs. Arkady again. Liza was more reflective this time but still said she thought they could get by without her. Ted didn't argue.

*   *   *

DAY 9 WEDNESDAY, OCTOBER 20

Anticipating official permission to go to New York, Ted made an appointment with a Doctor Landsdorf at the Scandinavia House, for nine-fifteen a.m. on Friday.

Late in the morning he got a call from a Montpelier assistant that her first call, to NY Upstate Tele, turned up a number. The number was a 518 area code for a pay phone in Whitehall, NY. Ted figured Whitehall to be about twenty miles from Bee pond. He told the assistant there was no need to call other states. Ted thought about Stan Angle, who had spent the summer working weekends in Whitehall.

The meeting with the Lieutenant earlier was, mercifully, brief. There was a new major case in the Northeast Kingdom and Rondell had to drive up there right away. Very little about Ted's slow, actually lack of, progress was discussed. They each agreed the feds' investigation appeared poorly informed and likely had already faded. The Lieutenant told Ted he also agreed the missing pathology assistant was probably involved in some way with the John Doe case. That seemed to make Ted's strange stone a possible part of this case. Rondell cleared Ted to go to New York.

They ended as Rondell got up to leave for the Kingdom. "You probably don't want to bring your firearm to New York. You could bring a knife, I guess, if you want."

"Okay. Hadn't thought about that." He hadn't thought, at all, about the nuts and bolts of the trip.

Ted planned to meet Scott Golde at the North Road at two to get the keys to the final camps left to check. His father's illness altered the plan to check them on Tuesday. Looking at his list of things to do he reached for his phone and called Lieutenant Tim Schaffer at the Burlington PD. He and Tim had taken several training courses together and a friendship ensued. Their families socialized occasionally.

"Ted, what the fuck? You got some *ESP* or something? Whole department's talking about you. Not sure exactly what you've been working on but was just picking up the phone to tell you our missing person is now a dead body. Jackson made it like you stamped a big-ass *'Top Secret'* or something on all this stuff when he was talking to you. What gives, Ted?"

Ted wasn't sure, 'what gives', himself. The diener's car was found at the Rutland Bus Station, at least sixty-five miles from his home. But his body was found at the head of the Winooski Falls, in Winooski, maybe two or three miles from his home in Burlington. The corpse was a mess, probably from being in the water a few days. Tim said there was no obvious sign of injury; drowning was most likely. The M.E. and another pathologist were starting the post shortly. The other diener couldn't bear to be involved.

Even with a friend Ted saw no reason to spread conjecture, which was all he had, about a bunch of pieces of a puzzle which continued to defy meaningful organization. He shared the basics about finding a murdered John Doe in a lake and that was about it. Even in his own mind he continued to have difficulty tying the dead diener to a case that looked, more and more, as though it could hinge, totally improbably, on some small stones.

Ted stressed the need to avoid public statements for as long as possible and he wanted nothing released to the media until he and

Lieutenant Rondell had a chance to discuss things later in the day, after the autopsy. Ted startled his friend when he advised him to have someone from the BPD at the post. Everyone was a suspect in this case.

*   *   *

All afternoon he waited for dispatch to beep him to call the M.E. It worked out the page came as he was returning keys to Scott Golde and was thanking him for all the time and help he had given the last week. Some effort to get inside every structure around the lake, except the Graham's, was finally complete, with only the Joiner's containing any apparent evidence.

He drove north and found a payphone in fifteen minutes. Doctor Raymond gave Ted the report. James Hardy had been murdered. Probably on the day he disappeared. The cause of death was two gunshot wounds to his brainstem. He was shot in the back of the neck, at close range, with two small caliber bullets neatly entering one half inch apart. Doctor Raymond, who was not a forensic pathologist, said Doctor Roller guessed the bullets were fired from a double barreled derringer. An unusual weapon, Ted thought.

Lieutenant Rondell called Ted at home around seven and they conferred about the murder of James Hardy and Ted's case. They concluded the Lieutenant would speak with the BPD Chief, Ed Hinshaw, and ask him to do everything they would normally do in an investigation like this but to stay away from the M.E. office and all its personnel. The State Police would manage that part of the investigation. When Ted returned from New York, or early next week at the latest, he would compare notes with whoever was directing the investigation for the BPD.

*   *   *

In the evening he rummaged around and found his old three-inch folding blade whittling knife given to him by his father when he was around twelve. He saw a small flashlight in the same drawer and decided to pull it out also. Tuesday, when the decision was being made for him to go the city, he envisioned himself carrying his things in something like his gym bag. Maybe that wasn't going to be so easy to get his stuff into. For the first time he seriously thought about what he would need to take. The plan was for him to be there two, maybe three, days tops. Since he wasn't to wear his uniform Ted realized even the business of packing was getting complicated. He eyed the blue latex gloves he liked on a shelf in the utility room. Liza brought them from the hospital. He picked up a wad of them to bring.

"Man, worrying about my crap. Am I turning into an old fart, already?" He spoke out loud, to no one in particular. He reconsidered his thought. "I am pumped!" and he felt real excitement about going to New York tomorrow.

"What was that? Were you saying something to me, Ted?" Liza was in the kitchen.

"No, babe. Talking to myself." He was quite aware Liza had been cool to him from the time it was clear he would really be away from home for a few days. He knew she wouldn't say anything but she wasn't happy. As always, that meant more arrangements had to be made and, of course in this situation, more work for her. They each often put in crazy hours to keep their careers and family afloat. Ted figured he was actually ahead of Liza in having periods to manage the kids alone. They each did significant weekend work. But on her rotations with no night call and, even the months with Mrs. Arkady, he had a lot to do.

He wasn't pleased with her demeanor. Shit, how much more domesticated could he be? No overnight hunting or fishing trips since the kids. A rare evening with Jamie and some of the others to watch a game or play some pool. Almost everyone was married now so nobody did much more than family things. Why not look forward to going to see a big city. And, fuck, it was police work anyway. He told himself he'd scout out some neighborhoods while he was there for Liza and him to come back to on a visit sometime. Just like everyone else with kids, he knew the first big family trip they would take, in a few years, would be Disneyworld. He was okay with that.

For a time, Ted thought he might have to take a bus or the train to New York since headquarters initially didn't want him driving in the city in his cruiser. He couldn't use his own car because Liza had to have a car and she couldn't very well take his cruiser. They thought about sending him in an unmarked and even checked to see if any standard state cars could be used. Ted pushed for his cruiser or, really, any vehicle. Any kind was preferable to considering riding many, many hours on a bus.

He called Janice at the 10th precinct. She greeted him like an old friend and gave him a number for the police garage building on west Twenty-sixth Street where a pleasant guy told him he could leave his cruiser in their building as long as he wanted if he didn't need to keep going in and out. And he needed something official from Ted's 'boss to his boss'. Headquarters bought it and Ted was very pleased.

"If you're taking your cruiser you either have to wear your uniform or get dressed up. Driving all over the northeast in a Vermont State Police Cruiser in your jeans runs the risk of lots of stops and lots of explaining for you." Liza's tone was not friendly, continuing to reflect her general dissatisfaction with what he was about to do.

You either liked (or were impressed) with the Vermont State Police uniform or you thought it was a bit much. All khaki, lighter shirt with darker cuffs, darker pants. Lots of piping and trim in yellow and green. Fancy pocket covers and epaulets and plenty of brass buttons. It was striking. Ted liked it. So he decided to drive down in his only suit, but also put his uniform in a plastic cleaner's bag and bring it along. He figured you just never know.

The idea of Ted going to New York City became reasonable after the murder of the diener, James Hardy. Almost everyone agreed it was likely his death was somehow related to the homicide Ted was investigating. The State Police were willing to escalate the investigation as necessary. The trip finally seemed mandatory when Ted's thinking and efforts hit pay dirt with the finding of a stone that might be part of the case.

* * *

DAY 10 THURSDAY, OCTOBER 21

After loading the cruiser early in the morning he went back inside to get something. All three of them were lined up in the living room watching him get ready. Kathy, the almost five-year-old, stood there with her arms folded across her chest and a slight frown on her face, a striking mimic of her mother. He suspected she had no idea why her mother disapproved of what was going on. Henry, almost two, was excited.

"Brumm, brumm, vroom daddy? Lights go on?"

"Right, Henry. Vroom, vroom. No flashing lights just yet."

Whether any of the four of them were thinking about the inherent danger police face when they go off to do their job was unlikely. Nothing about this assignment seemed to suggest danger in the city.

Once on the road he thought about his interaction with Doreen Miller, one of the payroll ladies, who also did disbursements. She had him sign the appropriate forms and also got some cash for his use. Doreen made a few comments about the out of town policeman going to the big city and he realized the image from TV shows of the hick cop or, usually, the sheriff in cowboy boots and hat, going to the big city (and, of course, showing up the city cops) was not likely going to be lost on lots of folks.

Ted really had virtually no exposure to urban life. He had been to the occasional Bruins game at the Garden and some Red Sox games at Fenway. But his very few overnight stays were never more than one or two days with Liza, in Boston and Montreal.

*   *   *

On his way to New York Ted made a quick stop in Whitehall, New York (a land-locked appearing location on the Champlain canal which advertised itself on a sign as the 'Birthplace of the United States Navy') and drove to the pay phone for the number in the dead man's pocket. It was in an enclosed booth at the edge of a service station on the main drag of that tiny town. Ted figured it would take about thirty or forty minutes to drive from there to Bee Pond.

He removed his camera from his trunk and took a few pictures, which generated a small gathering. He confirmed the phone worked and the number was correct. North of where he was standing, perched high on a hill, Ted could see the façade of the venerable old Scone Castle, a legend in the area, now a 'B&B' and the restaurant Stan Angle had worked at. Then Ted followed country roads and interstates south to the city for the next four hours.

He drove over the George Washington Bridge and navigated to the West Side Highway, which he took all the way down to the Twenty-third Street exit. Just as on the way down from upstate New York, most cars pulled into the slow lane and patiently or impatiently waited for him to pass when they saw his cruiser in their rear view mirrors. Twice on the Thruway New York State Troopers gave him a quick 'hand on hat brim' movement as they passed him.

The garage was on Twenty-sixth Street and Eleventh Avenue. There were two men in the small office. Both looked more like mechanics than cops. There was a note about him coming on the desk. One asked him to fill out a form and looked at his ID and the other walked to the door, waiting for Ted to finish, and then directed him where to put his cruiser. That fellow was a black man, who introduced himself as Chris Smithers as he shook hands with Ted and asked Ted to follow him in his cruiser as he led the way to a corner at the back of the building.

"Dat's a colorful vehicle, Trooper. Almos' like green cammo for all dat green forest up in Vermont, huh?" He said it in a pleasant way and Ted was glad to chat. He expected contrasts between Vermont and New York would come up frequently, in both his mind and in the reactions of New Yorkers.

"And I bet a police garage in this city is open and busy twenty-four hours a day. I hear the city never sleeps."

"Well, Trooper Vallan, I sure don' anyway. Dis place is a wonderful opt'tunity for me to rack up lots and lots of ova'time. I do so much of dat, I pract'lly got a reputation. The guys think I live here. So, you need sometin' you come on over. I'll proly be here."

Ted pulled his things from his cruiser. Smithers pointed him to a squad car that looked like it was fixed and waiting to be picked up. He directed Ted to get in and drove him the few blocks to his hotel. Ted dumped his gear, took a pee, washed his face, and brushed his teeth. He kept his suit on. Then he headed for the precinct a few blocks south and east.

He walked into the 10th precinct and asked a duty clerk to direct him to Jack Nichol's desk. The clerk pointed to an officer just down the hall who was running what looked like a metal detector machine. Ted put his brown bag with the sixteen-ounce, grade B, Vermont maple syrup he brought for Janice, on the conveyor belt. The officer, with some annoyance, told him to take it out of the bag.

There was a short line forming behind him and the officer and the folks on the line all stared at the brown syrup jug with surprising interest. The cop looked at Ted with some confusion. Ted said,

"Look, I'm…." and started to go to his back pocket to get out his wallet and badge. That movement put the officer on guard, reflexively placing his hand on his sheathed revolver. Ted stopped his motion and explained who he was and suggested he remove his wallet to show his ID's.

That done, plus an explanation the syrup was for Janice Delario, he was motioned, by the skeptical appearing cop, to empty his pockets and go through the walk-thru metal detector. Ted got anxious when he dropped his small knife into the basket. The cop looked at it for a few seconds and then passed it on, apparently comfortable enough with Ted's credentials not to make any fuss about a small knife. Ted had no doubt the small pen-knife found in his John Doe's pocket would have been confiscated at this place.

He was directed to go down a short corridor and through the wide double doors at the end. As he had imagined, the duty room was enormous. There was a woman at the closest desk. She was in a uniform but he couldn't be sure if she was a clerk or a cop. He took a chance and walked to her desk and stood there for a few moments. She looked up and asked what he needed. The woman turned around in her chair, looked across the expanse of the large room, turned back. She told him Detective Nichols wasn't at his desk, which meant he wasn't there right now. Then Ted asked for Janice Delario. She turned to her other side and pointed to the first cubicle, along a wall, with frosted glass and a window. He thanked her but she was already back to her prior business.

Ted walked to the cubicle and peeked his head into the open door. Janice looked up and he identified himself. Her face brightened and she told him to come in and have a seat. Before he sat he placed the sixteen-ounce jug of grade B Vermont maple syrup on her desk. She lifted it from the bag and flashed a big smile at Ted. Ted, as all Vermonters did with people who didn't know anything about maple syrup, began to explain to her that, although there is a grade A, the grade B is thicker, with more flavor, and generally the preferred syrup to have. Janice clearly didn't care about what he was saying but she seemed genuinely appreciative. From what he knew and surmised about her, now seeing the choice location of her cubicle, he was glad he brought the syrup. Being on the good side of Janice was probably a good thing.

Janice knew Nichols was out and pulled a tagged key from her top drawer for the Sixteenth Street apartment he was headed to. Ted handed her his John Doe's prints. She asked him how parking his cruiser worked out and gave him her card and Jack Nichol's card. Ted asked about the metal detector and she quickly pulled out a form and filled it in with some input from him. She took his badge and ID card and went to make a photocopy and returned them.

"No mor da'tecta Ted." She stood up so he did also. She handed him a temporary precinct card and offered her hand. "Good huntin' Ted. Hope youse find what ya came for."

* * *

It was getting to late afternoon when Ted left the precinct to find the building on his John Doe's business card. The day had turned cloudy and people carried umbrellas or wore hats but it didn't look like rain. He walked, happy to survey the activity of the huge city and its inhabitants. He assumed he only had to go about seven blocks but at sixteenth street the long crosstown blocks turned it into a longer walk. The neighborhood and the building appeared more commercial than residential. The Sixteenth Street address was a skinny building compressed between more obviously business use structures, maybe clothing industry related, he thought.

He learned what a 'sooper' was when the fellow who answered his buzz for 'superintendent' came out and directed him to the third floor, where he found the number he was looking for. The yellow tape was neatly placed and easily moved aside. He still wasn't sure if it was an apartment building or commercial building.

Inside, he was immediately struck by how small the room was; no more than about ten by ten feet. The place was notably stylishly decorated. Two plush arm chairs and a small, but fancy looking, old desk with a straight backed chair. The wall covering was the same on all four walls. It was some expensive looking woven material that reminded Ted of light green seaweed. The walls were otherwise bare. There was carpeting and, finally, a bookcase in the corner which took up about three feet of the far wall. It held some catalogs, including a stack of the "ABC", and a few brass animals. That was it. He guessed the place was meant to be a showroom.

He put blue latex gloves on and, probably just like Jack Nichols, sat in one of the armchairs and looked around the room. Someone's office. Nothing defining or incriminating. Same few things Nichols had found and that was all. It was not a good moment. His first big hope was looking like a strike-out. Then he heard a phone begin ringing.

Instinctively he went to the sound. It was near the bookcase. Standing there he realized he had missed the well-blended in outline of a slim, wall paper covered door. There was a small recessed handle only an inch from the end of the bookcase making it less likely to be easily seen. There was no lock and he pulled the door open. The ringing became much louder.

He was in a slightly larger room with a window that appeared to be a living quarters. An old murphy bed was down, strewn with clothes, surrounded by a tiny kitchenette on one side and a bathroom on the other. A small TV and desk, with the ringing phone, were against the wall where the door was.

The phone had an answering machine that clicked on a few seconds after he walked in. He heard no message but then there was a beep.

A woman's voice, despondent. "Sammy, Sammy, Sammy. Oh my god. What did you do? How could you this happen to you?" A long pause. Resignation in her voice: "I guess there really is no reason to ever call anymore. I…"

Ted quickly picked up the phone. "Hello! This is Trooper Ted Vallan of the Vermont State Police. I believe you recently contacted the Medical Examiner in Vermont about......"

She hung up. "Shit."

He stood for a minute with his hand on the phone. What could he have done to keep her on the line? He sat in the fold-up chair at the desk and looked at the phone. He inspected the answering machine. It was basic; still blinking, suggesting more messages were on the tape. Ted took his pad out and pressed the messages button. It re-wound for only a short time suggesting few messages and playback would be the earliest first. He could see nothing with time, date, or phone number of the callers.

The first message was from a man with a voice like stone. All it said was: "I need ta' hear from ya soon."

The next one was a female who sounded like the woman who had just called. "Hon, awfully long time not to hear from you. Hope your trip went okay. Call me."

Then that woman again, this time sounding frantic. "Sammy! This is not good. There's someone following me and I don't know where you are or what's going on. Please! I need to talk to you, now! I'm scared. I'm afraid to go back to my place. I packed some things and I'm staying at my sister Sara's place. Her number is 555-0103. Sammy, please call me!"

The fourth was the man with the voice like ice, again. "Dis time you done. Ya got one mo' day to get me what I sent ya' for. I tink you a dead man, fucka'."

That was it. Obviously some kind of deal had gone wrong. Not a surprise since he knew his dead man was murdered. Sounded like the man with ice in his voice caught up to this 'Sammy'. He looked at his notes from the messages and he looked around the messy room he was in. He found no papers or anything else he could tie to this man being in Vermont. How much of the whole story did he have now? Should he try to call the phone number from that woman's message?

The phone rang again. After a few rings he decided to answer it rather than wait for a message.

"Hello", in a soft, neutral voice.

"Is this Trooper Vallan, who just answered the phone before?"

Pretty good how she remembered his name after he had barely introduced himself before she hung up. She told Ted her name was Kendra Akers and she had been making the inquiries about her friend, Sammy, who was missing and, she presumed, now was dead. He asked if he could meet her to find out what she knew about him and why he was in Vermont.

She agreed, but advised him she was worried people were after her so they both had to be careful. She declined Ted's suggestion he and the NYPD meet with her now and secure her safety. She gave him an address and said he could come, alone, late afternoon, between five and six, on Friday. Ted closed up the apartment and replaced the crime tape. He doubted he would ever need to go back to this place again.

*   *   *

DAY 11 FRIDAY, OCTOBER 22

It was noisy most of the night. The heavy drapes and lighter curtains kept the room dark enough. Ted knew he would never sleep well on this trip. He got out of bed earlier than he needed to but he was up so figured he'd shower, get dressed, and get something to eat. Then he would find his way to the museum to ask about the rock with the probable rune figure on it. He hoped to spend only a short time checking out runes then meet up with Jack Nichols by around noon.

After that, later in the day, he was supposed to meet the woman on the phone who called herself Kendra. The story with that lady was sketchy but she seemed to be a clear link to his dead man so he felt he had to follow-up with her. Her story and emotional reaction worried him. He wasn't sure if she really knew anything or if, in reality, the things she was hinting at might be very important. Ted decided to see how the day went today before determining if he could return home some time Saturday after interviewing the renters who were staying east of the Graham's. They lived in the Riverdale section of the Bronx.

When he stepped from the lobby outside into the hotel entrance he was amazed at the activity around him. It was only a little after seven but the street was filled with cars and the sidewalks were crowded with people rushing both ways, deftly dodging one another as they hurried on.

"Taxi sir?" A doorman queried. Ted reacted acutely, quickly reminding himself to try to relax and limit the chances he looked out of place, like the hick he really was. He remembered all the people who told him 'don't keep looking up at the tall buildings' or he'd stick out a mile.

"No. No thanks, anyway", the first 'no' more emphatic than it needed to be. He walked down the avenue looking for a place to get something to eat.

Back in his room he wanted to call home but realized it was already too late to do that. He got his maps and put them in his suit coat pocket careful to make sure the maps, which he worried would brand him as a tourist, didn't show. He reflexively touched the side of his waist to check for his revolver which, of course, he didn't have, then put his hand to his pants pocket where his old whittling knife and that rock were.

In the hotel lobby Ted made his first mistake of the day. He thought about going to the desk clerk, showing him the address he wanted to go to, and get advice about getting there. But he had looked on his map and it didn't appear very complicated, although it was on the other side of town and rush hour was amazingly busy and everything was congested. So he walked outside and, again, waved the doorman off and started to walk down the street.

At the intersection he stood for a while, watching a few people hail taxis. It looked straight forward enough. He had plenty of cash and he saw no reason not to try one. He stepped, tentatively, out into the street. The number of cars rushing close by un-nerved him a little. He reached out his arm and, to his amazement, a bright yellow taxi practically shot from one side of the street over to his and slammed its brakes on in front of Ted.

The cab was off before Ted even gave him his destination. The driver reeked of cigar, had more than a few day's stubble, and was wearing a leather version of the typical cabbie's hat from the movies. Talk radio was blaring sports. "Where to this great mornin', pal?" he said without turning around.

"I'm going to the Scandinavian Museum on Park Street. Do you know it?"

The cabbie glanced back at Ted. "Pal, you can't be a cabby unless you know where ever'thin' is in this burg. I know the really minute stuff, and your destination ain't an everyday place. Park Street's in Brooklyn and the East Coast Scandinavian museum is just off there. Am I right? Bit of a trip, right? But mostly against traffic right now."

Ted really didn't know what the guy was talking about, so he said "Right" and sat back to take in the activity around him. He was glad the cabby didn't engage him in conversation. He had no interest in sharing anything with this guy beyond the basic pleasantries. He had no intention of telling him his job, where he was from, or ask questions about the city that might give away his ignorance.

Ted, like most people riding in a cab, was watching the meter in the front, just to the right of the driver. He was trying to figure out what made the dollars and cents move. Whatever did it, the values were going up faster than he liked. He realized he had no idea how long it would take to get to the museum and what it was going to cost. Ted admitted to himself part of the reason he was in the cab was because he had been reluctant to try to figure out how to do the subways. Liza told him to tip ten percent for a taxi and about twenty percent for a meal. He kept re-calculating as they drove.

They went over a bridge and then were back on city streets. In a few more minutes the cab turned onto a street lined with small trees and pulled up to an old, stand alone, brick building with a sign lettered in gold leaf on a black base: 'Scandinavian East Coast Museum'.

"That's Park Street up at the light ahead, but here's the entrance I know." The cabbie manipulated his meter and came up with a final charge of $18.80. Ted peeked at the bills he was holding in his hand and decided to hand over $21.00. The cab driver didn't react one way or the other and Ted took his suit coat and got out. He decided the driver was unhappy with him but that's the way it goes.

The museum was small and no one was walking around. It only opened about ten minutes before he arrived. Ted walked to the information desk off to the side of the large hallway he had entered. "Hi, I'm Ted Vallan and I'm supposed to meet Thayer Landsdorf here around nine-fifteen."

The fellow at the desk looked up at him with an expression of confusion or miss-understanding on his face. "I'm sorry sir, who did you say you have an appointment with?"

"Thayer Landsdorf. I believe he does his research here."

Again, he apologized, "I'm sorry, we have a small staff here and there is no one affiliated with the museum with that name."

Now Ted was also confused, and he looked dismayed.

"What kind of research are you talking about mister? Maybe I can find someone to help you."

Not knowing who he was really talking to Ted kept his words very general. "I was planning to discuss some things about 'Old Norse' artifacts with Professor Landsdorf" he answered.

"Let me call John Eriksen. I know he's involved in scholarly activities. Let me see what he knows. The man at the desk called someone and briefly explained Ted's problem. He hung up and smiled at Ted, "Mr. Eriksen will come right down and speak with you."

John Eriksen was a fit appearing middle-aged man with a warm smile, ruddy complexion, and small goatee that came to a point about an inch below his chin. "Can I help you, Mr. Vallan? I know Thayer Landsdorf. He and I curate Scandinavian artifacts and antiquities. Unfortunately, I think you are in the wrong place. He's at 'Scandinavia House', on Park Avenue in Manhattan."

Ted's face drained and he was visibly upset. In an instant he realized he was far from where he intended to be and had just blown more money than he should have on a taxi ride to the wrong place.

"I can direct you to Thayer's office but why don't you come upstairs with me so I can call him and let him know you won't be there for a while. It will take some time to get there no matter how you decide to go." Ted was a little dizzy contemplating an even more expensive taxi ride now. He was barely responding during the brief pleasantries they exchanged and Ted only told him he was an 'investigator' from Vermont. Eriksen had no special reaction to that introduction.

"Can I ask what you plan to talk about with Thayer? Maybe I'll be able to help a little. Of course, Thayer is an internationally known expert in our history. He studies the ancient past. I study more modern Scandinavian history." Eriksen leaned to the side of his desk to look at his Rolodex.

Ted liked the guy. What was not to like. He seemed courteous and was being helpful. He didn't really know what he had or where this stone business might lead so he figured the more input, probably, the better.

Ted pulled out his small flat rock and showed it to John Eriksen. Initially, he said nothing about it and just placed it on Eriksen's desk. Eriksen picked it up, held it up in the air, spent some time looking at the engraved side and just a quick moment looking at the back, then he set it back down on his desk. "Well I don't know what you already know about this stone, but the engraving, albeit quite faded, is what we call a *rune*.

Eriksen continued, "The configuration suggests it is some kind of charm." That designation immediately caused Ted to take a deeper breath and reminded him of Dr. Gruber. Ted wondered if an ancient charm is what Mrs. Gruber meant when she mentioned the Doctor's idea that ancient artifacts were magical to him.

"Professor Eriksen, how old do you think this stone is? I mean can this be dated in any way?"

"Well, Mr. Vallan, It's a stone. So, by definition, it's pretty old. Can't really carbon 14 date that kind of object. I wouldn't be able to say if it was shaped and engraved one thousand years ago or a few years ago. It does look old though, doesn't it? I do have a thought but you'll do better to speak with Dr. Landsdorf. Thayer can probably help with that kind of question. Where'd you get this Mr. Vallan?"

"Oh, it was found by a boy in a lake." That was all he was going to say. He saw no need to tell Mr. Eriksen the UVM ancient languages folks had told him pretty much the same thing. Although they had talked about coins, decorations, and good luck the word 'charm' never had come up. "You've been very helpful professor Eriksen but I think you're right, I guess I still should try to get to meet with Professor Landsdorf to hear what he thinks about this."

"Surely. Let's call him right now." He pulled the Rolodex over and flipped to a page and started dialing. He was connected to Landsdorf shortly. "Thayer? It's John Eriksen. I...yes, I'm fine. Hope you and Nan are both doing well. Good. Listen, Thayer, I'm sitting in my office across from Ted Vallan, who was supposed to be meeting with you this morning... Yes, yes. He came to the wrong museum...Right, right. Surely not the first time, eh. Well he wants to show you a very interesting stone that I take to be some kind of rune charm. Should I put him on or do you want to have someone in your office look at your schedule and talk with him to set up a time? Oh. Okay, No, no, it's fine. Mr. Vallan and I can chat a few minutes while you see what you'd like to do. No problem Thayer, it's my pleasure."

Eriksen cupped his hand over the speaker on the phone and told Ted Landsdorf's staff was going to see what they could do. He and Ted then reviewed the story of Eriksen's one trip to Vermont to ski years ago. Then he nodded and said "Okay" and handed the phone across his desk to Ted.

"Hello Mista' Vallan, dis is Imogene. The professor is happy ta fit ya in dis morning. I think the best thing ta do is send a car over ta get you in Brooklyn ta make it easy fa you ta get here."

"That would be great ma'am." Ted's mood lifted perceptibly.

"I'll get a car over dere within 'bout an hour, okay? Just try ta be outside the main 'antrance by den. The driver will probably be Jimmy, in a dark green sedan. Okay?"

Ted thanked her and thanked John Eriksen profusely for all his assistance. Eriksen told him where the reading room was off the main lobby if he wanted to sit until he was picked up. Ted went and sat there for a few minutes but decided to go outside and walk around for a while to see the city and think about his already eventful morning. He wasn't overjoyed with how he had managed things so far.

He turned right after leaving and walked up to the intersection the cabbie had said was Park Street. Of course it wasn't Park Street. The driver was all fucked up and just took him to the only Scandinavian Museum he knew. Ted pulled out his paper with the address on it and saw it said 'Park Avenue'. 'Shit'. Then he wondered if the correct address would've made any difference.

It was a beautiful day. Still pretty warm here even getting close to late October. He wandered around the block and noted there was only the one entrance. There was a bench in front of the museum so Ted stood in front of the seat, put his hand in his pants pocket to make sure the rock was there in its plastic bag, and sat down.

About ten minutes later a dark green sedan drove up. It was washed but had some dings and was not a new vehicle. Later, when they were on the road, he realized he might have looked to see if it had livery plates. There were two men in the front. A slight, thin, middle-aged black man quickly got out of the driver's side and came around the back of the still running car. He smiled and came up to Ted and offered his hand. "Mista Vallan? That you? I'm Jimmy Smith. Ya know, like the jazz musician." He carried a black limo driver's hat in his other hand.

"Yes, That's me" Ted didn't know who the musician was but he did note this was another Smith.

Jimmy Smith looked around. "Ya got no suitcase, huh?" He opened the back door for Ted to get in, then slammed it and ran around back to the driver's door and got in and put his hat back on. "Okay then, let's get back to the city. Mista Vallan, this here's my assoc'it, Glenny Miller, He gonna be with us for the ride." Ted looked at what he could see of Glenny Miller. Somehow he reminded him of his John Doe; fat, mostly bald, older middle age. The fellow in front barely turned and seemed to grunt something, apparently to signify acknowledgement. Whatever conversation they were going to have it looked like it would be Ted and Jimmy.

Jimmy had a lot to say, jumping from non-descript topic to topic. At one red light he turned back towards Ted, like the cabbie had done and said, "So you a PI, huh?" Ted assumed he meant a private investigator and saw no reason to set him straight or find out why he asked that. He also noticed Jimmy's hat had some embroidery on the front, maybe something indicating nautical symbols. That seemed a little strange.

"So Jimmy, tell me where we're at now."

"Oh we still got a ways to go suh. We got ta evade the lunch time traffic in the midtown. We skirtin' that and goin' up the east side for while. Then we will cut back in ta the middle of the city again and work our way ta the museum." There was a lot of traffic. It wasn't noon yet but getting close. Ted had no idea where they were and he was too uncomfortable about looking like a rube to get his map out to try to follow along with Jimmy's route.

"Which river is this Jimmy?" Since it was on his right he assumed, from his map reading last night, it was the East River. "The East River?"

"Dat's very correct, Mista Vallan. We zooming along the East Rive right now."

The city was filled with one imposing structure after another. Virtually every building was taller than any he had ever seen. He only recalled a few streets in Boston with large buildings. This went on forever. He saw a building he thought looked familiar. He wondered if it was the United Nations. Even if he knew he was right, the fact they were heading north and the UN was blocks north of where he was supposed to be going was something Ted would not have known.

They were travelling faster than the taxi and Ted wasn't going to have to pay anything so he felt relaxed and was anticipating his meeting with Professor Landsdorf might be very helpful. He was impressed and pleased the Professor seemed interested in their meeting and actually helped facilitate it.

A huge complex of roads developed in front of them. Jimmy seemed to know where he wanted to go and navigated, without apparent concern, through an octopus of entrances and exits with roads travelling above and below them. He took one big arm of a cloverleaf and they were off the highway. Shortly, Ted noticed a wide straight boulevard with mid-rise buildings, probably apartments by their appearance.

This neighborhood resembled nothing like the city where his hotel or the museum in Brooklyn were. As they drove up the avenue everything looked remarkably worn and rundown. Ted sat up straighter and felt something was wrong. Was he in trouble? Could his life really be in danger because someone thought he had some kind of stone? What?

"Jimmy, where are you going? This doesn't look like Manhattan." His voice was firm but not angry.

"Mista Vallan, we almost there. You please jus sit back and relax. We stoppin' soon." His tone was flat. Glenny Miller shifted in his seat. Jimmy stopped at a light and tapped his fingers on the steering wheel. This wasn't right. Ted began to consider his options. He was equally angry and fearful. He had to push away his anger and yet was wondering how he could keep winding up in bad situations when, first with the taxi and now, there really were no obvious warnings he could have acted on sooner.

His fear was about what the hell he was going to do. Free ride, shit! Too much time had passed on the road. He obviously wasn't in any regular part of the city anymore. He was well aware this city was huge and had troubled neighborhoods that probably were barely policed, if at all.

It was broad daylight and there were some people and cars around, but not too many. Wherever Jimmy and this Miller were taking him was unlikely to be anywhere he would want to go. Ted was glad he was sitting with his suit coat folded over his lap. He was able to slip his hand into his pocket and slide his knife out. Under his coat he was able to open it and make sure it was locked open.

'Wait a minute', he thought, 'What the hell am I going to do with this?' Who knew how many people were waiting for them? Who knew how violent this thing was about to get? He had no idea what these stones might mean that more and more people were getting threatened and maybe killed over them. Ted had fleeting thoughts about his family during these anxious moments. He had been so hot to do something exciting and on his own. And here he was in some bombed out part of New York City with two obvious hoods, whose violence and abilities he could only guess at.

He kept looking at those guys in the front seat. They had tensed up also but, so far, Jimmy hadn't changed the way he was driving. His speed as he maneuvered a few turns wasn't too fast. He sat, patiently, at the occasional red light. Neither of them appeared to be looking back at him. He noted Jimmy hadn't used his mirror much to look at him early on or now. Ted glanced at the door. He didn't see any obvious sign the door was locked or had any special 'child proof' system. He wondered if it was possible these guys never checked to be sure he was locked in. Maybe they had no way to do that?

It was time to try to relax Jimmy and *Glenny*. "Hey guys, you know I've got a lunch date and this trip is going to cut into my time with a lady I really want to be with. You know what I mean?" Was this Ted Vallan talking?

Jimmy took the bait and started talking and *Glenny* looked over at Jimmy, seemingly interested in what bullshit Jimmy was about to offer. "Oh, Mista Vallan, now you…'

Jimmy slowed down nicely for a yellow light, and they all watched it go to red. For Ted that meant go. He pulled the handle and the door flew open. He held his coat, threw his legs out the door, and was out of the car in seconds. He couldn't see much of Jimmy or Miller but they seemed frozen. It was broad daylight in the middle of a road in a bombed out neighborhood in New York City. Ted felt like there wasn't anything moving or anyone else around. He was stunned. And he was furious.

He was playing the role of everyone's hick to a tee. And here he was about to face some jerks who were maybe getting set to kill him in a few minutes. Maybe right now. The wide open streets of a New York slum were unlikely to offer any protection. All he had to defend himself, probably from two revolvers, was his old knife. He moved slightly toward the rear of the car, bent over and plunged his knife into the right rear tire. He did it rapidly; three times. Miller was halfway out of the car when he poked the tire the third time. Miller was unable, with his girth and age, to move fast. Ted thought he could probably poke him also with the knife before he could react but trying to kill these guys, knowing nothing about them, didn't make sense. If they were going to try to hurt or kill him then his goal was to limit their ability and chance to do it.

As Miller lumbered out of the car Ted saw that Jimmy remained frozen in the front. So he went to the left rear, crouched down, and with a strong effort plunged his blade quickly, three times, into that tire. The rear end of the dark green sedan slowly slid down, like a *low rider* in reverse. He wasn't exactly sure what that accomplished but he had used his knife and for the first time that day he felt he had done something to interfere with this madness. Jimmy started to crack his door, and he could see Miller, trying to crouch down, slowly moving to the back of the car. It looked like he might have a hand at his front beltline.

Ted took another quick look around and, much to his surprise, some people were now standing at the corners of the intersection. Just watching. He considered running to the people on one of the corners to be part of a crowd. Or waiting a few seconds more for Jimmy to begin to climb out of the car and open the door more. He could quickly get to the door and smash it in on him. Then the question was whether he would have enough time to see if he was carrying and get his gun before Miller was able to use one on him.

Miller was hesitating, although his face was beat red with anger. Jimmy's door didn't move. The sense of a stand-off was fleeting and they all knew it. They weren't going to stand there around the car in daylight in the middle of a street for long. Ted wondered if he ran towards the street corner whether Miller would chase him; or fire. Or what Miller would do if Ted started around the car after him. He realized these guys, thinking he was a PI, had reason to worry he might be carrying also. The original plan for him probably included a setting completely under their control. It wasn't that way anymore.

Suddenly, Miller stood up and bolted towards the crowd on the corner. Jimmy's door flew open and Jimmy was out of it much faster than Ted thought he was capable of. Their eyes locked for a split second and then Ted heard the loud 'wup, wup' of the squad car as Jimmy also bolted for the crowd.

The two cops sat in their vehicle, one obviously running the green sedan's plates (not a livery; stolen) and looking at Ted. The other watched as Jimmy and Glenny Miller melted into the gathering crowd and disappeared. Ted was standing close to the open driver's door and when he glanced in saw a Beretta M951 sitting on Jimmy's seat. He so wanted to figure a way to bend down and appropriate that pistol for his own use… only while he was in New York. This place was too dangerous to be a cop without some proper armor. The chances of accomplishing that were small. What he did do was close up his knife and slip it into his pocket next to the plastic bag with the stone.

Both cops got out at the same time, each with a hand at their firearms. They were clearly in no particular hurry. Ted had a sense if he had run and disappeared into the crowd also that would have been a great resolution to this business for these cops. One crouched around the back of the sedan looking at the flat tires and the other came over to Ted.

"Those flats from bullets?" the one by Ted asked.

"No. A knife."

"Really. Please put your coat on the roof and then put both your hands on the roof. The other officer is watching you closely so I strongly advise you not to move at all." First his coat was examined and his big map and small subway maps were placed on the roof. Then Ted was patted down. "What's in your right pocket, son?"

"The knife I used to puncture the tires and an evidence bag with a stone that is part of a homicide investigation." From Ted's position he couldn't see how either one reacted to his statement, but he was hopeful this situation would improve now. He could see the groups of bystanders had grown and he hoped that wouldn't play any role in how these officers handled this. The officer told him to empty his pockets and put the contents on the roof.

They both pushed him aside a little and looked at what was there. None of it seemed to impress them much. One picked up the bag with the stone and tossed it a few inches in the air.

"One tiny bit of hash" the one doing the frisking said to the other. "Wonder how much time he'll do for this spit?"

"Please be careful with that. That's police property in a very active case." Ted was still spread-eagle against the sedan. One cop pushed up a knee, planning to cause some pain in Ted's back. But Ted was taller than the cop and the knee landed square in Ted's fleshy rear end. Both he and the cop lurched a bit and the cop's tone got angrier. Ted could only wonder what his face looked like (or what any of the bystanders thought was going on).

"Son, what in this fuckin' world do ya think brings white boys in suits to this god- forsaken neighborhood? I'm thinkin' of splittin' this tiny brick in half right here and we can all watch er turn into sand."

"Brick? Tiny brick? It's a stone, barely larger than a quarter, with engraving on it. Don't you do anything with that stone. I'm a cop too."

They stopped, glanced up frowning, unhappy with him but also a little unsure of themselves. "Who are you son? Are you NYPD?"
"No. My name is Ted Vallan and I'm an investigative State Trooper from Vermont. I believe I was about to be harmed by the two men who just ran away and I was able to get out of their vehicle to save myself."

The officers relaxed a bit but kept staring at him. He had a military bearing and was clearly more fit than they were. But here he was, a young white guy in a suit in the middle of what was a war zone for them, making a fuss about a tiny rock in a bag. And did he scare off bad guys by giving their car flat tires with a pen knife?

"What are you, some *Dudley Do-Right* kind of character? Where'd you say you from, Vermont? Isn't that one big forest?"

Once again Ted decided he was being too passive. He hoped neither of these guys were named Smith. "Listen officers, there's a Beretta M951 on the front seat of this car and I'm working with Detective Jack Nichols at the 10th precinct, Manhattan South. Can I bring my hands down? My badge and ID are in my wallet." Enough of this he thought. This was going nowhere. If these guys could either get him to Professor Landsdorf or to the 10th, which they were much more likely to do, he could try to get more active involvement from the NYPD in this growing investigation. He was glad he didn't give in to the temptation to pocket the Beretta. That would have greatly complicated all this.

That seemed to do it. They went back to their patrol car and called for a crime team to work over the car and asked for Jack Nichols to be contacted at the 10th. For once, something went smoothly and Jack Nichols got word to them he'd meet Ted at the Scandinavia House and find out more about this case.

An unmarked showed up with a uniformed officer, probably a sergeant, who listened to Ted's story but only cared about his time with Smith and Miller. The Officer asked him to consider taking some time to go through their picture books but everyone knew that was bullshit. Prints were much more likely to get a hit if they could lift some. The sergeant said he would drive him to Scandinavia House so he and the officers barely nodded terse good-byes and Ted returned to Manhattan…with his knife for protection.

*   *   *

Liza was not having a good day. She had a restless night and was up for the day very early in the morning. She dressed and read for a while until it was time to get Kathy and Henry up. The kids seemed to sense her temperament and they were a bit difficult to get going and off to daycare. Liza definitely had more to do than usual. But she sensed her mood was reflective of more than that. They all lived with the knowledge every day that danger was a part of Ted's job. The thought of life and managing her responsibilities without Ted was terrifying.

Liza came to realize she was feeling out of sorts because she was concerned about herself, but mostly she was worried about Ted. She saw him as a fish out of water in New York City. She recognized it was unlikely he would be involved in anything beyond routine investigative work while there but who knew what might happen or how he would handle it in a place so foreign to him?

At the hospital work was always busy and she hoped it would provide a helpful distraction. When the opportunity for a quick run came up around noon she decided, despite her tiredness, it might be helpful for her spirits. Dressed in cool weather running gear Liza had to weave through semi-urban streets until she reached the bike path and head north. She only had about forty minutes before she'd have to be back so she could take a quick shower, eat something, and return to work.

Liza felt on edge when she started out, but, gradually, she sensed herself calming and her body becoming less tense. The day was overcast but dry and traffic was nothing unusual. As she got close to the lake path she noticed a very dark blue sedan stopped at the end of the road she had run along. The car had seemed to regularly leapfrog ahead of her the last few blocks then sit and do it again after she passed it. The road ended at the lake with parking areas to the left and right but the car stayed in the road, brake lights on, like it wasn't sure what it wanted to do. Shortly after getting on the bike path Liza promptly got lost in her thoughts and forgot about it.

On her return, two blocks before leaving the bike path to run back through the city to the hospital, Liza remembered the car she noticed before. She decided to turn up hill, east, one street early and then went south again so she would return to her usual running street one short block east of where she had last seen the blue sedan. As she reached the intersection that put her about thirty yards east of where that car was last sitting she saw it remained idled there, basically still parked in the street; brake lights on.

The blue sedan had New York license plates. For some reason that observation seemed to re-kindle Liza's anxieties about Ted, what she had been through with the pathology lab incident, and her general worries. New York plates were not uncommon in Burlington. In fact, for one thing, a number of people using and working at the hospital came, daily, from across the lake, from Plattsburgh and other locales. Liza could quickly come up with ten reasons why a car with New York plates could be sitting at the waterfront. But the idea she was being followed was, unfortunately, one of them and was the one she thought about as she ran back up the hill to the hospital.

From her English lessons a phrase Mrs. Arkady used regularly with the kids, 'fleet of feet, fleet of feet' reverberated in Liza's head as she pushed a little harder. In Mrs. Arkady's usage it meant 'keep moving along'. Back on the wards she knew she had to leave the hospital a little early to get the kids and was pleased at how efficiently she got through her work in the afternoon. Liza was also anxious to get home to hear from Ted, who she assumed would be calling around dinner time.

* * *

Detective Jack Nichols was standing on the sidewalk when the squad car with Ted arrived at Scandinavia House. They walked down the block to a lunch place. Nichols struck Ted as easy going and low key. Nichols probably saw Ted as the opposite after what Ted had just been through. Detective Nichols was surprised and then embarrassed when he found out he had missed the hidden door at John Doe's apartment. Nichols showed Ted the rap sheet with, finally, a name for his John Doe. After all this time it felt a little anti-climactic. Putting a name and some background to the body didn't do much to explain his presence floating in lake Bee.

Prints indicated he was Samuel Paskovich, with a slew of aliases, probably around fifty-five, and had lived beyond the law since his late teens. It was all non-violent activity and, also consistently, all low level crime. Nothing to suggest a smart guy. More recently he had arrests related to moving stolen goods, but nothing (despite his card) suggesting any real high-class stuff. Ted and Nichols assumed this guy was in Vermont doing some kind of deal. Ted was thinking about the $1000 bills. They also agreed aliases like 'Harry James' made it a good bet the dead man was linked, in some way, to the 'Glenn Miller' Ted had just been involved with. He also told Nichols 'Sammy' was the name the lady he was meeting later today used when calling the answering machine.

Ted explained to Detective Nichols why he was meeting with the Professor at Scandinavia House and told him he wasn't sure what to expect from him. The stone he had come upon was like a bad penny that kept showing up in the case and he was hoping the professor would, once and for all, tell him he could forget about it. Shouldn't take long.

* * *

Professor Landsdorf was cordial when the detectives were shown in, but he was, admittedly, distracted. In an upset and worried tone he told them one of the secretaries, actually the one who recently talked with Ted, had left for an early lunch and hadn't returned.

Ted was afraid this type of occurrence was becoming the norm for this case. He told himself to learn to accept that nothing was unusual from here on out. He knew the Professor was concerned and worried about the secretary, but Ted wanted to learn more about his stone. Nichols briefly questioned if 'Imogene' and her disappearance could have anything to do with Ted's fateful ride. But once Ted pulled the plastic bag from his pocket and emptied the stone onto Landsdorf's desk the discussion changed instantly.

The Professor startled and sat bolt upright in his chair. He was a small man with a full head of gray hair. His eyes remained riveted on the stone.

"Professor, do you have any ideas about this stone?"

"Of course I do, Officers." His reaction and words surprised Ted. Professor Landsdorf barely paused. "I'm sure it's one of the sixteen pieces of the *'Bracelet of Learning'* from the Norse village at L'Anse aux Meadows. I wondered if we would ever see it again."

It wasn't a reach to assume this stone meant a great deal to the Professor and there was an important story related to it. He wasn't completely surprised. Landsdorf held the stone in his hand and turned it around a few times. He looked like he was thinking about how to begin to explain to the police the significance of the stone he was holding.

"Officers, there are many parts to the history of this stone. I'll try to be brief, but I think you need to know a few things about why it's so exciting to me to be holding this stone now. As you know, the engraving on the stone shows it to be a rune. But what a rune!

"For centuries, especially the last two, there have been great efforts to find out if 'Norse men', commonly thought of as Vikings by the public, sailed and settled in North America. We know Leif Erikson visited Greenland and definitely spent extended periods of time there. There is greater mystery about any possible visits or settlements further west, even as close to us as Massachusetts. We're talking about centuries before Columbus *discovered* the Americas, somewhere around the years 1000 to 1100. A lot of people have made a lot of claims about uncovering signs of Norse villages for the last two hundred years.

"In 1960 inhabitants of a tiny village at the very northern tip of the peninsula of Newfoundland, in the Canadian Maritimes, encouraged two archeologists from Norway to investigate a series of mounds on their coast. The location is called L'Anse aux Meadows. Excavations unearthed indisputable evidence of Norse activity. It has been a most important and amazing find. As a matter of fact, we are working very hard with the Canadian government to have the area declared a UNESCO World Heritage site so it can be protected from exploitation forever.

"A treasure trove of artifacts has been found at the site. Throughout the sixties many interesting finds were reported. In 1963 a nearby farmer with a small mound on his property said he found a few things when he dug into the area. Quite naturally, the great preponderance of the findings in L'Anse aux Meadows are objects like iron rivets and pins for ships, but also, some bronze, stone, and bone implements for everyday existence have been found.

"The farmer's mound contained a most amazing sixteen small stones, one of which we are looking at, each with an engraving to match one of the sixteen letters from the *Younger Futhark* alphabet, which is considered the most likely runic alphabet in use by the Norse at that time. With the holes in each stone it is assumed the stones were at one time held together with something like rawhide, kind of like a bracelet, thus the title the collection has been given.

"It is assumed the stones could have been used for educational purposes since there are definite signs at the excavations that women and children were at the site. It's also possible there was an attempt to teach indigenous people their alphabet. But that is unlikely to have succeeded since there are no findings for this in artifacts from the few tribes known to have been in that area.

"Officers, runes are very interesting. Except for short inscriptions, like memorializing or identifying a location or event, they were not routinely used for writing in the way we use our alphabet. Each rune was also considered a symbol and had its own meaning or meanings. It's also likely some considered them charms or that the stones had magical importance."

Ted, who had several reasons to be very interested in this stone, was fascinated by the story the Professor was presenting. But Detective Nichols was shifting in his chair, looking around the room, and was much less engaged. The Professor continued.

"In the later sixties the bracelet, or stones, showed up on display in the antiquities section of our Metropolitan Museum of New York. Right here in Manhattan. How that came about also generated some stories and, in any event, caused quite a bit of ill will between Canadian authorities and preservationists and the museum administrators.

"After being displayed at the L'Anse aux Meadows site, which has become a Canadian National Park, the original owner, the man who found the artifacts, threatened legal action if the bracelet wasn't returned to him. As soon as it was reclaimed it became clear he had made a deal with the museum to sell it to them. This caused lots of bad feelings in Canada and with archeologists too. The Met went ahead and displayed it anyway until just a few years ago."

"Besides scientists who study all this are artifacts like these stones considered to be worth any significant amounts of money?" Ted asked.

"That's, in some ways, a difficult question, but the short answer is yes. And, especially in the last ten or twenty years, all antiquities seem to have skyrocketed in monetary value as public and private collections seem to be willing to pay increasingly large prices for artifacts."

"What about these stones, in particular?"

"Well I don't know, but when they showed up on display the Met treated them like they were worth quite a lot. Special display case; guards always around and things like that."

Ted had questions. "You're implying the stones were taken off public display. Why was that? Were they stolen? If they are so valuable there must be a path to trace how one showed up on a lakeshore in Vermont?"

The Professor noted Ted was all ears, but Detective Nichols appeared less than interested.

"Detective Nichols, now the story of these stones may become more interesting to you also." Nichols looked more directly at the professor. He remained slouched in his chair and looked as though it would take quite a lot to convince him.

"The reason the stones were taken off public display related, as with so many artifacts from antiquity, to concerns about authenticity." Ted looked puzzled and Nichols showed no reaction.

"The people at the Met were embarrassed about the possibility at first and then wrote vigorous and angry defenses in the literature. The stones were taken off display but the Met never wavered in promoting their significance. Some of us felt the lengths they went to talk about the stones were an indication they must have paid an enormous amount for them. So a kind of folklore grew about the stones and the whole business, making the stones even more mysterious and probably more valuable.

"That brings us to about the last year when I began to put together a special exhibit about the challenges of determining authenticity of artifacts, which I called 'Uncertainties of Antiquities'. The Met has a new administrator, John Snell, and he seemed happy when I asked him, after all the years of confusion, to have his people make their case for the bracelet. Then something terrible happened.

"About eight months ago, when the stones were sent over, the stones and the elderly security guard who was bringing them disappeared. He was driving one of their small vans and he never arrived here. A day later he and the van were found over by the East River. He was grievously beaten and had no memory of what happened. The windows were smashed and everything in the car had been rifled through, including the guard's belongings. The stones, of course, were gone. Detective Nichols, the police were involved from the time the guard was well overdue here the day of his disappearance."

Ted and Nichols looked at each other. To them it was pretty clear the guard most likely had been intentionally targeted. That he might have pulled over, for whatever reason, in the city or at the river, and became a crime of opportunity, not planned, by thugs on the streets, or if someone made him pull over and attacked him, was another possibility, however.

Knowing the history of the stones and their likely role in the crimes he was investigating, Ted was clear, in his own mind, the loss of the stones was a planned theft. Sadly, the Professor told them, the old guard nearly died and was permanently disabled, so his major felony assault became the main interest in the case for the police.

Despite the Professor's spoken assumption recounting these events would be of interest to Detective Nichols, it wasn't happening. Actually, he began to show signs of impatience. He yawned noticeably. Ted looked out the window but not at anything, certainly not out of boredom. He was imagining a few scenarios that might have led one of the stones to Lake Bee.

"Professor Landsdorf, I'm sure the stones were insured, so both the police and the insurers must have investigated the theft. No one tried to ransom them? Nothing turned up?"

"Not that I am aware of… Until your visit today." The Professor paused, then leaned forward slightly, indicating he had more to tell.

"The entire business was unusual after the stones disappeared. Several of us spoke but only among ourselves about it. I guess I should say I doubt anyone even would have considered mentioning it to the police at the time. Well it just seemed the folks at the Met really weren't very upset about what happened and they didn't pursue the investigation especially actively. Nor even did their insurance company. I think they were upset about the guard but we didn't hear much from them about the stones anymore."

Ted spoke as though he was trying to continue the Professor's line of thought. "So, if the stones were intentionally stolen, the mugging and then the felonious consequences of the assault to the guard might have made a thief wary of getting involved in making a ransom demand. Trying that could have exposed the thief to greater risk for a bigger crime than was intended. What about moving the stones to a private party? How much worth could there be in that?"

"Yes, of course, Officer. That's really the only option for a thief to make any money on the stones now. He would need a private collector to buy them. They say there are many serious collectors of art and antiquities who are quite satisfied to own pieces they can never display or speak about publicly. I suppose objects are sold out of public view among those types of people also. Unfortunately, that market is growing rapidly lately."

Ted was very interested. "I assume the police know what the insurance company paid to the museum for the loss. I wonder what a collector would pay for those stones? A thief who went to some trouble to steal them must have known they are of significant value and might have planned to ransom them but also would have considered their value after having them fenced. Can't imagine anyone doing this unless those stones are very valuable."

"Well, Officers, here's the thing about all this. What I meant to sort of imply about the way the Met acted after the theft was that some of us considered the Met was not entirely unhappy the bracelet disappeared. No, not for a minute did we think they planned any of what happened. But when the stones did disappear they accepted the loss without much public response. You know Officers…" at this he leaned forward as though he was about to tell them a secret. "I, for one, would not be very surprised if the folks at the Met and their insurer made a deal after the loss that saved the insurer a lot of money."

Ted, and even Nichols, were confused and appeared perplexed. Ted asked the obvious question: "Why? What do you mean Professor?"

"The stones are fakes; clearly fakes." With that pronouncement he paused and sat back for effect. "Some scholars have debunked them and the Met knows it also. The farmer who sold it to them was accused of trying to sell more objects, with much less provenance, over the last few years. In truth, when I studied the bracelet, even years ago, it seemed clear to me there were marks on some of the stones suggesting the stones were machined. Yes, modern machines used to shape and smooth them."

Ted remained confused. Even Nichols didn't sense the Professor's attempt at offering his idea of a bombshell explained everything.

"Then why did you have such a reaction to seeing the stone? And if everyone knows the stones are really fakes why were they stolen? Why would a thief think they were valuable enough to steal and expect to squeeze enough profit for the risk?"

"Gentlemen, in the world we live in these days museums battle to compete over having the most exciting new find. And with so many people with so much money even a fake, with a good story, can be worth something. Sometimes, maybe even stones like these actually can be worth quite a lot. Perhaps many, many thousands of dollars still. And, of course, not everyone agrees the stones are fake so that also helps preserve some value. They are not real. I'm sure of that.

"And one more thing, related to value. Now, since you have brought one of the sixteen stones here today, Officer Vallan, everything changes. For whatever value the bracelet might hold for a museum or a collector, especially for a collector, missing even one stone dramatically diminishes its worth. Museums, rightfully, can still display even small pieces of artifacts so the public can see and learn about the past. But a private collector needs to have a complete meaningful object or set to justify its worth. Having fifteen stones from the bracelet is greatly less collectable, and therefore worth much less than owning all sixteen; the entire bracelet. So, if there is someone out there who paid for or expected to receive all sixteen stones that individual is probably very unhappy you possess one Officer."

Rather nonchalantly Professor Landsdorf then asked Ted, "Officer Vallan can we keep that stone?" Neither Ted nor Jack Nichols, who Ted glanced at, felt the need to explain to the Professor the stone might be evidence in a capital case.

"No, I'm sorry Professor Landsdorf. Thank you, very much, for everything you have helped us learn about this, though." All three stood, shook hands, and Ted and Jack walked out of his office.

*   *   *

What the Professor told them was a lot for Ted to digest. Nichols had only been polite and was anxious to get on his way. The Detective and Ted, standing outside the research wing in the atrium of the beautiful building, agreed the Professor's story didn't justify the NYPD doing anything further right now. The police were going to try to get more information about the characters who tried to *take him for a ride* in the morning.

They talked a little more as Nichols drove crosstown to the 10th precinct where they shook hands and Ted walked the remaining distance to his hotel. On his walk he was more occupied with thinking about the case than taking in the sights around him. The next day he greatly regretted how he had foolishly forgotten to use this opportunity to buy some souvenirs for his kids.

As he reviewed the Professor's final words in his head he remembered what he had been through earlier in the day. Had he considered, seriously enough, that his possession of the sixteenth stone made him, personally, a target for whoever might possess the rest or even several? Ted continued to tend to reject that thought. Not especially convinced he told himself 'that would be insane'.

Most of his thinking was directed to the character, Sammy Paskovich (his John Doe), whose business card, 'Object's D'Art', seemed to deeply implicate him in this case. But, so far, everything was circumstantial. Just like trying to tie Dr. Gruber to the case just because he was a collector. The most unsavory character he knew about on the lake was Stan Angle. Ted had questions about almost everyone he had interviewed, but he figured if Stan Angle lived in the Gruber house instead of the Grubers he would have a more likely suspect. Location, location, location.

He continued to be amazed with the twists and turns coming up in a case where homicide was involved in the stealing and apparent buying of artifacts that had a good chance of not even being genuine. Back in his hotel room Ted lay down and dozed for about twenty minutes. When he awakened he worried he'd be late meeting Kendra Akers and promptly forgot to call home. He started to think about what he wanted to accomplish meeting with this Kendra. He turned the TV on while he washed up and changed into jeans.

*   *   *

Ted's Night in the City

The sound from the TV was almost uncomfortably loud. The nature of the program was unclear. It seemed like some sort of quiz show, with lots of people and lots of yelling and laughing.

"So here's what we are gonna do. We want to find out if it means anything to watch how women respond to being told they are on camera and to yell and cheer when the camera catches them. We have fifteen women in this line and let's see what we get." [*About three times the camera slowly pans down the line while young women shouted and jumped around when on view. Most waved and yelled, some jumped up and down, and some clearly wiggled their hips while doing that.*]

The MC looked at three people in a line next to him and said:

"Panel, what do you think? Can we draw any conclusions about the sexual, shall I say, interest [*loud laughing in unseen audience*] of these women… or ability? [*very loud laughing and yelling*].

"Now I want you to know each of these ladies agreed to fill out a pretty *down and dirty* [*howls, hooting, and laughter*] questionnaire before we asked them to line up and cheer on camera. So what do you think? Was there anything about the behavior of any of these ladies on camera that is a tip off to ladies who, shall we say, are a bit more into the sex thing? [*hooting and laughing*]. Seriously, [*hoots and laughter*] don't you think this could be very important information, guys? I mean you're at the bar watching the big game. If you knew that the way some chick responded to a big play meant how she feels about *you know what* [*hoots and howls*] you could be way ahead of the other guys. You know what I mean? [*hoots and howls*]

"Well Bret, what do you think?"

"I have to tell you Don, these gals all look great to me. But I sure did notice some pretty suggestive hip swiveling [*hoots and howls*] from a bunch of them and I bet some of those ladies might be the ones we're talking about Don."

"Okay Brett, so you think you've found a tip off, eh? What about you Missy, is Brett on to something here?" [*Audience cheers*]

[*Missy shoots her arms up in the air and shakes her hips --- place goes crazy. Audience, host, and other panelists start jumping and hooting and yelling*] "Frankly Don, I didn't see anything that makes me think that any of these ladies are signaling anything about themselves, especially sexually." [*loud boos and hoots from audience*] "Gee, I don't know Missy but if that's your thought, then okay. Jeff, I guess it's up to you to say whether you think we can know something from what we've just seen. Do you think we saw anything interesting [*howling and hooting*] just now?"

[*Laughing almost uncontrollably*] "You bet! I think those 4 or 5 gals who were wiggling [*hooting and howls*] themselves every which way; I mean they looked like they're ready to go." [*loud, sustained hoots and howls*]

"Well thank you panel. I guess the guys think they're onto something…but Missy isn't too sure [*laughter*]. So we're going to take a short break and when we come back we'll introduce Sam Smith, who is a psychologist and expert on body language. Doc Smith will give his interpretation of what we're seeing and then we'll learn whether what you just saw and the questionnaires are going to help us guys in the bar." [*hoots and howls*]

The phone rang. Ted picked up the controller quickly and pressed power, which turned the set off. As soon as he did it he realized he meant to press mute, not turn the TV off. He wanted to see what was going to happen and realized he was a little turned on by the show. As he answered and started to speak he also tried to get the set back on, with the idea to quickly press mute to see if he could still follow what was happening. As soon as he said hello and recognized it was Lieutenant Rondell he dropped the controller and never got back to the show. Later, while he was walking to meet Kendra Akers, he wondered about what he would have done with the TV if that call had been from Liza instead of the Lieutenant.

After he made his way crosstown and then a little uptown, without being diverted this time, he found the address and was buzzed into Kendra Aker's building. Yesterday meeting with Aker seemed like a straight forward lead to follow-up. Now Ted found himself second guessing what he was doing heading to the apartment of a woman in this huge city where he was clearly on unfamiliar turf. They exchanged handshakes and he was invited in. Akers was the kind of person with a natural ability to put people at ease. She acted like they were old friends.

"Oh, Sammy was a fuck-up but such a sweet fuck-up. He couldn't help himself. He always trusted people and he was in a business where you can't trust no one." There was true affection in her tone. "He worked for that jerk he called Forlenza from time to time. I think Forlenza knew he couldn't count on Sammy for anything violent. That just wasn't Sammy. And, as I said, Sammy often screwed up. But, for some reason, Forlenza let Sammy keep doing some jobs for him. I don't know why he put up with Sammy. I think this Forlenza is pretty high up in someone's mob. You know, look at what he's doing now." Kendra kept talking while she got up and brought back a beer for Ted.

"A deal went bad and he's having people killed and maybe wants to kill me and, who knows, maybe you're on his list too." Ted wondered just how much this lady knew about everything that was going on. "Maybe Sammy finally did something Forlenza wasn't going to forgive. Sammy told me it was a *commodity* deal. He was supposed to drop something, and pick something up; a quick turnaround.

"Only that fat fuck would call the job that got him killed 'a piece of cake'. How he loved to eat!" Ted was beginning to match a bit of a personality to the face of the body he had pulled out of the lake. "Sammy was a dreamer who got lost in his dreams. You know what I mean, Officer?"

Ted reflected on her words. He didn't think he had stumbled onto a deep thinker, but he had to admit to himself he had never really thought about what she had just said. He wondered about himself...and his father.

"He was so sweet to me. He always had a bunch of deals going on. This year he was working with some guys fencing fancy stolen stuff.

Sammy called it *artsy* stuff and considered himself in a high class business, even though everything was stolen."

Ted showed her one of the 'Objects D'Art' cards they had taken off the body. "Yeah. He didn't know shit about art, but he had a couple of deals that paid off so he started studying about all kinds of collecting and stuff.

"When Sammy got back he said we were gonna go to Florida and maybe stay there a long time if his connections worked out. Sammy wasn't the only *egg in my basket*, if you know what I mean, but I might have gone with him if it had worked out. He told me he had a feeling this Forlenza had had it with him and wouldn't cut him anymore slack if he screwed up anymore. So I guess he had his guys wack him." *Mob* language, Ted thought. Where was this business going to go? "Now It looks like he wants me. He must think I've got something."

"Have you ever seen or talked to this Forlenza?"

"Are you kidding? Of course not. Sammy did, but Forlenza runs the show from somewhere in the Bronx. Sammy thought it was so funny. He was always spouting out 'numba' 111, 148th Street.' He thought that was great. He'd always say 'the numbas add up'. I guess meaning the first four add up to four and four plus four then are eight or something. No, that Forlenza creep, he's never around. He has thugs who do all his dirty work. Don't for a minute think he's the guy following me. It's one of his boys. You kidding? I'm telling you he's high up."

Ted finished his beer. He had taken only a few of the Ritz crackers with cheese spread on the platter between them. Kendra was finishing her second mixed drink of some kind. As soon as Ted finished his beer she got up and brought back another one. He took it from her and put it on the table, intending to just leave it there. He felt comfortable sitting there talking with Kendra. He suspected if they continued to talk he could get more useful information from her.

What he had difficulty figuring out was why this Kendra, by any measure an attractive woman, who was ten or more years younger than Sammy, was so attached to a fat guy she happily called a fuck up? As he talked with her and watched her he sensed he had never before looked at or talked to an older woman like this, who seemed to move and react in such a sexy manner. The slightly throaty, husky tone in her voice and the way she positioned her body, sitting across from him, was a bit of a turn on. He picked up the second beer and took a chug. He remembered the crazy TV show before he left the hotel.

"Kendra, tell me what Sammy told you about this deal he was doing for Forlenza."

"I told you, Officer...can I call you Ted since we're sitting here sharing drinks?..." Ted nodded. "So Ted, it's like I said, Sammy's job was to do the legwork, like on other deals. Day before he disappeared he told me he had to make a call upstate at an exact time. When I saw him that evening he told me he was going to be out of town the next day and would be gone at least one and maybe two days. He said the deal was on. He did say, from talking to him, there was something funny or different about the guy he was going to meet."

"You mean something he said or the way he talked?"

"Beats me."

He wondered what that could mean? If it was the way he talked, Ted thought everyone in New York City probably would say *he* had an accent.

She took a big sip of her next drink, picked a cigarette out of a pack on the table, then bent over and used a lighter on the table to light it. She motioned to Ted, who waved her off, and indicated with the same movement it was okay with him if she lit up.

Ted was close to finishing his second beer. He was getting an idea she was just waiting him out. Sure, she was giving him valuable information and maybe her last comment meant something important (although too vague to be helpful now). At the same time this was all going really slowly. Kendra was no longer acting nervous or frightened as she had sounded the day before. She seemed a little too comfortable in this tiny apartment that was supposedly her sister's. It was never made clear where her sister was or if she was going to return. Ted had lost count of how many drinks Kendra had. She was, ever so slightly, beginning to slur her words. She got up and brought back another beer for him.

She was drunk; he was half way there.

Then Kendra sat up straight and spoke directly. "I'm hungry Ted. Do you think we should have something to eat?" Immediately Ted thought that was a good idea. Food might settle some of the potency of the alcohol, for both of them. Kendra was clear she was reluctant to go out since she felt threatened. She told Ted about a Chinese place just down the block and he said he'd be glad to get it. No, he told her, no one had reason to be looking for him, and if he was being followed he wasn't worried about it. And he really wasn't.

She had a take-out menu and they sat together going over it, making a list of what they agreed on. Ted recognized he was excited just sitting next to her. They didn't plan to get much. Ted put his coat on and set off with his instructions.

The cool air felt good and the restaurant was only a few doors down from her sister's (or whoever's) building. While he waited for the order he thought about what more he wanted to try to learn from Kendra. Anything more about Sammy's deal that took him to Vermont and anything about people like Glenn Miller and Jimmy Smith would be useful.

He paid for the food and walked back up the street. He stopped for just a moment and looked around. The area was filled with people. Kendra buzzed him in and he started up the three floors to the apartment. Who knew if anyone was watching for her outside or if anyone was looking for him, he thought. He had just seen about half a million people going every which way at eight in the evening.

He knocked on her door and waited while he heard several locks being adjusted. Kendra had a drink in her hand when she let him in. She walked to the couch and then turned around. Ted stood in the doorway and his jaw dropped and the bag with the food literally started to fall from his arm. He grabbed it. He knew he was flushing. There was sweet perfume in the air and Kendra stood there, in a short black robe. It was doubtful there was anything underneath. Ted hesitated and she motioned him to close the door and come over to the couch. He walked over slowly and she sat down. Ted just stood there, staring at her. She looked good.

"Ted, aren't you hungry?"

He put the bag on the coffee table and sat down slowly. She didn't touch him but leaned into him so they were flush against each other, arm to arm. It didn't take Ted long to figure where this was going. He couldn't recall being this excited in forever. He flushed again just thinking how embarrassed he would feel if she put her hand over his expanding crotch. She smelled wonderful. She seemed glad to be doing this.

He knew they were both drunk. He sat there and felt his brain exploding. This case; this city; and now this woman. They were alone and he was turned on; way on. Did any of this make any sense with this woman? Holy shit! Her robe was coming open and she was leaning over and bringing her arm up his leg. Ted pulled back. He sat up and slid himself a few feet away from her to the end of the couch.

All day, at least, he knew he had been making one bad decision after another. Tonight was really exciting but doing this wasn't going to be any good for the life Ted had. Initially, Kendra appeared surprised. Looking at her now he could see she was very drunk. She stiffened, made an exaggerated motion closing her robe, and sat up also. She quickly flashed her anger at Ted.

"Well that's really something, Ted. You know your father wasn't so goddamn choosey!"

Ted jumped off the couch. "Jesus Christ! Holy shit! You slept with my father?"

"Your father."

Kendra retained her anger but softened a bit. She clearly felt hurt and rejected. She was happy to hurt Ted. He was all red again. He could feel his heart pounding.

"My fucking father?" Barely a question; more a declamatory statement.

"Well he wanted to. I think. We got undressed and sat on the bed. I told him we should drink some wine first; kind of a toast. I turned to reach for the glasses. His was spiked. But he started pawing me all over. Suddenly he sat up. He looked pale. He said he was gonna vomit. He ran to the bathroom and threw up, then pulled his clothes on and ran out of the motel room. I haven't heard from him since." She sighed, and her body kind of deflated on the couch. "I think he was fucking with me anyway about saying he had what I wanted."

Ted didn't know what to say. While some of the gaps this stunner began to fill rushed into his brain he also felt flashes of anger, embarrassment, confusion, and a million other things. He had avoided making another huge mistake, but he still felt like a jerk for how far it had gone and now for what he was learning about his father, and even Kendra. If he had any suspicion this lady had her own agenda it was now obvious. It seemed like everyone around him knew more about what was going on than he did. How could that be? It all kept repeating in his head.

That was a consistent thread throughout this business. He wasn't nearly as suspicious of everyone as he now knew he should have been. Even his own, literally, *fucking* father. No one had been square with him.

He looked over at Kendra and she looked truly sad. Well that was going to have to be her problem. Ted had to find out what she knew and what she was trying to get from his father no matter how embarrassing for either of them. His rejection of her advances seemed to allow Kendra to act differently from the last hour or so. She dropped her effort at seduction and seemed to accept his need to get more from her.

Kendra offered Ted a huge piece for his puzzle when she proceeded to tell him Sammy had told her some special money, old, valuable, big denomination bills, were part of the deal he was doing. This seemed to confirm the $1000 bills they found on Sammy were involved in the case. He didn't have to ask much more to construct the scenario in his mind of Kendra following the "ABC" for a lure about the bills. Sammy obviously had educated her about the "ABC".

Even though Sammy made his phone contact in upstate New York, Kendra, and probably some others, figured out taking the train to Rutland meant there was a good chance Vermont was involved. It wasn't difficult for Kendra to contact the few hospitals in Vermont when Sammy didn't return. When his description fit a John Doe in Burlington and she saw the ad in the "ABC" she thought there probably was a connection.

Ted's father sounded like he would be an easy mark. Not a surprise. Kendra had concerns for Sammy but also thought some of the money involved in the deal was kind of rightfully hers. Ted accepted now that Kendra was a hustler also. She contacted the ad box and spoke with Ted's dad the next day. He told her the name of a motel and a fake name, A. Symthe, to sign the register. They planned to meet late the next afternoon.

So she took a bus to Burlington and a cab to the motel. She figured someone in Forlenza's operation could have found Sammy skimming a few extra from his cut and Forlenza had him killed. But maybe some unknown person or people interrupted the deal or robbed Sammy and took the money and maybe whatever the other *commodity* was being traded. Forlenza's killers wouldn't be advertising to fence the money if they had it. They had professionals to do that kind of stuff.

When she spoke on the phone with Ted's father he kept asking her what the bills were worth to her. She kept saying it depended on how many he had. She didn't even know what size bills Sammy had been talking about until she saw the ad. She made it clear to him any deal had to be done right then so he better bring the goods. Kendra admitted to Ted she began to feel she was getting in over her head on this. But the two calls she had with his father made her feel he was going to be easy to roll, just like Sammy, and she doubted any reason for this to be any kind of plant from Forlenza's guys.

Her words about getting together really seemed to turn his father on. When she went up there she assumed her main problem was to figure how to get however many bills there were away from the mark. She packed a few barbiturate sleeping pills and put thirty obviously fake $1000 bills from a toy store in an envelope in her bag. She wrinkled them up to make them look old. For some reason they had 'Doc', from Snow White, on the face instead of Grover Cleveland in the circle in the center. For a quick look they would be fine. Of course, she didn't know his father's collection of fakes was exactly the same, also with 'Doc' on the face. Not even any fake money ever changed hands.

When Ted left her building this time he knew he wanted to do some walking. He definitely needed to clear his head. He set off crosstown, happy to walk however many blocks it was back to his hotel. The cool, crisp air felt good. Everything in his mind was racing but no longer exploding. His father; his truly *fucking* father. How close he himself had come to temptation. Why this Forlenza was having people killed after a deal gone bad? Why this city was so fucking crazy? It was about nine-thirty on a Friday night and the place was lit up like a festival. People and cars and trucks were everywhere. He was drunk and tired. Why weren't all *these* assholes tired and home somewhere?

Walking along some of the quieter side streets, for the first time all night, he had a sense someone might be following him. When he turned corners and glanced back he saw two guys, maybe twenty, thirty yards back, walking at his pace. One on each side of the street. 'Who knows?', he thought. They each had old time plaid tweed hats on their heads. Didn't look skinny like Jimmy Smith or fat like *Glenny* Miller. Neither frightened him.

What Ted wanted was time to work on thinking through all that happened during the long day. He was trying but wasn't able to come up with some way to spin what he had just been through with Kendra to make it seem less gross than he knew it was. After a short while he decided it would be best to figure out if he was being followed. Distracting his mind might be the best way to actually begin to clear it. Everything was so jumbled.

As far as Ted could recall Vermont State Police were never given any training in tailing on foot or being tailed. He thought it would be hard to feel physically threatened by these guys, if they actually were following him. Most of these streets were as busy as Church Street in Burlington during a holiday week. He caught himself. This was New York City and he was quickly learning lots of strange shit happened here. Anyway, he sped up for a while then slowed down. He walked into a store and looked around at housewares for a few minutes. Then he back-tracked one street. After all this his conclusion was only one of the tweed hats was tailing him. There was some dark humor in all this. With some nervousness Ted wondered just how many 'troops' this Forlenza had to do his bidding?

Figuring a way to confront the guy seemed pointless to Ted. He knew he was being followed; the man following him probably knew

Ted had figured it out. Unless some speeding car filled with goons drove up he guessed this guy was just doing his job, keeping an eye on Ted. At this point Ted assumed this guy probably knew little about what Ted wanted to know about this case, and the NYPD wasn't hanging at the phone waiting to discuss this man with him. So Ted would go to his hotel and he and the man with the tweed hat would keep tabs on each other along the way.

His tail stopped at the final intersection, about twenty yards south of the hotel entrance. Ted walked into the lobby and was passing the front desk when the clerk called his name, a bit loudly and with some urgency. "Uh, Trooper Vallan? Is that right?" Ted diverted to the desk. The clerk handed two slips of paper to Ted and said, "Sir there are two messages for you. One appears to be quite urgent and just came in no more than three or four minutes ago."

Ted opened the first one and all it said was 'Remember us? Home'. Oh shit! He had never called home all day and now it was too late. Shit! He opened the second and immediately forgot about the first. 'I'm about to be taken. Call my number: 555-0103! Kendra'. The desk clerk stood close by, watching him the entire time. Unprompted, he spoke up, "She was terrified and screaming Trooper Vallan. We were just talking here about whether we should call the police but then, fortunately, you walked in."

Ted was thinking. He was pleased to finally be called 'Trooper' by someone but he was immediately distracted. He said, "Yeah, right." He looked around. "Hey where is the nearest phone I can use?" The clerk quickly produced a phone from under the desk. Ted dialed the number from the message. It only rang once and was picked up. He could hear banging and Kendra shouted into the phone,

"Ted! Ted! They're about to break down my door to get me!"

"Kendra, did you call the police?"

"Of course, but they put me on hold so I hung up and called the number of your hotel you put on your card. Ted! They're taunting me! Talking through the door, telling me I have a date in the Bronx! Ted!" She was frantic.

Ted heard a large crash and Kendra dropped the phone and was screaming. He assumed there was a struggle. Ted kept shouting "Kendra!" into the phone. Then it got more quiet. He could hear someone was at the phone. "What is going on?" he shouted.

A husky, but mid tone voice spoke into the phone. He might have guessed someone like 'Glenny' Miller would sound like this, but he had never really heard him say anything. "Listen, asshole. Youse gonna need to learn to stay outta dis business. Don't concern ya self, ya hear? Know what asshole, ma'be youse should be watching youse own backside fra now on, shithead!"

Ted had to be quick, so he took a chance, with little to lose, and shouted to whoever this was, "You call yourself 'Glenn Miller' but the word is out on you dick head, all about you, and you're fucking up again…bozo asshole!" Who knew, but maybe Ted hit a nerve. He could hear it. The guy was seething, like Miller was at the car.

"Fuck off, youse piece of shit!" and the phone slammed down.

Ted looked up. The two people at the desk and the few people in the lobby were standing like statues, riveted to his conversation. He pulled out Jack Nichol's card and dialed it. He got his voice mail. He had no other number for him. He considered trying to work through a duty desk officer and talking with any detective around but the chance that would lead to a quick emergency response wasn't very good. He hung up and bolted for the stairway and ran up five floors to his room.

He had to get back to the South Bronx. He wasn't sure if what he heard had been staged or if more killing was about to take place. He couldn't just sit there or go outside and hail a cop. How would he get to the Bronx? The only solution he could come up with was his cruiser. He peed and washed his face.

Ted started for the door, then realized, no matter how he travelled in the cruiser, he was going to attract police attention. He literally moved back and forth into the room then back to the door several times before deciding to put his uniform on. After changing he started for the door but, again, found himself being tugged back and forth for a second time. He was fed up with this city and all he was going through. Tomorrow he was supposed to meet at a place called the Cloisters in the Bronx with the renters who were east of the Graham's at the lake, and then go home. He pulled out his bag and threw all his toiletries and clothes, including his suit jacket and pants, into it and headed downstairs. Maybe he could stop somewhere later to get the souvenirs he had promised his kids. He didn't want to come back here.

Ted rushed down the stairs and the thought some might think he had changed into his superman suit didn't escape him. He didn't feel like superman. He felt like he was running behind a fast train and was unable to catch up.

His arrival in the lobby was anticipated. People who were there and also at the desk got bigger eyes as he walked rapidly in his distinctive, almost form fitting, trooper's uniform; tan with green and yellow piping. No hat and carrying his bag. He headed for the door but noticed the dropped jaws at the desk as he headed out with his things. He stopped, pulled a business card from his wallet, and tossed it on the desk. "I may not be back or, I guess, I may be. The State Police won't stiff you." And he was out the door.

He foolishly stopped to look around to decide how to proceed. Long enough for the tweed hat at the south intersection to take notice this was his guy, albeit in something like a scout's outfit. The man was probably on his tenth cigarette since Ted had gone inside.

In the time the fellow tossed and stepped on the cigarette Ted had headed north. At the first cross street he turned left, which was west, towards the police garage. He put an arm around his entire case and took off in a jog. At the next avenue he went north again until west, again, at the first cross street. The streets were more desolate now and he could easily tell it was doubtful his tail was still around. He continued at a comfortable slow jog, working his way toward the Hudson River and the garage on Twelfth Avenue.

Ted broke to a walk at the entrance. It was well lit and he could see activity inside. If that Chris Smithers was telling the truth there were mechanics always doing shift work and overtime here. He showed his NYPD ID and his Vermont badge to the clerk behind a locked door in a tiny anteroom. He said he needed his car. He also asked if Chris Smithers happened to be around. The clerk looked at some log sheets and said Smithers was there, on second shift today.

He buzzed Ted in and Ted asked how he could find Smithers. The clerk paged him. There was quite a racket going on in the large open shop with people working on cars and vans, some on lifts, but the paging was loud enough to be heard. The clerk repeated Smithers' name a few times.

Looking like a mechanic, rubbing his hands with a cloth, wearing an apron over what seemed to be a blue uniform Smithers smiled as he walked up to Ted only a minute or so after his page. He had been working on this floor. He decided to give Ted a slight wave rather than offer his greasy hand.

"Hey, Trooper Vallan, that's right, isn't it? You headin' back to Vermont this time of night?"

"No, but I need my cruiser. You still putting in lots of hours, huh?"

"Shit yes. I'm jus ending second shift but 'spect I'll be here few more hours. Trooper Vallan, you sure you should be drivin' now? Your face all red and you got booze on your breath."

"Chris I've got no choice. I've had trouble with really bad guys all day and I can't reach the cop I'm working with. I think a lady in big trouble is being taken to the Bronx, right now."

Smithers tipped his head back and scratched the back of his neck with a look of disbelief on his face, even if his manner was always to try to make light of everything. "I…I dunno," as he was shaking his head no.

"Smithers, listen to me. Are you a cop or aren't you?"

"Well, Trooper, it kind of depends. I'm a police mechanic, but I got spec clearance, tru this job, to do some police things. And I got the police benefits, which…."

"You sound close enough to be a cop for me. Listen I need my cruiser and I need you to help me. You have to get me to an address in a bombed out area of the Bronx where I suspect this lady is going to be held."

"Oh shit, Vallan, you must be crazy nuts. Never been in State Trooper vehicle befor but goin' with a drunk cop to Bronx don' make any sense tonight."

"Fine, Smithers, then just help me get the cruiser and quickly write down how I need to go. You know, I'm a cop and I can't just let someone maybe die cause it sounds nuts to you and the rest of the NYPD. People are dead already." Smithers shook his head again as he went into the clerk's office and came out with Ted's key, which he flipped to Ted. Ted then followed Smithers to the other side of the shop. The others on duty watched as they walked by each bay to a corner way in the back where his cruiser sat.

Smithers started to write some directions for Ted then stopped and looked at him. He knew it was useless. Ted told him he wouldn't even have to punch out because this was police business. Ted figured with all of Smithers' overtime he probably earned more than twice what he made. Smithers, reluctantly, agreed to go. Ted even talked him into getting a Police .38 Colt Special revolver from the office. Ted said he was the first man with Smith in his name he trusted. The reference meant nothing to Smithers.

Ted started out with only his solitary, large blue emergency roof light flashing. Smithers shouted to him he couldn't drive city streets that way or he'd get broadsided in twenty of one hundred intersections. Ted turned on the siren. Smithers looked at the radio but decided this was not a setting where he could figure a way to contact the NYPD.

As they really got going and settled in some during their frantic drive to the Bronx Ted tried to engage Smithers and build some camaraderie: "You know, I saw that plaque with your name on it on the wall in the office. You and I each did MP work in the army."

Smithers was quite surprised and smiled as he turned to face Ted. "Yeah, they drafted my sorry ass the day I graduated high school. I told them I was good with engines and, as fucked up as that army is, they sent me for vehicle repair and main'ance trainin' and I spent my war in the Motor Pool. You too, eh?"

"Well, sort of. My MP time was Military Police. Right out of high school also. Guess I'm still at it...just like you. Hey, but you know, Smithers, before the Motor Pool you had to have basic. So you do know how to handle a weapon?"

"Trooper, if you are looking to me as your back-up you talking to the wrong guy. I keep the cruisers going, not you. Do you hear me?"

Smither's facial expression changed. But what Ted noted more was his manner of speaking was completely different. No more New York accent and no more *black* vernacular.

"Look Trooper, you may think I've got an easy, good thing going here. Things aren't always what they seem. I've learned how to do a lot of things to get what I think I want. 'Mister Charlie' thinks I'm a happy-go-lucky darkie, just happy to be bringing in some bucks, so I don't challenge that."

While he spoke he continued to look straight ahead, using his arms to direct Ted and the cruiser. "But, you know, when you crack an egg sometimes it can get messy. I've got my own racket here and I don't intend to see it get fucked up doing something crazy for you. You know, I told you I work extra for my wife and kid. Well I actually have two wives and two kids. I brought a lady back with me from 'Nam. She's in Jersey and my other wife is in Queens. So I work so much overtime to make money I need to keep this fragile situation going. Everyone always thinks I'm working, even NYPD,…and my ladies, if you know what I mean. I got a feeling being with you might fuck up the whole business."

By the time they were near the northern tip of Manhattan a squad car was behind them, also flashing lights and wailing its siren. Ted thought he heard something from that car's loudspeaker but there was way too much noise. After a brief time on a highway Smithers directed him to a wide one-way road that approximated the bombed out area Ted was in earlier. They were in the South Bronx. The cars screamed up the avenue, with some caution at intersections. Two more squad cars joined in, each noisily flanking Ted's cruiser. He yelled above the din to Smithers asking how much farther they had to go? About twenty more blocks was his reply. Ted kept at it.

With no more than three or four blocks remaining the NYPD preformed a maneuver Ted thought was very impressive. As he came to an intersection two more squad cars arrived, one coming out of each side of the side street. They effectively blocked his ability to keep going. He stopped and turned off his siren.

It was instantly quiet. Ted got out and stood by his door and two or three policemen did the same at their vehicles. A Sergeant who was a passenger in one of the blocking cars slowly walked over. Ted thought he better give the NYPD a few minutes before he made his case. The Sergeant stopped a few feet away and looked around, like a dog might initially move slowly to smell a pile of dog shit. He was frowning. He bent over and looked in at Smithers, who sat looking forward, wearing police blue that probably confused the sergeant. The .38 was on the front seat.

The Sergeant spoke out loud, to no one in particular. "So you the *Boy Scout* Pappas been tellin' ever' one 'bout today, huh?" Looks at his name tag. "Trooopa' Vallan, I tink you fucked up dis time, eh? Shit, now youse racin' tru da city again, dis time in ya *full O shit* play car. Ya know trooper, youse always seem to have a weapon on the seat of the cars you in, from what I hear. Don ya? Well enough of dis shit fella. Ya sure don belong here. Ya…."

Ted thought he might rattle on endlessly, and Ted agreed: Enough. Enough of this reactive policing. "Sergeant, we don't have time for this exercise. I'm after a lady who's been taken and I'm sure she's being held practically around the corner from here." He started to list all his NYPD contacts, especially the Sergeant from this precinct who drove him downtown earlier. "I need to speak, immediately, with someone who will help me go to number 111, 148th Street."

In a way, Ted understood how crazy this all must sound to the New York cops and realized it was a big decision on their part to consider assembling a force to go into 111, 148th Street, basically, only on his urging. He also understood it would be useless to try to go into that building on his own.

Ted thought the mention of that address evoked some recognition. "Listen Trooopa', take ya fuckin story up wit the Lieutoonant. Here he comes now." The Sergeant motioned to a flashing black sedan coming up the avenue.

The Lieutenant did not appear to be a pleasant man. He acted like he was eternally tired of everything, on a chronic basis. He did, however, manage to find the energy to unleash a torrent of expletives right into Ted's face. Then he spoke more quietly. He looked over at Ted's name tag. "Trooper Vallan, you been drinking?"

Ted didn't answer that. He mustered an earnest and demanding but not disrespectful tone and reviewed as much of the last twelve hours and NYPD names as he could quickly manage before the Lieutenant stopped him. The Lieutenant started screaming at him again. He thought he heard him saying something about already knowing about this, but he wasn't sure. Then there was a sudden, prolonged pause and he spoke in a normal clear voice: "Northeast SWAT hasn't been out in a couple of days. Let's shake things up." For the second time that day Ted's jaw literally dropped.

In minutes a flashing armored vehicle was visible in the distance. As it closed fire trucks could be seen also. The Lieutenant told Ted to get in his cruiser and follow him.

"Trooper, you stay in your fuckin' cruiser and I'll come get you when this is done. I think you'll agree this is an ass bustin', un-fuckin'-believable thing that's about to happen. If we don find nothin' it'll be your and your boss's asses, but at least our guys will get some trainin'."

On 148th Street they turned right, off the main avenue, and drove through one more avenue. SWAT actually had even more vehicles that had approached from farther east, so 148th Street was now blocked at both avenues. The place was instantly lit up with extremely bright lights aimed at the building making it difficult for anyone inside to see what was going on in the street. No one wasted a moment after their arrival. Ted parked his cruiser at the curb, facing east, about two hundred feet from number 111. Smithers stayed in the cruiser. Ted got out and stood by his door. By the time he was on the sidewalk SWAT was in the building. The show of experience and teamwork was impressive.

There were one or two flashes and booms from stun grenades and one brief burst of automatic fire. Then more sirens from everywhere. Ted walked forward, trailing the Lieutenant, who walked up the steps like MacArthur returning to the Philippines and ignored Ted. Inside, the area was a mess. A Swat Officer was on his radio swearing at whoever was listening. Basically he was telling them to keep searching the building.

Suddenly two shots and then a burst of automatic fire from below them. Several men rushed to a corridor, ran down it to a stairway, and the sounds of many boots on stairs pounded the air. Then it was quiet again. The SWAT Officer and the Lieutenant moved to the hallway corridor waiting for word from below. "HQ, bad news. Dead middle-aged white woman beat to shit down here. A punk proly took one in the leg getting out some other way. Advise need to search whole fuckin' place and will need ambulance down here. Squad two."

*   *   *

"Why did they have to kill her? She really didn't know anything?"

The Lieutenant was unimpressed with Ted and responded impatiently. "You a-hole, don't you get it? That's *why* they killed her. Once they satisfied themselves your body was really their guy and, with her connection to him, her nosing around didn't get her any of the stuff they think is theirs, they didn't need her anymore. When small timers cross paths with guys like these they usually wind up disfigured, dead, or something bad anyway. Frankly, her connection to you probably sealed her fate." Ted winced in his chair. What was he supposed to do as he had worked through this case?

"Why does this shithead do all this for a deal gone bad that could never add up to justify this toll in lives already?"

"Vallan, you know what? There are some things you should know about guys like these: They generally don't stop until they get what they want or they think they're owed from any deal. And my guess is they are not at all happy with you and your efforts here, Vallan" Ted got the drift of his words. "So, Trooper Vallan, if I were you I'd go back to Vermont now and let us see what we can find out here from now on."

It was the middle of the night. Ted got nauseous when he had to ID Kendra. She was viciously beaten and strangled. He couldn't reconcile still smelling the remnants of her sweet perfume with what she was now. He only knew her a few hours. By any measure she was alive then. She *was* in over her head.

It was time to get out of there and the night air felt good. His thoughts were a jumble. He owed it to Smithers to get him back to Manhattan. He walked out to the front steps of the building. Only the Lieutenant's and another squad car were there, parked in front. Ted looked west down the street where his cruiser was and assumed Smithers was waiting; also angry with him.

Suddenly a fat figure came out slowly from a building about eighty feet away and started west down the street. Ted shouted and took off after him. The fat man began to run. Ted was catching up but as he got close he saw a pistol in the man's flailing hand. Just as the man determined to stop and turn to face Ted with his weapon Smithers pushed open the cruiser's passenger door and sent the guy tumbling. He came up surprisingly quickly and he and Smithers grappled, but only for seconds. As Ted arrived there was a shot and Smithers fell back.

"Oh no!" Ted shouted. Then he was on the man also and pushed the weapon out of reach. Police came running from the building and secured the fat man. Ted was sure it was 'Glenn Miller'. Ted went to Smithers and saw he had been shot in the lower leg but was alert. He took some rope from his trunk, cut it with his knife, and made an effective tourniquet. Smithers never said a word. An ambulance and more squad cars arrived. Ted told Smithers he would visit him later in the morning. He could only imagine how Smithers felt now that his worst fears were coming true.

* * *

There was some daylight now; dawn of a new day. Ted walked slowly down the block to his cruiser again. He was exhausted. Only one squad car remained in front of the building and the crime team was finished with the scene at his cruiser where Smithers was shot. Vallan broke a slight smile and told himself everyone named *Smith* was not an ass-hole after all. Smithers was a good guy and he was glad he was all right. He got into his cruiser and sat for a minute, still thinking about Smithers. He was sorry Smithers was going to lose some of the overtime he was devoted to, but he had acted like a cop and Ted hoped he would eventually accept what happened.

There was no reason to disagree with the NYPD Lieutenant about going home now. He wanted to get away from this city even last night. What more could he learn here? He wasn't sure how to get out of the city and he thought he should call home first. He had a piece of paper from one of the cops at the scene directing him to the nearest precinct station.

He started the car, made a sharp U-turn, and slowly rolled to the intersection, turning left onto the one-way avenue. It was just barely light and he forgot to turn his lights on. As he pushed lightly on the gas pedal, about thirty yards down the road, a black car started to shoot out from an alley. The sedan, probably a town car, slammed on its brakes just feet from running broadside into the cruiser. All motion stopped for some moments. There were two men in the front. The driver started twisting around in his seat.

The passenger door opened and a tall, thin old man got out slowly. He had a black felt fedora and a long black camelhair top coat. His face was thin with a red moustache and pointed goatee, probably dyed, given his apparent age. Mostly the expression on his face projected consternation and exhaustion, but Ted also could sense anger. Both hands were in pockets. Whether he had a weapon in one of them was something Ted decided to assume.

He calmly walked over to Ted's door, took one hand from his coat pocket and motioned Ted to roll down his window. Ted was stunned. As he slowly lowered his window he felt for the .38. It wasn't on the seat anymore.

"Offica' Vallan. You all over the place, eh? You come out of th' fuggin woods an' make some trouble, eh? Dis whole business turn to fuckin' shit for some time. Never a good deal, Vallan. Time you gotta know now you got outta ya league down here." He couldn't completely hide his hunched shoulders and his exhaustion. He continued on in a matter of fact tone, no visible signs of increasing anger or emotion. "You got little missus and two little youngstas back up there in your Vermont, eh? I tink you best go back ta keep an eye on them now, eh?"

Ted was blindsided. Did this asshole just say what Ted thought he said? Was this really happening?

There was fire in the old man's eyes now as he spoke louder and firmly, "Now pull ya piece a shit ca' up so I can be on my way."

Ted left his window down and sat there while this man, who he assumed was Forlenza, put his hand back in his pocket and strolled back to the sedan and got in through the still open door. Before putting the cruiser in gear Ted thought to reach with his left hand into the back seat and was able to feel for his camera on the floor. He pulled it up front. Instead of going forward as he was told he slowly inched backwards. The black sedan started ahead when there was some clearance. Ted had clicked the camera on in his lap. He figured this self-important bastard wouldn't deem him worth looking at and he was correct.

Without checking the viewfinder Ted held the camera out the window and took three shots; two aimed at the passenger window and one at the car's plate as it turned left to the avenue. Then he sat there a few seconds. He was in a cold sweat and had no doubt he had flushed during his moments with that guy. He gave no thought to whether he would ever even look at what he just did with the camera.

Ted turned on his flasher and siren and headed for the precinct close-by. He would call Montpelier and Liza and get home as fast as he could. No New York City souvenirs for anybody this trip. No stop at the Cloisters.

* * *

Liza's Night in the Country

Liza loved her home. Almost in the woods but just enough suburban convenience. Even with non-stop activity when the kids were awake she saw it as her and Ted's refuge from the too busy world that was increasingly swallowing their time.

At home the kids were cranky but so was she. That seven and then eight o'clock passed and still no word from Ted made her angry. She tried to reach him at the hotel and left a curt, nasty message at the desk when he didn't pick up. Part of her anger reflected worry about Ted but she recognized it was also from frustration that she had no one to share her day and concerns with, including her own anxiety about all that had happened this week. She tried, again and again, to rid herself of the rising paranoia she began to feel ever since thinking she was being watched in the morgue and her interaction with the now dead diener.

Months when she was doing hospital overnights Ted had Mrs. Arkady to manage the house and even provide some company, although he said she definitely talked too much. Liza liked her more. She enjoyed Mrs. Arkady's constant flow of English homily's, maxims, and platitudes as she worked on her English. Mrs. Arkady was a key to managing the family, at least for the three years of Liza's residency.

Actually, the only real extra they had paid for in their new house was fitting a full rather than half bathroom downstairs next to the den, which served as bedroom for Mrs. Arkady when she was with them. Having a nanny/housekeeper was a great expense for the Vallans but she was essential since Ted and Liza were very directed towards getting through these tough years without sacrificing good support for the children. Fortunately, Mrs. Arkady, in her late fifties, had close family in Albany, NY and was happy to spend extended time with them, in blocks that totaled up to six months each year, when she wasn't needed. Tonight Liza wished Mrs. Arkady was around.

With the kids asleep Liza tried to reconcile herself that it was no longer likely she would hear from Ted. Briefly, she thought about calling the Barracks and have Lieutenant Rondell call her to find out what, if anything, he had heard from Ted. She quickly laughed off that idea. She could just picture Ted's reaction to hearing she called the Lieutenant to check-up on him: 'You what? You tracked down Rondell to find out if I was okay? Are you serious? Am I your third kid, on his first overnight?' No, that wouldn't be good.

She was un-nerved by all the events of the week. At least her in-laws hadn't called to find out what she heard from Ted. Telling them he hadn't called yet would be been bound to set off very verbal worry and upset from them. The last person she wanted to see upset was her convalescing father-in-law. She could picture Mother Vallan, all elbows, trying to take control of this situation. Maybe Ted called them and not her? Unlikely, she decided.

About nine o'clock Liza let the dog out for the last time. The Vallans lived in a rural area, about fifteen or twenty minutes east of Burlington, but on a street that was a fairly new subdivision of about ten similar houses just off a main town thoroughfare. There were enough houses so there would always be kids to play with as their kids grew older. The Vallan house was the last house on the south side of the street, with woods to the east and beyond the backyard to the south. The back yard was fenced in for the dog and the kids.

As soon as the dog was out he started to bark. Liza was tired, but she, grudgingly, raised out of her chair to get him after only a short time. While she was walking through the mud room to call him in the dog let out a fierce, loud, high-pitched, almost ghostly howl that startled her. She turned on the back floodlight and went outside. George galloped to her and seemed to be okay. She quickly inspected him but found no sign of any obvious injury or bite. Liza looked up and gazed into the yard. Twenty or thirty feet away, near the east fence, she thought there might be a piece of wood or something. As she looked at it she immediately became distracted. Liza noticed an odor in the air. It took only a few seconds for her to recognize it smelled like a cigarette. No one she was aware of in the neighborhood smoked.

She hurried the dog in. She wasn't sure what to make of the cigarette smell but, given her already heightened anxieties, it un-nerved her. She locked the back door but kept her hand on the door knob while she thought a little more about it. Then she unlocked the door, exhaled, stepped out the door, and took in a big gulp of air, which confirmed her initial suspicion. She, indeed, smelled cigarette smoke. She locked the door and hurriedly went to the front of the house, pushing the picture window curtain aside, and looked to see if anything, like a car, was on the street. She tried to see the driveways of contiguous neighbor's homes to see if there might be any different cars parked there. It was too dark by now to see anything more than the street and there was nothing there.

Liza often remarked on how she loved how dark the neighborhood became at night. There were no streetlights and often, when she let the dog out, she would step into the yard and marvel at the innumerable stars that blanketed them. This night she was fearful of the dark.

What was going on? Was anything going on? Where the hell was Ted, and why hadn't he called? Exhausted from her fitful sleep last night she wondered how she was going to get any rest this night. The dog practically clung to her, one more unusual occurrence of the night…so far. Liza abhorred weapons. She insisted only Ted know the combination to the safe he kept his revolver in and that it wasn't written anywhere in the house. Unless she heard from Ted she could not get it. (She doubted she would try to get it even if she could. She felt strongly weapons in a home were usually more dangerous to those who lived there than anyone else, like an interloper.)

One of Mrs. Arkady's Russian maxims came into her head, 'The lid won't blow off if the cap is on tight'. She took that to mean 'keep cool'. Must make more sense in Russian she thought. She wished Mrs. Arkady were there tonight.

She decided to do a few things to the house and go upstairs to try to rest. While she moved things she mulled over the option of leaving the kids in their rooms or bringing them in with her. She took kitchen table chairs and propped them on an angle just under the door knobs of the mud room door, basement door, and front door. She had no idea if they would withstand any effort to open those doors but assumed at least getting by them would be noisy and give her some warning.

She took a large flashlight from a cabinet and turned off the lights. Liza stood at the foot of the stairs and listened. No sounds, no odors. She stood there, motionless, for several minutes. Then she started up the stairs, with the dog closely in tow. On the stairs she stopped and tried to decide if it would be better to leave some lights on downstairs or to keep them off. Liza could certainly navigate the rooms in pitch black if need be. But then she assumed anyone who would be in the house would have a flashlight so darkness might not be an impediment. She decided to go back down the stairs and turn the kitchen light on and leave it on for the night.

Upstairs she looked in on each of the children. They were obviously out for the night. They were good sleepers and were unlikely to be up until about six unless she roused them by carrying them into her room and put them in her bed. If she did that they might be up and down all night. Making decisions about all these things was a challenge for her. Liza realized her self-confidence was faltering, something very unusual for her. Despite still assuming it was very unlikely anything dangerous was going on outside, she also knew she couldn't shake her anxiety after all that had been happening. Smelling cigarette smoke frightened her. Someone had to be smoking nearby.

She admitted to herself she was afraid. Afraid for herself and for the kids. Everything was making her nervous, even the way the dog stuck to her and looked at her. She was angry because she worried about her fears getting the best of her but mostly because she wasn't sure what to do. Ted? She envisioned Ted, shoes off, laying on a fancy hotel bed, maybe drinking a beer from the mini-bar, watching TV, and planning some sight-seeing for the next day. 'He better remember to get some souvenirs for the kids… Why the hell didn't he call?'

The kids would stay in their rooms. A chair from her bathroom was placed at the top of the darkened stairs. She would sleep in her jeans and a sweatshirt. She asked the dog to sleep in the hallway at the top of the stairs but it wasn't going to happen. He was glued to Liza. Before she got into bed she went to the windows that overlooked the back yard and east side of the house and cracked them a few inches. She kneeled down to where one was open and took some deep breaths. Nothing. No odor. She got Ted's baseball bat out of the closet and, fully dressed, got under the blanket only and thought she would try to read. On her night table she saw the latest mystery she was reading. Seeing it made her decide to lean over and pick up the phone to confirm there was a dial tone. Too many crime novels.

She lay in bed, listening… for minutes. A clock ticking, nothing else. She tried to remember which doors creaked when opened. She stayed completely still, eyes looking up but not really seeing anything, trying to concentrate on listening. Would she hear a slowly opening door creak?

There was a night-light in the bathroom and she left the reading lamp on Ted's side of the bed on. She could still read and figured it would be less distracting for her if she were ever able to get some sleep. She opened a seven hundred plus page Infectious Disease textbook knowing from long experience there was nothing better, when tired, to induce sleep. It was after ten and after less than two pages she was out.

When her eyes opened she felt like she had slept only a few minutes. But her mouth and throat were dry and eyes crusted. She looked over at the clock on the night table and it said almost three-thirty. She was astounded she had been asleep that long. She looked down at the dog and it was snoring, as usual. She didn't move and tried to listen and smell for what she fervently hoped wasn't there. Nothing; nothing at all.

Liza felt herself, palpably, relaxing for the first time since the evening. Wherever that cigarette smell came from it wasn't anything to do with her and her family. At first she blamed Ted for all her worrying. Then she stared up at the ceiling and half smiled as she considered what kind of a family protector she was if she could fall deep asleep in the midst of danger. She leaned over to Ted's side of the bed and turned the light off. But she stayed in her clothes. Liza dozed again.

Before she was really sure why she woke up again she immediately thought she smelled smoke. Now the dog was stirring, holding his head up, but making no sounds. Liza looked at the clock. A few minutes after five. She lay back, almost paralyzed, thinking her worst fears again. She felt sweaty and had an awful headache and stiff neck. Once again, for a few moments she lay, motionless, testing her auditory and olfactory senses. The phrase 'where there's smoke there's fire' reverberated in her head.

She got out of bed and kept the light off. She picked up the flashlight and carefully navigated around the still recumbent dog. The dog showed no obvious interest in going with her as she walked into the upstairs hallway. She went into the baby's room, which was on the northeast corner of the house, facing the street. Very slowly and quietly she went to the window and barely parted the curtains.

It was the cusp of first light. Liza surveyed what she could make out of the front yard and then tried to scan the street, starting from the west to the east. Her eyes stopped at the very east end of the road at the dead end and the woods. She stared intently. After a minute or so there must have been a faintly perceptible increase in light and

Liza was convinced she saw something. Nothing was moving. A car? Backed into the woods with only the front end sticking out? That was enough for Liza. Her initial reaction was perplexing to her. At first she was furious and angry; not so fearful. But, as it often will, fear and a cold sweat then also welled up in her. Her heart was racing and her arm holding the curtain was just barely shaking. Before getting the kids she swiftly returned to her bedroom, turned on the light, and picked up the phone. She called the Montpelier Barracks.

"State Police." Just hearing the dispatcher's voice Liza almost felt they had been saved.

"This is Liza Vallan, Trooper Ted Vallan's wife, and I have an emergency. I need a trooper out here *stat*" For a moment Liza worried the medical term for urgent might not mean anything to the dispatcher. "My husband is out of town and I think someone is watching my house."

"Yes, Mrs. Vallan, Trooper Dipscht should be arriving at your place in just a few minutes."

Liza was confused. How could a trooper be on the way before she had called? And Ed *dipshit* Dipscht of all troopers.

"I don't understand." There must have been some desperation in her voice because the dispatcher was very patient in her response.

"Lieutenant Rondell called about ten minutes ago and ordered us to find a trooper to get right over to you to monitor your house. We weren't told why. Did you call your husband?"

"No…Please, have the Trooper come in flashing. Tell him to come in hot. Something's wrong."

"Honey, I'll radio him. And why don't you stay on the line until Trooper Dipscht arrives?" Before Liza could respond there was a loud crash of breaking glass downstairs.

"Oh my God! Someone just smashed a window in the dining room!" Liza wanted to hang up and get the kids, but the dispatcher yelled, firmly, into the phone "His ETA is only one minute. Please stay where you are. Let me tell Ed what's happening."

The dog was barking away at the stairwell, but she heard no sounds from the kids yet. Liza picked up the bat and walked as close as she could get to the hallway with the bat in one hand and the phone in the other, the cord extended as far as it would go. Then she heard the siren. There was sound outside. She went to her east window and looked out. It was light enough now to see two figures running to the woods where the car was. She knew now it was unlikely anyone was in the house.

Liza told the dispatcher she thought two people were running to where she had told her the car was. Ed came in flying, with lights flashing and siren wailing. His spotlight lit up the end of the street. He pulled, head to head, in front of the car and lit it up with his lights. He wisely stayed in his cruiser for five minutes until a local policeman, who had probably been roused out of bed, arrived.

It was mostly light now. Trooper Dipscht carefully got out of his cruiser. There was no response to his amplified command that anyone in the car or the woods come forward with hands in the air. Weapon in hand, local cop right nearby standing with his revolver behind his car door, the Trooper carefully moved forward and inspected the vehicle. Whoever had been in it was gone, likely off into the woods.

* * *

Thirty minutes later the street was filled with all kinds of police vehicles. Even a local volunteer fire truck was there. Neighbors were already busy cleaning up glass and boarding up the broken window.

The immediate denouement of this long night was unremarkable. Ultimately no one in the Vallan family was actually physically harmed, except maybe the dog. Liza had been terrorized and any impact on Ted was yet to be known, but physically they were all okay.

Trooper Ed *dipshit* Dipscht was his usual inappropriate self, smiling away, while picking up the brick in the house that had been thrown through the dining room window and pronouncing it a *New York City* brick. Liza was only briefly glad for his company. He meant well, but it was his personality that he always tried to make light of whatever was happening. Dipscht was cursed with a slight perpetual grin on his face. Even when he did try to be serious it was hard to accept. Today his demeanor and manner were notably annoying. When Lieutenant Rondell arrived Ed happily described the car outside as loaded with candy bar wrappers and empty cigarette packs. Cigarette butts were everywhere, even near the fence in the backyard.

The New York plates and the VIN number from the dark blue sedan were being traced. The crime scene lab team was coming to look for prints and anything else that might be helpful. The Vermont State Police did not have resources to mount a major search in the woods or elsewhere for this type of event. So the local area and woods were briefly searched, but no dogs were brought in. An alert was sent out for two people, but no descriptions could be offered.

Liza and Rondell talked about the events of the last day.

"These assholes were pretty brazen and sloppy going about their business" he said. "But just what they were doing is unclear. At first they were following you and then they sat there all night, stinking up the neighborhood with their smoke. They probably are so used to continually smoking they never even considered the smoke might stand out. But, of course, out here it would. Probably not locals. Sorry to say it, but I suppose they came from New York City. Un-fuckin'-believable!...Oh, sorry Liza.

"But why did they wait all night to do anything? No way they could have known Ted had a run in with some kind of crime boss guy a little before five or so. No, their orders were probably to tail you home and then only to frighten you early in the morning. They probably planned to throw the brick and then drive off. How they figured out who you were, to be able to initiate following you, is another concern. In some ways, Liza, that worries me more than what happened here last night."

"I get it Lieutenant."

The kids had slept fine all night. They were parked in front of the TV for the time being. Liza was in no condition to go to the hospital for weekend rounds. A trooper was stationed outside and was to stay at least until Ted got home.

The next day Rutland police called the Barracks to report an officer checked with the folks at the train station and they remembered selling a ticket to New York City the evening before to a scruffy appearing man, likely in his forties or early fifties, wearing *city shoes* and smelling like cigarettes. A day later a farmer called after hearing there had been a home invasion in Richmond. He told of picking up a hitchhiker the day of the incident just south of Bristol, a good fifteen to twenty miles from Richmond. He said the man was wearing *city shoes* and offered him twenty dollars to take him to Rutland. Both the farmer and the train agent remarked on the wad of bills he was flaunting.

There was never any news about a second person. But the car was teeming with prints and further information was likely coming. The car, not surprisingly, was stolen, as were the plates. The car was registered in Long Island City, New York, and the plates were from a vehicle registered in Brooklyn.

The crime lab sorted out the prints and concluded they came from two people. The prints were express mailed to New York City. The day after that there was a call to Montpelier from NYPD that only one of the prints was a hit. The match was a fellow with a string of aliases and a record to match. Armed assault and robbery were on the list. His sheet suggested he had spent more time in jail than out since he was a kid. He was a known low level worker for one or two of the established mobs in the area.

Someone had been so sure both men were from New York that person never considered running prints in Montpelier. The unidentified prints were shipped back to Vermont where they were run through the state database and there was a match. In the meantime, that guy, who turned out to have a Vermont record was, by then, long gone from his last known address. At least this finding better explained why only one of the criminals was tracked to a way back to the City.

Finding the local hood became a priority for the State Police. Rondell wanted him for his criminal acts, but just as much for his desire to find the connection to a New York mob that allowed them to find and threaten a trooper's family in Vermont.

* * *

The ride back to Vermont was very unpleasant. He hadn't slept in over twenty-four hours and was exhausted. Ted couldn't shake thinking most of what he had done either ended up causing more trouble or about half of the things he did wound up wrong. Even his decision to put off calling Liza until later in the morning so he wouldn't disturb the family too early had back-fired.

He had stopped for coffee on the New York Thruway about seven and called home and found out what had happened. Liza was furious with him; he got that for sure. But he actually wasn't entirely clear why she was so angry with him and that made him more unhappy. She didn't even know about the whole business with Kendra. No one did. He wasn't at all sure whether he was going to tell Liza; ever. Feeling like a fuck-up was unusual for him. He was dismayed that in settings requiring quick decisions about action he had often done things that didn't work out well, especially for other people.

His flat, almost subservient, response during his interaction with Forlenza also bothered him even though he figured the way he had handled that brief face to face with the presumed crime boss was correct. Ted took the opportunity of the long ride home to review the entire case and try to evaluate and weigh what he knew. But each time anything related to Forlenza came up he was distracted.

Every time he thought of that smug face on Forlenza and his impassive manner while he threatened Ted, and then considered the potential of risk to his family, his own wife and kids, he turned beet red and seethed with anger. Going after a trooper like that and, unbelievably, going after a trooper's family, was something he thought could happen only in a movie or on TV. How brazen could anyone be?

Ted's anger and exhaustion led him to aggressively imagine what he would or could do to the man who threatened his family. He desperately wanted to grab him and smash his face hard into something. Provoked only hours before, he was so consumed by his anger he wasn't sure if he would ever be able to drop his own vendetta against that man. Whatever he did he knew he would never make that ass-hole's family a part of it; it was between just the two of them. After he made the stop on the Thruway and found out what had happened at his home, his anger welled up again and hate filled his head.

Just trying to picture what Liza had gone through that night practically overwhelmed him. In the State Police there was a kind of sick joke about hoping not to wind up as a name on a road sign, memorialized by a stretch of highway. He, like the others, accepted that possibility. But his family? For them to be in danger or, even worse, harmed because of police work, was unimaginable.

The guilt he felt was difficult for him to sort out. Was some of all this his fault? How? Had he gone beyond any reasonable boundaries of police work? It was difficult for Ted not to moralize even his only fleeting attraction and temptation with Kendra as a kind of imagined payback for which his family had suffered. Whatever he had done so far in this case was impacted by terrible consequences for his family and maybe even for Kendra also. What had he done wrong other than, just for a few minutes, considered infidelity? He had stopped himself. Nothing really happened. But he felt guilt and thought the threat to his family was punishment for his sin.

He wondered if his father felt guilty for *his* attempted infidelity and its consequences?

Then Ted surprised himself and found himself rejecting some of the *retribution for sin* idea. Previously, Ted had lived an image allowing him to distance himself from much of what he saw in the world around him. Drafted into the army when he finished high school he was sent to train as an MP. There he learned to pull one man's dick out of another. He saw many levels of behavior he never dreamed could exist. As a trooper he, routinely, had to intercede in terribly sad and upsetting family situations. And he once found a teenage prostitute dead with a needle in her arm. But he hadn't been involved in a case like this before, with so many levels of complexities that would no longer allow him to be dispassionate about his work and his own life.

Relying on his past attitudes and even the remaining few glowing embers of having been an eagle scout weren't going to hack it anymore. Ted was changing as his world was changing. You do the best you can in a far from perfect world. Beating up on himself wasn't going to solve anything in his personal or professional life. After all he and, as best Ted knew, his fucking asshole father also, may have lusted in their minds but never actually completely acted on their opportunities.

Again his thoughts drifted to ruminating about Forlenza who provided a more acceptable focus for his frustrations and anger.

*   *   *

DAY 12 SATURDAY, OCTOBER 23

Homecoming was anything but pleasant. He would be looked at more like a returning prodigal son than someone who was successful at the task he set out to accomplish. He spoke over the radio with Rondell one last time for the day about forty minutes before he arrived home. They agreed to meet at the Barracks Sunday morning and spend as much time as it took to update each other and fit as many pieces as possible of the several puzzles together. Ted had a lot to share but he wasn't looking forward to the session given all the recent events in both Vermont and New York.

The kids didn't understand all the excitement and they were a little wild. Around ten his sister, Ellen, showed up, popped the kids in her car, and said she'd bring them back around four. Totally worn out and tense, both Ted and Liza became rather emotional in response to Ellen's thoughtfulness. They reacted as though they had been given an extraordinary gift of love. Ellen *poofed* them off. All business, like all the Vallan women.

It annoyed Ted when he realized the cruiser parked at the end of his road was apparently going to stay there for a while. He didn't need that. He figured the guy sitting there was probably happy to be getting some overtime. He would go out to chat with him if he was still there later but didn't feel like chatting with anyone just then.

Throughout the day Ted and Liza did not speak much. Once the kids were gone she took a shower and fell asleep on the bed. Ted sat on the sofa and then slid his body down on it, legs stretched out straight to the floor and dozed, on and off, for an hour. A couple used to being tired most of the time had managed to take exhaustion to an even higher level.

There was a formality to their interactions and it was obvious all was not right. Liza was anxious and angry. She had been collecting terrifying experiences; something all too unique for her. Ted interpreted her mood completely as a response to his actions. Some which she knew about but there were still some he knew she could not know about. He projected a palpable guilt throughout the day. He kept apologizing and aggressively empathized about the terrible day she just had.

Initially, it all made sense to Liza, and she appreciated the extent of his concern and their shared upset. She knew Ted took his job seriously and was doing it to the best of his ability. She knew what had happened to them last night was extraordinary in law enforcement. There were no easy answers for the past twenty-four hours, for both of them, she presumed. They ate something and sat around most of the day. Ted was pleased to notice the cruiser was gone around three.

During the afternoon Liza told Ted her mother, Kay, was coming on Sunday from Rhode Island to stay for a few days. It seemed anyone who heard about Liza's nightmare wanted to do something to try to offer support. Liza was fine with it but guessed Ted wouldn't be especially happy. She suspected Ted would see her visit as punitive in some ways.

Liza was right, but Ted was in no position to say anything but 'fine'. Ted liked Kay Hart well enough. But more and more her presence troubled him because he, increasingly, sensed the old adage he had been told at his bachelor party might be coming true. They joked 'you marry your mother-in-law'. Kay was okay but she wasn't what

Liza was when they married. He was dismayed when he saw how much alike their mannerisms and attitudes were now that they had kids.

Some sense of normality resumed when the kids returned. Ted went out to get pizza and a movie and they all watched a really dumb dog movie on the VCR. Liza fell asleep. After the kids were down Liza was awake again and Ted was too keyed up to sleep. With the night and time to think about everything without any tension Liza began to feel a subtle change in her reaction to Ted's continuing self-deprecating and apologetic behavior. She wondered why he continued this way so persistently?

"Ted?" They were Ted and Liza right now, not 'babe'. "I know you're feeling bad about what happened yesterday and I know none of it is really your fault. I get it. Why do you keep telling me how badly you feel about it, even tonight? Is there other stuff out there that I don't know about that's upsetting you?"

Ted was exhausted, furious at Forlenza, confused, and feeling guilty as hell. It was not the best time for talking through personal issues with Liza, much less even beginning to have an idea of thinking of a plan. He truly wasn't sure how he wanted to answer her question. He hadn't even considered when, if ever, they might have a discussion about the personal parts of his New York trip. Now, with her comment, he felt Liza could see right through him. Had exposed him. At the same time he had true empathy for what she had gone through and, as odd experiences can do, felt a very deep love for his wife and family. Again his guilt surfaced. Maybe he would feel better after it came out and was done. That ruled the day. In reality, maybe it would have been better if he had delayed until they each were rested and in better moods.

"Liza, a whole lot happened in the short time I was in New York. I learned a lot about the case. But, instead of solving it, I think I may bear some responsibility for the death, homicide, of a woman who was only peripherally involved. And my own life was also at risk again, I think."

Of all that, Ted felt even more exposed when Liza chose, in her response, only to react to him bringing up Kendra. "How were you involved with a woman's death? Who was she?"

And so Ted, in a flat monotone, told Liza about how he came upon Kendra Akers, or whatever her real name was, and wound up in her apartment only the night before; about twenty-four hours ago. He described her as an attractive, slightly older, sometime companion to his John Doe. He looked down, not at Liza, and told her he had gotten a little drunk sitting with this woman and she came on to him.

"In her apartment?" Liza stated more than questioned. She wanted to be sure of the facts. Her eyes were wide open but she was trying to remain neutral in her reaction.

"Yes."

"Well, Ted, so what are you trying to tell me or not tell me? What did you and this woman do?"

"Well, that's the thing. I don't know how to say it, but I caught myself. When I realized what was happening I stood up and she closed her robe." Bad last sentence, he thought. "So, Liza, nothing happened. I had gotten confused because I guess I let myself get a little drunk. She wanted information from me, just like from my father."

"*YOUR FATHER?*"

Ted flushed. "Yeah. It's a very long story. I'm not allowed to speak with my dad about what he did yet, but he did something crazy about my case and this Kendra came to Burlington to meet with him. I guess they were getting close to having sex when he started to have his heart attack."

Liza wasn't planning to wait for any more details. She was sitting bolt upright. She shouted: "I'm worrying about being watched when I go for a run, and I began to worry about the kids. I've been downright frightened ever since you made me poke around for some stupid stones in the creepy autopsy room. Then last night I might as well have been in a *Friday the 13th* sequel. And all this time you and your fabulous father have been trying to diddle some middle-aged woman in Vermont and New York City. That is something Ted."

"Liza, you've got it all screwed up. Wha…"

"See! That's it! It's all about screwing, isn't it Ted?"

"Liza I knew this was never going to go well whenever it came out. I guess this might not have been a great time to tell you since we are both so out of sorts. But the thing is I always knew, deep down, I would eventually tell you. I love you too much to want to have secrets between us. I feel awful for what almost happened. But it didn't. The whole two days became overwhelming. I let someone get me drunk, but we never did anything at all. And now she's dead, maybe because I helped her killers find her."

Ted thought he probably had done the right thing by responding honestly to Liza's assumption some odd things happened in New York. He decided when he mentioned his father's connection to Kendra was when it got out of hand. He assumed he could explain more about his trip over the next few days. No, Liza's response suggested tonight was not the best night for this discussion.

"Ted, if my mother wasn't coming tomorrow you'd for sure be sleeping in Mrs. Arkady's room for the foreseeable future." Sarcastically: "Glad to have you home. Good night."

* * *

DAYS 14 – 17
MONDAY – THURSDAY, OCTOBER 25, 26, 27, 28

The week passed slowly. It seemed interminable to Ted. All week he was plagued by two great worries. First, he was still unable to put aside his anger and obsession with that Forlenza because of Forlenza's threat to his family. Some of his worry was even why he continued to be so acutely haunted by that man and his actions. No doubt about it, just a thought about any part of what he held Forlenza responsible for made him tense; set off a tightness and dryness in his throat.

As details about the case dribbled in Ted considered whether Forlenza ever finally got what he was after from this mess? Clearly the job had been botched at least once but maybe several times. Why else were people killed over some stones, probably fakes besides? He wondered if knowing they were fakes would have made any difference to any of the murderous idiots involved. And even if he got fifteen of the stones back, did Forlenza know their value had plummeted without the sixteenth? If he got a few or even a lot of the $1000 bills Ted assumed were traded for the stones you would think he would have at least stopped killing people, like Kendra and the diener, and punted on the stones.

As upset as he remained about Forlenza, this week he began to recognize a new, second, thought was beginning to greatly upset him. This was a new worry and he was aware it could become a pressing and ultimately consuming fear also: He was terrified his case had quickly gone cold.

Practically the entire week he was at his desk. That did not seem like the way to do a homicide investigation. Nothing really new had turned up since the weekend he returned from New York. He had a palpable sense the NYPD never had any great interest in any of this and he barely heard from them all week.

His contacts with people in New York on Wednesday (an assistant Borough DA) and Thursday (a 40th precinct detective) made him worry he had fallen into a hole like that Alice. The New York City law and legal systems were a mess, he thought. Dealing with them had become closer to a fiasco than anything he could have imagined. After two days of trying he had finally obtained those phone numbers, actually through Janice Delario, for the precinct and the prosecutor's office in the Bronx (who knew?) where Kendra Akers was murdered and Chris Smithers was shot. Neither interaction went well.

The prosecutor's office for the Bronx gave him a name and number to call. No one asked him exactly what he was after. It wasn't clear to him why that name was given to him. This assistant DA was a woman, Angela Parsimone. Ted, initially, reacted to her name with some excitement. As he dialed her number he had an imaginary conversation in his head where he told her his wife was also a professional, to imply how neat it was women were achieving success in so many areas. She answered the phone:

"Hello." And then a pause. Ted started to say a cheerful hello.

"You have reached the desk of Angela Parsimone, Assistant Deputy District Attorney for Bronx Borough, New York City, State of New York." Another pause.

"I am on another call or away from my desk. This week, October twenty-fifth to the twenty-ninth, I will definitely be out of the office on" pause again, "Monday, the twenty-fifth, eight a.m. until noon; Tuesday, the twenty-sixth, eight a.m. to nine-thirty, and from one p.m. to three p.m.; on Wednesday, the twenty-seventh, I will be in court all day…."

My God, she was going on forever. She spit it out like she was
a machine and she sounded, literally, like she was ten years old.
When she finally finished mapping out her office availability for the
week, she ended with:

"Of course my schedule may change. You can try this number from
time to time. If this is an emergency or for immediate assistance
please call 222-555-0198."

So much for kindred souls. This lady was not Liza. Pride misleads.
It was already Wednesday. She only updated her message weekly.

There was no mechanism to leave a message. So he had to call back
and listen to the entire fucking message again to get the 'immediate
assistance' number and then call it. He was glad he called. 'All day
in court' turned out to be just the morning. Attorney Parsimone
was out to lunch and he was advised to call back around two.

He had an hour so he put in a call to the 40th precinct, in the
Bronx, to try to get hooked up with a detective who could give
him information about the arrested man and Kendra's murder
investigation. Everyone was pleasant, but he was bounced from
place to place and had to give a synopsis of his case to three
different people before he thought he found someone finally taking
ownership of his call. The detective who was handling at least the
murder was in court and could not be contacted. The fellow on the
phone assured Ted he had written down *the particulars* and would
be sure to have Detective Timothy Mangione call him; probably
first thing in the morning.

With the enforced break until he could call the DA back he reached
into a bag he brought on Monday with five big red apples in it.
Much better idea than a candy bar. But, sitting at his desk eating,
there was time for his mind to wander. Concentrating that day on
the action in New York he unhappily thought about Smithers. He
knew he should get in touch with him and find out how he was
doing. His reflection included his awareness Smithers might not be
interested in talking to him.

When he saw him off in the ambulance Smithers barely acknowledged Ted's presence. Ted told him he would come to see him the next day. That was before his confrontation with Forlenza when everything changed. The next day he was in Vermont. And now a bunch of days had passed and Ted had made no effort to find him or find out how he was doing. His few encounters with Smithers still stood out quite clearly in his memory. What an unbelievable story. And he knew from Smither's point of view Ted had fucked everything up, quite royally. Eventually he would have to track him down. For now, he really wasn't sure what he would say to him if they talked.

This time when he called Angela Parsimone she answered on the first ring.

"Parsimone, Bronx DA's office." Small voice; no nonsense. Ted identified himself and offered a brief introduction to the cases he was concerned about. He told her he called because he really wanted to know if the man he knew as Glenn, or *Glenny*, Miller was going to be prosecuted for the murder of Kendra Akers and the shooting of Chris Smithers. He wasn't sure why but he decided to tell her, in some detail, about his odd car ride in the Bronx and wanted whatever information she had about his own attempted kidnapping. He, briefly, mentioned something about the mysterious Forlenza, a name Parsimone said meant nothing to her.

To her credit, Attorney Parsimone's initial reaction to Ted's story was to ask him to hold on while she looked to see if there were files she could find. He didn't know if that meant she knew about the case, or cases, or not. After quite some time she returned to the phone. She stayed all business.

"So, now what is it you want to know about the investigation of the homicide of one Kendra Akers, Trooper Vallan?"

'Well, basically, its status and if that fellow, believe he might be called Glenn Miller, is considered a suspect in her homicide."

"I'm looking at the report we have filed under that woman's name and I do see your name noted in it. Attached to it is another name, Sarah Javonivich, from her prints, and a copy of the rap sheet for those prints. Not much else here. There's an autopsy… Oh, yes, and there is also a page for someone else. Let me look. Says nothing about any Glenn Miller, but there is a mug of a middle-aged man with a kind of fat face. His attached prints carry the name Sidney Danilio. Very lengthy sheet for him.

"Trooper Vallan, I'd have to say the file suggests a connection has been made but that's about it. Let me go back to the files and see if there's anything else about Danilio."

Ted wrote everything down. Nothing really surprising so far. It was interesting, in a sick sort of way, it seemed like they had so many homicides down there a capital case was just another file in the system; unknown and unfollowed, as best he could tell.

She came back on the phone, "Trooper Vallan there has been some activity for this Danilio. Just perusing the file to see the latest. I see here there's a petition from a lawyer for his release from detention; dated Monday, the twenty-fifth. Let's see…. He must be at Riker's. Preliminary judgment indicates that, pending a requested urgent report from his probation officer, he can be released on $2000 cash bail on Friday, the twenty-ninth. He has quite a long record."

"So he's appeared before a judge and a DA and the police have testified about the cases?"

"Not necessarily. The caseload is so extreme some petitions are handled at a lower level."

Here Ted was a little at a loss. He wasn't sure how to formally address the attorney. He had heard of a new way to refer more formally to any woman as 'Ms.' but did not want to offend. She sounded so young he decided to try 'Miss'.

"Miss Parsimone, if a man is on parole and is found with a pistol and has shot someone how can he be allowed out on bail?"

"There is nothing here that directly ties Mr. Danilio to a weapon at the murder scene or to the murder victim."

"But Miss Parsimone, he shot a cop. He was arrested while running away from the murder site and shot the officer after he was tackled."

"Really." It was an earnest response. "I see nothing about that here. You say he actually shot a police officer? Is he part of the 40th precinct?"

Now Ted was at a loss, again. It was never clear exactly what Smither's relationship to the NYPD force was. But there sure was a shooting. He was there.

"No, not the 40th. Actually you could say he's in …er, *logistics* or *transportation* maybe"

She latched onto the latter. "Oh, so he's a Transit cop, is that it?"

Ted wasn't entirely sure what that meant but it seemed close enough. "Yeah, I think so."

"So it sounds like there is something missing here, doesn't it? You know, I can't just put a hold on a pending judgment, even what we have here, without better evidence to justify canceling it. This Danilio needs to be interviewed and you, Trooper, need to clarify with the 40th the facts about this shooting you're telling me about.

"Do you know how difficult it will be to arrange to get out to Riker's and for this man's lawyer, and probably his probation officer, to be there? I don't like that place. It literally takes all day to get in and out of there. And, frankly, they treat me like crap there."

Ted had never envisioned this discussion turning out this way. He was reminded of his interview with Fred Graham. One more time he was at a loss, this time how any of this was his problem.

"Miss Parsimone, I have no doubt if you look through that file on Sidney Danilio you will see he's forfeited bail before and has a history of violating parole. How in the world could he have tried to kidnap and harm me, be present at a murder, verbally spit into a phone at me while kidnapping the person found murdered, and finally shoot an officer as he was arrested and be eligible for bail? How can that be even considered?"

She didn't miss a beat and her voice began to suggest she was getting tired of the discussion.

"Look, Trooper Vallan, defense lawyers can be very well financed and aggressive. The State's side of the judicial system can't respond quickly to every petition, and defendants have rights, you know. You want to stop this bail you get someone from the 40th to go to Riker's with you, talk to Danilio, even you just ID him, and I'm sure you can have them continue to detain him. Okay?"

Enough. He should have found Detective Mangione first and reviewed everything before he looked for a DA.

"Thank you for your time, Miss Parsimone. Please let me give you my information so you can contact me if anything more comes up or if you have any questions for me."

"That's fine Trooper. I'm sorry you are uncomfortable interacting with a female DA. And, by the way, I don't know how it's done in Vermont but here we address all women as Ms… Goodbye."

* * *

Some of what he got from the assistant DA helped him get started with 40th precinct Detective Timothy Mangione when Mangione called him on Thursday morning as promised. Ted noted a number of the people he was making contact with had names with both Irish and Italian origins. He guessed that was part of why New York was known as a melting pot. Foremost on Ted's mind was to find out why the DA had nothing about Smithers.

"Smithers? I got nothing on a Smithers. The guy was shot, best I know, he called himself Smith. You may not remember, but I was still in the building when the shot went off down the street. A couple of us ran down there where you and that Danilio were wrestling on the ground. We pulled you two and the black guy apart and arrested Danilio. It was morning by then. I tied up a few more things and went home to hit the hay. Later that day, on my way in for my shift, I stopped at Lincoln hospital to talk to the black guy. He was gone.

"Not much info on him. Name he gave was Smith. But in the ambulance he gave someone an insurance card and so they told me he had something to do with NYPD, and the black guy I talked to in hospital security gave me a wink and said everything was taken care of.

"I come across some guys like that before. They got secrets they don't want disturbed. I did six years in the navy and there even were guys who actually had a lady, even wives, in every port. You know what I mean? Man, some of them had to work really hard to keep track of everything. It was real effort. For those guys the continuing need for deception became a job in itself. You know what I mean? Imagine. Who knows what this guy's story is?

"Bullet passed through his calf injuring no vital structures and he was never officially admitted. He was outta there after a few hours." Detective Mangione paused, then he continued on, but his tone turned harsh and nasty.

"Of course, I tracked the nigger down, just so he'd know we knew about him, so if we ever need him he's stuck." Then pleasant again. "Sure wanted to keep himself out of anything and everything to do with that night. So we played along and helped make it like it never happened. Even heard something about the guy managing to get time off pay while still doing some shift work. Guy who knows the system, that's for sure."

With a firm voice, asking a question but really telling him like it was going to be: "Do you have a problem with that Trooper? Any of this gonna be something for you?"

Son of a bitch. Smithers had an angle on everything. He probably figured it all out while in the ambulance. At first, as Mangione unfolded the strange story, it gave Ted a good feeling knowing Smithers was okay. Then he realized the disappearance of any trace of him being shot was a disaster for making a case against Danilio. He spoke out loud: "Son of a bitch!"

"Yeah, you could say that." Mangione replied, although he was referring to the other situation.

Ted had been feeling badly assuming he screwed Smithers by upsetting his complicated and delicately balanced life. The reality was Smithers, naturally calling himself a Smith, had screwed Ted.

Any case against Danilio was fading fast. The chance of using Danilio to get to Forlenza would be gone with the loss of Danilio. Ted knew Kendra died from strangulation. She was beaten, but never shot. Detective Mangione described, again, the scene of SWAT bursting into the room Kendra was in, with two or more of the thugs running out back hallways like rats surprised when the lights go on. Among a whole slew of bullets from SWAT weapons only two of the slugs found in the walls were assumed to be rounds shot by those guys as they ran out. Unclear if any bad guy was hit. Ballistics from the bullets in the wall didn't match the weapon they took from Danilio.

Ted sighed, audibly, then hoped Mangione hadn't heard him. He was discouraged. That night a woman he had been talking with only hours before was murdered. Quite alive before then. She was dead now and no one was going to be held accountable. He fretted, fleetingly, about what he might have done, could have done, so it didn't turn out that way. Turning his thoughts to Forlenza had become his more accepted method for diverting himself from such self-incriminating worries.

"Detective Mangione, what about the crime boss, Forlenza, I told your Lieutenant about that night? You know I ran into him as I was leaving the scene and the fucker threatened my family in Vermont. He actually had some shitheads throw a brick through a window at my home while my family was in there the same night the lady was murdered."

"Oh my. No…No that name means nothing to me. But, you know, we got all kinds of wop families doing what they call *organized crime* up here. Whole set-up that night very consistent with their modus."

This Mangione appeared to be an equal opportunity disparager of race and ethnicity.

"You want to pin down that shit or other mobs: wops, the chinks, spics, or whoever, you got to talk with the jerks in the Organized Crime Task Force. lotsa different cops, and feds too."

Mangione hadn't missed the significance of the threat to Ted's family. "Boy, you mean that shit actually went through the effort to find and threaten your personal family way up there in Vermont? Man, I get it. You're more than pissed. And you should be. I get yelled at and threatened a lot but nothing, no nothing, remotely like that has ever happened to me or any of the guys that I ever heard.

"You definitely run into a weird one. You should talk to those idiots in Organized Crime, but I don't think they ever do anything much. They'll tell you they're monitoring this an that but you hardly ever hear of them taking any action. Some of them come around every now and then an ask us some questions. Guess they do lots of paperwork. They're rats, putting in their time waiting for their pensions."

The last thing Ted needed just now, as he suspected any case against any of these people was dissolving down the drain, was a reminder it was an almost unique situation for his, a law officer's family, to have been physically threatened during a criminal investigation. He was supposed to take the threat personally and he certainly did. The obvious corollary to the threat was he was impotent to stop it. Some of that was coming more true than he ever would have believed.

The harsh reality was there probably never was any good reason for Forlenza to threaten him like that because he must have known there really wasn't anything Ted, or anyone else, was going to be able to do to him. Those criminals worked a tried and true system they had honed over a long, long time. Those assholes got away with most everything they did. This Forlenza must be something else. Just crazy with his sense of his power to have done that to him. Or maybe really just crazy. But it was looking like he would get away with it all: murder, threatening Ted's family; every fucking part of it.

Every law enforcement shithead he ran into who heard his personal story was truly pissed and shared Ted's anger. But who was going to do anything about it? No one, apparently; not from Vermont to the NYPD or probably even the feds. Some verbal outrage and then sympathy. But that's it. No action.

Then again, Ted went over in his mind what little Forlenza may have gotten out of all this. If he had some or a lot of $1000 bills why was he still at it? The only thing Forlenza said in that alley which really made any sense were his words disparaging ever getting involved in the 'fucking shit' deal.

Or, maybe he was crazy. When that deal blew up he got that much crazier. Ted fervently hoped the shit lost on that deal. Might not have cost him money but, hopefully, he lost what he hoped to get anyway; possibly the only, very small, consolation Ted had for satisfaction. It wasn't much. No, probably not anywhere near enough.

The pause in his conversation with Mangione had gone on ridiculously long while Ted's brain played through all this. Mangione wondered if Ted was still on the line.

"Hey Vallan, you still there?"

"Oh, I'm sorry Detective, I was thinking things over."

"We done here?"

Ted was trying to think if he had any options. He just wasn't ready to have all this explode on him for good. He wasn't ready to let it go.

"Listen, Detective Mangione, I have a favor to ask of you."

Mangione sighed and his tone was flat and non-committal. "What you want Troooper?"

"Detective, I've got to go over all this with my superiors and some other folks in enforcement. All I'm ever going to ask you for, I think, is only this one favor."

Still non-committal. "What is it?"

That Danilio is probably going to get out on bail tomorrow if his probation officer doesn't fight it. Once he's out I doubt I'll ever find him again. While I work all this out I'd like you to make sure he stays in jail for at least another four to six weeks. That's the time I need right now."

Grave, low tone: "You mean you want him dead, Vallan?"

"Wha….?"

Laughing now. "That old, fat fuck stays on that rock any length of time he'll get killed for cigarettes… Just kidding, Vallan. That's no problem. I got all the sheets here. I'll call his probation group and they sure won't give a shit us asking to keep him. And I'll call

Rikers so's they don't let him go. But Vallan, I got to put your name on this, so when his lawyer goes ape-shit with the DA the DA may come running to you. Got it?"

"Sure... Hey Detective?" Because of the way he spoke about him Ted was about to ask Mangione if he actually knew Danilio. Then he decided it probably didn't make any difference so he dropped it. "Yeah, that's great. I'm fine with that and I really appreciate this." When he told Mangione he owed him one he knew, with this guy, he really did.

They ended the call and he tried not to get stuck thinking about how that assistant DA was going to react to getting caught in the middle of all this when Danilio's lawyer raised a fuss about his delayed release. He probably should alert her but simply did not want to go another round with her.

*   *   *

DAY 18 FRIDAY, OCTOBER 29

He was learning a little more about the dead diener, but not much. BPD wanted more from Ted, but he was holding back. How was his investigation going to continue? Would Rondell let him continue to work full time on it? Would the force give his case to someone else? It was getting very unsettling. He had been over all he had a hundred times this week. Too much time with too little to show for it, especially this week.

And what had he actually accomplished the week before either? Sure, he had been incredibly busy, everything was active and, certainly, a lot happened. Then he realized he was drifting again into self-recrimination. Could his actions really have contributed to some of the awful things that happened? Immediately, he tried to shake off those thoughts. Nothing helpful would come from dwelling on them. His pager went off. Liza wanted him to call her.

The operator at the hospital paging service came back on the line, "Dr. Vallan has been paged. Please remain on the line." Sixty seconds passed. "Here is Dr. Vallan."

"Hi Ted, thanks for calling me right back. You busy? Got a minute?"

Ted had more than a minute. "Sure Liza. Just sitting at the Barracks working on the meeting set for Monday morning with the

Lieutenant, and who knows who else, to talk about my case." His tone was flat.

"Oh, sorry…well, sort of sorry that everything has died down since last week."

"I have a feeling that meeting is going to be trouble."

"Well, I thought I should call you because something a little strange happened at the hospital just a short while ago. You remember that patient I had two weeks ago, just as you got called for your case?" She assumed his response and continued talking. "Well, today is my last day on the ID service. I was supposed to talk about that case two weeks ago at the Rheumatology conference. After she died the case discussion was moved to today so more of the results from the autopsy would be available."

Ted knew only one significant thing about the one o'clock medical conferences. Liza had told him the meetings often were a good place to go and sit behind someone tall. When the lights went out for slides to be shown many house staff routinely closed their eyes and took short after lunch naps.

"I went to the room a little early since I had to present for ID. There were only a few people already there. I sat near the front since I was going to have to speak. Don't know if you noticed I was working extra hard this week to prepare.

"I was sitting there, studying my papers, and you know when you get a feeling that someone's looking at you? I looked up across the aisle in the middle of the room and on the other side there was a man who quickly averted his eyes when I looked over. He was an older man, kind of fat, balding, with a gray moustache. He was sitting in the second row.

"The Chief of Rheum came in and placed some papers on the lectern and then walked over to that man. Dr. Wyley had a smile on his face and they greeted each other, shaking hands, like they were friends. I couldn't hear much but I thought I heard Dr. Wiley call him 'Franz'. Thing is, the whole time, I kept seeing that man look over at me. The expression on his face was grim.

"I presented my part of the case and sat down. I should still be there but I was uncomfortable about that guy. Then I thought I remembered you had mentioned one of the people at that lake you were talking about is a doctor. And I thought you might have mentioned a name like 'Franz'. So I staged a coughing fit so I could get up and leave and I knew, even if that man had any interest in me, he would not be able get up to follow me in the middle of the conference. Now I'm calling you. It's probably nothing; still some nerves from last week."

For a few seconds Ted thought about it. "No. No Lize. No, this may be something." Dr. Gruber had stubbornly stayed very high on his list of who at the lake might be involved in the homicide of Sammy 'Harry James' Paskovich. If he was a known visitor in Burlington what might that mean for some of the other things that had happened? And why would he be looking at Liza? What connection could the man at the conference, especially if it was Dr. Gruber, possibly have with Liza?

"Listen Liza. I'm going to come over there, now. Tell whoever you are working with you have to be with someone or a few people for the entire afternoon. I'm sorry, I know it sounds awkward, but I don't want you to be alone for the rest of the day. Go to the library or something. Don't go to your car or drive home until you talk to me. Do you understand? Okay?"

"Well I think you might be over reacting, maybe because of last week, but I'll stay in a crowd until I hear from you."

"How can I track down Dr. Wyley? I need to speak with him as soon as I get to Burlington."

Liza told him to page the Rheum Chief. She said he had at least two offices; one in the hospital, one in the university faculty practice building across the street and, maybe, still another one in one of the research lab buildings.

It was just two then and possible the conference was still going on or, more importantly, this Dr. Wyley and whoever the man was who had attracted Liza's concern were still in the same room. So Ted walked over to the small lunch room and bought a few candy bars from the vending machine. Then he walked to the corridor where the Lieutenant's office was and seeing his door open walked to his doorway. He told the Lieutenant some possibly important information had come up and he was going to Burlington.

What he wanted from the Lieutenant was a rough timeline of where Ted might find him to discuss things if he found something he might need to act on quickly. Lieutenant Rondell looked interested but didn't ask any questions. He did make a point of letting Ted know he expected to be in his office until after six this evening. Ted faux saluted with candy bar in hand and quickly went to his desk and called the hospital paging service.

Dr. Wyley came on the line and was, initially, quite pleasant. Ted didn't mean to upset him or put him on his guard but that happened and his tone was much more cautious after Ted identified himself and rather quickly asked the Doctor if he was alone or in an area where there was anyone else around. The Doctor had no idea why Ted had such a query so it created some alarm. He said he was alone in a ward charting room. Ted told him it was urgent police business he meet with him as soon as possible. He was leaving Montpelier momentarily and would arrive in Burlington in about forty minutes.

Ted suggested they meet in the Doctor's clinic office, not at the hospital. Dr. Wyley almost certainly knew he had little choice in the matter and said he would be there. He sounded frightened. Ted wished he could put him at ease but he thought it best to say nothing until they met in person. Dr. Wyley also probably raised an eyebrow when Ted said he would meet him in forty minutes. The drive from Montpelier to Burlington was usually about an hour, on a good day.

Ted had some ability, especially on certain roads, to shorten his travelling time. He put his lights on and stayed in the passing lane on the interstate the entire trip, maintaining eighty to eighty-five the whole trip.

He arrived at Dr. Wyle's office around three. The Doctor had emotionally regrouped and probably decided it was best to be affable with the trooper. As they shook hands and each sat down Dr. Wyley recited a short litany about Liza Ted had almost come to expect whenever he was in contact with anyone involved in the residency program.

"Trooper Vallan, after you called I remembered you are married to Liza Vallan, one of our residents. Well I guess I don't have to tell you she is a remarkable woman who has greatly impressed us all. How she has managed…I guess I should say how you both have managed so she is so attentive to her training responsibilities while raising a young family is just remarkable. Many doctors are still quite biased against having women in medicine but Liza has started dismantling some of those barriers for other women to come. And I'm sure they will be coming." Ted had heard variations of this ever since Liza was in medical school so he had learned to be patient during the exercise and then signal his agreement and appreciation for the kind words.

He wanted to feel out the Doctor about the man Liza had noticed but planned to do it in a way so he, hopefully, would be able to exclude Dr. Wyley from any suspicion, if the man in the room did turn out to be one of the case's persons of interest.

"Doctor, I'm sorry to have been so uninformative on the phone before but it was necessary I speak to you in person, privately, about a major criminal case in the state." The Doctor's face returned to one of confusion. "I need to ask you some questions about a person you may know. Regardless of whether you know this person or not it is essential you not speak with the person we are about to talk about or, for that matter, anyone else, even your own family members, about any of this. If, at any time while we are speaking, you feel you can't abide by that then you must tell me."

"No. I mean yes, Trooper Vallan. I will speak up if I'm not comfortable with what you ask me."

"Doctor, there was an older man at the one o'clock conference today who is not one of the residents or students. I believe he was sitting very close to the front of the room." Ted wanted to see what the doctor might volunteer rather than remind him he had greeted that individual. "Do you have any idea who that man is?"

It looked like the Doctor wanted to relax and his facial expression answered yes to the question but he still was a little wary. "I do know that man. He is a retired physician who frequently comes to our specialty conference. His name is Franz Gruber; a very sweet fellow."

Ted had to contain his reaction and tried to only slowly re-settle himself in his chair. He already knew Liza obviously had been right when she said she thought she was being watched and followed last week. The question now was no longer if, but by who, and, maybe, how many people were following her?

"Dr. Wyley, do you know why this man comes to your conferences?"

"My understanding is Dr. Gruber is a retired internist, I believe from New Jersey, who, over the years, added rheumatology as a special interest in his practice and remains interested in our field. From time to time retired or emeritus physicians come to our meetings. Dr. Gruber had no fellowship training but he's obviously a very smart guy who often asks good questions and we've enjoyed having him at our sessions. I think he's a good model of a physician who always wants to keep learning. I think he's been coming to our conferences for at least a year."

"During the time you have known this man have you ever had any social activity with him outside of the hospital?"

A little wary, again. "He's an old man, why would I do that? No. Is Dr. Gruber in some kind of trouble?"

Ted didn't answer that question but thought he could offer some reassurance. "Doctor, I just need to get an idea of how frequently this man is in Burlington. Do you remember the last time you saw Dr. Gruber before today?"

The Doctor was visibly more relaxed. He probably had come to the obvious conclusion a man he didn't know very well was the subject of the Trooper's concern. He might have wondered how it was the Trooper had in some way associated him with Dr. Gruber but he didn't ask.

"As I said, he usually comes up to Burlington every other week for our conference. So it must have been two weeks ago. Months ago we had coffee together after a session and he told me what he and his wife do. I guess they have relocated to an isolated area just south of Middlebury. Conference weeks they come up to Burlington early Friday mornings and stay at a local hotel. He comes to our meeting and he might do some other things at the hospital or school; maybe the library. I really don't know. She shops. Then they go out for dinner and, sometimes, have tickets for a venue in town. I gather they may do some shopping Saturday and usually return home later in the day. Maybe he said they occasionally stay over till Sunday. I'm sorry, I'm just not sure about that."

Ted knew, right away, Dr. Wyley was about to place Dr. Gruber in Burlington the weekend the diener disappeared. That was a crucial connection he needed if he ever was going to push Dr. Gruber harder. But, at the same time, Gruber was known to this Doctor, and probably several other people, to routinely be in town every other Friday anyway. He decided he would try to find out if this Doctor might have noticed anything unusual about the last time Gruber was in Burlington.

"You think Dr. Gruber was at your conference two weeks ago?"

"Yes, I believe so."

"Two weeks ago when you last saw Dr. Gruber on that Friday do you recall anything unusual or different about him? Did he participate in the discussion the way you said he usually did?" Ted was fishing, hoping to jog something from the doctor's memory if there was anything else to recall. The doctor began to express his response as Ted was finishing talking.

"Well, I can tell you what I do remember because talking with Franz today reminded me of it just now when we chatted for a minute after the meeting. Today, just like last time, two weeks ago, Franz said he regretted he was going to miss a fine dinner in Burlington tonight because he had to pick up his wife now and head home to take care of some things. That struck me as funny because I recalled what happened after he said exactly the same thing last time.

"I stopped in my research lab mid-morning the next day, Saturday, to pick up some papers. The building is attached to the hospital and I cut through the hospital to go to where I park my car. Walking through the lobby I saw Dr. Gruber come out of one of the stairwells. I waved over to him and I know he saw me because he gave me a slight, half wave back. He looked distracted and I thought he kind of mouthed the words 'I got lost' and then he went off in a different direction. I was a little surprised to see him."

Far from incriminating and maybe not perfect, but despite its circumstantial nature Ted felt it might be a good fit for answering some of the case's questions. Now there was definitely more than enough reason for Ted to go back to Bee Pond and put some pressure on Dr. Gruber. Gruber may have lied again to Dr. Wyley about going home right away, but Ted thought looking for Gruber at Bee pond today was a chance he wanted to take after the inactivity of this dull week.

He rushed back to Montpelier to quickly review what he learned with the Lieutenant so they could devise a strategy for his anticipated interrogation of the Doctor. Over the radio he alerted Rondell he was on his way to the Barracks. He also requested the Lieutenant have a cruiser follow Liza home and make arrangements for a trooper to stay outside their home until he could be there later in the evening. Rondell agreed there was a small chance Liza could be at risk and set it up.

As he walked down the hallway to Lieutenant Rondell's office Ted heard Rondell talking with someone in the office. He stopped. He thought it might be Sergeant Dixon's voice. Even though the Lieutenant's door was open he quickly turned around and walked to the main room. He went to his desk to look for messages. He was anxious to get going to Lake Bee and hadn't counted on having to wait to see the Lieutenant. He walked to the small lunch room and got a couple candy bars. Ted was hungry and hoped he'd be back on the road very shortly.

Impatience won the day and he mustered up his courage and started down the hallway again to Rondell's office. This time he made sure his heels clicked loudly on the granite floor. At the office doorway he stopped. Both Rondell and Dixon stopped their discussion and looked to Ted at the doorway.

"Come on in Ted. Sergeant Dixon was leaving when you called me and he decided to stick around to hear what you said you've found."

Sounded reasonable enough. This was kind of a big case by now for the force. Dixon was Internal Affairs, but he was also a state trooper. No one waved Ted to a chair to sit. So he just went ahead, standing in the doorway, holding a candy bar, and told his superiors what he just discovered. He tried to be brief. After reporting details he learned from Liza and Dr. Wyley Ted began a cogent, well organized discussion of the possible and probable implications of this new information. He recognized some of the thoughts he put forward included speculation.

Ted doubted Sergeant Dixon knew much about several of
the details and nuances of the case that made up part of Ted's
presentation but he hoped the Lieutenant remembered most of it.
When he finished what he wanted to say he paused. No one gave
any indication of planning to say anything. So he went ahead and
introduced the questions he felt he needed answered before he went
to see Dr. Gruber.

For Ted there were two critical issues to decide. The first was how
aggressively to confront Gruber. The second was whether or not
there was anything Gruber might say to him that would justify
arresting him tonight.

First Rondell, and after a few minutes Dixon, weighed in on this
part of the discussion. There was pretty good consensus right from
the start, but Ted knew he was more likely to value comments from
Rondell than Dixon. If he disagreed with Dixon he thought he
better be careful, though, because he definitely feared the power of
Internal Affairs. His recent run in with that department was enough.

Not surprisingly, Lieutenant Rondell was more cautious than Ted
about what Ted might be able to do with what the Doctor might
say. He advised Ted to try to confirm a justification they had been
looking for to do a thorough search of the Gruber home and car
before contemplating an arrest. He said he was willing to get the
paperwork for search warrants started tonight and, depending on
what came out of Ted's informal interrogation, plan to get a large
detail and the crime lab back to Lake Bee early in the morning. He
also suggested, unless Ted became less interested in Gruber after
talking with him tonight, they meet sometime Saturday with a
State's Attorney.

Ted didn't disagree with the plan advised by the Lieutenant. There
were still plenty of steps to climb before more formal legal action
could be expected to be sustained. Given signs of some kind of
New York mob activity in the case he decided to ask the officers
what they thought about him working words of caution or warning
into his conversation with Gruber; risks that might impact his and

his wife's safety. Rondell was non-committal about that. He said if Gruber was a killer he doubted he would much care about anything like that by now.

Ted wanted to get on the road. The discussion was very helpful. He thought he had a good idea how he should handle things. He moved as though getting ready to leave the room and looked at the candy bar in his hand, which was beginning to melt in his sweaty palm. He stopped. A thought hit him. He worried what might happen if he left the Grubers later that night and they were alone, able to try to leave the area, or whatever, in the hours before a task force showed up in the morning? He expressed his concern.

"Lieutenant, maybe I should spend the night in my cruiser at the Gruber house to ensure they don't leave?"

"Ted, I'm already startin' to worry about how you are goin' to stay in shape with all the candy bars you seem to subsist on. I don't think you need to stay at that lake all night. I'm worried if you do we might find your cruiser filled with candy bar wrappers and, who knows, even empty cigarette cartons in the mornin'. You remember the last vehicle we found that looked like that? Whenever you are done with the Grubers why don't you give me a call and we'll make a final decision about how we should handle the rest of the night. But we will have a cruiser in your driveway until you get home."

"Fair enough. Call you later." Ted couldn't help it. He was energized. He felt he was back on the trail of something big after a long period when all the 'gears' had seemed frozen for a time.

* * *

Distances Vermont State Troopers frequently have to travel to get where they want to go often allows ample opportunity to mull over and re-visit concerns and plans for a case. As he drove he thought it over again. It was time to confront the Doctor now. So many paths were either leading to him or seemed to involve him. Ted had suspicions about Gruber early on but you can't make or, certainly, finish a case based on suspicion alone. The revelation Gruber and his wife were in Burlington and Gruber was at the hospital the weekend the diener was killed, was too much for Ted to accept as coincidence.

It also was time, Ted really believed, to make sure Gruber was aware of the lengths the New York mobsters who had their hands in this deal were willing to go in this mess to get what they deemed was theirs… And their apparent casual use of violence as a means.

In all his previous interactions with the Doctor, and even his wife, they each projected an air of detachment from obvious realities in this case. If he was involved Ted doubted the Doctor had any idea about who he was really dealing with. He seemed to have a collector's obsession with achieving his vaunted goal as the only justification he needed to maybe be part of all this.

The idea Sammy Paskovich wasn't alone and could have been killed for some number of $1000 bills by a confederate on the county road as soon as a deal was done was plausible when considering something as violent as murder. But that didn't begin to answer why Sammy had some of the stones in his gut, and where those and the remainder were.

Ted had little expectation Gruber would respond any more honestly after he educated him about the likes of guys like Forlenza and how they managed their business. Accepting any potential for the Doctor, himself, to be a cold-blooded killer was difficult. If so, legal efforts by the state of Vermont to establish that probability would be only one of the challenges he suspected the Doctor faced. If Forlenza had resources to find out who Ted was married to then he probably also had a good chance of having people who could eventually identify the collector he had done business with. Things had gone wrong and more people might have to pay.

Leaving Montpelier he worked his way south and west over a network of two lane roads, which comprised the overwhelming travel option in Vermont. Ted knew these roads well and maintained decent speed as he wound his way. Five miles north of the lake he turned onto the county road that ran by the lake.

After about a mile he saw a farmer running out of his house with his arms flailing in the air. Ted quickly figured it was a response to two teenagers running away from a cart at the edge of the road, who, more than likely, had just raided the cash box left at his roadside egg stand. He slowed for only a second and saw the farmer's anger become directed at him as Ted decided he needed to keep going and not intervene. Ted did turn on his lights, indicating he was on his way to an emergency. He hoped that might help, at least a little, to assuage the upset of the abandoned farmer. What Ted couldn't know was turning on his lights frightened the young thieves, who then dropped the stolen money by the side of the road, easily retrievable by the farmer.

It was getting dark and was about to rain. It would have been better to start with the Grubers in some light but he was losing that battle. Dusk was brief this time of year and it was almost gone as Ted approached the north road entrance to the lake from the county road. He was driving south through forest and there was no view of the lake from that direction until another half mile ahead on the county road. The entrance wasn't marked, but the one lane north lake road began as a short fork at the county road. Generally, cars left via the south spur and came in from the north spur.

A drizzle started but nothing was very wet yet. As Ted turned onto the north spur dirt road he saw a car coming up the road and approach the south spur at rapid speed. The car turned on its lights only as it reached the south spur. It looked to be a black sedan but that was all Ted could determine in the seconds it was visible. The car never stopped at the county road intersection and sped off to the south.

Ted headed west along the one lane dirt road. He smelled it well before he saw it. Wood was burning. He had to drive slowly because of the meandering nature of the road. After passing the first one or two houses closest to the county road there appeared to be no lights on in the homes he was passing. He continued the almost mile distance looking for signs of a fire. The rain began to pick up.

When he reached the Gruber house it was essentially engulfed in flames and he knew it. Whatever secrets it held probably couldn't be saved. An immediate worry was whether the flames from the large conflagration were going to jump to surrounding trees and, possibly, the Joiner or even Hurley homes. If that happened the whole lake might go up. He reached for his radio mike but hesitated when he saw Gruber's car, crashed into trees across the north road from his driveway, just slightly directed towards the east. Lights were on inside and the front passenger door was open. As he stopped his cruiser near it he could hear the engine. Ted got out quickly and un-snapped his holster.

Mrs. Gruber was slumped over the wheel; not moving. Blood was all over her neck and back and the front dash of the car. She had been shot, at very close range, right through her skull. Ted figured the shot was from behind her. She was definitely dead. He pulled out his weapon, turned off the Gruber car's ignition, and looked around the area. It was bright from the fire but the cold rain was having an effect on the flames. Thick smoke was increasing. He couldn't see anyone moving or hear anything other than the crackling from the fire. There were occasional 'poppings' more likely from exploding solvents than gunshots.

Ted went to his cruiser and called both of the emergencies in. He asked for the fire department, an ambulance, and a major crime investigation unit. He requested the dispatcher caution everyone about the tricky road turns for large vehicles near the beginning of the north road.

In the middle of his call, while looking at nothing in particular, Ted thought he glimpsed a small light moving in the woods. Done with the call he quickly managed to walk completely around the Gruber house, shining his flashlight to see if there was anyone around. At water's edge both the Gruber's dogs were laying, dead, half in, half out of the water. With the heavier rain smoke was over-taking the flames and apocalypse for the Lake Bee Pond community appeared unlikely.

Ted hurried back to the end of the driveway intending to get his slicker. As he rushed to his cruiser he directed his flashlight down and looked again to the woods just north-west of him. He saw the small light again, higher up in the hilly woods and now stationary. He was afraid to lose the light again so he started off after it. He used his own light, directed straight down, only to illuminate a foot or two ahead of him. He climbed through brush and around trees for about fifty yards until he heard movement. Ted killed his light and unholstered his revolver.

He approached the light, carefully, in the dark then turned his light back on and directed the beam at the stationary light. Gruber was lying on the ground, barely moving.

"Trooper Vallan. I tink it's good you happened to here just now. Dere are some problems. Some men, hooligans I do not know attacked me and, as you can see, burned our home down. I suppose it's gone by now.

"I been shot on my left arm and left leg and unfortunately dere is great deal of bleeding from da wounds. I assume, since you are here dey have gone now. Tank goodness Ida was able to get away while dey chased me up here in da woods. Even though Ida doesn't have da directions to everythin' she knows what ta do."

Ted looked around as Gruber spoke. The pelting rain was a little less here, deflected by foliage remaining on the branches of trees. But even if the wet magnified the amount of blood on Gruber it was obvious the wounds were serious, and possibly, fatal. Ted decided there was no purpose, right now, in telling him his wife was dead. He told Gruber to lay still and leave his light on. Then he moved as quickly as he could down the hill to his cruiser. He called dispatch to alert them to his position up the hill. Then he broke out his first aid kit, grabbed his slicker and a tarp in his trunk, and managed to get back up the hill without falling. From his belt and a strap he had he fashioned two tourniquets above the wounds and pulled tight.

Gruber looked awful. Even with only the two small lights his face was dusky and it was easy to see his breathing was increased. Ted had to lay on the ground to gain some traction with both tourniquets. He pulled as tightly as he could but it was hard to think Gruber would not die soon.

"Doctor, I have an ambulance coming but, as you know, it will take some time to arrive. You should know Doctor Gruber, we know the body in the lake and your wounds are all related to your effort to obtain some possibly ancient Norse artifacts previously stolen from the Metropolitan Museum in New York City about a year ago."

Gruber exhaled audibly and sighed. His face softened and he looked away. His body managed to collapse even a little more and he took on the appearance of giving in to his fate. Then he turned his face and looked up at Ted who had perched the doctor on his own left hip so he could try to keep tension on both tourniquets.

"I knew he was a dumb fuck da moment I picked him up at da train station in Rutland."

The Doctor was probably dying. He seemed interested in talking and Ted had no inclination to stop him. He had no idea how long it would take for a rig to get there, and even then, what they would be able to do? He held both tourniquets as tightly as he could. Gruber's arm was dusky but dry, but his leg wound was high up and continued to ooze despite Ted's efforts with the tourniquet.

"He tried, at first, ta act like he was da guy I had been doin' da deal with but I quickly figured him for some kind of deliveryman sent ta make da exchange. He was a nitwit. I don't tink he really had any idea what we were dealing with. He jus wanted to smoke and drink coffee. He really annoyed me. Stupidly, I didn't just make da exchange right dere and leave him dere to let him figure himself out for getting back ta da City. After I got him some coffee an a donut he sat dere, in my car, making a mess. He whined dat da return train wasn't until eleven-thirty at night so I had ta let him stay with me until den. He had no idea how far away I lived.

"I sat dere watching him for a while. I was a little worried he might not have da stones. Den I figured jus maybe he actually was who he said he was, just dumber den I had thought after all da time we worked on da deal. His voice and City accent weren't dat different. I was getting so angry at da way dis guy was handlin' dis and seemed so sloppy. I den made my biggest mistake and began ta tink about giving him fewer bills den I had agreed ta.

"I drove back da long way by driving up ta Brandon and cut over from dere. All back roads so he'd have no idea where he was. It was dark by then. At da house he ate some crackers and had some mor coffee. I suggested we toast the culmination of da deal and he quickly agreed ta some scotch. I kept refilling his glass. I brought out da thirty $1000 bills and asked him for da stones. I counted out da bills and he casually pulled a small plastic bag from a side pocket of his jacket and tossed it on da table. I jus didn't like anything about dis guy; he made me angry tinkin' I was getting dis wonderful famous bracelet from dis idiot who knew nothin'.

"I counted out da sixteen stones and den stupidly left dem in da bag on the kitchen table. He folded da money and put it in da same pocket and stood up. He was shaky. He took da coat off, folded it over his arm, and said he wanted ta lie down for a little while. I pointed ta da couch in da livin' room. But first he headed for da bathroom. He din' stay too long an I could hear him peeing. He came out staggering a little. He placed his coat on da back of a kitchen chair and den went into da livin' room and lay down.

"I waited about thirty minutes trying ta decide if he was out and how many bills ta take back and when was a good time to move da stones ta da place I was planning ta hide dem. I walked over ta da chair with his coat and easily removed a wade of bills, quickly pocketing about half of what I pulled out. Den I folded da rest and slipped dem back in da coat pocket. I looked at him again and he was snoring. I decided ta go ta da bathroom and went upstairs ta da one in our bedroom. I was washing my hands when I got done and I heard a kitchen chair move.

"As I ran downstairs I picked up da baseball bat I always keep near da bedroom door as a defense against intruders. I walked into da kitchen and I saw the remaining bills were scattered on da table. And den I saw this dumb shit, whose back was ta me, had opened da bag with da stones and was calmly swallowing dem; one by one! I couldn't believe it! I couldn't imagine how he could so easily be swallowing something dat size. He only took a sip from da coffee or scotch each time and you could see him gulping it down. Oh my god, he was killing himself! Dere was no way any those stones was going to pass through his gut. Da dogs started barking furiously.

"I screamed at him ta stop. He turned his head slowly and had such a supercilious grin on his face. He reminded me of some dumb kid who knew he had done somethin' dat was goin' ta get him in trouble. Den he frowned, a dark nasty look, and turned ta swallow anotha' stone. I was furious. I told him ta stop again, and told him those stones were going ta get stuck in his stomach and he would get a bowel obstruction and die. He turned away again and I was so angry I din really tink and I raised up da bat and slammed it into da back of his head. He immediately slumped over on da table. He looked like he was out but den he stirred a little.

"I put da remaining stones and all da bills on da table in my pockets and ran upstairs ta my bathroom. I found a small bottle of ipecac in my medical bag and ran back down da stairs. He was bleeding, but not too much. I tried ta raise his head up and get him ta take the ipecac but I wasn't sure if he did get any. I sat down and tried ta tink da situation through. What could I do? I left him dere and went back upstairs ta find da number I had used ta arrange da deal.

Da old man I arranged da deal with, who I was told ta call 'Vinnie', answered and it sent a chill through me. Da guy downstairs was just a messenger. I tol him dere was a problem. Dat whoever he sent here said he had no stones. He must have sensed da terror in my voice and he tol me ta shut up and put his man on da phone. When I said I couldn't do dat, dat he was gone, he started screaming and swearing at me and threatened me dat I wasn't goin' ta be able to walk away from dis deal. I hung up. I din know what else ta do."

Once again, Ted's brain was filled with threads he was rushing to connect. Gruber's interest in talking while he was dying seemed to reflect his personality more than his situation. Ted didn't think he should, but he went ahead and asked:

"Didn't it worry you to make a call on your party line?"

"Oh, posh, no. Da only udders on our line are da Joiners and da Greys and needer of dem have been around." Gruber acted like it was a silly question.

Ted wondered if this 'Vinnie', who he was sure was Forlenza, was able to track Gruber to his location with phone records? He liked that possibility. That made his lingering worry Forlenza might have gotten to the Grubers by having somehow followed Ted a little less likely. Gruber seemed oblivious to Ted's interruption and continued with his story.

"I couldn't imagine what I was goin' ta do with da guy in my kitchen. I went into my basement, just looking and tinkin'. Den I went into my shop dat's attached ta da house. I kept tinkin' dere might be, had ta be, some way for me ta get those stones; make him vomit and get him out of dis area. I just couldn't tink well. I wondered about some plastic tubing I could shove down his throat an provoke his gag reflex, if he still had one after all dat alcohol. I came out of my shop ta go back in da house and decided ta go over ta da Joiner's. I knew Harry had a good shop in his basement. I went in through da metal storm doors and looked around for about five or ten minutes. I took a small rubber tube from a drawer but it was too thick and probably too short.

"The dogs kept barking an I knew I couldn't shut dem up while I was running all over. I came back in da house and walked inta da kitchen and da bastard was gone! He had gone out through da kitchen door onta da lakeside deck. I went out on da deck an looked around. Dere was a flashlight in da kitchen an I could have turned on da deck lights but I was afraid ta call attention ta what was goin' on. Especially when da dogs kept barking constantly. Den I saw him in what little moonlight dere was. He was right at da edge of da shore moving towards da mouth of da lake.

I knew da last house, da Hurley's, was empty. I started down da deck steps an saw him stop an put his hands ta his belly, den hunch over. I figured he was vomiting inta da lake. He stood up, and den he just flopped over inta da lake on his belly. With da way he fell he jus seemed ta be propelled out inta da lake an he slowly floated off towards da middle of da lake.

"I din know what ta do. Everythin' had gone wrong. And, because of my panicking, even Vinnie knew I was involved in dis. I wanted ta walk ta da shore but, with dat jerk floating out dere, I was afraid. I wondered if he would shout out or do somethin'. I hoped he would sink and be out of my life forever. I stood dere, staring at da lake for some time. I never thought dese tings would happen. I had got angry and greedy. I started up da short path ta da deck and stumbled on somethin' dat turned out ta be da idiot's shoe. I was in no condition ta know what ta do with it. His jacket fit me so I put it in my closet."

The air was acrid from the thick smoke that continued to pour from the remnants of Gruber's home. Gruber's confession, offered without prompting so far, plausibly reflected his own presumption he was dying. There was a lot more Ted wished to know, but he was torn about pushing Gruber in this setting. He decided he had to find out about the diener, James Hardy, if he could. If Gruber was responsible for his death the implications for any involvement of the New York people were very significant and, in fact, contrary to most of Ted's theories.

"Doctor, you were in Burlington the weekend James Hardy was murdered." Offered as a statement of fact, not a question.

"Yah. I was desperate to tink of a way ta complete da set of my stones. I had been ta da autopsy area several times before ta view specimens with a few others. I actually had struck up a casual acquaintance with dat fellow during my visits. So I called him the day after I assumed da post had been done. All I said on da phone was I knew dere was some money ta be made related ta some strange objects in da dead man's stomach. He was interested immediately. He din come right out and say it but da way he talked made me sure he was aware of da stones. We agreed ta meet early Sunday mornin' at da Williston boat launch on da Winooski river. We agreed on five a.m. so Ida an I could do what we planned ta do and get out of Burlington as early as possible. I told him I knew someone who would pay a thousand dollars for all six of da stones.

"On Saturday morning, I went down ta da pathology area tinkin' I might be able ta find somethin' myself. I bluffed my way in. Den I got very scared when I heard someone coming and stood behind a door ta hide. A young woman walked in and seemed ta be looking for somethin' also. She seemed ta know more about da path lab den I did so I watched her. If she found anythin' that could be the stones I determined ta try ta go up behind her and hit her with my hands an da small pistol in my pocket."

Ted felt sick. He knew what Liza said about her visit to that spot but he had never imagined the true danger she was in. His revulsion at Gruber and the matter-of-fact way he described his violent quest for those stones sickened him. Gruber was insane. And, of course, he felt revulsion with himself for ever having allowed a family member to be involved in police business. His wife and family, and even his father. 'Oh shit!' What a mess.

"Suddenly lights went on and James Hardy came inta da room. At first he started ta yell at da young woman, who he seemed ta know. Den he tried ta find out from her what she was doin' dere. He told her she should leave. After that Hardy looked around and den unlocked a cabinet with many drawers. He pulled somethin' out but I couldn't see what he was doin'. I was afraid to try to jump him dere. And he was a big guy. He locked da cabinet, an turned off da lights on his way out. I assumed it was somethin' to do with da stones."

"Why did you kill him?"

"Oh I din. Ida said we couldn't let anyone ever know we were involved with da death of da stranger in da lake. Dat diener was another dumb fuck. He din even seem ta notice we each were wearing gloves when we got inta his car. So when we met dat mornin' I sat in his passenger seat an Ida sat in da back. I showed him da twenty fifty dollar bills from da deal.

"He reached inta his pocket like he was going to get da stones. Den he said on Friday afternoon da pathologist, Dr. Roller, called an asked him an Jackert, da other diener, where all da stones were. Dr. Roller said dere should be six. Hardy told us he already had them so he figured to put different stones in da specimen case Saturday mornin' and he told Roller he would be sure ta find dem for him first thing Monday mornin'. Den he smiled at us and said, after da switch, when he was back home he realized he had five, not six, stones like he put into the bottle.

"Well I was furious. what good would da bracelet be ta me if a stone was missing? He was obviously holding out on me and would make our lives miserable from den on. Ida understood what was happening immediately. As we were making da exchange she shot him with da derringer; both barrels.

"We pulled him out of da car and down ta da river. It was still dark an no one was around. I put some bricks in his pants and we pushed him off da bank and da current was strong enough ta take him downriver and we hoped he'd sink after a while. We cleaned his car up with alcohol we brought. Den I drove his car, an Ida followed me, ta Rutland an parked it at da bus station, an we drove home. We thought about taking it ta da border an leaving it dere, but we were too tired."

Ted lay there on the ground with Gruber's torso partially on Ted's left side. He continued to try to pull as tightly as he could on the two tourniquets. He was amazed how clear and persistent Gruber was in telling him this part of his disastrous story. He saw Gruber's blood dripping onto his uniform, beginning to match the location of Gruber's own deep thigh wound. They stayed in that position a few minutes. No one said anything more.

Finally, with Gruber barely awake and notably pale, Ted heard sirens wailing in the distance. He thought he could probably fill in likely scenarios for several loose ends, like how the shoe got into the Joiner's closet. Probably sometime shortly after Sammy's death; another act of lingering panic and poor judgment after what Doc had done that night.

There may have been no violent criminal intent when Gruber started out to make a deal for the collection. But the whole business, from very early on, was tainted with shady trappings and people. Gruber, himself, seemed to suddenly descend to a level where he ultimately acted in a more lethal and criminal way than some of the others. Although the name Ted now was sure he knew, 'Vinnie Forlenza', would, hopefully, ultimately aid in completing the picture of the apparent mastermind of this sordid mess, he knew he still had a way to go.

He had obtained all the information he was going to get from Dr. Gruber. Gruber died in the ambulance on the way to Rutland Regional Hospital.

Ted wondered where a bunch of $1000 bills and a bag with some small special stones might be. Since the diener, James Hardy, and now Gruber and his wife had been killed for those stones, it was unlikely whoever wanted those nuggets wouldn't also want that cash too, if it could be found. In any event, with the killing of both Grubers there were still homicides in Vermont for Ted to solve.

*   *   *

DAY 19 SATURDAY, OCTOBER 30

Ted appreciated the Lieutenant's consideration, giving him time to settle his mind about all that had happened this month. They were sitting in the lunch room in the basement at headquarters. It was just after ten a.m. and no one else was there. The windowless room was brightly lit by several fluorescent light banks. Cream colored plastic laminate tables were each flanked by three or four brightly colored laminate chairs with spindly silver metal legs.

The Lieutenant had pulled his chair away from the table and sat, slouched, with his legs straight out in front of him and his hands clasped behind his head. Ted sat up close to the table with his folded arms resting on it. He had trouble finding the words he wanted since he had difficulty making sense of all his thoughts. Some of what was troubling and made him anxious were things he guessed the Lieutenant already understood. The Lieutenant didn't rush him.

"I thought this whole thing really hinged on a New York mob and they were killing people left and right."

"Well, I guess they are capable of that."

"They got to the lady in the city and they sure killed the Doctor and his wife. But after the Doctor killed the guy at the lake, even though he probably hadn't planned to do it, he became so sure he could beat whoever set up the original deal. I guess after he killed the diener and got most of the stones and most of his money back he might have thought the whole business was done. Wonder if he had any idea who he was really dealing with and their resources?

"I guess I now think there's a good chance if I had stayed around the lake, eventually, I would have focused on the Doctor. He didn't seem to be too worried about me or the mob but they got to him first. They are violent bastards. In reality though, as far as this case went, Gruber and his wife were just as violent monsters. And they lived right here in Vermont, not New York City. I just would never have believed this case might have been solved without me ever going to New York. But maybe so."

"Yes, Ted, maybe so." He didn't sound terribly judgmental but Ted got his point.

"At least those assholes never got the money they wanted or those fucking stones back. There could be some big bills buried somewhere but unless they drain the lake and look at every stone on the ground in the woods there's no way fifteen of them will ever turn up. If there really ever was a map it probably burned up with the house. Treasure hunters can try but even the mob isn't going to get into a mess like that. I sure hope those stones really were fakes.

"My run in with that fucker they call a mob boss was something I'll never forget. I still don't have any idea how he knew who I was. He just had a lady killed and he looked calm but I could tell he was seething underneath. He was so fucking like ice in his manner while threatening my family. Lieutenant, you surprised about the way some of these mobsters in that city act like they own the world and manage to get away with just about anything they want?"

Rondell sat up straighter. "I guess so. I'd like to think that couldn't happen here. But who knows? From what you've been through you can see the chances of anyone bein' held accountable for the murders of Gruber and his wife are slim. You and I are goin' to do our policin' up here and ask for help from other jurisdictions when we think we need it. There are more and more tools being developed for the police work we do to track and catch guys like these. I think we're gonna get better and better."

Ted was drifting off from the conversation. Would he ever be able to forget the threat to his family? Right away he sent the NYPD the license plate picture from his encounter with the town car. He decided, for a few days, to keep his picture of the reclusive man to himself but then went ahead and sent it to an FBI Agent in the Organized Crime Task Force.

Ted recognized so much of him had changed because of his disastrous time in New York. After all that happened, even his own blunders, his anger at the threat to his family while he was doing his job haunted him more than anything. Maybe that bastard even thought his intimidation succeeded. Did he think he won? Ted wasn't ready to quit.

If the mob couldn't forgive and forget, could he? After all, there were still two murders in the state of Vermont for which no one had been charged.

*   *   *

Halloween celebrated

Around five thirty in the evening Ted walked along and monitored the progress and activity of one Tinkerbell and Superman as they trick or treated at each of the nine other homes on their block. Liza stayed home and doled out candy to the neighbor's kids.

*   *   *

DAY 21 MONDAY NOVEMBER 1

Fall remained in name only. It was consistently cold and for the next five months it was not if it would be cold, only a question of how much colder it would be. Sunlight, certainly bright sunny days, would be at a premium for a long while. November, in particular, was known for its tendency to be a more overcast, and to some, gloomy introduction to hard winter.

In Vermont the major forms of large vegetation are deciduous. Just west, in the Adirondacks in New York, plentiful pine forests sustain some green through the long winter. But in Vermont, the 'Green Mountain State', winters reveal forests often free of most branch vegetation. The state forests are notable for 'old growth' higher up its mountains, more isolated from its population, and huge areas of 'new growth' forests. Colonial and post-colonial Vermont were periods of herculean effort by pioneer farmers who scrambled with their families all across the state trying to tame both fertile flat land and inhospitable rocky, forested hills and mountains.

It is said by the late eighteen hundreds two thirds of Vermont had been turned into pasture and farm land. To create this massive agrarian conversion much of the forest had been harvested. The wood of the forest was not wasted. Burlington, mostly, and a few other Lake Champlain ports developed into industrial cities packed with processing and shipping access for the wood, greatly disfiguring the shoreline. Only in the second half of the twentieth century was popular opinion starting to seed organized efforts to re-develop the shore, especially since forest harvesting and commercial water use were long gone, even before world war II. Land use also had been radically altered and thus the new growth forests had been growing from many fields and hills for almost a century.

Most Vermonters tried to pick out and highlight the good and pleasant from each of the inevitable changing seasons, including winter. Ted was no exception. He had his own name, in particular, for early November. When the trees were free of leaves and the sun was out he thought the bare branches gave the forest a silver hue and so he called it the *silver season*. It was especially noticeable when there was just a thin dusting of fleeting snow from the night before to highlight the trees. But this first day of November, which had dawned bright and demonstrated several hours of silvery hue across the hills, Ted was oblivious to any of it.

On Sunday, with Henry strapped to his back, they all had gone on a short hike. It turned out to be a good way to divert his over active mind from thoughts and doubts, especially lingering self-doubt. With so much over now, for better or worse, he did feel some relief. He was feeling especially good about his improving relationship with Liza. How much she really had to forgive him wasn't completely clear in Ted's view. But he accepted she was hurt by some of the things that had happened, and he was certainly in the middle of it all, surely responsible for some of it. Beyond what happened with Kendra, though, Ted still felt that he also was more victim than instigator in so much of all that had taken place.

A great deal had changed by Monday morning. The Grubers were dead, clearly on orders from Forlenza, who remained responsible for Kendra's (Sarah Javonivich) murder. But, to Ted's surprise, neither Harry James (Sammy Paskovich) or the diener (James Hardy) were Forlenza's direct responsibility. Go figure. Forlenza would have killed Sammy if he ever found out he planned to keep some $1000 bills. But he had no information that would have led him to go after the diener. Ted realized he should have figured that out.

Ted wasn't sure if his case was over. The story of the stranger in the lake was explained. The diener's murder was explained. After the hour he spent with Rondell on Saturday morning he was left with a strong sense the Lieutenant was trying to let him know any further or more formal pursuit of this Forlenza was best managed by law enforcement in New York City. Ted seriously doubted the Lieutenant had any continuing interest in New York, at all, except for the connection to some young Vermont thug who had connected with the mob and went after Liza.

After all that happened on Friday, especially following his unsatisfying phone conversations on Wednesday and Thursday, he was more than apprehensive about what he would hear when he answered the call from an FBI agent on the line first thing that morning. How much worse or complex could all this get? More unsupportive words from law enforcement was what he expected.

It had taken several tries before he was able to connect on the phone with Aubrey Blaustein the Organized Crime Task Force FBI agent he was directed to contact last week about any mob involvement in the case. Now two more people were dead, no doubt ordered by Forlenza. When they finally were speaking Special Agent Blaustein put Ted at ease by saying he appreciated Ted's patience and he now had ample time to try to help answer Ted's questions. Ted was wary but appreciated his time and had no reason to even question, in his own mind, why every FBI agent was a *Special* Agent.

"Yeah, Trooper Vallan, I had that photo you sent of the guy who threatened you and your family looked at. Yeah, we think that's Vincent, Vinnie 'Skinny' Forlenza, in that shot. He sure is looking old, isn't he? Forlenza was a minor 'capo' boss whose name was out there for a while in the late fifties into the sixties. His thing was intra- and interstate truck theft. They'd divert trucks on the road or break into trucks parked at warehouses. Lots of stolen stuff to sell. When the interstate theft part began to attract the feds he backed off and was pretty small time after. I think we thought that schmuck was dead.

"If he's still around would have thought he'd be out of the game by now. My guess is the big guys now have no use for him and he has no control, at all, over them. If he's still doing some small change stuff it's because they tolerate an old man and he stays out of their way.

"Violent? Sure. All those bastards use brutal violence to do their shit. It's the only thing they know. I don't think we ever sent Forlenza up for anything or certainly not for much. I think he had a bit of a rep for allowing his little guys wind up doing the time. So his boys were not always the brightest. But they were tough.

"At the same time these bastards aren't in the kind of business where you would ever try to say you are retired even though you leave the action. Too many enemies. Always have to watch your ass; forever. From what you've described to me sounds like he's trying, or wants, to keep his hands in the business, even in some small way.

"There is one thing I can tell you and maybe, from what you've told me, you've figured this out: These bastards don't like to lose. A deal gone bad is a big thing to them. Trying to put it right in their eyes can turn out to be a bigger thing than the original deal. Violence is an accepted and preferred method for satisfaction."

As the agent suspected, Ted had come to understand this. "So I'm learning. But what about actually going after a law officer and, especially, even his family?"

"Well, Trooper Vallan, your story about the way they made threats and tried to scare your family is, fortunately, nowhere near what we usually see. Of course some bad stuff has happened over the years but that's clearly the exception. No, there is a sort of line out there even those murdering bastards usually don't cross. Know why? Because when it happens the world comes down on them. No good for them or their business.

"No, my guess is 'Skinny' Forlenza, if he really is still out there, has lost his marbles. Old man who thinks he was screwed and got pissed off and is striking out everywhere. This shit's actions definitely constitute a federal offense. We would love to help you come down hard on him but, frankly, we would need more hard evidence. The low level pricks caught so far are shared around since 'Skinny' wouldn't have enough work to keep them busy enough anymore. We'll work with you, if you'd like, but my strong guess is this story is over now. No one left for the asshole to go after.

"He may still hold you responsible for getting in his way, but I can't imagine he would ever try to act on that again."

"No…No. Even if I should be, it's not at all like I'm not worried about him or afraid of him. I'm angry, Blaustein, and if he can't be put away then I really would like to just see a scare put into that fucker. I want to see him lose that smug, smart-ass expression on his face that stays with me. I have to tell you, bringing him to justice, whatever that means for shits like him, is only a small part of what I think about. I want him to be scared shitless and to know it's me doing it."

Special Agent Blaustein's tone became more serious. "Vallan, that kind of thinking and the emotions that generate it often lead good people into trouble. I'd advise you to find a way to work your way out of any obsession or anything like that you might be developing over Forlenza and what's happened. Might not end well for you legally. And don't forget, these assholes usually have families with bonds that bind others to actions to aid family brethren. Vallan, you should find a way to let it go now." Having said that, the Agent's tone lightened again and he continued right on.

"Of course, the task force can get more information about Forlenza's whereabouts and family connections if you ask me to. Any information will be our effort to help you fill in the blanks of your active case. Don't count on the FBI or the task force to go after the schmuck unless something else turns up to interest us."

Ted thought about what Special Agent Blaustein had just said, and there was a pause in the conversation. The case for the Vermont State Police was, for all intents and purposes, over. Then he spoke. "Yes, Agent Blaustein, please get me as up-to-date stuff as you can on that shit. I'll look forward to hearing from you."

"Okay, Trooper Vallan from the Vermont State Police. We'll do it… but you should think about being done with all this. Good luck."

*   *   *

It was then Ted decided to task himself with writing down his recollections about the case, especially pertaining to Forlenza, his constant enemy; maybe for forever. He made his notes at night after everyone was asleep, over at least the next eight or nine days, often writing two or more hours. Part of him hoped, now that so much was explained, the exercise of writing down the details might help to assuage his anger and upset. He probably knew that wasn't likely.

*   *   *

By now, after several long conversations when the kids were asleep, Ted had also told Liza everything; everything about the case. Their lives and years together had made them inseparable to each other and neither could imagine any other way to live. But that didn't mean that they would always agree.

That night Ted recounted his call with Special Agent Blaustein. Liza looked right at Ted. Her face was like stone. Her words came out slowly and felt as cold as ice to Ted. "You think there is still a job for you to do. But you know the real reason is something with your pride. So many pieces to this case and you think you will set everything right by punching a senile monster who has hurt us all.

"Think about what you have told me, Ted. Terrible things have happened to a lot of people in this case who you have been around. But, despite it all, you have come through safe, virtually unscathed.

You think some of your actions may have actually helped those killers hurt others. Because a part of you feels some guilt you want to keep on this, hoping to set your mind at peace. But what if with the next step your luck runs out and something happens to you or all of us are back in trouble again? Even if you get that fucker in jail will the world be safer? Will *justice being served* mean much of anything, except to you? I don't see much upside here. Do you?"

They were sitting in the living room, each on an end of the sofa. Liza had her usual monster textbook on her lap. Ted looked at her while she spoke. When she finished he reached over for her hand, and for the first time since he had told her about Kendra, she lifted her arm and they clasped hands. Neither smiled. Liza had a feeling about what Ted would say.

"Of course you're right. Everything you say makes sense." He got up to let the dog out. They left the discussion there for the time being.

About ten minutes later Ted walked back into the living room and sat next to Liza. "Liza, what do you mean by *senile*?"

She looked at him. Her response was brief but pretty clinical. "Someone with dementia. A demented person has lost memory and also capacity to make reasonable judgments and a host of other things."

"So a person with dementia might do things differently now than in the past?"

"Sure. Often there is a loss of inhibitions. A demented person can lose understanding of the consequences of his actions."

Ted thought about all this and thought about Forlenza. "Then does a demented person have to be totally demented to act that way or can this stuff develop gradually?"

"Absolutely. There is often a period of a few years when things go from subtle changes to more full blown dementia."

"If someone is demented and does terrible things is that person responsible for his actions?"

"Ted, I think you know as well as I there are many different views about that; from doctors, lawyers, the legal system, and so on. You mean, is a man with dementia responsible if he sends people to kill a policeman and his family?" Instantly she regretted how she had phrased that sentence.

It didn't really matter. Even before she said that they each suspected Ted wasn't done with Forlenza.

* * *

DAY 23 WEDNESDAY NOVEMBER 3

Thom Vallan had been admitted to the hospital the afternoon before for his heart catheterization, planned for Wednesday morning. Ted purposely hung around his office doing paperwork until he got a call from his mom his dad was back in his room. She said she was told it went fine. At three p.m. Sheila, Liza, and Ted met with the cardiologist who had done the procedure. The Doctor was practically buoyant, explaining there really were no findings of consequence. The heart muscle and major arteries were fine. There was evidence of only a small blockage at the end of a non-critical vessel. He said he doubted this would ever happen again, certainly not for a long while anyway.

His listeners were pleased but, quite naturally, wondered why he ever had a heart attack in the first place. The cardiologist answered the best he could figure Thom must have been doing some kind of an activity requiring extreme exertion to cause this to happen with a pretty healthy heart. Sheila was puzzled. Ted and Liza exchanged glances. The Doctor forgot to include extreme stress or excitement, Ted thought. Well the bastard was well enough to be told how he had fucked things up for Ted, not just himself. He would still have to find the right time to do that. Then he wavered and wasn't sure he'd ever do it.

* * *

DAY 28 MONDAY, NOVEMBER 8

A week after speaking with FBI Special Agent Blaustein there was a long message from him on Ted's extension at the Barracks. It was riveting to Ted. The gist of it was the Organized Crime Task Force was onto something pretty big that added up to a law enforcement leak source for the mob. What that meant exactly was unclear to Ted. But Blaustein said during a Task Force investigation bits of things had come out, including some suggestive evidence which might explain how some Forlenza people knew where Ted lived in Vermont. Blaustein's inflection made it seem like Vermont was somewhere in the Himalayas, but Ted knew what he meant.

Blaustein then explained he had found out from another source Forlenza was a lone wolf, working totally on his own, pretty much dis-avowed by the families. Why he didn't know. Anyway, 'Skinny' recently asked for a favor. Blaustein's guess was the favor was information about Ted. His informant said Forlenza was given what he wanted but was told not to come around anymore; to fuck off, for good.

Finally, Agent Blaustein asked Ted to get him his 'facts' number so he could send him the personal information, last known address, etc. he had requested on 'Skinny' Forlenza. Ted had no idea what it was Blaustein needed from him. He wondered if he had to have something that served as clearance to receive protected information; something he'd have to get from the Lieutenant or someone.

Neither did he recall ever asking Blaustein for any personal information on Forlenza.

Shit, this thing was still crying out for continuing activity. This asshole, Forlenza, had something up his ass about Ted. What the fuck for? Was it what he did? Wanted to do? What he found? From Ted's perspective he had just done routine police work. An investigation with few unusual features. There was a hint, popping up from several bits of things he was hearing, this Forlenza was just crazy. Crazy like a fox, or plain crazy?

Ted got up and walked over to the administration area. There were two women sitting at small facing desks typing away on their new IBM Selectric typewriters. They both stopped when Ted stood between the desks.

"Ladies, do either of you know anything about any special numbers or codes I need to give to an FBI agent so he can clear it to send me some information? He left a message saying I need to get him my 'facts' number. Any ideas?"

They looked at each other and smiled. The younger woman deferred to the older.

"Ted, I think he was referring to our FAX number; you know, the new FACSIMILE machine. Everyone calls it a FAX, F – A – X lately."

Ted blushed ever so slightly as he understood the connection. He tipped his head and walked back to his desk to call Special Agent Blaustein. But he was already back to mulling over the details, and more importantly, the implications of his message. Was he at war with this prick Forlenza?

*   *   *

DAY 31 THURSDAY, NOVEMBER 11

Almost two weeks had passed since the deaths of the Grubers. From time to time Lieutenant Rondell let Ted know the second man who had been at his house that night, who was believed to live in Vermont, hadn't turned up yet. He made it clear to Ted they were still looking for him and had no plans to stop. Nothing else about that case was talked about anymore. If his superiors were bothered no one had been held responsible for the deaths of the Grubers no one told that to Ted.

Ted had met with the Gruber's children in Montpelier. They were stunned by what he told them and had little to say after. He told the Lieutenant he wouldn't be surprised if he or a superior heard from them again after they had some time to process what he had gone over.

He was glad he hadn't been able to tape record Gruber's confession. Gruber's tone and matter-of-fact telling would have chilled them even more. Half-way through talking to them one son dropped his jaw and his mouth remained open. A minute later the other son did the same thing.

The Gruber kids, at least for now, didn't seem to pick up on any of the subtleties that were out there. As they were leaving the younger one turned to Ted and gave the impression he, at least, had already started to move on from the horrendous crimes and end of his parents to developing anger at their murder. "Won't someone who killed them be caught and punished?"

No one asked Ted how he felt about the apparent closing of the case. His investigative division was busy and there was plenty for Ted and everyone else to do. He had made a conscious decision to try to leave it and move on. From Liza to every professional he interacted with about the case there wasn't anyone who encouraged him to continue.

That afternoon, after being on the road most of the day, Ted stopped at the Barracks to lock up some evidence before heading home. He looked over at his desk and saw he had some messages. The second message instantly brought the case, and his anger, back to him. The note had come in the morning. It was from Jack Nichols, the NYPD detective from the 10th precinct. All it said was: 'call me if you still are thinking about going after Vinnie Forlenza'. The tumult unleashed in him just seeing 'Forlenza' told Ted the case certainly was not dead, at least for him.

There really was a lot going on in his division and Ted's days were going to remain filled for a long time to come. He was heavily involved in two major investigations, one fraud and the other an embezzlement. He was making good progress with both of them. After what he had been through with the Gruber theft and homicide business he found he was appreciating these cleaner cases a little more and was, grudgingly, beginning to accept what others were telling him: he did, indeed, seem to have a talent for breaking and managing that type of crime.

Ted even found the word *embezzle* attracted him. He thought it looked and sounded neat. Certainly making this eight letter word at scrabble would be very difficult; but possible. Just like many criminal cases. A blank as a 'Z' and attaching to an open spot with an 'e' was possible but what a challenge. The derivation in the dictionary explained its origin as more French than anglo, meaning 'make away, or to steal money or property from another'. Definitely didn't look English. In fact, 'dispose of fraudulently to one's own use' meant, as Ted had always supposed, that embezzlement is just another form of fraud. But he agreed the unusual word did describe a particular pattern of behavior which distinguished it from other forms of stealing.

When he studied the derivation in the dictionary he noted the earliest references to any form of that word dated to only around the 1300's. He was reminded of the infamous *rune stone bracelet* for which blood had been spilled that, had they been real, would have been from an even earlier time. What if they were authentic? Gone now anyway.

The note from Nichols conflicted him. He sat down and read it over a few times. He knew why the anger still came so fast. But he was more reflective now. He wondered exactly what Nichols was going to tell him and whatever Nichols might say that would make Ted try to have the case go active again. Would that be good or bad? He just wasn't sure anymore. He decided he would not try to track Nichols down at this hour. He wanted to think about it and sleep on it for a night.

That may not have been such a good idea for someone like Ted. In the evening and then lying in bed he found himself gradually becoming, once again, captivated with catching Forlenza. He constructed an image of a task force of police and a look of extreme horror on Forlenza's old face as he was surrounded by law enforcement. Then the image became one of a very old man in prison garb in a cell, staring at a wall.

*   *   *

DAY 32 FRIDAY, NOVEMBER 12

Ted didn't say a word to Liza. By the morning the case and the anger he had for Forlenza continued to a boil, and he only hoped what Nichols had to tell him was actually something important and useful. He altered his plans for early Friday and tried to busy himself at his desk until he could start to track down Detective Nichols. At eight-thirty he thought he could call.

Nichols was at the precinct. Ted tried to keep his hopes muted and not to sound overly excited to Nichols. They exchanged pleasantries and Ted moved the issue.

"Jack. Jack, I got your message but it was very late so I thought it would be better to wait until this morning. Hope that's okay? What have you got?"

"This is nothing urgent, Ted. And, you know, when dealing with mob idiots you never know for sure what task force people and feds and such are going to want or be willing to do anyway. Know what I mean?"

"Sure." Ted didn't know what he was supposed to say. "What have you got?"

"Well, think back to the time we both met with that Professor at the Scandinavian Center place. When we got there he was all worried about some secretary who hadn't returned from lunch. Remember?

So that was the lady you spoke with on the phone who, we think, arranged the pick-up in Brooklyn that almost got you killed.

"You might not know not only was she never seen again but the cops in the 17th who did the investigating of that found out she once worked in a similar capacity at the Metropolitan Museum of Art at the time those stupid *lucky* rocks were stolen. Different name, but they think same lady. Called herself 'Imogene' with you. Right?"

"Right." Ted had never followed up on her absence that afternoon.

"Turns out this lady, Imogene or whoever, has kept herself busy with all kinds of jobs; day and night. Just picked up for prostitution."

Ted wondered why or how a busted hooker would be able to break open his case with an outcast from the mob like Forlenza. "A prostitute?" His inflection implied his doubt.

"No, not just a prostitute. This lady was running an entire operation. Obviously with mob backing. She's singing because she's looking at some big time for her level of involvement. Especially since they say a bunch of underage, *maybe not there by their own choice*, young ladies were found at her *shop*. Who knows what she's really got, but Detective called me says she can tie some old shit to some murders.

"You should at least come down and talk to her. This time bring the wife and kids. Make a vacation of it. Didn't you like your last trip to the city?.. Just kidding."

Ted couldn't really joke about it. He did remember what Rondell had said about sticking to Vermont and letting other jurisdictions support them if needed for future investigations. He assumed this case would apply. So he asked Nichols who he should speak with at the 17th precinct. He decided he would get more information before he even mentioned anything about this to the Lieutenant…or Liza.

*　*　*

"No, oh no trooper. If she so much as let out a squeak about the prost'tution mob she'd be a gonner in no time. Disappear forever in a minute. No, guy she's dangling is some old geezer. Guys here tell me they thought he was dead. Must be working alone if that lady thinks she can get away giving him up. Whaddya you after him for Trooper?"

Ted told the affable sounding Detective Emerson from the 17th precinct his story in as short a version as he could. As he went through it he came to terms with what was his own only lingering or continuing attachment to the whole sordid facts of the case. By now all Ted still felt or cared about was his inextinguishable fury at Forlenza.

Apparently, just listening to Ted this cop, who he had never met, determined what was really in Ted's head. "If you can't shake this jerk, then why don' you find him and go ahead and smash him in the puss a couple of times, and then maybe you can forget about him and move on."

Didn't make much sense to Ted at that moment. But it became a thought that stayed in his head and, over time, he began to play with in his mind. A police officer's goal was to apprehend the guilty and let the justice system prosecute.

Ted thought about what would be considered a vigilante action or, if he wanted to think about it, as sort of a sick joke: 'I touched you last.' No, Ted was no vigilante. He believed he was a conduit to justice. No, if he went after Forlenza it would have to be as part of a coordinated police action. Probably, at least, with the NYPD. Maybe others.

"So Detective Emerson, do you know the details she's offering that would make my case against this shit go?"

"Listen, Troop Vallan, all I know is this lady is looking at a good three to five, solid, and she wants to sing. Loud. She tells us your boy has forced her into some deals, including your case, and there's clearly no love lost there. You get it? Says she worked to get info so your boy was able to lift some fabulously valuable stones or rocks, which I take to mean jewels, ma'be diamonds. I get that lot of the deal went to shit. She says he's a crazy killer now and sounds like you and yours got on his list. Cop killer sometin' we don' hear much about, thank God. Some wacko.

"You want nitty gritty details and stuff she says she got on him, says you got to come here with other cops and a DA so you can vouch her story and she can make the right deal. Got it?"

Shit. It all made sense to Ted and his first response was quiet elation. Even with her pieces of the puzzle he knew there was still so much to put together to make the kind of case that wouldn't allow a guy with legal resources to have options and maneuvers to beat it.

Detective Emerson spoke again. "These days we don' often see even the easy cases go smooth. Trooper, even if she goes through wit' it and sings loud and it all fits, the dead people can't talk, and asshole lawyers play wit' everything so much those still living get lost. Know what I mean? Long road to go. Know what I mean?

"Hey, you should talk it all over wit' your people up there and ma'be some folks down here, too. Wouldn't be a bad idea at all for you at least to come down and meet wit' her wit' a DA. After what you been through and all this fucker has been doing, proly should have a pow-wow and talk it all over. Know?"

"I think you're right, Detective Emerson. I've got another low level guy stashed at Riker's Island for another week or so, so I got to make some final decisions about all this soon anyway. Please keep her for me and I'll talk with my superiors and get back to you in one or two days. Is that okay?"

"Hey, no problem man. She ain't got nowhere to go for long while. Call me."

* * *

DAY 35 MONDAY, NOVEMBER 15

A message was on his desk, marked urgent, to call Angela Parsimone, Bronx Assistant DA, at her office. It was dated five p.m. on Friday, the twelfth. Ted stared at it for a while. The case that wouldn't go away. He had known it was probably just a matter of time until he would hear from her. After all, he had pretty much dumped the Danilio case on her when he got Mangione to block Danilio from getting out on bond. When that happened he wasn't as interested anymore and saw no reason to do anything about it becoming her problem. But he hadn't forgotten.

He looked at other papers on his desk and finished his apple before he called her back. From his notes he saw the number he was to call was different than the one with the ten-minute message. That was good. Angela Parsimone, personally, answered her phone. For a minute he wasn't positive it was the same woman. He was careful to address her as Ms. Parsimone.

"Trooper Vallan, I'm glad you're calling back." She had been attentive last time, but this time there was less formality and more friendliness. "You know you're a hard man to figure out." How could she know anything about him? They talked exactly once for a few minutes. "I admire your determination. You can imagine my response when the Danilio case, which I assumed was finished, got dumped back on my desk again a few weeks ago." To her credit, she said no more about that. "Well, we finally were pushed by his fancy lawyer to a hearing I had to be part of. It was set for late Friday and his lawyer asked me to meet with him and Danilio an hour before. I guessed the lawyer wanted to try to talk my office into accepting a bail deal.

"You must have had some ideas this Forlenza guy and his boys wouldn't forget about you, even though I have no idea why. I pressed Danilio a little about that. When I made a little light of the knife in the tires incident this Danilio got enraged and spit out something like 'we gonna get that shit cop yet'. Can you imagine that? His lawyer aged five years. That fast-talking schmuck was speechless." So was Ted.

"So everything changed after that. Probably not admissible but happened to get it on tape. Cancelled the hearing. His lawyer has no choice but to let him sit in jail until some more of this case gets worked out.

"That's why I'm calling, Trooper Vallan."

"Ted" he interjected.

"Yeah Ted. We have to get everyone together to go over this. I don't see how we can ignore a, maybe, credible threat to the life of a law officer. I mean, by your story, they've already come after you more than once."

"That is quite some information, Ms. Parsimone."

"Angela", she said. They were best friends now. That was okay. Ted couldn't help but be appreciative. She seemed to get the importance of all this. Finally, from someone in New York, the kind of serious response that might mean something.

"Yes it is Ted. I need for you to FAX me the names and contact info for everyone from law enforcement you've been involved with in this area, throughout the case. I'll have my staff put together a meeting so we can decide how to move on this, face to face. It will take some time. If I can get it set for next Monday can you be sure to be here?"

Ted was a bit shell-shocked. Each time he thought he might be putting all this behind him and moving on the worst of it, at least for him and his family, managed to find him again. Angela's new information cut to the heart of his lingering worry so it easily rallied his anger and fury.

"Of course Angela. I will start to plan to get down there now. As soon as your office confirms a date and time I'll arrange to be there. Your call is upsetting but nowhere near a surprise. I will have to deal with it. If you and I can get law enforcement agencies to agree to act on this I will be very pleased. I really do appreciate the way you feel about this and your plan to approach this mess. Thanks again, Angela."

"Right Ted", and they hung up.

"Now that's something" he said, out loud, to no one.

* * *

DAY 41 SUNDAY, NOVEMBER 21

For this trip Ted was offered an older, dark green unmarked to take to the city. It had a siren and a small red flasher in the front grill, and a magnet based red light he could attach to his roof with the wire plugged into the lighter. He had permission to leave his prominently displayed in his driveway but all locked up.

This time Mrs. Arkady was at home with Liza. The State Police were planning frequent patrols and the neighbors all said they were on alert. With all that Ted was glad he had sat, face to face, with his father on Saturday and gained his promise not to keep driving by with a baseball bat in the front seat. Thom Vallan seemed to agree there was a good chance a neighbor, State Policeman, or a Richmond officer might very well go after him if he was driving around a lot.

Ted put his stuff in the trunk and turned and hugged and kissed everyone good-bye. Liza seemed to have made her peace with this trip. His family walked back to the house and, only a minute later, he followed them back to the house also, his hands filled with a bunch of chewing gum wrappers from the back seat. For the remainder of the trip he always looked carefully before sitting or putting anything in the car, to make sure neither he nor what he had got stuck to old gum.

It was a typically chilly, gray morning. He assumed there wouldn't be much traffic the whole trip. For days he had been studying maps of the entire New York Metropolitan region; city street maps for all the boroughs; highways, bridges, and tunnels; subway maps and bus maps. From asking around he got the idea nobody ever tries to learn subway or bus schedules. Subways, anyway, he was told, seemed to come all the time except late at night.

He felt and hoped he was much better prepared for the city this time. He even had *X'ed* out several locations that sold souvenirs. He wouldn't blow that again.

Ted had contacted Janice Delario since the big meeting at the Organized Crime Task Force office was downtown, not terribly far from where he stayed last time. She advised the same hotel and could secure him parking at the same garage on Twelfth Avenue. With some misgivings he agreed and she set it up. Just thinking about running into Smithers was a distraction he didn't want to think about then, much less how it would go if they met. But the price, free, was right and he figured he wouldn't use the car much.

The trip down was uneventful. He was dressed casually, in jeans. His carefully wrapped uniform was folded on the back seat. The knife that might have saved his life was in his pocket and, in his other front pocket, a small canister of some pepper spray he noticed when he placed his weapon in his safe at home. He figured, why not?

He stayed right at the speed limits, which slowed him a little, but without traffic it was a pretty quick trip. He found the garage and pulled in. His pulse was up a little and he realized he wasn't looking forward to running into Smithers, if he was there. On the way down he wondered, whether he came across him or not, if Smithers was the kind of guy who might give his car a flat if he found out it was Ted's.

No sign of Smithers and no one working that day seemed to remember Ted or remark on it if they did. Ted did not ask after

* * *

Smithers. He still had the temporary ID Janice had given him and it worked fine. He also was pleased the fellow helping him had no negative reaction to Ted asking if it was okay for him to come back in about an hour and take the car out for a few hours. It looked to Ted like the major activity at that moment was watching a football game on the tiny TV in the small office, which was crowded with men.

It hadn't occurred to Ted, especially dressed in jeans, that anyone at the hotel would remember him and his dramatic exit the month before. Since arrangements for this stay had also been set up by staff at Montpelier the hotel personnel were, indeed, all very aware he was returning. There was no financial issue; that had been taken care of. No, it was the excitement and drama of that night in October they recalled. Several staff were dying to ask Ted what had happened and what was the resolution, but fortunately they were too well trained. And Ted was clueless about their awareness of who he was, giving no opening for asking.

It was approaching three o'clock. He assumed it would start getting dark around five. He wanted to drive around the city to get his bearings. A BPD officer he knew who once worked with the NYPD told Ted using a car in the city was rarely practical except on Sundays when traffic was usually much lighter and parking easier. Unfortunately, Ted knew exactly where he wanted to go.

He retrieved his car and headed out, planning to work his way crosstown. When he was still at home in Vermont Ted rationalized to himself the trip he mapped out and was now taking was an exercise in navigating around the city. That his test destination was Forlenza's address in Long Island City wasn't something he planned to dwell on.

Given Ted's intense focus on Forlenza his short trip to Long Island City was very productive. Pulling off the highway at the appropriate exit his first impression was there must have been an error with his map reading or the address he was given by Special Agent Blaustein.

He was in the midst of endless streets of industrial buildings. There were clusters of small stores at some intersections, but mostly he was driving by warehouses and factories. The area didn't have that 'bombed out' appearance like the area of the South Bronx he had been in, but it had some lots filled with weeds and garbage, and the streets were dirty.

He kept at it and came upon several small, two or three street residential areas plunked down surrounded by industry. Even though the streets were tree lined the neighborhoods did not impress. The homes were all close together; some actually were attached, in a long row. Cars were parked in front of the houses, but he noticed there were alleys behind, where garages were.

Following his map, he navigated to a street not much different than the others but the smallish homes were not attached. They all looked the same. Tiny fenced in yards, steps, and a small porch. All the homes were multi-colored brick. Ted thought they looked kind of garish and the whole neighborhood was crowded. He drove the street slowly, then suddenly worried it was still light and his green Vermont license plates could be seen too easily.

As he had in other nearby neighborhoods he noted a few small religious shrines in several yards. Probably the Virgin Mary, unfolding her arms. On Forlenza's street the home he was looking for stood out. That yard had the Mary shrine, another statue, and a sizable cement fountain ringed by cherubs, too big for the small yard; dry now. He believed it was Forlenza's home anyway.

At the end of that street he turned at the intersection and went only a few yards and turned into the alley that served Forlenza's street. He had to keep driving, but quickly counted the homes, as he had done when he passed Forlenza's house from the street. All the yards were fenced and looked pretty similar. The one he pegged as Forlenza's back entrance was notable for a loose screen door noisily flapping back and forth as he passed the house. He completed the alley and turned as if to circle back to Forlenza's street.

As he turned he saw lights from a car he remembered all too well entering the alley from the other end. Ted slowly backed up and parked and turned his lights off. He was just off the alley. He watched the car in the alley stop at the house with the flapping screen door. The driver helped a man out of the passenger seat. Forlenza was sitting in front when he and Ted had their confrontation. The man was old and thin but held himself ramrod straight now, probably a reflection of his rigid personality. Same guy. He was sure. The man unlocked the gate and went up the steps to the house. The driver put the car into the garage across from the house. Too dark now to see any more.

'How about that?' Ted thought. 'The shit still lives where they thought.' Finding him was almost too easy.

*   *   *

DAY 42 MONDAY, NOVEMBER 22

Ted was up early, as usual, and finished off two oranges he had brought with him. He showered, shaved, and dressed, consciously not turning the TV on while he did all that. But he did take his time and thought about a lot of things. Angela Parsimone had suggested they meet for coffee at nine, an hour before the meeting. That was a nice gesture on her part, but he couldn't imagine how they would fill up most of an hour talking.

Downtown to the Federal building was a long walk but he was looking forward to it. The day was going to be bright and he thought it just didn't seem to get that cold in this city. He decided to allow an hour to get to the coffee shop address she had given him. If he was going to be late he assumed he could find a taxi for a quick ride.

For this meeting Ted had to wear his uniform. He knew he would be dressed like no one else at the meeting or, for that matter, also like no one else on his walk there. But he was acting in an official capacity so had to dress for it. He was all set to leave his room and then hesitated as his hand went for his hat. A State Trooper's hat was vastly different than the great majority of law officer's head gear. If anything it might re-enforce the Boy Scout look to many. So he did one of his *Ted Vallan* moments and visibly moved back and forth a few times trying to decide whether to grab or leave his regulation hat. He wondered if *Ted Vallan* moments like this were unique to him or if others, maybe everyone, had moments like this? Would he be this way all his life?

Ted decided he wouldn't wear his hat, but he would carry it with him. He had nothing else to carry. He had never lost a hat.

Ted left the hotel with some spring in his step. The lobby was already busy and, just the same as last time, the streets were already filled with people and traffic at eight on a Monday morning. As he navigated due south he was dismayed to recognize his uniform was having an impact on the other pedestrians. He stood out and people were making small adjustments away from his path or slowed slightly and gazed at him. It was so strange that in Vermont reaction to his uniform was generally deference and respect. His uniform made him proud and helped Ted and others on the force stay serious about their job. Deference here made him feel like he must have seemed outfitted like pictures he had seen of those Beefeater guards at the English Queen's Palace. He shook it off and took in the sights and sounds of the city around him. At least he was distracted from thinking, maybe worrying, about the meetings to come.

He found the coffee shop, right across the street from the federal building, about ten to nine. The temperature was shy of forty-five degrees. Ted was warm from his walk and waited, contentedly, for Angela to arrive. She walked up to him at nine. She was a small, thin woman wrapped, actually bundled up, in a long black coat. Her face was all smiles and she extended her hand as a friend does. With his hand he offered a friendly, exaggerated, "Ms. Parsimone" in return.

When they walked inside he figured he dare not help her with her coat. Even though small she had that bigger voice he recalled from a week before. More notable was her short haircut and her clothes, more typical for a man than a woman. In the army they would have called her butch. Ted was surprised but it provoked no other emotion in him. He couldn't not like Angela after all she was doing for him. She obviously had some obsessive-compulsive tendencies, but so did Ted and half the people he knew, including his wife. And if she liked girls, well, so did he.

He thanked her for what she was doing and they proceeded to spend the greater part of their hour talking about each other's lives instead of the meeting they had come for. Much to Ted's surprise he really did like her. They each laughed at similar *fish out of water* stories; Ted, of course, in the Bronx and Brooklyn, and Angela, briefly lost in the Adirondacks a year ago. She and her partner had never been to Vermont.

Ted immediately regretted telling her she should visit Vermont, where individual freedom and alternative lifestyles were encouraged. Angela took it as the supportive comment it was meant to be. Angela was, herself, surprised to find out about Liza and her progress with her professional career and family. What Ted didn't get, at least at first, was Angela was most impressed with the way he spoke about Liza, and the way he and Liza were facing the challenges of family and each of their careers together.

Towards the end of the hour Ted realized he was becoming more reflective about the many components of his life. His life was so much more than this case. He had heard Lieutenant Rondell use the phrase *reality check* before. He sensed Forlenza's face and threats begin, ever so slightly, to fade some.

About quarter of ten Angela reviewed with Ted what she planned to do at the meeting. But she told him she honestly couldn't predict how things would go. She told Ted after what he had been through he was entitled to this meeting; no matter what happened.

"Angela, you're exactly right. That's how I see this also. Kind of like my day in court, you know. My hopes are up a little, but I have to tell you, your words and support are helping me to make progress I hadn't been able to make fast enough to move beyond this episode in my life and career."

"Wow, my parents always said I should have been a therapist. My pleasure Ted."

*   *   *

After everybody sat down Assistant DA Parsimone took charge of the meeting she had organized. She asked everyone around the table to introduce themselves even though most knew who was who by now.

"Folks, I think we can cut to the chase about why we're all here. Trooper Vallan has been in the middle of a capital case and his investigation has taken off in a number of directions. We are here today because there is convincing evidence that during his investigation a law officer's life and family, actually Trooper Vallan's, were threatened in a significant way. There is reason to be concerned the threat continues to be active."

She then gave a concise but fairly complete review of Ted's case, highlighting the features that involved 'Skinny' Forlenza. Ted was impressed and satisfied with what she had put together. There was a pause. After that it all began to go downhill.

Special Agent Blaustein sat back in his chair. "You know, I guess you can never know how one old crook is going to react after you use a knife to pop the tires of a car he's using to kidnap you, can ya, huh?"

That changed everything. The mood in the room visibly lightened. It was almost as though Blaustein had given license for everyone to take the whole meeting less seriously. Ted, and to a lesser extent Angela, were furious. Was he doing this intentionally or was this his personality? Either way if offered opportunity for a consensus response that immediately removed a large part of the intensity and gravity from the discussion.

Not only were some others there now less intense but, it turned out, the relaxing of seriousness suited their own problems with the obvious reason for this meeting: to take action to resolve risk to the safety of a law officer. Detective Emerson and the assistant DA with him, Ernesto Rubio, were more comfortable now presenting their doubts about the usefulness of Imogene for Ted.

First Detective Emerson, with a sigh, told the group his investigation was now suggesting Imogene Janus may have had a much bigger role in the theft of the stones, and even Ted's brief abduction, than previously thought.

"Imogene Janus probably tipped Forlenza off you're a cop, Ted."

That was a blow. He was way too distracted by all the bad news, but what Emerson said gave him a shiver because it meant the guys who took him *did* know he was a cop.

Next Assistant Manhattan DA Rubio told them his senior supervisor didn't appear to be interested in making a deal with Imogene Janus anymore. Rubio's story was her case had political implications. The nature of her crime and the notoriety about it in the papers made her case too charged to consider a deal now.

Before Ted, or Angela Parsimone, or anyone else had a chance to react to all that, Rubio continued.

"I know none of this sounds good to you Officer. I'd like to make a strong suggestion we still go ahead with the meeting scheduled for tomorrow with Imogene and her lawyer. My supervisor promised he will be there. Who knows? Maybe you'll get some useful information. Maybe my boss won't be as intransigent meeting face to face."

As if Special Agent Blaustein hadn't already damaged the meeting enough, he wasn't finished. So diverted by what he was hearing Ted had lost track of Blaustein, who had pushed himself about two feet from the table and was reclining back, motionless in his swivel chair. Ted had an impression Angela was about to query Blaustein. But then he spoke up.

"Interesting stuff folks; interesting. I think I told you way back, Trooper Vallan, these kinds of cases are always difficult to really take anywhere. What's happened to you is terrible but I hope I and maybe the other folks here today didn't get your hopes up too high about taking care of this."

'No', Ted thought to himself. 'I've only been on a treadmill the past two weeks being fed a bunch of info that looked to be very actionable. No, I happily disrupted the life I'm trying to put back together to spend my time down here where everyone says I've just wasted my time.' He kept looking at Blaustein. Ted figured they all could read his expression.

But Agent Blaustein still wasn't done. "Trooper, your case did raise some heads and, as I told you, we worked with some of our contacts to find a link between law enforcement and criminals. Well it paid off and we found something, like I said. But, and here's the thing, what was exposed has generated some more findings. Our task force is onto something now we feel may be very big. Too big to allow what we learned about your case to come out for now. Keep your eyes out for maybe something out of New England, Ted. I honestly can't tell you when or if you will ever be able to use the information we found about your case."

Ted's optimism had degenerated into profound discouragement early in the meeting. Angela Parsimone had tried to remain positive, but by now she too knew there was nowhere else to go with this.

Special Agent Blaustein didn't appear particularly invested in the meeting from the start. In any event, as he started to stand, he, gratuitously, tossed out "you know, too bad that crazy fuck Forlenza couldn't know enough to just retire and do somethin' like write a dumb book instead of killin' people."

Angela stood up and thanked everyone for coming. Ernesto Rubio shook Ted's hand and handed him a piece of paper with the time, address, and pertinent phone numbers for their meeting the next day. It was scheduled for two o'clock. Detective Emerson, half-heartedly, said he'd try to make it. Everyone left except Angela and Ted. They sat down and looked at each other.

At about the same time each of their somber faces relaxed and in a short time they were smiling, and then laughing.

She said, "I mean, in this fucking world, you couldn't make more things go wrong in such a short time if you rehearsed it. You know? This morning you were talking to me about pieces of a puzzle in the case. Well, holy shit, we wound up in a chess match instead. And you and I ain't gonna be enough pieces to round up the bad guy. I think that was check-mate for *us*, Ted.

"Well, I suppose we could still talk some cops into bringing that Forlenza in for questioning. Just to rough him up and let him know he's being watched. Even if he's crazy that might help him to decide to get off your back. I really don't know what else to consider."

Ted's smile and laughter were genuine. He was warming to the insanity of the entire last few weeks, foolishly thinking he was closing in on Forlenza.

"Oh I don't know what I should do now. I'm not even sure what I want to do with this mess anymore. But listen Angela, honestly, you've been the only bright spot in New York for me. I really appreciate the way you listened to me, even way back, and then you tried to make something work. Really good of you to try. I'm lucky to have had your help."

She smiled. Ted continued on.

"You know what? I feel really good about having a laugh about all this with you now. I think some of this thing is finally starting to fall apart because of its own weight. I'm thinking enough. I'm going to go outside and walk around for a while. See some sights and get some things for my kids. I'll let all this sit for a while then I guess I'll go over it again and think about any options."

They took the elevator down to the lobby. Angela bundled up as they walked outside. Ted marveled because it just wasn't cold. He stopped for a second and wrote his home phone number on the back of his card and made her promise if she ever planned to pass through Vermont she would consider calling so she and her partner could meet his family and share some time in Vermont.

They had joked about it earlier, in the coffee shop, so they each smiled as they shook hands and Ted placed his hat on his head, tipped it slightly, and said: "*Ms.* Parsimone."

*   *   *

Ted was not foolish enough to think he had completely exorcised his obsession with Forlenza. He wasn't surprised a little while later that his anger was still close to the surface. He had a few ideas but no good options. Would anything satisfy him? What would satisfy him?

Enough of this. Like Angela said, bring in the criminal and make all those jerks in the justice system do their jobs. The thought reflected the sick feeling in his gut and true disappointment that those people would never get their act together and do something about all this.

The web weaved today was blocking Ted's need for justice to be served and an ending to all this. After all he heard from others about the shitty dynamics and problems involved, and all the time and effort he personally had invested staying on this case, disrupting his family and career, there still was no good resolution in sight.

He bought more than enough stuff for the kids. He did a lot of walking. He forgot about people gawking at his uniform. He found a street with nothing but jewelry and watch stores. He thought about Liza. Would their life together ever be the same again? Why couldn't it? If he bought her something would she think he was trying to apologize for so much of the past six weeks? Or could he convince her a gift was meant to be emblematic of the deep love he felt for her and the life they shared as a family.

He bought a nice watch with a large sweep second hand and numbers that glowed in the dark. He knew she could use that when she was taking a pulse, counting respirations, or whatever.

Walking down a street he stopped on the sidewalk. What the hell was he doing in New York? They hadn't made love since the first day of this case. He was amazed when he realized he hadn't even thought about sex with her for so many weeks. He was thinking about it now. And he had kids waiting for him at home. He had cases with real solutions waiting for him at home. As the daylight began to fade he started downtown to his hotel.

He went to his hotel room and around five o'clock called home. Liza detected a change in Ted's tone; a lightening of his mood even though the story he recounted about the day was bleak. He told her he was actually feeling better about the whole business and wasn't sure if he would even stay in the city or cancel his meeting set for Tuesday afternoon. Liza was sweet on the phone.

She surprised herself when she did it and she certainly surprised Ted. It was only a quick phrase but, as they say, it meant so much. Liza softly told Ted it would be good for him to be home. She was waiting for him.

He changed into jeans and went out to buy some take-out. He also stopped at a small grocery and bought some oranges and apples and a few cheap tools.

He was more tired than he thought he should be, but his mind was still busy. Could Forlenza and whatever crew of goons he used truly still be a threat to him or his family? It made no sense. The anger was ebbing now. With the passage of time so much of it seemed unreal. How could Forlenza's face mean so much to him? He lay on the bed in the dark, the noise of the jumpy city hum in the background. He dozed on and off. He woke up to go pee. It was the middle of the night. After that he found it difficult to fall back asleep.

It was a late night revelation, but Ted thought he was thinking clearly. He was tired of all of it. He wanted to go home. But this time *enough* didn't just mean he wanted to get out of there. This night he realized it meant it was time to be home and be with Liza and his family. He wasn't leaving; he was *going*; going to where he desperately wanted to be.

Wednesday was his birthday and the next day Thanksgiving. As he lay there the frequent image of Forlenza that haunted a place in his mind for so long was becoming more difficult to conjure. It was replaced by Liza, with her warm, welcoming face and smile.

*   *   *

DAY 43 TUESDAY, NOVEMBER 23

Close to three Ted got up and took a shower. It was quieter out on the street but there was enough noise to accept the city never sleeps. He sat at the small desk and wrote out what he thought he should write down and he put papers in various pockets. He made sure his knife and pepper spray were accessible. He carefully folded his uniform and packed it and his hat into his suitcase. He wanted to travel lighter over to the police garage. He wondered if his middle of the night trek to the garage might be the most dangerous part of his next twenty-four hours.

In the lobby he roused the somnolent desk clerk and settled his bill. Just like last time, he told the clerk there was a chance he would be back. He wasn't sure. The clerk only cared about trying to decide if Ted should be charged for another day or just a half-day considering when he was checking out. Ted told him he didn't care and asked him to move along.

The side streets were empty and very quiet. He felt okay and told himself anyone who might challenge him as he walked toward the river would be more at risk for his own life than Ted. Close to the river and the garage he was amazed to come across a huge number of garbage trucks getting mobilized to start their day. It was all lit up and noisy.

The officer at the garage office was pleasant enough. There were some workers there. Ted didn't look for or find Smithers; which was fine. He was walked to his car, put all his things in the trunk except his fruit, and climbed into the front seat, placing the fruit on the passenger floor. He checked his maps and cash for tolls and set off. The drive was uneventful. He arrived near his destination before five. He figured it would stay dark until a little after six. He hoped to work without a flashlight.

He was a police officer. He planned to do what cops do: arrest felons and place them under the control of the justice system. He thought there was more than enough evidence to arrest Forlenza. Whether or not the laws and the people who administered them had the ability, or even the heart, to fight to hold this felon responsible for his crimes was not something he could do much more to impact. Do it and then let the chips fall where they may.

He made sure, one more time, he had all his IDs and a paper with a list of the names of everyone he had been working with, including a 24 hour number for the Organized Crime Task Force. In his shirt pocket he had a piece of paper with a phone number and a name to contact at the Long Island City precinct. Armed with his knife, some rope, and a few small tools in his jacket, he placed his red portable flasher in the middle of his dash and got out of his car. He hoped that would help discourage any potential break-in at the run-down street location he parked the car, with its green Vermont plates, about five blocks from Forlenza's house.

Danilio was still in jail so Ted assumed no more than two, but probably only one man would be with Forlenza if he really had any bodyguards. When he drove by before parking he didn't see any occupied cars in the front or the alley in the back. He was pleased to see the back screen door he had seen flapping on Sunday was still flapping nosily, back and forth, in the wind. He was amazed the neighbors tolerated that constant noise.

Ted walked quietly up the dark alley where streetlights were only at the ends. When he approached the house he saw a dull light in the room with the banging door and a faint light at a window on the floor above it. The rear gate of the chain link fence that went completely around the house was locked with an old pad lock. The fence was no more than four feet high and Ted vaulted over it. He was concerned the back door would be his biggest problem, but hoped the constant banging of the screen door would have inured anyone in the house to any noise he would probably make breaking in. If there was someone sitting in that back room Ted might have trouble.

The door handle and lock were in bad shape. He had little experience, but what he brought was enough for Ted to actually pop out the cylinder with almost no effort. There was no dead bolt, or if there was it wasn't locked. Whoever lived in this place was sloppy about uninvited visitors.

The door squeaked as he slowly opened it, but he let the screen door continue to flap and doubted his actions would cause anyone to stir. He was in the kitchen. It smelled like burned tomato sauce or tomato sauce and burned toast. Ted made note of where the phone was located.

The hallway from the kitchen was dark, but there was a dull light on beyond it. Probably the living room. That room was furnished with wood chairs with ornate scrolling and brown cushions. He could see the tip of a bald head at the top of a plastic wrapped sofa facing the closed curtains for the front picture window. The walls were faded red and filled with oils and large photos of vistas and cities; he assumed places in Italy.

Ted stood, quietly, in the hallway for a few minutes listening to the rhythmic breathing until he was sure the man was asleep. He walked to him, slapped five inches of duct tape over his mouth, and reached down and bound his hands behind him before the man was really aware of what was happening. He had been in a deep sleep.

He pulled him off the couch and quietly turned the couch on its side so the man's face was looking at the seat cushion and, with the back now on top of him, was blocked from any view of what was going on. He used the remaining length of rope to anchor the man's hands to the radiator behind him, beneath the window frame. The man tried to make noise but he was wasting his breath. Ted looked around and headed upstairs.

He found his way to the room where Forlenza was sleeping by listening to him snore. There was a night light in the bathroom in the hallway at the top of the stairs and another one in Forlenza's room. Just enough light to safely manage his arrest. There was another phone on the far night table. He walked over to Forlenza.

Forlenza snored away. He looked ancient. A thin clear plastic shower cap covered his head, probably to keep the garish red dye in his hair from ruining his pillow. Ted stood and stared. This was not what he expected.

He was so old. Yet he still apparently had that sixth sense that somehow often wakes you up when someone is standing over you. Forlenza made a slow motion to reach under the pillow next to him. Ted easily pushed his arm away and secured the weapon that was there.

Ted spoke in a normal voice and cadence. "You know, I guess old assholes have other old assholes around to protect them. Now it's just you and me, pal."

Forlenza looked terrified. But he couldn't help himself and spit out, with his accustomed bravado, "Who are ya, ya testa di cazzo?" Ted assumed that was something like *shithead* in Italian. Ted pulled him forward by his nightshirt. Forlenza's fear overcame him.

"Whoever ya are, I'm an old man. Don't hurt me. Don't kill me!"

"No, I won't kill you. I'm going to smash your fuck face so that look of yours isn't going to haunt me or my family ever again. Nobody cares about you anymore except me. Your fucking *families* have written you off already. They let you screw around with small stuff just to keep you happy and occupied. But you are shit to them." Forlenza's look of terror did not fade.

"If you still have a face left after I'm done with you we'll let a prison hospital try to put you back together. You're never going to sleep in this bed again."

Ted started to pull him up even closer so he could make sure, face to face, he could tell Forlenza who he was and why he was doing this. The man looked really old; almost feeble. Could he hit such an old man? Forlenza started to turn gray and in just seconds went limp. Ted was shocked. He let him fall back to his bed. He was out. He choked and gurgled a little. Then he convulsed, foamed at his mouth, turned blue, and never moved again.

Ted pressed Forlenza's neck where he assumed his carotid artery was. He moved two fingers around all over the region but could not find a pulse. He tried the other side. He thought about taking one of his latex gloves off to get a better feel but decided it wasn't necessary. Wasn't going to make a difference. Forlenza's face looked like stone. Before Ted had a chance to remind him of his story, spit in his face, or deliver the punch he had dreamed about for so long the old shit was dead.

For a short time he stood there and stared at the dead man. The lives he hurt just to keep his fingers in the only business he knew, while he probably bragged he would never retire to anyone who would listen.

It was time for Ted to go home. No longer any need to call the Detective or the feds to tell them he decided to proceed with a case against Forlenza.

*   *   *

Ted walked quietly down the stairs and left through the kitchen door he had entered in the back of the house. The middle-aged fat man Ted had surprised downstairs was growling on his belly on the floor, hands still tied behind him with rope anchored to a softly hissing radiator. The shiny sofa covered with clear plastic remained pushed over so he could see nothing. Ted knew the man would be able to work himself free, eventually.

Later that day the bodyguard extricated himself and called his associates and then even the police, who sent a coroner so the body could be moved. The man tried to tell everyone the same thing: He was sitting, awake, in the living room. Someone unseen came crashing into the room from behind him, practically knocked him out, and tied him up. No one bothered to challenge him when he said the only thing he had seen was that the man had blue hands... Nobody cared.

*   *   *

EPILOGUE

Almost twenty years after Ted Vallan spent time near the end of the case writing notes memorializing some of the events I, his son Henry, found a folder with those notes at the bottom of a drawer in the den desk we all used. At first he brushed off my efforts to learn more regarding what the writing was about and why he had done it. Writing was already my passion but I had never seen my father write anything. At my urging he agreed to look at those notes with me later that night.

Around ten-thirty the house was quiet and mom was upstairs so I reminded him I was anxious to hear about what he had written. I could tell he was re-thinking his agreement. He looked at me and his right cheek pulled to the right, skewing his mouth in that direction, a mannerism that, for years, often betrayed some uncertainty in his thinking. The notes we reviewed and the discussion that ensued were the genesis of the story you just finished reading. Some of what you have read was taken practically verbatim from his notes. And some of this book was derived from the discussions those notes generated with both my parents.

For when my father referred to the case he always called it *our* case since, as you have read, Liza was, unintentionally, a major player in it. Describing what happened to her required her gracious and frank input. But since it was my father's first major case and his notes form the basis for my telling, most of the book recounts his perspective and thinking. Each of my parents has kindly accepted the license I have taken with their story.

All of us have secrets.
Secrets accumulate over a lifetime.
Some secrets go to our graves with us.
Well, some last for about twenty years anyway.
That should be good enough.

THE END